OMEGA ALPHA NX2

Spies, Missiles and Clouds of War

LOUIE GALLIO

CONTENTS

PROLOGUE

"Hey Dad, check it out!" Gunther Schueller pointed at the video game room with excitement. Inside, incessant whirring, chiming bells, and psychedelic lights surrounded a maze of electronic devices.

Hans van Schueller turned and chuckled. "Ah, yes. I can see where you'll be spending your time!" Canard's new cruise ship, the *Princess*, was a modern marvel. Schueller and his family looked forward to a well-deserved vacation on the liner's maiden voyage.

What they didn't know was that the gaudy cave-like video room would soon become young Gunther's eternal tomb.

Schueller, the European commissioner for the European Union, was returning to Brussels. The German statesman had just completed a landmark trade deal between top U.S. officials and the EU.

In fact, many passengers were the world's richest and most influential people, including the U.S. ambassador to the UK and European diplomats. A few hours earlier, the *Princess* had left New York with great fanfare; ports of call would be Britain, France, and Italy. Measuring 1,130 feet in length, the huge ship towered twenty-one stories from keel to masthead—the manifest named 2,400 guests of its 2,800 capacity.

But the festive crowd on board the *Princess* was oblivious to the imminent danger lurking below.

Some two hundred miles away, a Russian-made nuclear submarine prowled the ocean floor like a stealthy bull shark. The *Foxchase U- 486*, an Antyey-type attack submarine, was armed with twenty-four ballistic missiles. Banks of twelve were stored on each side, between twin layers of the boat's thick hull skin. On this mission, the missile of choice was the 100RU Veder, NATO code-named Stallion. The top-secret, rocket-boosted torpedo was specially designed to destroy American carriers and submarines.

The *Princess* deftly sliced the moonlit sea at thirty knots. Inside, guests were joyfully dining, dancing, and socializing. Lively music echoed against the ocean, then faded in the cool night air.

"Yes!" screeched young Gunther. He had scored another hit in a video game entitled, *Dead or Alive*.

In the dining area, Schueller and his wife, Elke, sipped a glass of red wine — Brunello di Montalcino, 1993. They had finished an elegant dinner comprised of chateaubriand, scalloped potatoes, and sautéed zucchini.

Wineglasses in hand and elbows propped on the table, and they interlocked their arms in a toast. His eyes fixed admiringly on his wife, Schueller said, *"Zur Gesundheit und zum Glück,"* to health and happiness. They drank some wine, then kissed softly.

Framing her heart-shaped face, Elke's short, golden blonde hair glistened in the candlelight. The smile on her ruby lips reached her dazzling hazel eyes.

Meanwhile, onboard *Foxchase* (U-486), the submarine commander, a short man, looked at the clock on the wall. A deep frown etched his round, weathered face. He twitched his head to the left and shouted into a snakelike microphone, "Prepare to launch!"

A launch technician wearing heavy earphones lifted the cover on the number one missile switch. "Fire control ready!" His unshaven, boyish face gleamed with beads of sweat.

On the *Princess*, Schueller tipped his glass and savored the last drop of wine. "Ready to dance?" "Yes!" Elke replied.

The couple rose to their feet in tandem. Hand in hand, they proceeded to the crowded dance floor in front of the main stage. A trumpet player in the sixteen-piece band was playing a soothing arrangement of "Moon River." They came together cheek to cheek and began dancing.

In the depths of the ocean, *Foxchase* (U-486) had reached optimal firing range. With his scrunched hat tilted, the stone-faced commander navigated the sinister iron whale. "Steady. Maintain course," he ordered. A red light on the bulkhead cast a creepy glow upon a row of engineers seated on the starboard side. They were motionless, eyes glued to multi-colored radar screens on an instrument panel.

"Two minutes to launch!" declared the navigator.

With a slight quiver, the launch technician rested his hand on the panel and loosely gripped the red toggle switch with his fingers. His bloodshot eyes were hollow.

"Minus sixty seconds!" said the commander. Intently following the second hand, he arched his eyebrows and took in a deep breath. "Three, two, one, fire one!"

"Fire one!" the technician blurted while flipping the ignition switch.

The attacking vessel shuddered and recoiled in a rumbling crescendo. The Stallion had shot out of its twenty-six-inch diameter tube. Target: The Carnard *Princess*.

After the nuclear warhead cleared the submarine, its rocket boosters ignited underwater. The Stallion burst through the surface, spitting orange flames and puffy billows of gray and white smoke. Guided by GPS-driven radar, it reached altitude and darted through the air at twice the speed of sound.

When the lightweight torpedo arrived at the drop zone, it shut down its rockets and slowed in velocity. A small parachute popped open with a sharp clap. The deadly warhead gently dropped into the dark sea, just three miles ahead of the *Princess*.

A few feet below the surface, its propeller motor started with a surge.

Armed with the equivalent of 200,000 tons of TNT, the projectile zoomed towards the innocent cruise ship for the final kill. Like a serpent, it slithered quietly through the water with diabolical intent.

Within minutes, the Stallion struck the bow of the luxury ship precisely below the waterline. It blew a gaping hole in the ship's hull. The huge liner momentarily wrenched.

On the dance floor, Schueller was thrown backward, but quickly regained his balance. Fear in her eyes, Elke fell into his arms, and they clutched each other tightly. People stumbled to the floor, furniture shifted, drinking glasses tumbled and shattered. The music stopped. A classic Steinway piano slid off the stage and crashed to the floor. Alarms sounded. Screams of terror filled the room.

In a matter of seconds, the timed warhead melted through the forward interior walls. When the second explosion occurred, the *Princess* became a massive fireball. Shock waves traveled hundreds of miles. The blast created a crater over 2,000 feet wide and unleashed a 1,500-foot-high waterspout. A colossal tidal wave followed.

The cruise liner had disintegrated. There were no survivors.

1

MCLEAN, VIRGINIA

At two o'clock in the morning, Bosco barked frantically. Outside, two men dressed in camouflaged battle fatigues were crouched near General Chet "Bulldog" Fuller's study in his McLean, Virginia home. When they heard the huge Lab bark, the intruders broke into a sprint. They dashed across the lawn and down the street.

Upstairs in the bedroom, General Fuller woke up in a cold sweat. He bolted upright. Trembling, the heart within his massive chest pounded like a heavy drumbeat.

His wife, Caitlin, reached up and gently placed her hand on his shoulder. "What's wrong?"

"Thought I heard something." Fuller pulled the covers back, got out of bed, and padded down the stairs into the kitchen.

In the distance, Fuller heard a car start up and drive away. Bosco stopped barking and looked up at his master. Rubbing his eyes, Fuller peered through the window. He saw nothing but the morning dew sparkle under the streetlight.

"It's okay, boy," the general said, patting the dog on the back.

Fuller thought nothing of it. He yawned and went back upstairs. "What was it?" said Caitlin.

"Nothing—just a car down the street. Actually, I woke up in a bad dream."

"What about?"

He paused to consider carefully, then shook his head. His crew-cut silver hair glowed in a ray of moonlight. "Can't remember." *Why alarm her?* He shrugged and slipped under the sheets.

"Goodnight," said Caitlin. She snuggled up on her side.

"G'night," Fuller said with a sigh.

As soon as his head hit the pillow, the general's mind began to reel. Replaying the eerie nightmare, he envisioned blurred images of soldiers scampering about, shouting orders incoherently. A giant-size projector screen displayed a group of missiles on a launchpad. He remembered banks of computers, flickering lights, and spools of tapes jerking back and forth. In his dream, he tried to move but was paralyzed—as if in a straightjacket. Suddenly, there was a blinding glow. He felt like a deer staring helplessly into the headlights of an oncoming eighteen-wheeler. Seconds later, a deafening silence. Then came darkness.

Throughout the night, he meditated for hours. Stolen nuclear secrets, missing supercomputers—how vulnerable are we? Young officers are leaving our forces in droves. Can we survive the evils of the new millennium? If we continue to ignore the rules of moral dignity, we've lost.

We're faced with the terrorists, the arms buildup, moral decay, one government rule, and God knows what else. Who are our *real* enemies, anyway?

Mentally exhausted, General Fuller finally went to sleep. Little did he know he would soon be fighting to save the entire species of humanity.

2

THE OVAL OFFICE

"When can we expect the final reports?" asked President Ryan "Mac" MacDuff. Hands folded behind his back, he stood at the array of windows, and gazed outside. He watched the mottled green leaves flicker in the sunlight. But on this day, after the *Princess* tragedy, his mood was grim.

"By the end of the day, sir," General Fuller replied, in a slight Texas drawl. The Marine shifted in his chair and added, "Seismologists in Nova Scotia registered the explosion at eight point five on the Richter scale." Behind Fuller, a sunbeam highlighted the presidential seal, embossed in the royal blue carpet.

The president grimaced. "It's messy, General. A sticky mess." The world's newspapers reacted to the Canard *Princess's* sinking with a flurry of reports, stories, special editorials, and banner headlines. Various theories flooded the media: sabotage by terrorists, a missile attack, and faulty equipment. The tragedy encouraged people of all nations to mourn. Most flew their flags at half-mast.

"So, what's your take?" MacDuff asked. "What caused it?" His bluish-gray hair complemented his intense, ice-blue eyes. He was not a big man. He was tall and had a soft build but was not egregiously overweight. Time on the golf course and tennis courts was ample exercise.

"Hard to say, Mr. President. It could've been any one of them—a bomb planted by terrorists, a missile, or even a torpedo. But until the evidence comes in —"

"We have security checks for ships, don't we?" The president's pallid, angular face contrasted his dark gray suit, white shirt, and red power tie.

"Yes, we do. We have the latest scanners. And bomb-sniffing dogs." Fuller sat erect, his jade green eyes straight ahead. Glimmering rows of medals lined his sleek olive-green uniform—among them, the Medal of Honor. The familiar eagle, globe, and anchor insignia dotted his lapels.

TV news helicopters continually buzzed above the murky water at the disaster site, sending live broadcasts across the globe. Flimsy bits of evidence were strewn over a three-mile radius. Many news stories evolved around personal tragedies suffered by relatives of the victims, particularly the prominent Schueller family.

"For Pete's sake, someone must have intelligence on this!" The President began pacing. "What about the CIA, the NSA, DIA, the FBI?" The National Security Agency, Defense Intelligence Agency, and the FBI were all investigating the tragedy.

"Nothing yet," said Fuller, shaking his head. "Any of our subs in the area?"

"The navy is compiling a report." Fuller paused. "Then there's the anonymous caller, identifying himself as a member of the pro-Iranian Shiite group, the Hezbollah. They're claiming responsibility. Who knows? It could very well have been them. But was it an accident, an act of terrorism, or an act of war? No matter what we call it, it's still people dying a tragic death." He flinched as visions of grisly combat scenes abruptly appeared—American troops dying on the battlefield. *There's no escape from the grief and stench of war*, he thought. *The endless rows of crosses at Arlington Cemetery and the untold number of MIAs are reminders.*

"Atkins is cutting his trip short," MacDuff said. Secretary of

Defense Charles Atkins and other U.S. officials were in the Middle East dealing with an oil crisis. They were negotiating with OPEC and the OIC, the Organization of the Islamic Conference.

Fuller nodded sharply. "We spoke this morning."

"What about your missile defense sites?" said the president. "Pick up anything?"

Fuller hesitated. "Sir, initial reports indicate there was a breach.

Possibly radar jamming at the time of the explosion."

"You mean, when we needed the radar, it failed?

"Not exactly. The THAAD system tracks missiles in the air, not bombs stowed on a ship or underwater torpedoes." THAAD, The *Theater High Altitude Area Defense*, was the first global program for defending against ballistic missiles.

"Okay, okay," MacDuff said, with flailing hands, palms out. "So, what's your gut feel, General?" He resumed pacing the floor, hands folded behind his back. "I think it's nuclear."

The president stopped in his tracks. He glanced over his shoulder and said, "You sound convinced."

"Gut feel, sir. Just gut feel."

MacDuff gave a low grunt and resumed pacing.

"Mr. President, if they jammed our radar, doesn't that speak for the need to upgrade our systems in the field?"

MacDuff spun around and squinted curiously at Fuller. "Oh, I see. You're leading to the Taiwan issue again?" Fuller nodded.

"Tell me, General. What does this have to do with Taiwan?" The veins on MacDuff's forehead ballooned.

"A lot. This *Princess* thing caught us off guard. We need balance. We need better equipment and more troops stationed in the right places."

"Places? What places?"

"The Asia Pacific, for one."

"Well, of course, General. I forgot; you're afraid of China—the dragon in the East," MacDuff smirked. "No worries there. They're just tough trade competitors, but nothing more."

Fuller ignored the remarks, considering MacDuff's corrupt ties with China over thirty years. "If we don't supply Taiwan with updated arms, China could squash them and conquer the whole region in one big sweep."

MacDuff's eyes darted from side to side. "Don't think they'll do that. China and Taiwan are heavy trading partners. No matter how much Beijing squawks, there's too much at stake. Besides, they're afraid we'll step in."

"Commerce won't prevent a war from breaking out. History is pretty clear on that," said the general. His square jaw was set. His thick dark eyebrows hung low over deep-seated eyes. "China has our computerized technology. They can nuke Taiwan off the map!"

MacDuff sighed, turned, and cleared his throat. "General, I believe it's not wise to provide more military aid to Taiwan. We would stir up a hornets' nest with the strongest geopolitical power in the region. Not to mention dependency on our trade deals."

Fuller fidgeted in his seat, leaned forward, and said, "Maybe. But allow me to review some facts, sir. Have you forgotten that the smaller Iraq inflicted serious damage to Iran with 190 missiles?"
"That's history!"

"Yes, it is history. But Iran, Syria, Yemen, Saudi Arabia, India, Libya, and others have ballistic missiles. And that's today! Besides, China's quest is to conquer the world. They've bought into and are deep-rooted in our political, economic, and cultural infrastructure."

MacDuff was reminded of the Marine's persistent, grating stubbornness.

"What's your point? China's going to invade us?" MacDuff's attitude locked down Fuller's jaw. It made the jagged three-inch scar at the right corner of his mouth more prominent. Inflicted by a piece of hot shrapnel in Korea, the wound added intrigue to his ruggedly handsome features.

Fuller scoffed. "Hah! China has already 'invaded' us with the COVID virus! That was their economic bomb that set everyone back, and them ahead. Aside from that, the point is, if smaller nations have to, they can and will defend themselves with modern weapons."

His words gave pause for thought. Nations in the Middle East had fought for centuries. But in Asia, the size and capabilities of China's growing military machine intimidated the entire region. "If they wanted to, China could easily take over Taiwan and the rest of Asia. They could upset the balance of power. We know that's their aim."

"C'mon, General, that's a stretch." MacDuff glared at the general, turned, and continued pacing. "I know what the Cox report said—they could use our nuclear secrets to build modern missiles. But that's not gonna happen anytime soon." His arms pantomimed his words as he paced the floor. "They're just as reluctant to go to war as we are." He moved towards his chair and sat down heavily. He swiveled around to face the cluster of windows. The American flag and the presidential banner stood regally against the stylish gold drapes. MacDuff thought, the eagle is a double pain in the butt—a stubborn old-breed Marine. He doesn't know how to soften up, bend with the times.

MacDuff tilted his head upwards and began delivering his rhetoric as if preaching from the pulpit. "General, we need to stay focused on human rights, and at the same time, continue our trade relations with China. That's what the public wants, and that's what I'm gonna give 'em. I'm not going against public opinion!"

He rotated his chair towards Fuller. He saw the look of disapproval on the general's face, which slowly changed into a scowl.

Whether on the Hill, in the Pentagon's secretive tank, or the White House, Fuller stuck to his beliefs. As a child, he believed he could overcome dyslexia, and he did; this experience formed the basic tenet in his life. He believed he could win on the battlefield against lopsided odds, and he did. Now it was a battle of politics, a leftist dictatorship in D.C.

The president stood up stiffly behind his desk. "Now, General, go do your job. Find out about the *Princess* debacle."

MacDuff lowered his eyes to a document on his desk.

Fuller responded, "Anything else, sir?"

After a long pause, MacDuff shook his head and fingered through the report. His face was impassive.

Fuller sprang to his feet. "Guess not." He pivoted around and sharply marched out. *There will be another time.*

3

WHEATON, MARYLAND

"In position. Clear," General Fuller said into the tiny microphone inside his sleeve. He had a rush of adrenaline. Tonight's assignment was risky but invigorating. It was not an authorized mission for him, but he missed the gripping thrill of the hunt, the sweet taste of victory.

In front of a low-budget motel, he sat in a rented car and waited. He checked his wristwatch. It was 21:49—eleven minutes before launch. The burly, six-foot-three Marine wore black warm-ups, dark sneakers, and a navy baseball cap pulled low on his forehead. It was a clammy, still night. The band of his cap was moist with sweat. His skin felt bloated, and his mouth was dry.

Fuller thought about Vietnam—the gritty battles, hot metal, hot beer, rock and roll music, and the torrential rains. *Man, those monsoons were a bitch. Heavy raindrops—like bullets—hammered the hell out of my helmet. Felt like buckshot. Trudging through leech-infested water, ducking sniper fire fourteen hours a day–my energy sapped, my brain fried.*

In firefights, squeezing off rounds from my M16 made my arms feel like rubber. When ammo ran out, I had to kill 'em with my bayonet. We were shot up pretty bad, and for what? Political screw—ups. Forget it. It's history.

Headlights suddenly appeared in the rearview mirror. Fuller watched a car turn from the main road. It steered to the left, towards the south wing. It parked in front of a unit halfway down. A couple got out and casually went inside.

The general turned back towards the rental office. Moths fluttered haphazardly around the light globe hanging above the drive-through. The small motel had two wings, both angling off the lobby with a twenty-degree offset.

Fuller studied his watch again—21:56 hours—four minutes to go. He raised his left wrist to his mouth. "Minus four minutes. Clear?" he said into the microphone.

"Clear," said a voice through his earpiece. A small transceiver was clipped to his belt.

Vietnam was nothing compared to what could crop up. Now, world power hangs in the balance. And the stakes are much higher. At last count, over 13,000 nuclear warheads worldwide. The next war could be nuclear.

Fuller's watch read 22:00. Time to start. He lifted his arm and spoke into the microphone. "Now."

"Ten-four."

Fuller opened the door and eased out of his car. He went into the motel lobby and registered as Grant Stevenson from Orlando, Florida. The night clerk, a frail, gnome-like man, sat behind the counter reading a magazine. His balding head shone like a taupe-colored bowling ball. He lifted his eyebrows and glanced over his bifocals. "How long is ya staying?"

Fuller kept his head bowed. The bill of his cap shielded his face. "Just one night."

The clerk shrugged lazily. "Sixty bucks," he said. He went back to reading his magazine.

Fuller paid with traveler's checks, using a fake driver's license in the name of Stevenson. Naval Intelligence handily supplied such things.

The night clerk took the checks and wrote out a receipt. He reached for a set of keys hanging on the back wall. "To the left. One thirty-two is near the end," he said, handing the keys over.

"Thanks." Fuller took the keys, turned, and promptly went for the door. He could feel the man's curious gaze as he walked out the door. He hastily padded down a long path and went inside the room.

Fuller gave the room a quick inspection. A double bed and a nightstand with a lamp half–filled the room. The faded gold bed cover nearly matched the stained beige carpet. A small table combined with a standing lamp and two chairs cluttered one corner. A television set on a wobbly stand stood next to a dresser drawer at the foot of the bed. He peeked inside a tile-faced bathroom. A faucet dripped water down a brown stain in the sink.

He went back outside. Locking the door behind him, he placed the key in a potted plant at the door. The general hurried back to his car and got inside. "Room one thirty-two. Repeat, one, three, two," he said quietly into the microphone.

"Roger," came a voice. This time, a different one. The hollowed sounds of a moving vehicle echoed in the background. "One, three, two."

Meanwhile, in a dark corner of the parking lot, Colonel Manny Gomez peered through a pair of *Enforcer 250* night-vision binoculars. "Ten-four," he too responded.

Inside his car, the warm summer air was muggy—the profuse humidity sopped up oxygen like a sponge, opening his pores wide. Beads of sweat speckled his face and hands. His binoculars were slippery, and the peepholes clouded up with condensation. Gomez was the trusted flank man.

Excited by the aura of danger, Gomez reminisced about real fighting, hand-to-hand combat. He remembered the skirmishes in 'Nam and his unique experience in Teheran—when the shah of Iran was forced to leave the country.

On that repressive day, Ayatollah Khomeini arrived from Paris to lay claim on a nation in turmoil. The religious maniac mobilized crazed extremists who wreaked havoc on Americans. Gomez was a Marine security guard at the American embassy when they raided the compound. The invaders shamelessly held chancery personnel hostage.

At 22:30, Gomez keyed his mike. "Did package arrive?"

"Negative," Fuller responded. "Stand by."

"Roger."

Gomez thought about the gruesome street fights in Central Los Angeles, where he grew up. Chains, brass knuckles, knives, and handguns were his opponents' weapons of choice. A smile came upon his face. He was proud of his victories in the ring as a scrappy boxer—a Golden Glove champion three years in a row.

General Fuller's heart raced at the motel as he watched a late model Nissan turn from the main street.

A short, robust man cloaked in a maroon shirt, navy slacks, and a *Payne Stewart* golf cap emerged from the car. He walked with short, choppy steps. Hands in his pockets, the man went directly to the potted plant. He looked around, retrieved the key, and unlocked the door. He slipped inside and quickly closed the door. The windows and drapes were shut tight. He switched on a lamp.

Colonel Gomez clicked his microphone. "Found the shopping list." "Roger," said Fuller.

Gomez continually scouted the area, searching for a tail following the man in the golf cap. Five minutes later, he uttered, "Going shopping—back in thirty minutes."

"Roger." Fuller stepped out of his car. His profile and movement looked like a football player—a tight end—tall, husky, supple as a leopard. He marched briskly to the room and tapped on the door, three short bursts of two knocks each. The door opened, and the general disappeared inside.

On this rare occasion, General Fuller chose to meet Lame Duck in person. The double agent from Beijing had vital information about China's nuclear missile projects.

While the two men conferred, Gomez tenaciously scanned the area. Suddenly, a black sedan, a Cadillac, turned into the motel entrance. The car slowed to a crawl. Moving past the lobby, the exterior motel lights silhouetted two men in the front seat.

The car turned sharply to the right, headed towards the room, and slowed nearly to a stop. Alarmed, Gomez reached for his 9mm, automatic Smith & Wesson, Mark 22 handgun. A silencer extended the barrel. Navy commandos in Vietnam called this model the Hush Puppy. "Car outside. Hit the deck!" Gomez shouted.

Fuller and Lame Duck dove to the floor.

The car crept past the room and around the corner. The taillights disappeared into the darkness. "All clear. Sorry 'bout that," Gomez said, holding his pistol at the ready.

Fuller chuckled. "No sweat. You're our eyes and ears." He and Lame Duck unceremoniously got up from the floor and resumed their talks. Thirty minutes later, Gomez spoke again, "Comin' home?" "On my way," the general responded.

Seconds later, the door opened, and Fuller left the room. He quickly- marched down the path to the car. He slid behind the steering wheel. Gomez continually searched the area. The light in the room faded, and the door opened. The man from Beijing stepped out, turned, and locked the door. He dropped the key into the potted plant and scampered to his car.

Gomez watched the agent get in his car, back out, and drive away. He sat for another ten minutes, relaxed but watchful. Then he started his car and drove away.

Mission accomplished.

4

BARE CORRUPTION

"They were brought in through a German firm in Antwerp," Hayden Boyd said to the president, "then transferred to China under a so-called technical consulting contract."

The relationship between president MacDuff and Boyd, the CIA chief, was bittersweet. MacDuff simply did not understand the methods or values of the intelligence service. Plus, the agency had suffered a poor image in recent years and had lost support.

But that didn't stop Boyd from tracing supercomputers and the misuse of U.S. technology. He called a meeting to discuss the growing problem, and the two men convened in the Oval Office.

On hearing Boyd's statement, the president cringed. "Who sold them to the German company?" He thought *I got a feeling it's Redding, pulling one of his tricks.* Instantly, his eyes flared. A rush of blood began to flow up his neck and across his face.

"MegaTronics," Boyd answered. "Two units were sold to the Germans directly from the plant. And here's the worst part. They were both equipped with special missile control devices."

"That freaking traitor!"

"Who?"

"Never mind," MacDuff growled abruptly, waving off the issue with flailing hands. He sprang to his feet and began pacing. He always paced when faced with an impending crisis. With hands clutched behind his back, he turned and walked to the array of windows behind his desk. He peered outside at the rain coming down in fine, wind-whipped sprays. *How could I make such a blunder?*

Boyd cocked his head and glared at the president. "The same thing happened in Russia. Know anything about it?" Boyd was on dangerous ground, and he knew it. The hell with it, I'm going for it. He knows something but doesn't want to say it. Wonder why? What's the connection?

The president pirouetted around. "No! What are you implying?" MacDuff looked directly into Boyd's penetrating eyes, as if to say, "Don't mess with me".

By now, his angular face was bright crimson, furrowed in a frown. Arteries pumped upon his temples. *Guess I've really screwed up. He's rooting me out. If anyone can, this guy can. And there's no telling which side he'll come down on.*

"Nothing really," Boyd replied coolly, showing no regret. He shrugged his shoulders. "Sorry, Mr. President, just asking—a force of habit, I guess. My job is to interrogate people."

MacDuff grunted incredulously. "Indeed." Like a chameleon, he straightened his posture and assumed a relaxed, presidential demeanor. His bluish-gray hair gave him that mature, distinguished look. When necessary, and in a deceptively charming manner, he could make his ice-blue eyes twinkle in the presence of anyone. "Never mind," he said smilingly. "Now, let's talk about those units. How long has this been going on?"

"Not sure," the CIA chief replied. Boyd was the scholarly type, but he was no professor. He was the nation's top sleuth, a person with years of field experience. His ruffled gray hair and wire-rimmed glasses adorned a full cherubic face. His large, brown eyes were probing, intrusive. "We think at least six months, maybe more. Hard to keep track. You know, because of our budget, we've had to downsize in the field."

MacDuff cleverly ignored the lure of a debate over finances. "See what else you can find out. I want to know names, dates, and places. Get hard evidence—whatever you can muster." He turned his back to Boyd and lifted his eyes to the ceiling. *Gotta create a diversion fast, dig up some scapegoats and cover this up. It could blow up on me.*

MacDuff turned and said, "Thanks for the report."

Boyd took this as a signal of dismissal and emerged from his chair.

"Right."

"Stay on top of it. Give me weekly updates."

Precisely, Boyd thought. *Now that I know there's a connection, I'll be watching you too, Mr. President.* "Yes, sir." He turned and walked towards the door.

MacDuff remained standing as Boyd left the room. Then he sat down hard and swung his chair around. He stared out the window. He watched the misty rain spray the trees, then drip from the leaves like heavy teardrops. The rich, green landscape was serene, but there was a burning madness within him. He was seething. *That conniving Redding. He's going behind my back—cutting me out of the action—that greedy, double-crossing weasel.* Sensing possible chinks in his armor, MacDuff was poised to retaliate. He knew the ravenous press corps would eagerly accommodate a smear campaign, however ridiculous. But he needed a good story and well-picked characters. He leaned over his desk, pushed a button, and spoke into the intercom. "Tiff, I've got an item for you."

Within seconds, Tiffany DeNeaux ambled through the door with a pen and notepad.

"Call the FBI," he said. "Get Scott Brummell on the phone. Tell him to send over the files on Redding and key people in his company. And while he's at it, get everything on General Fuller too."

AIR FORCE ONE

"Mac, please stop." Liz Ledgewick was becoming irritable. The president was getting aggressive with her in the executive lavatory, but Liz was not amenable to his advances while on Air Force One. MacDuff muttered, "Okay."

She had not condoned such strident crudeness, but only for his insatiable desire did she concede to it.

Seconds later, MacDuff gave a throaty chuckle. "Sorry, Liz."

The alluring brunette had a crooked smile on her full, sanguine lips.

Thin, dark eyebrows outlined her large raisin-like eyes. "Coming up on D.C. anytime now," MacDuff said. Liz straightened her clothing. "Need to tidy up."

The two had had an ongoing affair for the past six months and MacDuff couldn't resist his urge for Liz. While the rest of the White House press corps were in the next cabin, she was privileged to have private conferences with the president. Other journalists scoffed but reluctantly accepted it as part of the game. Her method was effective. Relaxed, MacDuff leaned against the wall. "Liz, these excursions are becoming awkward. I want to set up something a little more permanent. Like an apartment, maybe?"

Ted Whittington, MacDuff's vice president, had arranged MacDuff's first meeting with Liz Ledgewick in a late-night interview nine months earlier. She was an ambitious GNN news correspondent who often went on MacDuff's whirlwind fundraising tours.

Liz paused. "You mean, a long-term relationship?" She sprinkles her upper-class British accent with American inflections.

The president put on a devilish smile. "Sure. Why not?" To him, it was simply domesticating their salacious affair. Indeed, he had been in far worse follies. A supplicating lover, he was a beggar of her flesh, and he was driven by it. It made perfect sense to surround the relationship with convenience.

In a twisted manner of justice, he considered it a noble motivator. After all, on-demand sensual gratification would enhance and confirm him as the most powerful man in the world. It was for the good of the people, a stabilizer for the presidency. Much like a pleading criminal would rationalize his acts, that made it okay.

Liz gave him an icy cold stare. "What about your situation? Your wife and family?"

Relinquishing moral instincts, she felt some remorse for his wife, Claire, and his daughter, Bridgett. She empathized with them. She could sense the pain and humiliation if the affair were exposed.

He looked at her sternly, but he was not altogether upset. "We've been through this before. What's the harm?" he said with a shrug. "As long as we deny it, everything will be all right."

"Mac, what about my career? I'd like to get married and have a family too!" She stared intensely into his eyes, hoping to draw a commitment. Liz was determined to have a fulfilling life. And she was steeped in one's loyalty to political and moral standards. Reginald Ledgewick, her father, was a University of Cambridge graduate—Trinity Hall—and a British diplomat stationed in D.C.

Following her father's tradition, Liz attended New Hall—a women's college in the Cambridge school system. She earned two degrees—one in political science and one in journalism. Though not as quaint and historical as Trinity, the prestigious New Hall was close to the Cambridge city center, nestled on an old Roman site on Castle Hill.

After graduation, Liz worked as a BBC correspondent in Paris and subsequently spent two years in Russia. While there, she lived in a flat at metro Baumanskaya, near the famous towns of Russia's Golden Ring—a group of historical cities in Moscow's northeast. She spoke fluent French and Russian. Her impressive credentials and foreign experience won her the job as a White House correspondent. She was also equipped with top-level references from her father's friends and previous employers. By all accounts, she was destined for stardom in the competitive world of broadcast journalism.

Liz's canvassing words grated on MacDuff. His face reddened with frustration. He turned towards the mirror, clenched his jaw, and gritted his teeth. His scarlet cheeks rippled as he looked at himself in the mirror. You could only hear the hum of the jet engines, the hiss of rushing air, and the rattle of cocktail glasses in the galley.

After a long pause, MacDuff said, "You know the deal. My career is first and foremost. What's with the guilt trip, anyway?"

Her cheeks flushed. Liz felt used. But at the same time, she had deep emotional conflicts about the relationship. Admittedly, she had come to enjoy the intimate relationship and being part of a world power brokerage. Besides, it was certain advancement in her profession. But still, it was an ambivalent feeling and often difficult to deal with. She had hoped that he truly loved her—hurtfully, words that he seldom uttered.

Then again, Liz had a yearning mission in life, and she was determined to see it through. She loved her career and the exciting challenges of handling risky situations—and demonstrating her grit against the male class. She actually savored intrigue, risk, and danger. Her trysts with MacDuff provided for many of these needs.

And again, the direct line access to White House information would advance her success on a fast track. The payoff would be huge, rationally offsetting his sometimes-brutish treatment. But at the moment, the hurt was deep. The emotion was undeniable. With a cold stare fixed on him, Liz snapped, "I have feelings too." Close to tears, her small straight nose wrinkled on her smooth oval face.

MacDuff lowered his eyes and nodded stoically. Though a rarity, his face revealed an inkling of regret.

Now Liz had a glimmer of tears in her eyes. "At some point, you have to make a decision. You either break it off with me or divorce your wife." She failed to quell the oncoming whimper in her voice. "This can't go on forever, you know." She thought about the personal sacrifices she had made to be with him in secret. And the many dates she had passed up. Most of her suitors were handsome, rich professionals of position, willing to make sacrifices to be with her.

"I understand," MacDuff said quietly. "But we'll have to ride out this next election before we do anything. Okay?" He angled his head and gave her an appealing boyish look, hoping for a reprieve. Exploring her eyes, he could see he had succeeded. Her submissive expression and the slight gleam in her eyes revealed her surrender.

The president cleverly suppressed a ghost of a smile, a smile of victory.

Liz gazed at him, searching for his true inner feelings. Then she turned away abruptly. Even in a sensory way, she feared exposing her vulnerabilities, her deep-rooted motives in life.

At that moment, Ted Whittington rapped on the door. "Mac, fifteen minutes from landing!"

"Just a minute!"

MacDuff and Liz hurried to freshen up. Liz rummaged through her purse for a hairbrush and makeup while MacDuff combed his hair.

MacDuff gawked at Liz in the mirror while she put on her makeup. "Liz, you're so beautiful. I'm crazy about you," he muttered in a raspy voice. "Are you just saying that?"

"Sometimes I think about you all day long. I wish we could be together all the time."

Liz paused, then glanced at him incredulously. His voracious expression confirmed his motives. "Let me translate. You want to make love to me every day, but not necessarily marry me."

There was an awkward silence. "Well, I guess so," he said with a thin, nervous smile.

"Sounds like plain lust."

"Maybe so, but I'm still crazy about you. Your intelligence is captivating. Being with you can enslave any man on earth." He paused, muffled a deep sigh, and opened his arms. "I, I need you."

His charm was disarming. Liz began to retreat. She held his eyes with her own and softened her reproach. And after all, lovemaking was only one aspect of the partnership. But most importantly, she was achieving her professional mission in life.

"We have to be careful," Liz said. "I'm concerned rumors will get started." She continued to put on her lipstick, pat her face with powder and fluff up her hair. She turned and squinted at MacDuff, suggesting caution but discernibly conveying her willingness to continue the affair. "You know, we can't risk a scandal, especially this close to elections." After which, she cracked a thin smile, beckoning his advance.

Instantly relieved, MacDuff grinned, ear-to-ear. "Don't worry, sweetheart; we'll be okay." MacDuff hardly got the words out before they embraced. Mouths opened, they locked into one last passionate kiss. He hesitated to release her but was prompted by the "Fasten Seat Belt" sign and the chiming warning bell.

Later, Liz stood before a Global News Network (GNN) TV camera. Using the White House as background, she wrapped up her news commentary on national television, "And those are the hard facts from a close White House source. Liz Ledgewick reporting live, from the White House."

TOLEDO, OHIO

Like a huge ivory ball, a new moon hung in the sky over Toledo. It was a summer evening, warm and humid with a gentle breeze. At an outdoor amphitheater, people sipped cold drinks as the president came to the end of his address.

He had just delivered his usual stump speech and was getting to his boilerplate crescendo. "And for the first time since the dawn of the nuclear age, on this night, this beautiful night, we are not targeted by nuclear missiles." He stood at the podium wearing charcoal slacks and an open collar shirt. The moist, oppressive night air caused armpit stains on his light blue shirt.

A few days later, Vice president Whittington spoke at a national convention of party supporters in Canton. He summarized by saying, "And our strength at home has led to renewed respect abroad. American cities, our homes, and our families are safe from a missile attack."

MacDuff and Whittington were on the campaign trail—misleading the American people into a false sense of security. The notion that no missiles were aimed at the U.S. was ludicrous. Statements coming out of Russia and China blatantly negated their contrived message.

5

SITUATION ROOM, THE WHITE HOUSE

"General Fuller, if we provide more weapons to Taiwan, China would be furious!" With hands folded behind his back, President MacDuff paced the floor.

"But we need to protect our advisors," responded General Fuller. "At the least, we should shield Taiwan under the East Asian Theater Missile Defense System."

"Not necessary," MacDuff shot back. "We should replicate what's going on in the Middle East."

Cabinet members glanced at one other with a puzzled look. The Middle East situation had a little comparison to East Asia.

"Sir?" Fuller asked.

"Well, General, I can see you're wondering. I'm talking about the Organization of Islamic Conference. They want to eliminate all weapons of mass destruction. They're urging Israel to go along with the nuclear non-proliferation treaty."

Instantly, Fuller had a dreadful vision. He saw Israel being disarmed, then ruthlessly ambushed. It would be the same for Taiwan. "But China's got over two hundred missiles fixed on Taiwan. What if they attack?"

MacDuff hesitated. Heads turned, and muffled conversations drifted around the room.

"My goal is to let Beijing and Taipei solve their own problems," the president said. "As long as we continue to have peace conferences, we're off the hook. I intend to use the diplomatic approach, and most importantly, preserve our trade relations."

"You really think China's interested in peaceful coexistence?" Fuller retorted. His face was like stone. "I don't think so. And if they do attack, we should whack 'em. Hard!"

MacDuff anticipated the display of emotion. He stretched his lips into a sardonic grin. "Planning on a political career after retirement, General?"

Fuller glared at him with fire in his eyes. Okay, so I'm not politically correct. I'm a ragged fightin' Marine. "Sir, I'm simply concerned about our country!"

"Indeed, General. There's nothing more boring than dogmatic self-righteousness. Like I've said before, 'there's nothing to worry about.'

There's no need to prepare for war!" All eyes switched to Fuller.

Fuller struggled to control his emotions. MacDuff was a master at humiliation. *The bunker mentality, that's what he has—take cover until things blow over. Sooner or later, we'll have to square off with them.*

The general took a deep breath and let out a sigh. "Sir, no one wants war. But let's analyze the facts and determine the consequences of not building up our allies. That's the least we can do."

Fuller continued, "Global military power has tilted in favor of a few enormous, powerful nations. And like it or not, we're being infiltrated in many ways. Besides the issue of China, we have terrorists within our own borders. They're already entrenched and have orders to strike. We either gear up for a fight now or pay a higher price later."

MacDuff gave a low grunt. He sensed the strength of his argument was ebbing away. "I want to maintain our image as peacekeepers. It's a complex situation."

"True enough. The politics in Asia and the Middle East are too unpredictable," said Fuller.

MacDuff's eyes darted from side to side. "No. I'm not sending more arms to Taiwan!"

Fuller's craggy eyebrows dropped low over his eyes. "And what about our people stationed in Korea, Japan, Okinawa, and Taiwan, where the Chinese are most likely to attack?"

"We'll be forced to retaliate."

Fuller shook his head briskly. "Too late. It would be a freaking slaughter!"

"Then, you tell me. You seem to have all the answers!"

"Deter them now, before they strike!"

"No way!" MacDuff shook his head vigorously. "Besides, the Chinese wouldn't attack our soldiers."

Fuller paused. He leaned towards the president. "I'm not convinced of that. And heaven help them if they do." A dog was buried in his throat, and everyone could hear it snarling.

All eyes shifted from Fuller to the president.

After a few seconds, Charles Atkins, the secretary of defense, spoke up. "Gentlemen, we should think this over very carefully."

MacDuff cleared his throat. "I want to maintain our image as peacekeepers," he uttered solemnly. "On the other hand, with our troops in Taiwan, China is kept aware of our support in the region. But I don't wanna ruffle any feathers either." MacDuff glanced around the table to study reactions. Some looked at each other and said nothing. Others fidgeted, leaned forward, attempted to comment, but held back.

"I have a problem with that," the battle-hardened general grumbled. All heads swung towards Fuller. "If I have to, I'll take this up with Congress. I don't want the blood of Americans on my hands!"

The opaque skin of MacDuff's face turned a bright crimson. He bowed forward and said, "Now just a minute, General." He leveled a cold stare directly into Fuller's smoldering eyes. "Aren't you being awfully presumptuous?"

"Not at all," the general snapped, stoic before the president's challenging stare. "I'm realistic." Fuller squinted his probing eyes. His defiance and clenched jaw that many associated with the tough Marine remained firmly in place.

You could only hear the ticking of the clock on the wall. Around the oval conference table, everyone waited to see who would back down first. Ted Whittington sat rigidly in his leather chair next to the president. He gripped a pencil in his fist, looking back and forth between the two. Colonel Manny Gomez, the general's aide, had a wry grin on his face.

The president balked first. He looked away, taking a long drink from the glass of water at his elbow.

"Look, we're inviting big trouble with the Chinese," Fuller said. "If they hit our troops, they'll win a psychological battle. Besides, if push came to shove, I think Russia would join up with them in a major coup. China's been real cozy with them lately."

"C'mon, the Chinese and the Russians fighting us in the same camp? Absurd!"

"Don't forget, China and Russia were together in Korea," countered Fuller. "Instead of welcoming Russia to join NATO, we've essentially ignored them, isolated them, let them wallow in economic disarray and political decline. Why should they want to join the West?"

"They need our help. That's why. I've been holding back on playing that card—waiting for the right time, the right circumstances."

"Wouldn't count on it," Fuller said. "The Russians don't have any particular love for the U.S., and they still have a few cards of their own. A hefty nuclear arsenal, for one. That's enough reason to sway them into our corner."

"I'm telling you: we don't need the Russians!"

Fuller paused for effect. "Well, sir, what if they decide to revert to a cold war attitude? As it stands, they can pull that nuclear trigger anytime they like."

Bristling, the president paused. "I'm not an unreasonable man. I'll consider your opinion. Even if we raise the issue with the general Committee, and no matter what the outcome, changes have to be cleared with Taiwan and the ASEAN organization. Understood?"

"Understood," Fuller replied, grim-faced. Inside, he was smiling.

6

CRISIS MANAGEMENT

Outside the White House, the streets were slick from a drizzle, causing delays for homeward-bound workers. Making matters worse, Pennsylvania Avenue was blocked off—protecting the White House from terrorist threats. It was a period of *glasnost*. International terrorism and Third World intransigence were on the rise.

Intelligence pointed to the Palestinian groups AMAS and Islamic Jihad and the Algerian Armed Islamic Group. Threats also came from the Egyptian al-Gama' a al-Islamiyya.

Then there was the despicable Lebanese group Hezbollah Ummah. They were responsible for the bombings of the Marine barracks and the U.S. Embassy in Lebanon. Hizballah still holds the dark distinction of having killed more American citizens through terrorism than any other group.

But at the moment, terrorism and traffic were secondary to MacDuff and Whittington. In the cocoon of the Oval Office, they were dealing with damage control.

"What'll we tell the press?" MacDuff said, gazing across the room.

Whittington leaned forward in his chair and stroked his chin.

"Maybe not such a problem." He smiled broadly. "This could be a golden opportunity."

MacDuff snapped out of his trance and looked at his VP.

"You know, spin the story in our favor," said Whittington. "And release the news on Friday night for the low coverage. We've done it before."

MacDuff put on a crooked smile. "And we can do it again!" He sat behind the historic Resolute Desk, a requirement of his role model, John F-Kennedy. They made the desk from the British ship's timbers, the HMS *Resolute*, abandoned north of the Arctic Circle in 1854.

The ship was later found by the crew of an American whaling ship, refitted, and sent to Queen Victoria as a token of goodwill. They made the desk when they dismantled the ship. Queen Victoria gave the desk to U.S. President Rutherford B. Hayes in 1880.

"Mac, you can charm anyone." Whittington said. By all appearances, they were an odd couple. Whittington was short and clever, MacDuff tall and suave. "Charisma, Mac. That's what they call it. Charisma."

MacDuff beamed over his choice of words. He spun his chair around and faced the window. He watched the misty rain trickle small water pellets from the leaves.

"Amazing," MacDuff said. "Twist the logic, say some words, spend a little money, and they'll believe anything!" He rocked back in his chair. *Ah, life is good. And getting here was fun! The days at Oxford were often boring, but the political debates were invaluable. And those wild parties— marijuana, hashish, and exciting female encounters. I was able to hone the art of political persuasion while seducing British women. Cripes! I hope that stuff never comes out.*

The president swiveled around. "Ted, I've got another ingredient for the mix." He reached out and pressed a button on the intercom. "Tiff, bring me the China report."

Tiffany DeNeaux came in and handed MacDuff the top-secret document. A holdover from the election campaign, Tiffany was an attractive platinum blonde with sea-blue eyes and long legs. She wore a powder blue blouse and a short, snug-fitting white skirt. "Anything else, sir?"

"Yes. Call Lee Redding. MegaTronics Corporation."

Tiffany flashed a coy grin. "Of course. There's only one Lee Redding, isn't there?" She smiled seductively, turned, and strutted away with the gait of a model. Tiffany was in her early forties but didn't look it. Whittington was less interested, but with craving eyes, MacDuff stared at her mocking invitation. He handed the report to Whittington and watched Tiffany disappear through the door.

Whittington gingerly fingered the pages. The six-page report confirmed two MEGA-Star computers were in China's missile programs. He shook his head. "Not good."

"C'mon, man, tell me something worthwhile!" Arteries pumped up on MacDuff's neck. "Strategy, I need a strategy!"

Whittington glowered at him with his rosy cherubic face. "Sure, sure. Of course, Mac." His jaw was tight, but he spoke smoothly. He had willed himself calmness, ignoring a groundswell of frustration.

"We're in this together."

As quickly as he flared, MacDuff shrugged it off. "Okay, forget it. Just get to the bottom of this."

"Sure, sure!" Whittington responded evenly. He was extremely adept at weathering emotional tirades. His moody mother unwittingly cultivated this extraordinary skill at repressing emotions. He was also callously tested when told of his alcoholic father's death while at middle school.

"Mr. Redding, line one," Tiffany said over the intercom.

MacDuff leaned forward and said, "Redding may fess up." He punched line one and picked up the telephone. "Bill, how's business?"

"Great, Mr. President!" Redding's squeaky, metallic voice exuded excitement. "Of course, I still have to deal with my competition, Dante Martin at ComTech. And my problems with the DOJ." He chortled nervously.

MacDuff rolled his eyes and ignored his lure. "Competition? What competition?"

Redding hesitated a second. "Well, not much competition, anyway."

"Listen." MacDuff lowered his voice in a serious tone. "We've got a bit of a problem."

Whittington's ears perked up.

"Oh?" Redding's voice was tight. "What is it?"

"Illegal foreign exports. Your systems in China."

"What!"

"Precisely. Now, tell me, what the hell is going on?"

"Jeez, don't know anything about it, Mac." He paused. "Honest!"

Silence.

"Cut the crap," replied MacDuff, wearing a deep frown. "It's me you're talking to. The spooks are finding your stuff all over the world."

"But Mac, we just supply the CPU chip. We don't market—."

"Don't market? Bull!" He glanced at Whittington's smiling face.

"Listen, if I go down..."

Redding swallowed hard. "I get the picture."

"Good," the president said. He sighed heavily.

"Now, you know, we have to take care of each other."

He closed the conversation and cradled the telephone. They had nurtured mutual servitude over the years and Redding's computers were key to MacDuff's economic strategies.

"Think he'll eventually end up in deep trouble?" Whittington said, with a lopsided smile.

"If he does, to hell with it! We'll just fill the gap."

"Right. We've got computer makers, aircraft companies, carmakers, Fortune Five Hundred companies, and most importantly, social media and the press in our corner."

"We're set," the president said with a smug grin.

"Manipulate the trade deficit and leverage our high-tech card—especially in China, the world's biggest market."

"What about the supercomputers and missiles in China?"

"Ted, Beijing's not going to screw up! They know better. They're not gonna risk international trade leverage."

Whittington bit his lip and abruptly turned away.

7

____

THE PENTAGON

With cold steel eyes and his jaw set, General Fuller emulated a Roman soldier in a suit of armor. He sat at his desk in his perfectly tailored, olive-green uniform. Behind him, the Stars and Stripes and the red and gold Marine Corps flag framed him like a statue.

The Cox report on the Chinese spy scandal, combined with Lame Duck's information, confirmed the stolen information severely breached our national security.

"Lame Duck's report didn't stop Mutt 'n' Jeff from preaching the 'no missiles' bull," the general said to Colonel Gomez, sitting across his desk.

"Surprised?" Gomez replied sardonically. "It's obvious they want to divert attention away from the nuclear threat. Then eliminate the export ban on shipping high-performance computers overseas."

According to military intelligence and the CIA, U.S. supercomputers were showing up in Russia, China, Korea, and other banned markets.

"Expansion of global commerce," Fuller mused.

"More like global greed," Gomez voiced abruptly, looking at Fuller with stabbing ebony eyes. Gomez raised his brow and said,

"Scuttlebutt is, the White House cleared MegaTronics and others to enter these markets. They're in cahoots with the high-tech industry. Especially with Lee Redding at MegaTronics."

"Don't think he's the traitor type," Fuller said. "Egocentric and gullible, maybe, but not a real traitor."

"No matter how you cut it, it's disgusting." Gomez grimaced. "They're promoting slipshod trade policies and transferring critical technology. At the same time, they're downsizing the defense budget." He took a moment to ponder the situation. "They're giving our technology to crazies who would nuke us! That's what it boils down to."

Gomez's statement triggered the general's recollection of a conversation he had had with his agent in Beijing. He remembered Lame Duck's exact words on how the PLA, the People's Liberation Army had "hit the jackpot with U.S. secrets." The Chinese were outwardly making progress as players in the nuclear weapons game. The 3-B launch vehicles, their improved *Long March* series, were heavily sought in international markets because of their low cost and high reliability. The Loral Space & Communications company had helped the Chinese correct the LM series guidance system, and Hughes Electronics advised them to shield multiple warheads during launches. Lame Duck also mentioned the Chinese were using the latest MEGA-Star computers as missile control units.

"Well, you're right!" said Fuller. "It's our own fault. Using our technology, the Chinese have cut at least fifteen years from their nuclear research and development. Lame Duck said China could now mount small warheads on lighter, mobile, covert missiles. And they've already combined multiple warheads on a single, larger ICBM—one that could reach the U.S."

The facts stirred Gomez's emotions. His Filipino-Mexican blood was bubbling, and retaliatory instincts kicked in. "Hey, we can still take 'em! Despite their modernized nuclear arsenal."

Gomez stopped short of revealing his deep-rooted feelings. *We need to stop them now! Combined with the president's misguided foreign policies and weakening defense systems, China's an existential threat.*

Gomez suddenly had flashbacks of his experience in Iran, and Khomeini's venomous hate for the U.S. Gomez was on temporary assignment when, on the morning of February 20, 1979, thousands of Iranian soldiers stormed the gates of Doshan Tappen Air Base at Farahabad, and seized automatic rifles and hand grenades. Embroiled with mob rule, truckloads of armed Iranians drove past the American embassy jeering, and yelling, "Yankee, go home!"

When the Shah of Iran left the country and Khomeini arrived from Paris to take over, the situation rapidly deteriorated. On February 14, 1979, an Iranian police officer arbitrarily began directing traffic away from the embassy. Suddenly, gunfire came from an Iranian perched on top of the wall surrounding the embassy. Without warning, Molotov cocktails came flying over the wall into the compound. Then rapid- gunfire came from an adjacent eight-story school building, just across the street.

Armed with only shotguns using number-nine skeet shots, Gomez and his troops could not reach the attackers. So, the gung-ho leathernecks threw tear gas canisters over the wall, then retreated inside the chancery to protect personnel and classified material. Sensitive documents were quickly burned just before the Iranians scrambled over the wall and riddled the two-inch thick wooden doors with AK-47 gunfire. Gomez ordered everyone to go to the top floor while his men released tear gas at all lower levels.

Later, much to Gomez's chagrin, the American ambassador ordered the Marines to give up their weapons and surrender without a fight. From that point, they were held captive for over fourteen months. Gomez recalled how our government could not muster the intestinal fortitude to send a rescue team or negotiate a hard bargain. In his mind, it remains an embarrassing event in history. Sadly, American citizens were again faced with that same weakness in MacDuff's administration, only worse.

Failing to restrain himself, Gomez blurted, "Before you know it, the rest of the world will get the strange idea that we're a bunch of wimps!"

Fuller gazed into Gomez's impervious tiger eyes—penetrating, alert, and yet unrevealing of themselves. The general was delighted to see the can-do fighting attitude—a trait that saves our country from defeat time and again.

Ah, the Marine Corps, the strongest brotherhood in the world. A unique force, a cut above. No matter the cost, the sacrifice, a Marine delivers results. While on the battlefield, there's no time for being tentative or doubtful. Once the mission is defined, there's no other way, he thought, *but to charge ahead and win. ONLY DURING PEACETIME MUST WE KEEP OUR HEADS UP, BE ALERT AND DEPLOY A PEACEFUL STRATEGY TO SAVE LIVES. It's about diplomacy before doing battle.*

Still peering into Gomez's eyes, Fuller said, "Yes, I agree. On the ground, we can beat the pants off 'em. They're no match for us. But then again, neither was Syria or the Islamic terrorists when they drove us out of Lebanon. We mustn't forget Beijing has the power to wipe out our forces in East Asia easily."

Fuller constantly worried the Chinese were quietly forming military alliances in the East with the idea of overpowering the region. And if they did attack us, they were clever enough to hold their position for the optimal time.

"The difference in ground troops is staggering!" Fuller snapped. "We have about hundred-thousand men and women under arms in that theater. China has twenty times that number. And they now have miniature warheads and the use of MIRVS—Multiple Independently Targeted Reentry Vehicles. As many as five to ten W-eighty-eights can be clustered on top of a missile to split and strike at separate targets. They could quintuple their land-based warheads."

Gomez's tight, the smooth face didn't look scared, but it showed apprehension.

"By supplying nuclear weapons to others, one of their loony partners could easily flip a switch and start a freaking star war," said the general. "No way I'm gonna let them use our troops for target practice!"

Gomez cringed. "Target practice?"

"That's right. Target practice. Marines in Okinawa and Japan and army troops based in South Korea are being targeted in mock missile attacks."

Gomez fidgeted in his chair and felt squeamish. Then a wave of rage swept through his body. The thought of using fellow Marines for target practice curled the hairs on the back of his neck. A stream of expletives ran through his mind. *Will there be another face-off with the Chinese?*

"And we have to consider Taiwan," uttered Fuller. "The Chinese missile threat against them has gone up from thirty missiles in 1996 to over two hundred and rising."

"Think Taiwan will buckle under pressure, join the mainland?" said Gomez. "They fought together once before when they expelled the Japanese from China."

The burly general let out a long sigh. "Who knows? As long as they're not in our missile defense system, they're vulnerable." A well-known fact, China is vehemently against the idea of Taiwan having a missile site of any kind. Mainland China regarded Taiwan as an aberration in history, a place of refuge for renegades. It was a nagging irritant, an embarrassment to an egotistical government in Beijing. They would not allow outsiders to add salt to the wound.

Fuller stood up and walked to the window. He gazed at the puffy clouds in the sky, seemingly analyzing them for rain. But the weather was simply a diversion. He didn't want to be pessimistic about the China affair, but his tendency to be practical usually won over flimsy hope and false optimism. The U.S. commitment to support Taiwan had been a solid policy for many years, but Fuller had a nagging feeling—the U.S. protection of Taiwan wouldn't last forever.

Disturbing inertia had loomed over the Taiwan situation, and Beijing was bursting to demonstrate its military prowess. "Manny, China could call our bluff and force the Taiwan issue to the breach of war—a war the U.S. cannot afford," he said quietly.

"But doesn't Beijing want to conserve trade relations?" Gomez replied. "Big business in the U.S., the Chinese government, and Congress have loaded up on trade deals." These factions had jointly mobilized a lobbying army of CEOs, targeting lawmakers with daily propaganda blitzes. The MacDuff administration, the U.S. Chamber of Commerce, the U.S.-China Business Council, the Business Round-table, and the Emergency Committee for American Trade led the drive for normal trade relations.

Congress's vote on permanent NTR would be a referendum on China's entry into the WTO. And Beijing had already threatened U.S. companies. They would not get the same market access as other WTO members if Congress did not cooperate. Odds were MacDuff, and Beijing would get their way. And Taiwan would be saddled with a much larger handicap.

Several seconds had passed while Fuller pondered the complex question. With hands folded behind his back, he turned and said, "Manny, in my opinion, this China-Taiwan thing is a glorified family feud. If we show any signs of reneging, it's no telling what Taiwan will do.

"They're part of a deep-rooted culture that's thousands of years old. Sure, there have political differences. But they're the same race, the same blood. The Taiwanese are just as Chinese as they are across the strait, even as far as Beijing."

8

———

RENAISSANCE MAYFLOWER HOTEL, WASHINGTON, D.C

The gala at the Mayflower's historic Grand Ballroom was a flamboyant affair. Huge chandeliers hung from the ceiling like glittering planets. While below, the rich Washington elite co-mingled in all their grandeur. Adorned with the finest, the colossal room had hosted U.S. presidential balls since Calvin Coolidge.

President MacDuff began his wrap-up. "Look at the fact that we survived the Y2K fiasco," he conveyed in a smooth, convincing manner. "And because of the scare of nuclear missiles being accidentally launched, we now have almost one hundred eighty nations committed to never getting involved in the nuclear arms race. Russia and other nations have de-targeted their nuclear missiles." His oratory skills were somewhat ordinary but effective. Over the life of his career, he had been coached by the best. Professional courses in acting, speech, and a special Dale Carnegie class for heads of state enhanced the president's natural charisma.

He paused to allow a round of applause. His smiling wife, Claire, standing at his side clapped gracefully. He relished the accolades from supporters sitting near the podium. It was no secret—MacDuff enjoyed being the object of adulation. Camouflaged by a thin coat of makeup, his sallow face stretched wide with a grin. He inhaled a deep breath of air and blurted, "For the first time since the dawn of the nuclear age, there is not a single, solitary nuclear missile pointed at an American child tonight. Not one. Not a single one!"

The audience exploded with applause. Beaming, the president turned and hugged his wife. "How'd I do?" he whispered in her ear.

"You did well," she answered. The First Lady's pearly-white skin radiated against her plum-colored evening gown. Her intense auburn hair and startling turquoise eyes radiated in the spotlight. And it was obvious she came from money. Claire had that look of contentment, the pampered lifestyle that the rich most often enjoy. Her family had gained millions in photography and public relations. In fact, her father's political influence and PR shrewdness were the prime driving forces in getting MacDuff first elected vice president.

How MacDuff became president was a twist of fate. His running mate, President-elect Bradford Chalmers, was assassinated during his first few months in office. A sniper shot him at a speaking engagement in Los Angeles. And to this day, the crime mysteriously remains unsolved. Oddly, the FBI, the CIA, the LAPD, and the district attorney's office teamed up to keep details of the case under wraps. They even pushed laws through the California legislature to lock up evidence. But going against strong resistance from local officials, an investigative committee was eventually set up by Congress. Ever since MacDuff had remained under a cloud of suspicion.

The president smiled as he gazed at Claire but felt a twinge of guilt. Their strained relationship had worsened in recent months. "Thanks for toughing it out," he said. "I know it's been rough."

Claire gave him a spurious smile and said nothing. She peered at him with a trace of spite in her eyes. In reality, it was only for the sake of their daughter that she chose to endure the hardships of his philandering, dirty politics, and impending scandals. Whimsically, she fancied herself something of a martyr.

As for MacDuff, he was in his element. Life couldn't be better. He spun away from her, and with a wide smile, he repeatedly blew kisses to a multitude of cheering people. The 7,656 square foot ballroom was filled. "Thank you—thank you," he said with a smile. The tuxedo-clad chief executive and the First Lady carefully stepped down from the platform. Surrounded by watchful Secret Service agents, the White House couple mingled with the crowd, shook hands, waved, and moved towards their seats.

Outside the hotel, like a school of sharks in a feeding frenzy, a gaggle of reporters with TV cameras had gathered. When the banquet was over, and people began to stream out, they first approached Lee Redding, the billionaire founder of MegaTronics Corporation. They questioned him about a new computer bug called AMOEBA, a unique virus that had infected Redding's MEGA-Star supercomputers.

Smartly dressed in a black tuxedo trimmed with a red sash and bow tie, Redding stated, "We're working diligently on the AMOEBA problem. And we are very close to a resolution." A contemptuous smile crossed his face. His wafer skin appeared paper-thin and very pliable. He gaped at the reporters through his round, wire-framed glasses and continued, "We're well aware of the possible conse-quences that AMOEBA can cause. That's why I've had engineers working on it around the clock."

Curiously, the virus had not affected any other computer brand. But the MEGA-Star was quite different from other systems. It was built with leading-edge, protein-based technology called *molectronics*–a bold divergence from conventional computing. The virus was a new strain, one with a strong resistance to antivirus soft-ware. It was an anomaly in the industry, and no cure was readily available. Redding had said more than he wanted to about the bug.

Then he raised his arms to wave off the jostling reporters. "No more, please," said Redding, now wearing a slight frown. As he marched off, the flock attempted to ask him questions. His demeanor was especially haughty since his new CPU chip had amassed billions of dollars in windfall profits.

His systems were in great demand worldwide, and his company played an essential role in the president's economic strategies. But more important to Redding, he had leaped ahead of his main competitor, Dante Martin, a respected war hero and a formidable rival. Though Martin's company lacked financial influence, he was gutsy, sharp, and his employees were extremely loyal. Redding spurned Martin because he was well respected for his character and not his wealth.

As Redding went to his limousine, Senator Kent Garrity, a presidential hopeful, approached the microphones. The handsome, bronze-tanned senator was often mistaken for a movie star. Garrity meticulously straightened his bow tie before he stepped in front of the cameras and pulled at his silver cuff links. He moved in front of the microphones and looked at the nearest TV interviewer.

"Senator Garrity, during the president's speech, he avoided the subject of the AMOEBA virus," articulated the reporter. "What's your opinion on this new computer threat?"

Garrity eyeballed the correspondent, and for a moment, he studied the cluster of people. He suspected what he was about to say would strike a nerve with the hyped news-hounds. And he was intent on countering the president's demagoguery. "My opinion is this: the AMOEBA computer virus could create a living hell for all of us. In other words, what we worked so hard to avoid in the year 2000 transition, a Y2K disaster, can strike at any time."

The senator paused. He took fleeting glances at the eclectic group in search of a reaction. His statement had astonished many. Listeners had turned to one another in muffled conversations. He pressed on. "We must recognize the fact that the AMOEBA bug can easily cause a global financial meltdown. Computers could crash unexpectedly. Electronic commerce would shut down. Financial markets around the world could be devastated." "Technically, how could that happen, Senator?"

"Well, many of the MEGA-Star computers are linked together in major financial institutions and business enterprises all over the world. Like the biological plague—COVID-19—that started in Wuhan, China, and spread worldwide, the Internet can spread the AMOEBA virus electronically. The Internet acts as a colossal electronic conduit—an unharnessed carrier of the virus to all corners of this planet."

Many were unable to grasp the profound meaning of Garrity's statement fully. And for them, the bleak reality of what was yet to come was elusive, and yet they were fully aware of the ominous nuclear threat.

Meanwhile, General Fuller and his wife, Caitlin, had appeared at the threshold of the hotel entrance. As Garrity wrapped up his talk, a flock of reporters scurried over to cajole General Fuller to speak. When Garrity ambled away, the cameras swung around and focused on the general.

Fuller proceeded towards the array of microphones.

"General Fuller, what do you think about the AMOEBA virus? Does it pose a threat to our national security?" a perky GNN journalist asked, slanting her microphone toward the general. It was Liz Ledgewick.

In full dress blues and standing under a canopy of stars, the general cleared his throat and said, "Well, yes. Since the MEGA-Star is used to control missiles, I would say this bug is a serious threat. But I can assure you: we're trying to prevent any accidents from happening."

"What kind of accidents? And what are we doing about it?" the reporter asked anxiously.

"The accidental firing of missiles. That's what I'm talking about," said the general. "As we did in the Y2K plan, we've offered to set up an early warning system with Russia and other nuclear-equipped nations." Looking squarely into the eyes of the broadcaster, he paused to seek out the right words. Fuller's eyes reflected wisdom, fortitude, and compassion.

He spoke in a slow, sharp tempo. "Frankly, after the unpublicized close calls over the years, we must reduce the risk of a war caused by a computer defect." There was a hush. "But unlike the Y2K problem," he continued, "this glitch is far more dangerous. We can't predict when or if it will strike on any given system." Fuller paused momentarily. "This virus moves slowly. It reproduces itself, taking on a different shape and character. It's elusive, deadly."

Six months previously, Fuller explained to the Russians, "The AMOEBA virus can affect your nuclear arsenal. We know you have supercomputers in sixty-five nuclear plants spread over nine countries."

When the general asked the Russians to participate in the missile defense system, they said, "Why should we? We cooperated in the Y2K project and nothing went wrong. We are adamantly against a missile defense shield of any kind." Moscow had essentially rejected the idea of modifying the 1972 Anti-Ballistic Missile Treaty. Further, U.S. allies in Europe had voiced concerns about whether the plan would trigger a new arms race.

Fuller shook his head, and sighed but did not waiver in his posture. "I also approached the Chinese with the same idea. A Beijing official said to me, 'Only a few businesses failed during the Y2K transition. So, we don't need your anti-missile program. Besides, we already have one.'"

"Not surprising," one of the reporters quietly commented to another. "China wants to demonstrate their mighty influence. In the past few years, Sino-U.S. relations have really deteriorated." He turned to the side and muffled his voice with his hand. "We're almost back to name-calling!" He hesitated, then put on a serious face. "Scary thing is, each nation has enough nuclear power to destroy the other."

General Fuller had failed to convince other nations to link up with a global missile warning system. Most troubling were rogue nations like North Korea, Syria, Libya, Iran, and Iraq. They were powder kegs with short fuses. All were anti-West, in highly volatile feudal environments.

The Iran-controlled Hizballah issued the mission statement, "We are America's arch-enemies. We view Washington's arrogant policy as one of self-interest, seeking to exploit peoples and intervene in their internal affairs. We confront this policy forcefully and firmly."

"We have to be concerned about the hair-trigger nuclear missiles in the world," General Fuller continued. "Wars tend to begin in unpredictable ways. Anything can spark a nuclear war. Just a build-up of petty irritations can lead to a conflict. And not necessarily about things that would *justify* a war."

That night in the Wheaton motel, Lame Duck made General Fuller aware of China's nuclear threat. The double agent conveyed a crucial message: "Of grave concern," he said, "there are at least thirteen missiles aimed at the U.S with a range of more than eight thousand miles."

The Beijing operative further stated, "China already has twenty-five missiles with ranges of more than thirty-four hundred miles. Now we are building two new ICBMs able to hit targets up to seven thousand miles away. And production has been increased. In the next several years, we'll have over a thousand in stock."

Fuller had already learned the Chinese were equipped with yet another series of missiles–the silo-based units with a range of nineteen hundred miles and the road-mobile model with a range of thirteen hundred miles.

Once in a meeting held months earlier, Hayden Boyd, head of the CIA, told Fuller, "China has missiles aimed directly at U.S. military forces deployed all over Asia. And it's been confirmed that they have mobile antiship missiles fixed on our patrol vessels in the Taiwan Strait."

The CIA chief also reported, "Stolen U.S. information has undoubtedly improved the reliability of Chinese rockets, useful for both civilian and military purposes. For example, in their *Long March* series, the Chinese have already successfully launched sixty kinds of foreign satellites. They're in the business commercially."

A 700-page Cox report detailed how a "Network of spies has transferred thousands of computer codes. These *legacy codes* provide a detailed history of nuclear weapons development in the U.S." Unmistakably, China's ballistic missiles were being built with miniaturized, multiple-warhead technology either stolen or commercially transferred from the U.S.

China's vast network of spies had infiltrated the Los Alamos

National Laboratory and important military bases. With well-organized operatives and in a twist of irony, they made heavy use of a system invented by the U.S. Department of Defense—the Internet. They had established a virtual private network over the Internet, a means of protected communications. The cyber spies developed an encrypted messaging system using secured digital lines.

Fuller and Senator Garrity were intent on avoiding computer failures and with good reason. Recently, the NSA's intelligence-gathering computer system mysteriously had become overloaded and failed. Amazingly, technicians had to virtually rebuild the programs and databases heavily relied upon for national security. That same month, a hacker could electronically transfer funds from an online banker to his personal account without detection. The FBI and the Computer Emergency Response Team were still on the case.

For global coverage, the Senator and General Fuller set up a security control center in Washington. The computer facility monitored critical government systems, the World Bank, and the IMF. It is guarded against breaches by hackers and the growing threat of cyberterrorists. The cowardly groups used the Net in a new kind of war. Information sabotage, electronic viruses, and political propaganda could spread across the globe within seconds.

"We mustn't be lulled to sleep by the docile outcome of the Y2K scare," said Fuller. "Most governments depend on computers. And what we avoided during the year two thousand crossover could happen without warning."

Busily jotting down Fuller's remarks, a wide-eyed reporter inquired, "General, what are the *real* chances of computers accidentally starting a nuclear war?" The low resonance of chattering in the background came to an abrupt halt. The young reporter's face mirrored the anxiety of the moment.

He looked intently into the reporter's eyes and answered in a deep baritone voice, "High. Very high."

9

———

WESTIN HERMITAGE HOTEL, NASHVILLE, TENNESSEE

"Liz, wake up, gotta get ready," MacDuff said, nudging Liz Ledgewick, lying at his side. They were enjoying the Westin Hermitage Hotel's plush presidential Suite. It was a French country styled suite with a master bedroom, a study, and two bathrooms.

Outside the room, the hotel's lobby and halls were elegantly decorated with Grecian and Tennessean marble. Downstairs, a spectacular three-story arched ceiling loomed above the lobby. The hotel had hosted many famous visitors including Gene Autry, Bette Davis, and past Presidents Franklin Roosevelt, Nixon, and Kennedy.

MacDuff and Liz were tired. They had worked a fundraiser the day before, arrived at the hotel late, had a long night, and just a few hours of sleep.

Liz rolled over to face MacDuff. Bleary and disoriented, she said in a sleepy voice, "Hmm, I smell coffee." She lifted her head and looked around.

"Yup. Kurt brought some up. I can always count on him. He's one of the best Secret Service guys I've had. He knows how I like things."

Liz sat up, brushing through her shiny dark hair with her long fingers. Then she yawned with outstretched arms.

MacDuff fixed her a cup of coffee and placed it on the nightstand. He glanced at her shapely body, gave a low grunt, and smiled. Liz was just as beautiful in the morning as the night before. There was something about the way she looked without makeup. She really didn't need it. The soft, smooth, youthful contours of her skin made her appear rather innocent and virginal.

"How was my speech last night? MacDuff said. "Sound, okay?"

"Yes, of course," Liz mumbled. "You did a good job." She sat up and bent forward, arranged a pillow up against the headboard, leaned back, and sipped her coffee. MacDuff propped his head up, hands clasped behind his neck and arms buried in his pillow.

Following a long pause, Liz said, "Mac, the talk about the Russians and Chinese doing missile testing—I mean, are you going to mention that today?"

"No way. Can't chance bringing that up now," MacDuff said while gazing at the ceiling. "Better to stay with the disarmament story. As far as anyone is concerned, there are no missiles pointed at us. That's it!"

"Of course. Tell people what they want to hear. You can't rock the boat now, this close to elections. But you'll probably ease into it after the election, right?"

MacDuff shrugged slightly. "Yeah, suppose so. Getting those votes is what's important. I'll worry about the military stuff after I'm reelected. What they don't know won't hurt 'em." He picked up a mirror from the side table. He checked the puffy, heavy bags under his eyes, which had worsened since taking office.

Liz turned and murmured, "Better stop looking at yourself, or you'll develop a bad case of—what's the word?"

"Narcissism," MacDuff said. His swollen eyelids crinkled together as he smiled and gave a deep throaty chuckle. "Already got it. Had it for years. It's an occupational hazard."

They laughed. After a while, the president's expression turned to apprehension.

Liz sipped some more coffee and momentarily stared across the room. Like a layer of peach ice cream, the plush carpeting set off the imperial furniture nicely. Then she looked at MacDuff appraisingly. She said,

"Something's bothering you. Wanna talk about it?"

MacDuff shook his head and sighed. "Yeah, a little bothered. But I can't talk about it. It's top secret." He paused momentarily in thought. *On the other hand, why not? The right-wing hawks have let the cat out of the bag. They've published a lot of the information already.*

"It's about the real truth of our missile defense system."

Liz looked at him in surprise. "Oh, I get it," she muttered. "You're worried they'll use the truth against your campaign slogan of 'no missiles pointed at us.' Right?"

He nodded. "I'm walking a tightrope. We can't defend ourselves against a nuclear attack." In an instant, he was tempted to tell her everything, the bare truth of how bad it really was—how other nations had actually caught up with the U.S. in nuclear capabilities.

Then Liz offered encouragement. "I'm curious," she said. "How do we really stack up? I mean, against Russia, China, and the others? How vulnerable are we? Besides, there's a lot at stake economically."

MacDuff hesitated but then felt an overwhelming urge to confide in her. "Let's put it this way. I shudder to think about a nuclear attack on the U.S. We're ill-prepared to sense oncoming missiles quickly. And the counterattack could be cumbersome."

Liz repositioned herself and leaned forward. "What does that mean? We could be hit without advance knowledge?"

"Well, not exactly. It's too technical to explain. But any way you look at it, we could be surprised. The technology is there, but I've held back on defense spending to get other countries to go along with nuclear disarmament." He shook his head slowly. "I've lost a lot of sleep over this."

Liz swung her head around and looked at him with searching eyes. "Really?" She paused. "Tell me, how long would it really take to detect the missiles, and—"

"Couldn't tell you," He interrupted. "I've purposely avoided the issue and locked that information out of my mind. It's too damn worrisome."

"But shouldn't you be prepared? Because the press will–"

"Hey, enough politics," MacDuff interrupted. "And enough business talk."

Liz fidgeted, drew in a deep breath, and exhaled. The excitement of learning more about the sensitive subject had evaporated. She put her coffee cup back on the nightstand. "Whatever." Liz was concerned about more than a few things. MacDuff showed signs of early dementia, and according to her sources, MacDuff could be ousted under the Twenty-Fifth Amendment. The process could expose his web of business dealings and destroy his empire.

OPRYLAND HOTEL CONVENTION CENTER, NASHVILLE, TENNESSEE

The Opryland hotel complex had nearly three thousand rooms and two hundred suites. Nine acres of lush interior gardens, waterfalls, rivers, and fountains surrounded the massive convention center. A glass roof crowned four and a half acres of interior tropical garden space, with interleaved multilevel walkways.

The fundraiser luncheon was served in the state-of-the-art, fifty-five-thousand square foot Delta Ballroom. "For the first time since the dawn of the nuclear age," MacDuff orated, "there are no nuclear missiles pointed at an American child, and I am proud of that." He had wrapped up an address to six hundred casually dressed supporters.

The ballroom was adjacent to the *Cascade Conservatory*, a gigantic atrium. A four-story fabricated mountain that ejected water over a cascading waterfall centered the water park. The huge gush of water supplied a maze of winding waterways that threaded the elaborate vestibule.

That same day, as MacDuff was giving his speech, *The New York Times* reported a briefing by a former U.S. assistant secretary of state. His brief was the first public revelation of what he termed "an indirect threat by China to use nuclear weapons against the United States."

SUSSE CHALET HOTEL,
SALEM, NEW HAMPSHIRE

There were two hundred voters at the one thousand-dollar, black-tie fund-raiser. Most were upscale politicians and businessmen from the local area. Just over Maine's border, Salem's strategic location was its greatest asset since the town sat midway between Boston and Concord. Salem, served as a convenient stop for politicians on the campaign trail, a town of only 27,000.

MacDuff's supporters were excited and keen to hear what he had to say about missiles and national security. The subjects had emerged as important issues in recent weeks.

But the president had rehearsed for the role. He stood at the podium with a serious, deadpan expression. Unable to ignore *The New York Times* report and indirectly referring to China, MacDuff cleverly addressed the issue of nuclear weapons:

"The Russians and *others* have de-targeted their nuclear missiles. So now, for the first time since the dawn of the nuclear age, there are no more nuclear missiles pointed at any American homes. Since I've been in office, that's not the case anymore."

THE OVAL OFFICE

Three days later, peering through his fashionable bifocals, MacDuff sat at his desk in the Oval Office reading a CIA intelligence report. The report stated that *Ogonek*, a Russian news weekly, published remarks by Rear Admiral Vigor Poltrushev, Chief of the Operations Directorate of the Russian Navy General staff.

The admiral said, "Yes, the presidents of the United States and Russia have signed the document—the Comprehensive Test Ban Treaty—according to which our missiles are not targeted at each other's countries anymore."

The report continued with an analysis of Poltrushev's position. The top Russian official considered the agreement irrelevant to his strategic mission, as he stated: "The missiles can be re-targeted within an hour, even without returning our ballistic missile submarines to their bases."

The CIA report said the next day, Russia test-launched a six-warhead SS-19 ICBM from Baikonur, Kazakstan. All six warheads reportedly hit their targets around Kamchatka on the Pacific Ocean. At the time, General Yikatorev Yieliesin, Strategic Rocket Forces chief of staff, said it was Russia's twenty-sixth ICBM test launch in five years.

The president had had intermittent feedback about this, but to actually see it in an official document was incriminating. He winced at the report, picked up the phone, and dialed Whittington. "We need to talk."

The VP walked into the Oval Office and eased into a soft, peach-colored armchair. "What's the story?"

"The Russians," said MacDuff, seemingly staring through Whittington. "They're at it again. According to this report, they're testing nuclear missiles again and again." His face was now frozen in a frown. Security was so lax that he knew it would open information leaks to the press in a matter of hours.

Whittington sat quietly, pondering how the report could affect public opinion. He stroked his chin and said, "We need to treat this one differently. We'll claim it's a lie. Get with our friends in the media, play it down, quell the story. Use plenty of euphemisms. They know the drill."

"Yeah, no big deal," MacDuff said, looking more at ease. "We can always discredit anyone who argues the point."

"Sure, sure. We keep on trucking," said Whittington. "We don't have to backtrack on missile speeches."

Two weeks later, *ITAR-TASS*, the Russian newspaper, reported Russia's Pacific Fleet conducted a test-launch of nuclear missile submarines. Three Delta-class submarines fired multiple missiles from the Sea of Okhotsk, just north of Japan, to a target range on the Barents Sea. Curiously, the Barents Sea, just north of Europe, is of equal distance between the launch site and the western United States. According to a Pacific Fleet spokesman, the large and complex test was designed to confirm Russia's naval strategic forces' 'actual combat readiness.'

That same day, in an interview by a television commentator in Washington, MacDuff made a statement on the Comprehensive Test Ban Treaty: "Reducing the nuclear threat is one of my highest priorities. As a result, there are no Russian missiles pointed at our people."

At general staff headquarters in Moscow, the minister of defense Vakaslov Chernoblick personally oversaw a complicated test involving the "nuclear briefcase," a tactical missile operation where a submarine launched a Topol-M ICBM and strategic bombers air-launched cruise missiles.

Shortly afterward, in a debate with presidential opponent Senator Garrity held at Georgetown University, MacDuff concluded with the remark: "There are no nuclear missiles pointed at the United States. And I will keep it this way."

Senator Garrity appeared to be standing at attention, heels locked together military style. He fiddled with his tie, then gave his summary. "And the rhetoric goes on. What is a myth? What is reality? If we listen to Mr. MacDuff, we'll be lulled into a 'sleeping giant' syndrome. When I'm elected president, I will awaken the American people to the real world – a world of nuclear threats. I'll do whatever is necessary to protect this great nation of ours."

The debate was over.

10

GENERAL FULLER'S HOME, MCLEAN, VIRGINIA

Designed to take advantage of the Virginia climate, General Fuller's English Tudor house made the most of a pitched roof, brick, stone, and exposed beams. The elegant two-story home blended in with the surrounding wooded landscape.

Fuller parked his car in the garage, walked into the kitchen, and kissed his wife, Caitlin. He put his briefcase inside a small study off the dining area. Desktop computer systems, modems, a red telephone, and cables lined one wall, and bookshelves covered another. Various photographs of the general with top world leaders and military paraphernalia covered the remaining walls.

"Met Lee Redding today," he said, walking back into the dinette area.

"What's he like?" Caitlin stood at five-foot-ten in a classic straight-up posture. Shiny chestnut hair framed her soft face. She carried herself as a great athlete would, effortless and with precise physical grace. Fuller and Caitlin had been high school sweethearts, courted several years, and were married shortly after graduation. "Bright guy," Fuller answered. "Really aggressive and on the ball. Don't think I could be his drinking buddy, though." He poured himself a cup of coffee and sat at the kitchen table. Leaning on his elbows, his large torso and wide shoulders dwarfed the table and Caitlin.

"Why not?" asked Caitlin, her sable brown eyes cheerfully inquisitive.

"Don't know," said Fuller, shaking his head. "Can't put my finger on it. He acts like he's still fighting his way up from the bottom of the heap."

"Well, we know he's not there!" she said amusingly, tilting her head to the side. Caitlin's facial lines accented classic Greek features.

The general looked at her admiringly. He had always thought of Caitlin as his best advisor. She was no slouch when it came to political sense and diplomatic protocol. Partly due to formal training in the diplomatic corps, she knew what to wear, how to act, and what to say at social events. She was intelligent, somewhat bookish, and took an interest in politics. Since her roots were in the demure culture of aristocratic Texas, she had old-fashioned values.

But she and Fuller were opposite in many ways. He had little interest in reading literature, going to the theater, listening to music, or indulging in the arts. Physically, Caitlin had the face of a delicate orchid and Fuller the face of a bull. But they did have common interests such as politics, dancing, and sports.

Fuller was a stellar athlete, having led his high school football team to all-state as a star fullback. Caitlin would be in the stands jumping and cheering him on, gleaming with pride. They enjoyed talking about the rules and duties of a democratic society, especially about protecting the poor and downtrodden. Their commonalities, native values, and a blend of diversity bonded the marriage. Naturally, it also helped that they were attracted physically.

Fuller shrugged at Caitlin's remark and sipped his coffee. "Yeah, he's already worth billions." He paused for a moment. "Rumor has it; he's trying to build his company even bigger by gobbling up competition. Or driving them out of business altogether."

"Playing the power game?"

"Yep. And he's got the rails greased. With his political ties, his company will get bigger, and he'll get richer. What's shaping up is a monopoly. If he manages to acquire his suppliers and their customers, he'll be in control of the market."

"Isn't that an antitrust issue?"

"Yes, it is," Fuller answered bluntly. "By the time the Feds catch up, he'll be sitting pretty."

"Ridiculous. How does anyone get away with that?"

"By being very cunning and using his connections with the White House," replied the general. "MegaTronics wields a big political stick. And a lot of guys don't have the guts to challenge him. I think the only one who isn't afraid of Redding is Dante Martin, the president of ComTech, Inc. Thank God for that!"

Caitlin smiled and cocked an eye at Fuller. "You sound excited." She paused and recognized the combative glimmer in Fuller's eyes. "Chet, something tells me you are getting into a skirmish!"

Fuller did not respond. He anchored his cleft chin, compressing his lips shut. But he had the alert look of a lion studying its prey.

"I know you, Chet Fuller!"

A mischievous grin came across his face. After Fuller drank some coffee, he said, "Indirectly, you might say."

"I knew it!"

"Well, he's in cahoots with the president. He's in trouble, Caitlin. I pegged him when we first met at a White House charity function. His charitable donations were grossly inadequate to his means. I think he's the kind of guy who contributes money for the recognition that comes with it." "Other than ComTech, what competition does he have?"

"Not much." Fuller shook his head. "Newcomers in the high-tech arena can really get burned—the biggest, richest players practice gamesmanship. They sometimes corner the market through high-level politics." Fuller was secretly investigating Redding's relationship with President MacDuff, and he was finding out plenty.

Redding was no neophyte. During his college days, he formed relationships with bright students and professors who could help him pass exams. Though Yale was a reputable school, Redding was up to dirty tricks. He often procured women and drugs for his suitor,

Ryan MacDuff being one of them. MacDuff was a regular in his "exams-for-whatever" escapades in college, and Redding could easily inflict damage on the president.

Redding had a penchant for being in the right place at the right time and for knowing the right people. He was bright and clever too, and his achievements were extraordinary. Much of his success was attributable to his relationship with MacDuff and the explosive growth of the Internet.

But General Fuller was more concerned with his reach into foreign markets and giving away missile technology—a threat to national security.

"One thing I'm looking into is the MegaTronics merger deal," Fuller said. "Redding is negotiating an alliance with Mike Branston, CEO of 3D Systems and one of the top three computer makers. Branston's company supplied a popular set of office management software that runs on Redding's MEGA-Star chip. Their strategy was to join forces and squeeze out competitors who rely on the MEGA-Star technology. And they'll do it!"

"Is that why the DOJ is after Redding?" asked Caitlin.

"Right. The DOJ doesn't like the idea of the MegaTronics/3D merger because they would control the MEGA-Star technology and eventually the market," Fuller said. "Investigators also found hidden personal profiling routines that tracked a customer's usage habits without their knowledge. The programs recorded what customers accessed while on the Internet, how much they spent, personal e-mail files and a host of other sensitive data."

"That's scary!" Caitlin exclaimed.

While researching MacDuff's connection with Redding, Fuller had learned a lot about Dante Martin. Martin was the son of Italian immigrants who climbed their way to the top in a predominantly WASP environment. To avoid the Mafia stigma, he had changed his name from Martinelli to Martin. He fought in the Vietnam War, which cost him a few years in his business career.

Martin despised the biased press, which played a role in defaming Italian Americans in their zeal for ratings and profits.

Italian immigrants had advanced in business, politics, and science was not sensational news, but they rarely told the story.

But Martin was a tough adversary, accustomed to winning. He was a star athlete in high school and college—a bruising linebacker in football and a skillful shortstop in baseball. He won an athletic scholarship and graduated with honors at Notre Dame.

Fuller related to Martin, particularly as a fellow Marine. Martin was also a well-decorated veteran, winning a Purple Heart and the Medal of Honor for heroic acts. He carried a wounded buddy five miles during an escape from the VC in a mission that went bad. They fought their way out, trudging through a torrential storm in a swampy area, to a secure Landing Zone for the pickup rendezvous.

Fuller learned high-tech companies were often involved in antitrust cases. Mergers were quietly planned and executed, often with mysterious government approval. This was not a difficult task, as there were few antitrust laws on the high-tech industry books. At best, defining and regulating new, sophisticated computer technologies in antitrust categories was extremely complex. Redding was a master at using loopholes and the White House.

The phone rang. Caitlin answered, "Oh, hi, Colonel Gomez. Just a minute." She handed the phone to Fuller.

"Yes, Manny."

"General, just got word the president is building a dossier on you. Thought you'd wanna know right away."

"Not surprised," the general grunted. "Who told you?"

"Blue Jay."

"At the bureau?"

"Yes."

"Then it's a straight scoop."

"You have instructions?"

"No, not for now. We'll talk about it tomorrow."

Fuller hung up. He had a conspicuous frown. MacDuff was digging for dirt. He could find it or create it.

Regardless, the general was determined to break up the Redding-MacDuff pact. Though both were Yale graduates, Redding used his father's connections with MIT professors to start MegaTronics. The DOD actually developed the new MEGA-Star chip under a DOD grant. How did they transfer technology into a private company? Fuller was suspicious, but he had no solid proof of malfeasance.

In return for MacDuff's influence, Redding set up a college professor as a straw man stockholder for the president—a vested interest in Redding's MegaTronics company. The arrangement was a steady source of wealth for both the professor and MacDuff.

Very few did so, but when Redding was challenged about his dealings, he was prepared to fight just for the sake of winning.

So was Fuller.

11

GENERAL FULLER'S OFFICE, THE PENTAGON

Fuller was fairly good at casting off the frustrations and pressures of a bureaucracy. After he met with MacDuff, he went back to his office and settled into his heavy executive chair. He relaxed as he waited for Colonel Gomez to arrive for their weekly brainstorm session. The informal interaction on current events kept things in perspective and often led to good ideas. For some time now, the president's slovenly regard for security had been the dominating topic. It was a sore spot for military men who had risked their lives to keep the country safe. The integrity of national security had deteriorated, and America's global political power was declining.

Gomez arrived, offered the usual greeting, and settled into the leather armchair in front of Fuller's desk. "How was the staff meeting?"

Fuller shook his head and gave a big sigh. "Dealing with MacDuff on the missile thing is a pain in the butt. Like talking to a freaking brick wall."

Gomez shrugged casually. "Elections are coming up. He doesn't give a hoot about missile defense or protecting secrets." He paused, then gave a mocking chuckle. "Security? All he has to do is use the same methods he uses to keep his health records secure. Then our nuclear secrets wouldn't be in the hands of crazy terrorists."

Fuller smiled wryly. True enough. But his smile quickly faded. "Manny, I know the Mid-east terrorists are nipping at our heels like mad dogs. But it's China I'm anxious about." China's military had grown stronger than its diplomatic corps, and the country was an enormous economic force in the East. Although most would not admit it, *the war with China had already started.*

For years the PLA smuggled arms into the U.S. through "legitimate" businesses while shuttling absconded secrets back to Beijing. And there were troubling reports of crack army units entering the U.S. under the guise of Chinese immigrants seeking political asylum or as students. Fuller was also apprehensive about China's military strength coupled with its rapidly expanding economy. And the fact that the PLA was already in control of the Panama Canal, a key influence in world trade patterns. About 14,000 ships pass through the canal every year.

China's unbridled arsenal was mushrooming, and they were in a dominating position in the region. "I only hope we wake up before we blow our lead. China's military advantage is like a vice-grip on that region," said the general. "They're getting too damn cocky. Selling nuclear technology to unfriendly nations and intimidating Asian trade partners goes against our agreements."

"Yeah, MacDuff should think more about *that* and less about getting reelected," snapped Gomez.

Fuller nodded slowly. "It's a freaking good thing the scum bucket nations the Chinese are giving the stuff to lack the nuclear clout to be an absolute threat."

Gomez paused momentarily and looked off into the distance. Then with a serious face, he turned and said, "General, if that weren't the case, do you think we'd be in *World War Three* by now? I mean, with the stuff those guys can throw at us, it's possible, isn't it?"

"Anything's possible," Fuller muttered grimly. "We really need a wake-up call before it's too late. We've got to break out of this freaking post-cold war stupor and lay out some solid strategy to deter nuclear war."

"It's a new ball game for sure," Gomez responded. "In China, the power shift has been going on for a long time under the label of 'global commerce.' They use the Japanese techniques of subsidizing exports and keeping imports in abeyance. And by moving export controls under the Department of Commerce, we've played right into their hands. I say the heck with global commerce for the time being. We need to pull back and regain control. I think we're doggone lucky to still have a lead in computer technology. They've been taking the stuff right out from under our noses, and it's gonna take a while to recover."

"Instant gratification," said Fuller. "That's what it's about." His eyes were of that baffling protean green color. They were never the same when contracted in anger. "Whatever voters wanna hear at the moment. Whatever appeases our trading partners. To the rest of the world, we must look like sniveling wimps!" At the start of the twentieth century, the U.S. was the world's largest creditor, Fuller thought. But now, the country was the centerpiece of a world debt economy—and losing ground. In the last decade or so, the U.S. had acquired the dubious honor of being the world's single largest debtor. "I'm no economist, but it seems obvious to me," he said. "I think the IMF, the World Bank, and other U.S.-backed institutions have piled up a ton of bad debts unlikely to be repaid. And concerning China, our economic relationship is against our national interests."

The general's secretary buzzed him on the intercom. "Yes?"

"Blue Jay is on the scrambled line, sir," she said. "It's urgent." The general reached across his desk and picked up his telephone.

"Yes?"

"Found two more computers," the voice said. Fuller arched his eyebrows. "Control units?"

"Yeah."

"When?"

"Three weeks ago."

"Okay. I'll bring it up at our meeting."

"Another thing. The Chinese purchased a nuclear submarine from the Russians."

Fuller dropped his jaw. "You don't think—"

"Don't know. Still checking."

"Thanks for the update." Fuller put the telephone in its cradle and turned to Gomez. His heavy eyebrows hung low. A look of disgust crossed his face. "China got two more of our computers. And they're buying Russian subs."

Senator Kent Garrity shared General Fuller's sentiment. He spoke about political issues at a fundraiser held at the Rotary Club in Des Moines, Iowa. Next to the familiar Rotary symbol on the back wall was another club logo. It illustrated a man and a woman holding a torch against the background of the globe. A small gearwheel was at the bottom. The plaque had the motto: "Build the Future with Action and Vision."

Approximately two hundred Rotarians dressed in business suits packed the room. Snack plates of cheese, vegetables, fruit, soft drinks, and coffee cups were scattered on white-clothed tables. The Rotarians were a lively group but serious spectators when it came to politics.

Garrity continued his speech: "President MacDuff is locked inside the Beltway and is completely out of touch with ordinary tax-paying citizens. But he is very much in tune to special interest groups and corporate sponsors who back his political career—groups that were embryonic in the sixties and wield voting clout today."

The polls showed Senator Garrity as the candidate most likely to beat out MacDuff. He had a lot going for him. Garrity was a well-known decorated war veteran, a true American hero. Garrity was a helicopter pilot who risked his life saving many of his brethren in Vietnam. At one point, he was shot down and captured by the North Vietnamese. Garrity spent three long years at the infamous "Hanoi Hilton" prison. He returned home to Dallas, where he finished college with a political science degree. Within a few years, he worked his way up to winning a seat in the U.S. Senate.

A capable, aggressive patriot, Garrity was compelled to reach for the highest office in the land. He wanted to help preserve our standards and help guide our country. Like many Americans, Garrity cherished the ideals that our founding fathers established.

Garrity was on the leading edge of the baby-boomer generation. He experienced the unique growth period in the late,40s and the 50s, after the Depression, World War II, and the changing times that followed.

Senator Garrity continued, "In retrospect, after World War Two, the period of reparation and peaceful reserve of the late 1940s and 1950s was the calm before the storm. The phenomenon caused a degree of social havoc, and sadly, marked the beginning of an age of crime, and immorality in America.

"Traces of crime, the drug culture, and a gloomy aura of discontent hovered over our prospering land. The baby boom period of the late '40s and early '50s was the crop that matured in the '60s and '70s.

"Baby boomers as a category cannot be faulted. Rather, it was a time of multiple social changes for a large body of ideological people. Most of the group chose mainstream values, but unfortunately, some leaned towards narcissistic, egocentric values.

"From 1960 to 1970, the crime rate increased by ten percent per year. From 1960 to 1975, the number of arrests of people under eighteen had tripled, and the rate of serious crimes rose over two hundred percent. Prosperity and youth, a lethal combination and the ingredients for social discontent and nonsensical violence, synthesized the connection between the population explosion and crime. People are fighting over religion. There's a building trend to suppress Christian practices."

The senator paused to take a drink from a tall glass of water sitting on a shelf inside the podium. As he glanced at his notes, a wave of mumbling swept across the crowd. Several people stood up and headed for the restrooms.

Garrity cleared his throat, took another sip of water, then continued, "Dangerously, crime has turned into a sport of youth. Young men especially feel their oats and yearn for adventure, danger, and promiscuity. Psychologists attempt to reason this behavior by citing unemployment, the school system, permissive parents, television, racial tensions, and poor law enforcement. The fact is we had a new crop of youth with a lot of spunk and prosperity, but also discontentment and pestilence. Starting in the 1960's, the 'drug culture' and an attitude of appeasement were penetrating our society."

As Garrity paused, white-jacketed waiters retrieved soiled plates and replenished drinks for the VIPs. One man glanced down at his watch to check the time. Another quietly talked into his cell phone.

The senator continued, "As predicted centuries ago by Nostradamus, the great French prophet, we are experiencing an era of decadence. Compared to other countries, on a per capita basis and as a two-hundred-year-old democracy, we have become the most violent nation in the world and the most corrupt. We have the highest divorce and crime rates; we waste the most resources and spend the most money to do so; we consume forty-six percent of the world's natural resources used annually. We have the biggest and most expensive public education system, but it produces the lowest-quality education.

"By the end of the 1960s, student unrest was compounding the problems of crime and promiscuity. At the end of 1970, inflation and unemployment mixed with this virulent brew with staggering consequences. It challenged the American standard system and was strongly protested by youthful malcontents. Unfortunately, this included future occupants of high offices in Washington."

At this moment, a commotion arose just outside the building. Garrity paused and looked towards the door. The crowd began to talk amongst themselves. Many stood up, stretched, turned, and looked around.

"Sounds like I've got some competition," Garrity quipped. A subtle roar of laughter emanated from the group of businessmen. Many turned to face the front of the building to see what was going on. Security guards blocked the front entrance, disallowing the protestors from entering. The dissidents shouted, "MacDuff, MacDuff. Down with fascism. Down with fascism."

Garrity ignored the ruckus and continued, "Out of seventy-six million baby boomers, many have permeated the halls of Washington and Mahogany Row of big business. The vast majority of boomers have assimilated very well into a conservative lifestyle and improved their quality of life. But some of those in public office have less than noble values.

"In my opinion, our president and some of his friends are of this zany new breed, radical in nature. While brave American soldiers were risking their lives in Vietnam, they dodged the draft and protested in foreign countries' streets. Yet, they enjoy freedoms and the right to speak to the extent of representing our interests in Washington.

"The global political scene has changed, and there's a demand for new and creative approaches. I'm especially bothered by the fact that the international community is 'the global capital of arrogance.' We must pause to ask the question: Why?"

Garrity glanced across the audience and caught the eye of a well-dressed man on the front row. He fixed a stare on him and said, "We are called that because, in some ways, we *are* arrogant." Then he looked out at the massive audience. "We are arrogant because we tend to force-feed our ideas, our materialistic lifestyles, and our social values in other countries.

"While we are helping other nations through financial aid and fighting their internal battles in the name of human rights, we are actually hurting ourselves. In the manner in which we do these things, and in the eyes of some, we are confirming that we are 'the global capital of arrogance.'"

Garrity paused and took in a deep breath. "Which brings up China. They've used this term against us for some time now. At the same time, they've accelerated military spending and have shrewdly bought into the *New China Lobby*." This group, of which Lee Redding was a leading player, consisted of a consortium of U.S. business, government, and academic leaders. They all profited from Chinese connections and exerted their political clout to shape Sino-American policies favorable to China.

The audience was captivated by Garrity's persuasiveness. "Let there be no mistake," Garrity went on, "in the twenty-first century, China represents a force to be reckoned with."

12

ESPIONAGE, SCANDAL

MacDuff, two White House staffers, General Fuller, and Colonel Gomez, convened in a small conference room. The discussion was about military matters in the Pacific Rim.

Fuller was in a somber mood as he looked over Lame Duck's report from Beijing, a ten-page document he had meticulously studied the night before. Following a short briefing by the president, Fuller took the lead. "Now, about China," he said. "What are we going to do about their nuclear program?"

The FBI's super-secret *Division Five*, the bureau's national-security arm, had recently obtained new information from China. But it was perplexing to them. A surveillance operation using satellite spymasters at the National Security Agency put out an alert. They warned that the Chinese government was funneling huge amounts of money into American politics. The FBI agents were peering at just tea leaves, whereas Lame Duck had painted a vivid picture for Fuller. In addition to espionage, the undercover agent reported as many as thirty candidates for Congress were recipients of Chinese donations.

"I realize they stole a bunch of secrets from us," MacDuff said, "but they'll go along with nuclear disarmament. They're still saving face over the spy scandal." He paused and stared at Fuller scornfully. "What's your problem?" Then he quickly studied the circle of men.

"We don't have anything in writing," said the General. "Sure, they've *claimed* nuclear testing has stopped. And they're putting the lid on development. That's simply not true. It's a ruse. They haven't stopped anything." He lowered his eyebrows and glared at the president with steely eyes.

"What proof do you have?" MacDuff countered scornfully. Frustrated, his face had turned a rosy color, and the arteries on his temples were bulging.

"My agent in Beijing," the general snapped. "Confirmed by the CIA. My contact said they've increased production and are testing all types of nuclear weapons." All eyes were now on Fuller. "So, what are we gonna do about it?" True to form, the stalwart, square-jawed, barrel-chested veteran held his ground. His troops used to say he was so hard-lined that he ate nails for breakfast while listening to John Philip Sousa.

One officer said, "He's the most gung-ho Marine I've ever served under. I was with him in Korea when we pushed back the enemy inch by bloody inch. All the way back to the Chinese border. We were constantly under a barrage of artillery and small arms fire, but that didn't faze the general. With rounds flying all around him, he just kept pushing forward."

Fuller was a *mustang* and a well-respected Marine officer commissioned from enlisted ranks while on the battlefield. A ladder of medals and ribbons evidenced his combat action from his shoulder to his rib cage's bottom. In addition to the Medal of Honor, he wore the DSC—the Distinguished Service Cross—the nation's second-highest award for valor. According to military folklore, winners of the DSC were entitled to the Medal of Honor, but somewhere along the line, they hacked off someone at a high level—an apt illustration of Fuller's legend.

MacDuff resented Fuller's challenging remarks. He stared at the defiant General and grumbled, "Well, we don't really know for sure what's going on in China, do we?"

Giving no time for Fuller to respond, MacDuff continued derisively. "You know, I wish you would present some hard facts before you go hypothesizing about China. I haven't heard anything about this new wave of nuclear testing from the CIA, the National Reconnaissance Office, or anyone else. I'm inclined to ignore your statement unless you can prove it." He fixed a cold stare on the general.

Unruffled, Fuller glared back with flint-like eyes and accepted MacDuff's challenge. He pursed his lips and spoke in hard halftones. "With all due respect, sir, this is no hypothesis. My source is inside the People's Liberation Army intelligence division, and his reports are accurate. China is determined to dominate Asia using military and economic pressure and diplomatic coercion."

Fuller acquired the nickname *Bulldog*—the Marine Corps mascot —when he single-handedly defeated five Chinese soldiers in hand-to-hand combat in Korea. Fuller shot two at close range and bayoneted one in the heart. Another was killed when he rammed the soldier's nose bone into his brain. The last one punched the general in the face. Fuller grabbed him by the neck, bit his ear off, and strangled him to death. An interpreter overheard a Chinese prisoner call the general *Devil-Dog*—a moniker given to Marines by German troops (*Teufel Hunden*) to describe Marines fighting in World War I. Eventually, it was converted to Fuller's nickname *Bulldog*.

MacDuff was steaming. His face was crimson, pumped full of blood. "Why wasn't I in the loop?" he scowled. "Why haven't you coordinated these activities through the CIA and other agencies?"

Fuller scoffed at his frail attempt to trap him in a petty snafu. The General shrugged and answered, "Look, the CIA's information on China is usually two weeks old, and some of their stuff comes from second-hand desk research. Frankly, in China, they're sometimes like the Keystone Cops. They have a few good operatives there but others flap around like fish out of water.

"As far as I know, no agency or ally has been able to penetrate the Chinese situation as I have with my contact—and by the way, someone I've known for a long time. I'm not about to risk blowing his cover!"

MacDuff looked directly into Fuller's penetrating eyes as if to say, don't mess with me.

Fuller brushed off the threatening gesture and continued, "We can't risk losing what few contacts we have in the Chinese system. If I corroborate with the CIA, the Justice Department, and the FBI, it's no telling how many leaks will open up. If that happens, we're sunk. My friend could be found out and executed."

Shifting miserably in his chair, MacDuff was reaching his wit's end. "Look, I don't want my embassy being used for a rendezvous with your contact!"

"Don't worry, bout that; I don't trust the embassy anyway. I think some of those people are tainted with political agendas slanted towards the Chinese. And in my book, that's treasonous!"

Like a reverberating echo, Fuller's remarks lingered in the air. Fuller's commanding demeanor was intimidating, even to MacDuff, who was obviously livid. Aides around the table stiffened up. The room was quiet, and the air was thick with tension. Eyes were riveted on Fuller, then on MacDuff, everyone waiting for the next comment. MacDuff was deeply offended by Fuller since most of the top people implicated were his political appointees.

Following a few tense moments, MacDuff said, "Well, okay, General, but I strongly disagree with your assessment of our intelligence community." Reluctantly, MacDuff continued, "If you think you're on to something, then go ahead and pursue it. I'm not officially condoning it, but we do need to be sensitive to national security matters. But remember this, keep me informed weekly. Nothing is to be said publicly without clearing it with me. Got it?"

"Yes, sir."

"The economy is thriving, and everyone is happy the way things are," the president continued. "I can't tolerate any rash disruptions." He was intent on maintaining an optimistic stage for his reelection campaign. And the economic stakes were high. His administration had become cozy with the Chinese, receiving campaign donations and plenty of trade deals.

General Fuller's concerns about China were warranted. China's armies were approximated at over 100 million, and their nuclear arsenal was growing exponentially. China was considered the dragon's head in the East and had demonstrated their military readiness through nuclear testing—spouting fire from the dragon's mouth. Reports from Lame Duck were accurate. While the Chinese faked a "no test" posture, nuclear testing was being conducted steadily. In the process, the Beijing military regime had become arrogant and bold, inching into new territories. Since the collapse of Russia's Communist bloc, the PLA was in a unique position of advantage, and they flexed their economic and military muscle.

Well-schooled on issues in the Pacific Rim, Senator Garrity addressed the topic in his speech at the Rotary Club in Des Moines: "Relations between China and in the U.S. are sometimes tense and heated, particularly because of human-rights issues. But on the economic front, China and the U.S. have developed lucrative relationships. This appeared to be good but also troubling. U.S. investments and the transfer of technology in China have chugged along at a rapid pace.

"Since 1993, U.S. businesses have forked over more than five billion dollars in direct investment. And the trade imbalance tipped further in China's favor. Now, the U.S. trade deficit with China has leaped to over *seventy billion dollars*, and they will dip into the well as long as we let them."

An undercurrent of mumbling drifted across the audience. "Yes, that's right, I said seventy billion a year. Furthermore, we can't ignore that they're taking advantage of our technology, using it for a military buildup, not for peaceful reasons.

"One thing to remember. As China's economic growth continues, inflation will set in, and they will eventually be forced to adopt retrenchment policies. And when that time comes, I predict we'll be left high and dry."

THE OVAL OFFICE

Tiffany DeNeaux had just delivered a fresh cup of coffee and was leaving the office. MacDuff was on the phone.

He watched the door latch shut behind her. "Ten million?" he said to Jack Blake, his campaign manager.

"They gave us ten million dollars?"

"Yeah. The way we handled it was—"

"No, no! Don't tell me how it was done," MacDuff barked. "I don't wanna know. Watch what you say. That freaking eagle Fuller is on the China case. Another thing, tell Chao Ling to cool it for a while, now that we've got that money. I don't want any more visitors from China for a while. That spy scandal is still fresh on everybody's mind, and we need to let it taper off. Okay?"

"Okay. Ling is a bit skittish about doing a whole helluva lot. I guarantee Beijing will feed him to the wolves if another scandal breaks. They'll sacrifice an operative before losing face."

"Tell him to wait for our signal." MacDuff hesitated briefly and said, "Schedule set for the fund-raising tour?"

"All set. We finished the schedule."

"Did you invite Liz?"

"Yes, of course." Blake paused. "Mac, about your speech. Wanna change or add anything?"

MacDuff paused to consider. "What did you have in mind?"

"Like, nuclear testing and stolen technology."

"No. If that comes up, I'll play it by ear. We need to stick to global human rights, and the 'no missiles pointed at us' theme. It strikes a chord. We can always change our tune after elections." MacDuff finished his conversation heartily. "Good work, Jack. Wow, ten million bucks!"

GENERAL FULLER'S PENTAGON OFFICE

"I know what they're up to. We've gotta stay ahead of 'em," Fuller said to Gomez, who was sitting in the leather chair taking notes.

"Obviously, they're only interested in permanent normal trade relations status, PNTR," the general continued. "So, they temporarily deactivated their missiles—just before the China visit by Whittington and his trade delegation.

Gomez looked up. "I'm glad some statesmen are gutsy enough to fight against PNTR. China doesn't respect any of the rules." His dark eyes revealed a daunting fierceness that would shrink the strongest of rivals. "Why should they be allowed to be different? They need to conform like the rest of us."

The general nodded. "Right. It's a smoke screen—a big smoke screen."

The leathery general narrowed his eyes. "Here's something we may be able to add to the mix. There's a group of Chinese dissidents who are giving Beijing a fit. Most of them belong to *NetForum*, that Internet outfit. We need to give them a dose of their own medicine— political subterfuge."

"Has Beijing jailed any of them yet?" asked Gomez. "I know they use filtering software to censor e-mails."

"Not that I know of, but according to Lame Duck, they've planted undercover agents in the group."

"It's a double-edged sword," said Gomez. "Plus, we've got a lot more information on the Web for the picking."

Fuller nodded his assent. He associated the Internet as the electronic version of Chinese business operatives spread across the globe. "And let's don't forget the other network—the *Overseas Chinese Businessmen*, the OCBs." Fuller paused to sip some coffee. His cup sported a dark blue F4U-1D Corsair picture, the famous bent-wing fighter airplane flown by the Marines in the Pacific.

Fuller continued, "OCBs are in every corner of the globe. They're well connected. They wield power and influence. According to Lame

Duck, some have links directly with Beijing. And since China reclaimed Hong Kong, the network of OCB contacts has expanded exponentially."

"The OCBs are a de facto spy ring?" Gomez asked. "Tied into Beijing?"

Fuller nodded again. "They're a big part of it. They've deeply penetrated the U.S., from grassroots business communities all the way up to the Oval Office. And a lot of companies over here are owned and operated by the Chinese military, the PLA."

"You mean, the president—"

"Nothing concrete," Fuller interrupted. "But we all know he has frequently hosted Chinese nationals—even known agents." Fuller leaned forward and lowered his voice. "Frankly, Manny, I think he's deep in the muck with the rest of 'em. At least one of his relatives has already taken bribes from the Chinese."

"Any evidence?"

"Put it this way; he may be the first president in history to be brought up for treason."

"Yeah. The sweetheart deals, lax security, Chinese spies with green cards. These guys are working in our universities and military bases! He's gotta be brought up on something!"

Eyes wide, Gomez squirmed in his chair and leaned forward.

"Not yet, anyway. People are burying their heads in the sand. But I want to expose that lowlife. That's why I'm sending Walters to Beijing. He was my top G2 guy in Nam; he'll help Lame Duck get the goods. Get him assigned to the embassy in Beijing as a commercial officer with some glorious title. But not military; he's gotta be civilian."

"What about the CIA station in Beijing? They know about this?"

"I don't give a hoot what they know!" Fuller lowered his bushy eyebrows and glowered at Gomez. "Those guys in Beijing have a problem. They see things the wrong way and don't know anything!"

Gomez shifted in his seat and changed his posture. "What's the best way to get this done, General?"

"Get in touch with Peter Barrett, the secretary of state. He's a straight-up guy and a friend of mine. He knows the score. In the meantime, I'll coordinate with Lame Duck and keep you posted."

"Yes, sir, General," Gomez responded sharply.

Following a brief period of silence, Fuller said, "On another matter, you been keeping up with that new OCB, Chao Ling?"

"No, sir, I haven't."

"He's that pompous rich guy who hangs out with MacDuff a lot. I think he's the new bagman for China. I'm trying to connect the dots, but a lot is missing. See what you can find out."

Gomez paused in thought. "Payoffs? You mean, the president is taking payoffs?"

"I don't know for sure. But Ling's a wheeler-dealer, a mysterious angle guy. He visits MacDuff a lot, then goes to China every other month. Draw your own conclusion."

"I'll get on it right away, sir."

Fuller hesitated, bent forward in his chair, and looked Gomez straight in the eye. "Colonel, it's time to take the freaking hill. I know he's our commander in chief, but we can't let our country down. Too much at stake. If we discover a money connection in Beijing, we'll nail Ling and the president to the wall! You copy?"

"Yes, sir!"

"Semper fi!"

"Do or die!" Gomez jumped to his feet and stood at attention. He snapped a salute, did an about-face, and marched out.

After Gomez left, Fuller sat quietly. He stared at a set of books neatly arranged on his built-in mahogany bookshelves. They were entitled, *History of the U.S. Marine Corps.* Okay, let's see now. The Marines and General Claire Chennault's Flying Tigers helped the Chinese fight off the plundering Japanese. Somehow, that morsel of history is seldom mentioned or recognized in history books.

On the other hand, maybe the Chinese can't forget the Boxer Rebellion. It was in June 1900. The Boxers and Chinese soldiers laid siege to foreign diplomats in Beijing. Captain John T. Meyers led the

Marines, the British, and the Russian troops. They overcame the Chinese and retook the wall.

Fuller rubbed his chin. *Or is it that they won't forget the Chosin Reservoir campaign in the Korean War? Ten Chinese divisions had orders to trap and annihilate the First Marine Division—a ten to one ratio. It was forty degrees below zero, the worst winter in centuries. Those long, cold nights in a ditch or a foxhole caused over Four-Hundred cases of frostbite. They blew bugles and whistles, came running at us shouting like animals, and we still kicked their butts. We annihilated them!*

He snapped out of his retrospect, picked up the telephone, and dialed the State Department. "This is General Fuller. Put me through to Pete Barrett."

Barrett answered, "Hullo, Chet. What's up?"

"It's the Chinese again, Pete."

"Oh?"

"Yeah. You know, we never really extinguished their network in that so-called cleanup last year."

"I hear you, my friend, I hear you," Barrett said, nodding. "What can I do for you?" He rocked back in his leather chair. Barrett was clad in blue pinstripe suit pants, a white shirt, and a white-dotted navy silk tie.

"Since you're the China expert, I could use your help in a special project."

Barrett had a tight, polite smile. "Expert no, experience yes. What can I do?" He placed his index finger at the bridge of his nose and gently pushed up his horn-rimmed glasses. Thick dark eyebrows topped his acorn-colored eyes. His soft black hair was flecked with gray, sheen, and slicked back.

"Whaddya know about the Chinese spy apparatus?"

Barrett chuckled. "Lemme see, you need the five-minute answer or the full report on Chinese espionage going back to the Second World War? If you want the latter, it'll cost you." His handsome square face had a wide grin. At the age of fifty, Barrett was considered young for his position.

"The five-minute version will do." Fuller laughed. "It's all I can afford!"

"For starters," Barrett began, "China found it difficult to recruit and plant foreign agents in other countries. They've been isolated under Chairman Mao's rule, so they never really established those types of contacts. But things have changed. The world has gone electronic. And so, have they. They use the Net and the OCB connections around the globe. They simply combined the two components and made it work."

Fuller responded. "Aha! That confirms my hypothesis. The OCBs do play a major role in the program."

"Of course, they do—in a subtle manner. No matter how they deny it, they're the underpinning of the whole damn machine! The Chinese have streamlined the art of obtaining and manipulating Western technology."

"Interesting," said the General, stroking his chin. "And, boy, have we felt the results!" Of course, they've taken advantage of our weaknesses. We've given them an open invitation. We loosened security measures and allowed a flood of Chinese nationals to get jobs in sensitive areas."

Barrett continued, "Especially through joint ventures with Western companies, they've openly obtained information or usurped it illegally."

"And buying influence?"

Barrett remained silent for a moment. "Chet, I can't comment on that." *Jeez, it sounds like he's dogging the Chao Ling affair.*

"Thanks, Pete," said Fuller, acknowledging the secretary's avowed discretion. His silence was revealing. Influence-peddling was indeed part of the Chinese connection. "One other thing, I need to put one of my guys in Beijing as a handler. Would you help me with this?"

"No problem," replied Barrett, aware of Fuller's pipeline but not of Lame Duck's identity.

Meanwhile, Senator Garrity continued his talk at the Rotary Club: "Despite so-called antinuclear agreements and bustling trade with the West, the Chinese and Russians keep their missiles pointed at us and other 'target' nations. It seems as though some of us have been in a sort of stupor in recent years. But the realization that nuclear missiles are ready and aimed at the U.S. should not be surprising.

"There's no mistake; our administration is aware of these missiles being aimed at us," said Garrity. "They can give their sanctimonious speeches about how no nuclear weapons are aimed at American children. But in the end, one can measure their demagoguery by the consequential loss of American lives. Our present leaders choose to remain in a state of denial. They don't like the real truth leaking out to the American public.

"Recent budgeting has been diverted from national defense, and focused in areas of special interest entitlements and promoting economic development in places like China. This is certain to buy the president a large percentage of votes during the next election." Garrity had an inkling of disdain in his voice. Despite China's decade-plus economic liberalization, he viewed the country as a monolith obsessed with growing ever stronger through unfair trade practices. Since China opened its borders to foreign investment, it encouraged progress in information technology and key nuclear weaponry.

Beijing believed it could export whatever it wanted while barring imports on any pretext it chose. They could undercut other manufacturing nations by the use of cheap labor. They could steal ideas and ignore copyrights without much risk of retaliation. China could blackmail companies into transferring jobs and technology at the price of entering a market of over 1.4 billion people.

Despite hearings about the Chinese spy scandal, nuclear technology's sale by the Chinese to other nations continued. Military strength was growing in Asia and Middle Eastern nations.

Senator Garrity concluded his speech in Des Moines: "Unfortunately, due to the nuclear buildup, a global missile defense system is a must. We need high-altitude theater missile defenses to intercept targets high in the atmosphere or even far above into space. But such a system could also provoke responses from Russia and China that would leave the U.S. vulnerable."

"On the other hand," Garrity continued. "Low-altitude theater missile defenses, which intercept their targets within the atmosphere, are not threats to future nuclear arms control. Fact is, we need both."

13

SABRE RATTLING

Fuller and the president sat at the small conference table, and for a change, both were in an amiable mood. They were to discuss missile defenses. MacDuff noticed sensitive budget information written on the whiteboard from a previous meeting. He got up, erased it, sat down, and poured himself a glass of water from a silver pitcher.

"According to the latest status reports, the THADD project is on schedule," General Fuller reported. "All major testing is complete. The missiles, communications, guidance systems, and radar units are functioning properly."

"Good," MacDuff mumbled. "Security in place? I don't want any leaks."

The THAAD project had experienced continual setbacks but had resulted in an advanced surface-to-air antimissile weapon, the MIM-99 Eagle. The Eagle was armed with a 200-pound high explosive warhead detonated by a proximity fuse. It would spray high-velocity fragments at an intended target. The Eagle, including the warhead, weighed 1,734 pounds, was seventeen feet in length and sixteen inches in diameter. It was powered by Thiokol TX-486 single-stage, solid-fuel rockets and was command guided with a radar-homing system.

"Of course," said Fuller. "We are under the guise of each country operating independently. As far as anyone knows, each THAAD site is sponsored and paid for by the local country. Practically, we're not subsidizing them, although we're supplying technical resources," Fuller explained.

Participant nations also paid a small part of the bill to launch and maintain satellites orbiting the globe—the satellites communicated with THAAD sites, NORAD, and the Advanced Missile Warning Center. The satellites continually scanned the earth, detecting flying objects, but especially sorting out and tracking those resembling missiles.

"I'm still concerned about security. I've bent over backward to get you funding, so I'm holding your ass responsible," MacDuff grumbled.

The president didn't want to rock the boat. He didn't want to provoke rogue nations like Iran, Iraq, North Korea, and Pakistan. He feared U.S. advancements in high-tech weaponry would leak out, which in his mind, was a hawkish program that contradicted his soft, liberal politics.

"I'll double-check security myself," Fuller replied. A definite contingency plan was in place. If the U.S. were under missile attack, the president would be evacuated to Cape Canaveral and launched into orbit in the national emergency command translunar integrator–known as "Necktie." The command-center satellite would communicate with NORAD and individual satellites manned by the army, navy, and air force while in orbit. All would be armed with antimissile proton beam weapons.

"Whatever, just get it done," MacDuff ordered.

Fuller verified MacDuff's orders in military parlance: "Roger, sir. One, maintain the status quo two, no security leaks; three, tighten down on communications; and four, maintain balanced relations with all provocative nations. Right?"

"Right. We need to come across as peacekeepers, the dove among warring nations."

"But the world already knows about THAAD. Sooner or later, we'll have to draw a line in the sand and hold our ground."

"Look, General, I want to lay low and keep the lid on this. We've got to remain neutral." MacDuff's nostrils flared, and his face turned red.

Fuller stared at the president with frigid eyes. "We've never won a war by being cautious or diplomatic."

MacDuff snapped back, "That's just it, General—we're not *in* a war!"

"You can say that, but I have a hunch another hot one, maybe a nuclear war, is just around the corner." Fuller thought, *Truman, where are you when I need you? I don't think this pasty-faced wimp has the cajones to declare war, much less drop the H-bomb.*

General Fuller delivered a speech at the J W Marriott hotel on Pennsylvania Avenue, just two blocks from the White House. The audience was a group of military personnel from the local area, and the subject was nuclear missiles. Two hundred fifty people from all branches of the military gathered to dine and listen to the general.

Fuller spoke above the clinking of silverware against bone China plates. "Fundamentally, missiles are made up of three major subsystems: the launcher, the delivery subsystem, and the warhead. The launcher is usually little more than a protective rack, which holds the missile until launch time. Once fired, the delivery subsystem takes over, steering the missile towards the target.

"The delivery subsystem is made up of a motor, guidance controls, and detonation controls. The motor can be either liquid or solid fuel thrusters or gravitic-driven. The guidance system can use manual operations, radar, or homing technologies: infrared seeking, mass seeking, neutron seeking, etc.

"A trigger device, the execution of which is performed by contact, proximity, intelligence, or command, controls missile detonation. Warheads fall into two broad categories: conventional and nuclear. Conventional warheads use standard high explosives and a focused force high explosive, which can only cause surface damage. Nuclear warheads involve fission, fusion, and enhanced radiation. Nuclear missiles cause both surface damage and radiation effects.

"Radiation effects include the prompt bursts of gamma rays and neutrons and the production of radioactive fission products. If the explosion's fireball touches the ground, a significant amount of radioactive fallout materials formed from the soil is swept up into the mushroom cloud." Fuller paused, cleared his throat, and sipped from a glass of water.

In the audience, a navy commander tapped the shoulder of a fellow officer and whispered, "I hear the General is on China's case about nuclear testing. Think something's up?"

"I'm afraid so," the other officer replied. "I think a fight is looming ahead of us."

Fuller resumed, "ICBMs are normally housed in silos in desolate areas away from the population. Modern rockets' nose cones can contain multiple missiles that split apart and travel towards preprogrammed targets as they enter the atmosphere. They are called *Multiple Independent Re-entry Vehicles* and are perfectly engineered for germ warfare.

"Missiles carrying biological weapons is a frightening prospect. Warheads can house germs such as the plague, smallpox, and anthrax as special *bomblets*. When deployed, the bomblets burst and spread the germ agents over a geographical target area. We've already seen modern germ warfare being used in Iraq."

Fuller continued, "The production of biological weapons is still an ongoing program in many regions of the world. For example, in a remote region of Russia, a germ-warfare laboratory developed some fifty-two biological agents as weapons of human destruction. And during the cold war, the Russians had their germ-bearing missiles aimed at most major cities in America." The General hesitated to review his notes.

For a brief moment, the audience became abuzz with talk. An army colonel leaned over and whispered to his aide, "They've been doing this all along — should've stopped them long ago!" The aide nodded in agreement.

Fuller continued, "Standard missiles designed for space combat come in two sizes: the larger ones designed to be launched from missile bays, and the smaller models are launched from missile racks. And anti-ship missiles can convert into planetary surface bombs or surveillance drones."

Fuller paused, then went on, "During the cold war, missiles were primarily aimed at large cities. Short of being just war games, testing and simulations of firing these missiles at targets are a continuous exercise. And the use of high-performance computers advances progress in this activity.

"Today, nations are expanding their military arsenals, and nuclear missiles are becoming the weapons of choice. It's a dangerous, almost childish game of tit for tat. If an adversarial country develops nuclear missiles, then their neighbors follow suit. Consequently, the list of countries with nuclear weapons continually grows.

"It is essential to concentrate on deterring the movement toward nuclear armament, to avoid an all-out nuclear war and possibly world destruction. Our inventory of missiles and deployment of the U.S. Navy's Aegis Cruisers, Tomahawks, and ninety-six Trident missiles on submarines, each with ten warheads, hopefully, sends the message that we are positioned and willing to fight a nuclear war if necessary.

"Despite the end of the cold war, the nuclear-weapon countries continue to rely on nuclear deterrence, with nuclear-armed missiles as its backbone. As long as they seek to deter each other, they won't be willing to reduce their missile defenses for fear that it would negate or weaken their retaliatory capability. We must be proactive in reducing the nuclear threat, but at the same time, we must ensure that a missile defense system protects our borders."

Back in his office sitting at his desk, Fuller said to Gomez, "India has been especially vulnerable to a nuclear attack. Nations surround them with their nuclear arsenals: China and Russia to their north and Pakistan to their west; but China poses the biggest threat to all nations in the region, and possibly to other parts of the world."

"That's why India tested their nuclear weapons—a show of force—to discourage potential aggressors," said Gomez.

"That's right, and there's more. India continued to develop the ground-to-ground missiles and expedited the overall upgrading of its weapons and military equipment." Fuller paused, rolled his chair back, and stood up. He walked over to the window. As his office was on the Pentagon's outer ring, he watched a stream of traffic flow like a regiment of ants along Washington Boulevard.

Fuller shook his head in dismay. "Then, China heightened its vigilance against India," he said. "China feels that, after Taiwan, India is a key enemy in terms of strategic campaign concepts and the deployment of equipment and troops. And they're planning accordingly.

"We know the Chinese army made a serious study of tactics they could use in mountainous regions, high in topography and cold in temperature," Fuller said.

"India's nuclear testing also prompted Pakistan to react," said Gomez.

"Right. They followed suit and tested *their* missiles. Now, China is in the middle of these power plays, but they sided with Pakistan, Iran, and Saudi Arabia. They've cooperated with them on nuclear missiles, creating a sensitive and dangerous situation."

Gomez responded, "The so-called world order is becoming a volatile, hazardous phenomenon."

"Yes. The Chinese think an enemy with hi-tech weapons and equipment will invade some of their territories in a big way. They're planning campaigns with similar weapons and equipment for a counterattack. This attitude is spreading throughout the region," Fuller remarked.

"It's insane!"

"They're treating weapons of mass destruction like tactical toys. A hot war hangs in the balance."

Fuller said, "I'm particularly concerned about their advancement in space weaponry, both defensive and offensive. China has tested their rocket, the 'Long March,' armed with a nuclear-capable, hypersonic glider as an attack weapon."

SENATOR KENT GARRITY'S OFFICE, THE DIRKSEN SENATE OFFICE BUILDING

Senator Garrity was giving his aide, Derek Stevens, a heads-up on the history of the nuclear arms race. Garrity kept an orderly office, with a portrait of George Washington hanging behind his desk. A bounded top-secret CIA report, entitled *Myths of Nuclear Disarmament,* was on his desk.

"When did it start?" Stevens asked Garrity.

"Basically, it started after the Second World War. In 1949, we thought we had a monopoly in nuclear technology and were openly developing a bomb way ahead of other nations. But the Russians surprised us."

"How?"

"They detonated a nuclear bomb that we knew very little about. It caused a major shift in the balance of power between the Russians and us. We knew they were working on an atomic weapon, but we thought they were at least three years from their goal."

"The Russians were working secretly, and we weren't?"

"You could say that. We kept our technology confidential, but security wasn't tight enough. An American named Ted Hall and others were spying for the Russians at the Los Alamos facility. They were feeding vital scientific and engineering information to Russian agents, and that's how they beat us to the punch."

"That's when we lost the lead?"

"Yes. Technically, they were behind, but with our latest technology in hand, they caught up real fast."

"Didn't we offer our technology to the Russians and others before that?"

"We did, for peaceful reasons," Garrity grunted sarcastically. "Of course, now we know why the Russians declined our offer, and we've been in a race ever since!"

Garrity continued, "Our emphasis was to develop a hydrogen bomb. We detonated the H-bomb on the tiny atoll of Eniwetok. And the AEC guys were upset over it." Garrity thought about the current situation. "Despite the administration's wishy-washy attitude, I think we're still in the lead!"

After a short pause, Stevens said, "But don't you think the administration has seriously deterred the U.S. lead in nuclear technology? I mean, in light of the Chinese stealing our secrets and using our supercomputers?"

"I'm hoping it will take the Chinese some time to catch up. It depends on how well they use our technology."

Back at the Marriott banquet, wrinkled cloth napkins lay haphazardly on tables. The audience of military men and women sat quietly at their tables, facing the floor-level podium where General Fuller stood.

The General concluded his speech: "My dear friends and colleagues, we must avoid the 'sleeping giant' syndrome. We should've learned this lesson at Pearl Harbor, but we've been lulled to sleep again. We've let our guard down in our rush to create a global economy. We mustn't forget to focus on our duty, to protect our country, our families, and friends." Fuller paused and said, "I implore you to support the missile defense program."

Receiving a standing ovation, Fuller waved to the audience and took his seat. In a moment of contemplation, a passage from the book of Revelations flashed through his mind: "The second angel sounded his trumpet, and something like a huge mountain, all ablaze, was thrown into the sea. A third of the sea turned into blood, a third of the living creatures in the sea died, and a third of the ships were destroyed."

He lowered his head, closed his eyes, and said a prayer.

14

THE OVAL OFFICE

"Yes, Mr. Cheng, we back MegaTronics. We support them in their efforts in China." MacDuff spoke over the phone in a choppy, loud voice to Liu Cheng in Beijing, China. It was uncouth of MacDuff to speak loudly—Cheng was not deaf—but he spoke that way to foreigners thinking they would somehow understand better.

MacDuff, Liu Cheng, and Lee Redding were on a teleconference call.

Cheng was in Beijing, and Redding was in California. Redding asked the president to make the phone introduction to establish his credentials and open the door to doing business.

The phone line to Beijing was crackling and wheezing like it was ready to disintegrate. Ironically, the Chinese were installing a nationwide Internet backbone using top-grade fiberglass cabling, but the telephone system was still 1930 vintage. Unless one was on a cell phone using satellite links, it was a crapshoot.

Liu Cheng was the Deputy Minister of the *China Council for the Promotion of International Trade*, the CCPIT, in Beijing. The group was also linked with the China Chamber of International Commerce. Cheng was a short man with a round face and dense black hair. He wore wireframed bottle-bottom glasses. He had on a Mao-style jacket, fashionably unbuttoned and wrinkled at the collar.

Cheng had been talking with the giant German company, *Siemens,* about computer equipment and services. And it was time for Redding to move into the lucrative market quickly.

"Sure, Mr. President, appreciate you call me," Cheng said. "We like a business with an American computer company, so I invite Mr. Redding to Beijing."

"Good," the president replied. "You know, we have the most advanced computer technology in the world, and Mr. Redding heads up one of our finest companies in the industry. I will work to support a joint venture with MegaTronics." MacDuff concatenated his words in a staccato fashion, making sure Cheng understood.

Redding piped up, "Mr. Cheng, I can make arrangements for a meeting in three weeks. Would that be, okay?"

"Sure, okay. You call me. We talk about meeting."

The timing was good. China had adopted a dynamic, aggressive approach to building a national communications infrastructure, and they needed companies like MegaTronics to supply technology. The Chinese regarded telecommunications, information technology, and the Internet as essentials to modernization, global commerce, and enhanced military systems. Plus, China's telecom-datacom industry was one of the most imminent, lucrative opportunities available to foreign involvement. But the industry was still under Beijing's central control, and it required heavy politics to make any deals.

China had committed serious funds to develop the information technology industry. MacDuff and Redding were drooling over a potentially big slice of the Chinese pie. The China consumer market numbered over 1.3 billion people, and if the computerization pattern was anything like in the U.S., MegaTronics could sell an astronomical number of computers. MacDuff's help set the stage for Redding's market entry strategy.

Lee Redding reached for his cigarettes on the nightstand and simultaneously lit two. He passed one to Tiffany DeNeaux. Tiffany took a long drag from her cigarette, exhaled, and sighed. She said,

"Bill, darling, when can we get married?" Tiffany DeNeaux was growing impatient. They had been secretly having an affair for more than two years, and Redding's promises were hollow. A wedding seemed like a distant fantasy.

Clandestine meetings with MacDuff and the purloining of classified information by Tiffany were distressing. She was committed to a fallacious triangle with a thickening plot. She was hostage to a world of lust, broken promises, and a breach of loyalty to the president, personal morals, and the country.

Lying back and puffing on his cigarette, Redding stiffened at her question. "Tiff, sweetheart, you know I love ya. Now, let me explain again. If we got married, that would create a conflict of interest since I deal with the president on business matters. You would probably have to quit your job at the White House. Then and I wouldn't be able to keep an eye on him. You know he can't be trusted."

"I know, but—"

"Patience," he interrupted. "Patience is the key. The time will soon come, and we can do what we want."

"Couldn't we get married secretly?" she pleaded, with a shred of breath. But after she spoke, she quickly realized she was grasping at straws. What was happening? And where would she end up? She started with a simple enough plan. Develop a career in government, meet a respectable, rich suitor, and get married. But somewhere along the line, her life became very complicated.

"Not a chance," Redding retaliated. He sucked on his cigarette and blew smoke rings that floated upward like wayward halos. "Look, if they found out, my dealings with MacDuff would come under intense scrutiny. Crazy stuff would happen. It could be a serious scandal. Too risky."

Tiffany frowned deeply. With a puzzled look, she said, "I don't understand. If they find out we're involved now, wouldn't that be the same thing?"

"Not really." Redding became impatient with the debate and was looking to end it. "Hah! Most everybody in Washington sleeps around. You know that! If they cracked down on sexual philandering, we wouldn't have a government!"

On that, they both cackled. But Tiffany's was a nervous, awkward laugh. She felt unsure of her destiny in the scheme of things. Was she hanging on false hopes? How long could they hide the truth? Was he just stringing her along? There were too many uncertainties. The room at the Renaissance Mayflower Hotel was a silent witness to a long, emotionally stressful night.

THE WHITE HOUSE

"Here's the deal. You fix me up with the Chinese bigwigs, and you get ten thousand shares of common stock. Whaddya say?" Redding made the offer over a cocktail in MacDuff's private office. As a rule, these kinds of deals were struck in this office, a personal conclave with a wet bar stocked with the very finest in booze.

Leaning back in his chair and looking up at the ceiling, MacDuff paused for a moment. He lowered his head and sipped his drink. Then he glanced at Redding out of the corner of his eye. "What's it worth? Quarter million?"

Redding grinned smugly. "More like a half million! Our stock doubled over the last few months."

MacDuff pasted a wide grin on his face and chortled. "How the hell can you stand being so damn rich?"

"It's not easy!" They laughed heartily.

"Deal!" MacDuff shouted as he darted his hand out for a handshake. "I'll get the ball rolling. We'll first get you in touch with the *Ministry of Post and Telecommunications.* The MPT is where the action is."

HONG KONG

Redding and his entourage endured the long trip to Beijing with a stopover in Hong Kong. Considering Hong Kong's bureaucratic imposition, he noticed the vibrant business environment was still present. According to Redding's research reports and based on venture capital flow into the local economy, telecommunications and networking were quickly growing in Mainland China.

The business mecca had been largely undisturbed under Beijing's rule, which regained control of the island when the British turned it over in 1997. At that point, Hong Kong had become a Special Administrative Region of China. In terms of history, in 1841, China capitulated to the British due to the First Opium War; and the British negotiated a ninety-nine-year lease on the island, which expired in July 1997. Eventually, Beijing imposed its brand of Communist control despite heavy protests by Hong Kong citizens.

Hong Kong had the nightlife, the bright lights, and other signs of the bourgeois decadence and opulent capitalism that Mainland China lacked. It had unique sights, sounds, and smells. The steady stream of people moving about, the myriad of nightclubs, fine hotels, restaurants, public transportation, and bustling street commerce highlighted an inspiring atmosphere.

Redding's crew checked into the Hilton hotel, made a quick visit to the MegaTronics branch office, and made dinner plans. The hungry Americans had their fill of caviar, dan-dan noodles, moo-shu pork, fish, bean curd, and chili, accompanied by rice. After washing down a meal with hot tea, they traveled the tourist trail up high on the mountain to Victoria Peak. They briefly visited with an officer at the U.S. consulate, but not before making the lofty Hong Kong scenery's usual photo shoots.

The group took their first ride on the Star Ferry on a thirty-nine-ton double-ended diesel boat. They crossed the Victoria Harbor between Central and Kowloon. Other interesting tours included the Stanley Market, a hodgepodge of stall shops that offered various goods; Repulse Bay, a popular beach in Hong Kong; and Aberdeen Fishing Village, a colorful and exciting glimpse of local fishermen folklore.

Eventually, they ended up at the *Bull and Bear,* a favorite hangout for expatriates who worked in Hong Kong. The club simulated a

British pub, complete with synthetic Tudor decor, British ale, and oversize mugs of *Guinness*.

Later, two men succumbed to the lure of Hong Kong prostitutes sporting silk skirts with slits running high on the hip. Their well-developed legs, dark almond eyes, and seductive giggling were a magnet to the young Americans. The well-experienced beauties in the ancient trade knew how to leverage the sexual frailties of Westerners.

CHINA MINISTRY OF POST AND TELECOMMUNICATIONS, BEIJING, CHINA

Redding's group was escorted into a spacious but drab, musty conference room. Chao Ling, MacDuff's confidant, had arranged the meeting and played host to the delegation.

The MPT was a powerful agency that owned and operated China's telecommunications and computer networking infrastructure. Akin to AT&T, the MPT was one of the most dynamic business monopolies in China and it was growing at a phenomenal rate. The Chinese representatives were anxious. One member was especially vigilant: Fuller's undercover agent, Lame Duck.

After the initial introductions, the heavy double doors were slammed shut, casting an echo down the long hall.

GENERAL FULLER'S PENTAGON OFFICE

Fuller trusted Secretary of State Peter Barrett's knowledge and judgment on China. The two discussed the Lame Duck report at the MPT meeting over the phone.

"It was about MegaTronics providing networking equipment and expertise in the construction of China's Internet backbone," Fuller said. "And, as I understand, the MPT promised that by cooperating with them, Redding's company was more likely to be awarded contracts with members of the multifaceted, all-encompassing CCPIT."

"Ah yes, the CCPIT," Barrett muttered. "China Council on the Promotion of International Trade. The *capo de capo*, the head of all China's trades associations. They represent every segment of the industry in China, with offices all over the modern world."

"Lame Duck said they have clout, and they used that as leverage in their negotiations. He also said Lee Redding already has confidential Chinese relationships through backchannels. Some are a threat to our national security."

"It figures. The Chinese expect you to build a relationship of trust and confidence, but some concessions go along with that. The Chinese are hardnosed negotiators, with an ample supply of tricks."

Barrett recalled his experiences as a top-level commercial officer at the American embassy in Beijing. After a four-year tour, he knew the *yin* and the *yang* of doing business in China. Specifically, how and when to stand firm and when to give in. And more importantly, never show one's true emotions.

Barrett also knew about the political fragility in China. During the demonstrations in Beijing over NATO's accidental bombing of China's embassy in Belgrade, one Chinese student outside the U.S. embassy voiced his feelings: "Do you know how many Chinese people there are in the world?" he shouted. "China should be a world power again, but the U.S. is always trying to put us down."

Barrett wondered if China would ever learn to get along with foreign nations, particularly the U.S.

Pondering Barrett's comment about concessions, Fuller recalled some of the details of Redding's arrangement with the MPT. He replied, "That figures. Lame Duck reported that as a caveat to getting a contract, the MPT officials wrangled a couple of MEGA-Star supercomputers from Redding in the customary '*trial-units*' ploy." The computers were provided as demo units, but the plan was to keep the units on trial forever—at no cost to the Chinese.

"And everyone would've known the transaction was illegal, not officially authorized because the units were high-performance computers," Barrett remarked. "What made Redding think he could get away with it?"

"He told the Chinese that if anything came up, he was sure the president would pull some strings in Washington."

"Really? I'm surprised. That implicates the president directly. Pretty bold stuff, don't you think?"

"Yeah. Not only for MacDuff's political career but because of what could happen to relations with our allies, world security, and lots more!"

"What was the Chinese position?"

"They weren't that bothered! Apparently, their main concern was budgeting the money. The officials at the MPT wanted to get the deal done before the remaining fiscal budget expired. Can you believe it?"

"Actually, I can. In their terms, Beijing plans the economy using five-year increments for setting goals, budgets, and governing rules for commerce. I can see why they set aside the legality issue and were more concerned about budget approval," Barrett said. "In fact, I just read the station report yesterday, and I can give you something else to digest. Hold on a second. Let me rustle up the report."

Barrett walked over to a row of sage green, government-issue cabinets with unfastened combination locks. He rummaged through one of the drawers and pulled out a document marked "Confidential." Barrett flipped through the *China Economic Report*. "Lemme give you some excerpts on the information technology industry in China. China is actuating a plan to reform its system from a planned economy to a market-driven, free enterprise system. They're playing catch-up after years of tight, economically stagnating Communist control. Economic reform has been steaming ahead at breakneck speed, particularly in information technology, defense systems, and key infrastructure industries."

Fuller fastidiously took notes as Barrett gave him the highlights. "According to China's five-year plan," Barrett continued, "the government sector alone plans to invest approximately twenty-nine billion dollars in advancing its information systems infrastructure. Chet, that's *billions, maybe eventually, in the trillions!*"

"Yep, I can see why Redding and MacDuff are working overtime," said Fuller.

"And this doesn't include foreign investments," Barrett continued, "The injection of these funds would also further boost the industry's average growth rate of thirty percent accumulated in the past years since 1992. According to the latest tally, there were over sixty thousand information service companies with over one million employees and revenues exceeding one billion dollars in 1994."

"Smart. Real smart," Fuller remarked.

"In 1996, China opened up its borders to the first commercial Internet gateway, perhaps unwittingly, to the world of free information exchange.

And for them to do that, there have to be serious advantages to them."

"Indeed."

Barrett continued, "In fact, they're putting in local Intranet systems in every province—twenty-six of them—over the next two years. MegaTronics and other Western companies are participating in this historic phenomenon by building China's Internet backbone."

"Didn't realize they were that far along," mumbled Fuller. "Better get our stuff together, and put them on our Internet radar screen."

"It won't take them long to catch up. They're at an advantage," said Barrett solemnly. "They're skipping over the old technology and putting in the latest and greatest. They don't have to go through the expensive upgrade cycle as we do. Technically, they can be close to where we are in just a few more years."

"No kidding, that fast?"

"It's possible. The big initiative includes custom LANs, WANs, and modern telecommunications." Barrett paused and glanced at a CIA report on his desk entitled *Myths of Nuclear Disarmament* and thought about the Cox report on Chinese espionage. He added, "And missile technology."

Fuller replied, "Exactly."

"The demand for computers and telecom equipment is high in the military and private sector too," Barrett said. "As we speak, satellite-driven cellular phones are in abundance in China, more than in the U.S., and conventional landlines are being upgraded as fast as possible."

"But their telephone system is pretty antiquated. Won't that slow down progress?" asked Fuller.

"Some, but not much. Beijing expects to have up to five million telephone lines, connecting forty-two percent of city residents and fifty-five percent of urban residents. The planned wireless infrastructure will accommodate millions of subscribers."

"Ambitious, isn't it?"

"Yes, but there's a horde of foreign investors ready to help in the movement. And the Chinese have plenty of bait to pass around."

At a press conference in the White House pressroom, MacDuff responded to the question of dropping Taiwan for China: "The problem is, it's difficult to establish equal support for China, and Taiwan without hurting relations with one or the other. But we must choose to align with Mainland China for several reasons."

Taiwan had lost ground with many nations. The Taiwan imbroglio was cause for concern—it could easily spark a war. Beijing went so far as to impose a break from Taiwan as a condition for establishing relations with many countries.

Such was the case in South Africa. On January 1, 1998, China and South Africa established diplomatic relations after decades of separation. The Taiwanese closed their embassy the next day. The flag over the new Chinese embassy was raised, while a few blocks away, the flagpole in front of the Taiwanese embassy was bare.

It was another victory for Mainland China, which considered Taiwan a renegade province that belonged to them. Since the 1970s, the number of countries maintaining diplomatic relations with Taiwan dipped from one hundred to a mere twenty-nine. Most of the holdouts were emerging nations in Central America and Africa, but developed countries began dumping Taiwan when China opened its markets.

When China was strictly a closed state, Taiwan built up strong economic and political ties with the West. But since China opened its borders under a "one government – two system" free enterprise environment, foreign capital poured into China's economy. America's corporate Sinophiles, members of the New *China Lobby*, joined the gold rush with heavy commitments but often gained no returns.

American and European visitors were also shocked to see the poverty that still existed in China. Beijing was trying to change these conditions through economic reform, and the Chinese people embraced the concept of a free enterprise system. They gave factories the power to determine production, inventory, pricing, and marketing practices. They could retain profits above a specified amount, to reinvest or to use as they wished. In some cases, they established employee incentive plans under merit systems. It was a capitalistic approach.

The state encouraged the growth of *collective* and *private* ownership of companies. A group of local owners ran collective enterprises. The government was faced with employing millions of restless urban youths, a society segment that threatened political insurrection.

Chinese leaders aspired to authoritarian capitalism as practiced in Thailand, Korea, Malaysia, and Indonesia. But they were running into trouble because of poor governance, fraught with cronyism, insider dealing, slack regulations, a weak rule of law, and a docile news media. The new formula for economic reform seemed reasonable, but there was also a downside. An economy heating too fast carried hidden dangers. But most viewed China as the biggest economic plum in Asia and were willing to roll the dice. Some naïvely planned to "make short-term profits, then get out."

But Beijing had heard this many times before and was prepared for eager carpetbaggers.

15

MINZU HOTEL, BEIJING, CHINA

"Hold out bait to entice the enemy, feign disorder, and crush him."
—Sun Tzu's *Art of War*

"*Wei?*" the interpreter uttered in a rising inflection. "*Uh-huh, shi. Hen hao! Shei-shei.*" He hung up the phone and announced, "Our car is waiting downstairs, Mr. Redding." The young man, in his mid-twenties, had a slight British accent. Educated in a British-run prep school in Hong Kong, he represented the new breed of Chinese yuppie, skilled in high technology. MegaTronics had recruited him to coordinate business with Mainland China.

Redding and his group rode in style. CCPIT provided them with a nice car and a white-gloved chauffeur. They got into a late model Citro that had cloth seat covers and red Chinese flags attached to each front fender. In Redding's words, the car was "A French-made wagon that looks like a pregnant hog but rides like a dream." Redding and his crew experienced their first tour of Beijing, a city populated with over eight million people.

A brownish-orange blanket of pollution hovered over the traffic in

Beijing. The city was teeming with thousands of bicycles, scooters, and bumper-to-bumper vehicles belching dark, toxic fumes.

The bicycles outnumbered everything else by a thousand to one. At intersections, traffic resembled a swarm of bees funneling through holes in a beehive. Horns blared constantly, and the battle between cars, buses, bicycles, and pedestrians was in all directions. The streets of Beijing were bumper-to-bumper with expensive cars, mini-vans, and even sport utility vehicles. Pedestrians hurried along, holding Motorola cell phones and wearing trendy Nike sneakers.

The scene was modern urban China, and it made Los Angeles traffic look tame. One glaring difference that was the Chinese reserved broad lanes for bicycles, which had special clearances. The CCPIT car, with a red flag attached to its right front fender, also had special traffic privileges. It was a VIP car, a car for the party.

CHINA COUNCIL FOR THE PROMOTION OF INTERNATIONAL TRADE, CCPIT BUILDING—GENERAL ASSEMBLY ROOM, BEIJING, CHINA

At two-thirty in the afternoon, the customary *xiu xi* had passed. The siesta period was over, and the Chinese were rested. In a Spartan conference room, the two delegations of four men congregated.

Besides Liu Cheng of the CCPIT, the Chinese group was comprised of Bao Fuzhang, deputy director of the Ministry of Post and Telecommunications, MPT, Huang Miao; the Ministry of Foreign Trade's regional director; and Economic Cooperation MOFTEC. Also, the present was Wang Zhang, managing director of China National Aero Technology Import and Export Company.

The two groups made formal introductions and engaged in small talk. Nodding heads and shaking hands, they greeted each other repeatedly, *"Ni hao, ma?"* The inexperienced *Meiguorens"*, Americans, amused the Chinese when they tried to speak Mandarin. Still, they appreciated the effort. At first, it was a bit awkward for both sides, but they had common goals. Eventually, they engaged in a vibrant dialogue.

Seated at the long, white-clothed table and using interpreters, Redding's men talked with the Chinese delegation while sipping hot green tea and munching on Chinese hors d'oeuvres. White-jacketed servers stood in waiting. Blue-and-white uniformed police officers guarded the area.

A pungent odor of curry, red peppers, and sesame-flavored meat emanated from the kitchen area. Cookies, fruit, steamed dumplings, spring rolls, a type of fried curry ravioli, and something resembling a fried starfish decoratively filled the platters.

"What are these things?" Redding asked as he put a starfish in his mouth and chewed. It made a crunchy sound.

"Chicken feet," the interpreter replied.

Eyes bulging, Redding stopped chewing, promptly cupped his mouth with his hand, and spat. He jettisoned the crumbled chicken foot into his plate. He lowered his head, wiped his mouth with a stiffly-starched napkin. He craned his head around the room to see if anyone was watching.

He grimaced as he washed the greasy residue down with hot tea. He reached for an almond cookie. The Americans were fortunate. The platter could've offered dog meat or fragment meat, a Chinese delicacy.

The day before, the MegaTronics group departed from Hong Kong for Beijing on a hazy, chilly morning, arriving with little time to check into the Minzu Hotel and get acclimated to the local ambiance. Beijing was much colder than Hong Kong was, in more ways than one.

In Beijing, the Chinese gawked at Redding's team curiously, as if they were indeed "foreign devils"—a phrase carried over from the Opium Wars–often used in contempt of Americans.

The city was huge, sprawling in all directions and crawling with people. Beijing was not very well equipped to host foreign visitors, especially Westerners longing for familiar food, service, and convenience. Redding's young crew was already uncomfortable. They craved pizza, tacos, hamburgers, and the likes of fast-food cuisine.

Agents of the *Public Security Bureau*—the ever-present plainclothes sleuthhounds—watched every move they made. The gruff agents restricted access to unauthorized areas, which were a mix of military and non-military sites. Nations often criticized China for slave labor using underage children, criminal prisoners, and other incarcerated social or political undesirables. Such criticism has been ignored.

At last count, more than 200,000 people were imprisoned without being charged or tried for a crime. In 1997, over 2,500 people were executed for various charges ranging from petty theft to murder. Thousands of Tibetan monks and nuns have been detained and tortured.

And of course, there was the massacre in Tiananmen Square in 1989: one student organizer of that dissident movement, Wang Dan, spent nine years in prison. He was released in 1998 and fled to America in exile.

Another, Chai Ling, escaped to France, then eventually to the U.S., where she operates her own Internet firm. High-level figures involved in the uprising were also persecuted. Fang Lizhi, an astrophysicist, sought refuge at the American embassy, left for England, and later ended up teaching at the University of Arizona.

Zhao Ziyang, general secretary of the Communist Party, was a sympathizer and reformist. The government put him under informal house arrest after the incident. Zhao's top aide, Bao Tong, was also arrested and put in prison, but later released in 1998.

General Fuller once described China as "A nation still ruled with tight reins by a ruthless, hard-ass regime."

By all accounts, Beijing was truly in a dilemma. The Communist government espouses atheism. But China's market reforms and loosening of social controls had spawned interest in religion and health sects.

Despite its willingness to embrace free enterprise, the totalitarian government was strongly intolerant of criticism or dissent—especially religious-based censure. It controls the numbers of religious believers through restrictions on worship and bans on proselytizing.

Authorities demonstrated their stalwart dogmatism in a recent campaign to curb religion. They closed or destroyed more than 3,000 temples and churches in Wenzhou's coastal city, a city known for its religious tolerance. Officials reasoned that the situation became "rampant superstition."

As far as Redding was concerned, moral or social issues were of little importance. He discounted negative issues and focused on China's immense computer market.

After the cumbersome get-acquainted period, Redding launched serious discussions with Liu Cheng. Putting on his best act of modesty, Redding addressed his Chinese counterpart. "Mr. Cheng, thank you for receiving our delegation." Redding paused, then continued his partly memorized introduction. "I've been reading about China's economic progress and your plans for developing China's computer infrastructure.

"As you know, our firm is the leading provider of the MEGA-Star chip technology, and we are interested in discussing joint venture opportunities. We can be your general agent for other companies, too, providing you a total solution for technological needs," Redding said.

Cheng listened to his interpreter. Cheng said, "My pleasure for having you visit China. Your company is known well in China." He continued, "Maybe, we think there are many opportunities in China for MegaTronics."

Cheng paused, searching for his best English words. "In China, we eager for computers to change to free enterprise system, our economic growth." Cheng delivered his punch line. "We know American technology is best in the world!"

"Nice of you to say," Redding replied.

Feeling more confident with his English, Cheng peered at Redding with narrow eyes and continued, "We want to make bigger friends with the U.S. and MegaTronics." Cheng had a half-moon smile, forcing his eyes nearly shut.

Redding took all compliments seriously. "Good, thanks for your comments. President MacDuff assures me that U.S.-China relations are improving all the time, and open trade with China, in terms of high-performance computers, will be approved soon."

Cheng's interpreter repeated Redding's statement. Cheng replied, "Yes, we work very hard and give sincerity to U.S. capital investment. We continue changing a controlled economy to free and open trade with foreign countries."

"Mr. Cheng, my company, aggressively supports proposals in Washington to remove trade barriers with China, and we will continue to do so."

Redding vocalized his pitch slowly. "Now, I would like to ask for your support in doing business with my company. We can explore ways of getting together before official announcements out of Washington." His voice was irritatingly strident.

Cheng listened to his interpreter intently, then spoke rather cautiously. "Can we do without an official U.S. government? Okay? China is careful to please America now because of MFN status. Understand?"

Redding put on a conceited grin. "Mr. Cheng, leave that to me. If you sign business agreements with my company, I will get government approval."

Cheng understood. He gave a toothy grin and nodded vigorously. *"Hen hao"*! Very good! I look forward to our next meeting. And meantime, I take necessary steps to make negotiations with MegaTronics!" Cheng was enthusiastic but calculating. Redding was like clay in the hands of a master potter.

The meeting ended with chit-chat about places to see in Beijing. Large tumblers and bottles of Wu Xing beer—Beijing's pride—replaced the green tea. A stamp collection was presented to each American as a token gift.

The meeting was adjourned with a toast to a prosperous future. *"Gambei!"* they asserted and drank up. Both delegations stood and shook hands while slightly bowing their heads; they finished their beer and exchanged good-byes, *"Zaijin!"* Redding's group filed out of the room as the Chinese stood, and with a habitual smile, bobbed their heads.

Beijing's traffic was incessant. By default, delays became a time-filler for sightseeing. They drove by a plaza near Tiananmen Square, where Mao's image adorned the Gate of Heavenly Peace. Then they passed the Forbidden City, a network of palaces that housed imperial dynasties for six hundred years. Inside was the stark-white mausoleum where the rubbery body of Chairman Mao lay under glass.

At first blush, the Chinese seemed more concerned for the dead than the living—a notion that was far from accurate. Based on history and its sheer size, culture, tumultuous times, and leadership, China had grappled and vacillated in the administration of social and economic issues over the years. They approached the task of governing their huge country following one of two philosophies: Maoist or pragmatic.

Founded in the struggles to survive the onslaught of the Kuomintang and the Japanese, the Maoist outlook contained an unusual degree of altruism and revolutionary zeal. The concept was to instill the Long March spirit—an epic 6,000-mile retreat by Chinese Communist guerrillas from Kuomintang forces in 1934—in every factory worker and peasant as a motivator.

The Maoist faction propagandized the approach to inspire the masses and achieve economic progress. They believed the approach was essential to the survival, modernization, and strengthening of China. But it was a one-dimensional solution to a complex, socioeconomic problem.

Consequently, some rulers, including Jiang Zemin and his allies, adopted a more practical approach. Their view was to achieve economic progress through profit motives without succumbing to pre-war capitalism. This notion contrasted with Maoism, but China realized it needed to change its posture in the global setting. Therefore, they adopted a more aggressive transition to a market-based economy. However, the fear of becoming a Western-styled society continued to be a major concern.

From 1953 to 1957, China formed a socialistic economic system by implementing mutual aid teams and cooperatives in the countryside. The government nationalized industry in the cities and encouraged farmers to enjoin their land and farming implements for centrally controlled operations. In the process, China had the fastest-growing industry in Asia at that time.

In 1958, Mao and his allies cleverly rekindled a revolutionary passion for economic progress using a central state-controlled approach. China's peasantry worked on local industrial projects to build the nation's infrastructure and industrial base.

The farmers were reorganized into colossal communes, whereby the land was state-owned and centrally managed. The workers lived in state-managed housing, ate in public mess halls, and the children were educated and cared for by state-run facilities.

However, from 1962 to 1966, the more pragmatic leaders, including Premier Chou En-lai and Deng Xiaoping, eliminated agricultural activities' communal approach to instill more personalized incentives. Private plots of farmland were permitted for the farmers to cultivate and profit from as a business. The Maoists feared this economically liberal attitude would return China to capitalism, and by 1966, Maoist factions had organized millions of activist youths into the Red Guards.

Subsequently, the Red Guards combined with the armed forces to oust the pragmatists and install "revolutionary committees" of workers and soldiers. Thus, the Great Proletarian Cultural Revolution had begun.

But by 1979, China no longer needed the Great Wall, and the Maoists were eventually purged from China's government system. Emphasis was placed on raising living standards, allowing profit motives, and fueling industrial and economic growth in all sectors.

Rather than using strict centralized planning and control, the trend was to let market forces dictate growth and enterprise survival and to rely more on foreign trade and investment. In 1982, the twelfth Party Congress adopted policies that confirmed that the pragmatists were still the dominating factor.

Lee Redding was oblivious to China's history and the sights in Beijing. He was preoccupied with the immediate business at hand. *This is a businessman's dream,* he thought, *but we need to hold on to our wallets. I've heard plenty of horror stories about dealing with the Chinese.*

They are tough scoundrels, and they will negotiate with every trick in the book. I'm not about to give up any of my technology, and they are not going to steal it either! I need to use my connections in Washington, especially with these guys.

MegaTronics was one of the first entrants into the China market, a market in existence since Marco Polo. Yet Redding acted like it was a newfound territory. Like a kid in a candy store, he was an aggressive opportunist in pursuit of a huge, emerging market.

Redding researched China's enormous potential, its special agenda to ramp up quickly, and decided to establish high-powered, strategic Beijing connections. Redding saw China as the juiciest, lowest-hanging fruit in the global market—he hungered for it—and he was determined to get it. All bets were off.

Redding convinced MacDuff to arrange another top-level meeting with the MPT, the group spearheading the development of China's telecommunications and computer infrastructure. MacDuff and Redding discreetly set up an itinerary for the China visit. The meeting was highly confidential, and the Chinese government continued to keep talks with MegaTronics strictly under wraps. There were no announcements in the *People's Daily* or the *China Daily.*

Redding pushed to clinch his first China deal with the CCPIT. He was also undergoing a course in Chinese Business 101.

CHINA COUNCIL FOR THE PROMOTION OF INTERNATIONAL TRADE, BEIJING, CHINA

"Tell him I want at least a five-year exclusive, or they have to pay regular prices!" Redding grumbled to his interpreter.

Redding had been haggling with Liu Cheng for several months, trying to close the deal and learn how the Chinese negotiated.

Ignoring his interpreter's advice, Redding made the mistake of letting the Chinese know what his departure schedule was on more than one occasion. Inevitably, Cheng would press for new conditions in the contract on the day Redding was to depart Beijing, often forcing him to agree or leave empty-handed.

"Okay, Mr. Redding, we give you five years. But you give us training for support of MEGA-Star," Cheng retorted with a heavy accent. "We need training for Chinese people."

The Chinese were sticking to their guns, figuratively speaking—guns with nuclear warheads attached. They cleverly deployed the two demo computers as missile control units at their *Xi'an* and *Qingdoa* missile sites.

Once the units were installed in their missile control program, the Chinese knew this would place Redding in violation of the Arms Export Control Act due to the restricted status and the encrypted software inside the MEGA-Star. And they could use this as another pressure point.

Redding was not fully cognizant of his precarious position, and in his eagerness, he ignored the possible consequences. "We will train your people, but a MegaTronics Sales and Service branch will also be set up in Beijing, Shanghai, Shenyang, Nanjing, Guangzhou, and of course, Hong Kong," he said to Cheng. "Your people can share our office space and expenses under a joint sales and service agreement, separate from our national blanket sales contract."

Redding wasn't a neophyte. By establishing his offices in China and having a five-year lead in the market, it would take competition at least seven years to get into the China ball game. By then, he could lock up the majority of the market.

Redding was up against formidable negotiators, but he used a few ploys of his own. By separating the service contract from the sales contract at the appropriate time, he could find fault in the service deal, claim a breach of contract and regain full control of services.

He was adamantly against giving up any significant technical knowledge on the MEGA-Star software. This was his hold on the market, and no one was to gain control over service.

But Cheng and his men were equally cunning. They plotted a course in the acquisition of critical proprietary information, including technical knowledge that would at some point allow them to duplicate MEGA-Star chips without the support of MegaTronics. They had used this strategy successfully with other gullible high-tech companies, companies that later found their products being produced by government-owned Chinese enterprises.

The victimized companies were lucky to recover any of the initial investment used for entering the Chinese market. Consequently, some corporations either gave up their effort or had a falling out with their Chinese partners.

Redding and Cheng finished their meeting with a *mao tai*, a popular local drink, and a toast; *"Gambei!"* They raised their glasses.

Later, in his hotel room, Redding chortled into the phone, "Man, did I do a number on those turkeys." Redding was talking to his soon-to-be partner, Mike Branston, in California. "They played right into my hands. I got the five-year lockout of competition and a separate service contract to boot."

"Fantastic!" Branston replied.

"Be ready to pop the champagne bottle when I get back!" Redding was certain to supply the Chinese with the new MEGA-Star.1 computer, well before the planned fourth-quarter release date. It would be difficult to manage the logistics of upgrading the MEGA-Star in China. Chinese counterparts were eager to deploy the MEGA-Star systems, without Redding's knowledge, in strategic missile control applications.

With the MEGA-Star supercomputer, their missile technology would leap forward five to ten years ahead of their adversaries. And the computer would manage the missile delivery system for multiple, miniaturized warheads.

GENERAL FULLER'S PENTAGON OFFICE

General Fuller cringed while reading Lame Duck's report on China's nuclear missile program. Along with the nuclear buildup, the

Chinese were developing laser weapons to block signals from U.S. radar satellites from penetrating a layer of clouds.

More disturbing, because U.S. bases in Asia had no missile defense system, the Chinese tagged U.S. personnel posted at these sites as hostages in case of a conflict. Missile strikes against these bases could mean the destruction of U.S. airfields, fuel dumps, weapons, and ammunition depots.

China also had submarines, warships, and ballistic, and cruise missiles that could reach U.S. ships on patrol in the region. They also had bombers with anti-ship weapons. The report went on to say China's regular mock missile attacks on U.S. bases were a clear message that any attack on its forces would bring missile strikes on U.S. soldiers, sailors, airmen, and Marines stationed in Asia.

"Besides setting up a missile defense system and targeting the U.S., China is installing mobile, short-range missile systems intended to target surrounding nations," Lame Duck reported. "Russia, India, Taiwan, Japan, and other parts of East Asia are in the sights of China. The Chinese military stationed 150 to 200 M-9 and M-11 missiles in southern regions, aimed specifically at Taiwan. And the number of missiles will increase to 650 by the year 2005.

"The M-9 missile has a 1,000-pound payload and a 370-mile range; the M-11 has a shorter range but carries a larger payload. Both can hit Taiwan, and both are nuclear-capable. And Taiwan is defenseless. China has 40 CSS-2 refire-capable launchers at six field garrisons and launch complexes. But some of the computer control units at these sites are outdated.

"The CSS-2 launchers are designed to interface with the MEGA-Star architecture, which highlights the need for doing business with MegaTronics Corporation. Undoubtedly, China's military readiness in modern nuclear weapons hinges on Mr. Redding and the president," the report stated. "You must take immediate action."

Fuller took Lame Duck's advice. He remembered the extent to which the Chinese had pilfered U.S. secrets on nuclear missiles. They had stolen information on every deployed thermonuclear warhead in the U.S. arsenal. Research material on our radar systems was also taken by the Chinese, which would threaten U.S. submarines.

Fuller surmised, "Perhaps China wants the world to know they can build a large, modern arsenal for a *second-strike* capability—not so much to launch the first strike.

Alas, what Beijing really wanted was respect—respect from the nation they considered an enemy.

16

RENAISSANCE MAYFLOWER HOTEL, WASHINGTON, D.C

Located four blocks from the White House, the Renaissance Mayflower Hotel was a convenient place for a rendezvous with Liz. Liz would discreetly check into a room and wait for MacDuff's incognito visits. MacDuff usually disguised himself with dark sunglasses, a stick-on mustache, the collar of his overcoat turned up, and a *Saxon/Dutton* hat. Secret Service agents shrouded his movements.

The Mayflower Hotel's grandeur was highlighted by opulent gilded ceilings, imported Italian marble, and ornately carved millwork. Liz's study had two working desks featuring ergonomically designed chairs and lighting, a fax machine, and the latest computer equipment. Having been the site of presidential inaugural balls for more than sixty years, the Mayflower was also rich with tradition.

"Oh, Mac, you're such a hunk," Liz said. The hotel was their preferred meeting place for a rendezvous.

MacDuff smiled broadly.

After a period of silence, Liz said, "Mac, what are you going to do about Russia selling rocket engines to India?"

"Well, if they go through with it, I'll be forced to at least threaten sanctions on both countries. The sale would violate the *Missile Tech-*

nology Control Regime guidelines, which Russia has agreed to enforce. I'd have to do something about it."

"But Russian and Indian officials deny they're violating the rules, claiming they cannot use cryogenic engines for military purposes," Liz said. "How are you going to get around that?"

"I know what they're saying. But they're in violation, and I'm forced to impose sanctions."

Liz replied, "But you know, they're also saying the guidelines are ill-defined. They point out those MTCR controls on launch vehicles with a range of three hundred kilometers and a payload of five hundred kilograms would include Russia's commercial space launch vehicles."

"They're accusing us of attempting to destroy Russia's space industry, and we are using the MTCR guidelines to quell all their deals," the president said.

"Russia and India have called for an international inspection to determine that the deal did indeed comply with the terms, but we're going to send our own team to examine the situation."

"You should use the soft approach with the Russians."

"Why bother? We're not going to do much commerce with Russia. Now, China is a different story. It's the juiciest market in the world. Already got some hot deals brewing."

THE OVAL OFFICE

Tiffany had just delivered a fresh cup of coffee and left the room. As the president sipped his coffee, he spoke to General Fuller over the speakerphone. "What's that? China did what?"

"I'll repeat." Fuller was impatient. "China has again sold our missile and radar technology to Iran."

"Confirmed?" MacDuff casually turned and looked out the window. It was a crisp, bright day. The sunlight lit up the Oval Office like a floodlight.

"It's true," Fuller said. "According to my contact, they also exported four hundred tons of chemicals to Iran, including carbon sulfide, an ingredient for nerve gas."

"Which department?"

"The PLA," Fuller replied. After two years of negotiations, the *China Precision Engineering Department,* an outfit owned by the PLA, decided to sell gyroscopes, accelerometers, and other missile guidance technologies. They did business with *Iran's Defense Industries Organization,* the main coordinating body for Iran's missile development programs.

"He also said they sold advanced air-defense equipment and some five thousand tons of other military equipment," said Fuller. "This included components to upgrade Iran's Chinese-made ASCMs, anti-ship cruise missiles."

MacDuff sipped some coffee, put his cup down, and frowned. "Well, maybe the top officials weren't aware of it."

"What? You can't be serious." The proliferation had become widespread. The *China Precision Machinery Company,* CPMC, shipped several ring magnets to Pakistan. Ring magnets are key components in the production of nuclear weapons fuel. But the administration would not impose sanctions.

Fuller continued, "Lame Duck also indicated that, for foreigners, it was difficult to determine which companies in China were truly privately owned and operated and which were adjuncts to the Chinese government."

"Business is business. And it's none of our business."

"But, sir, it is our business. Agencies within the U.S. intelligence community disagreed over the extent of the problem. The DOD cited multiple examples of suspected diversion or use of U.S. civilian technology in China's aeronautics and astronautics industries. I know the *CIA Nonproliferation Center* characterized the problem as an overstatement, but they did not question the potential for diversion in high-tech industries."

"General, let me remind you that the Chinese foreign minister furnished written confirmation that they will follow MTCR guidelines, provided we lift sanctions on the export of supercomputer and satellite technologies to China. And we're working on that right now."

"Well then, what about this?" Fuller said. "Lame Duck says that in a conspiracy to skirt the MTCR, China shipped short-range ballistic missiles—M-11s—to Pakistan. Now, the Pakistanis have the units in operation.

They've developed nuclear warheads for the M-11s."

MacDuff grimaced. "That's news to me."

"Also, in case the boys at Langley missed it, Lame Duck also revealed that China was building a missile factory at *Fatehgarh*, near *Rawalpindi* in Pakistan. It's designed to produce components for the M-11 missiles. He also reported that Chinese technicians were assisting the Pakistanis in developing a six-hundred-kilometer version of the M-11 at the Fatehgarh facility."

The General paused to allow MacDuff to respond, but he didn't. Fuller went on, "China has also been involved in proliferation in Syria and Iran. Lame Duck said the CPMC shipped special missile components to Syria for its Scud C ballistic missile program. And they're also helping Syria to develop solid-propellant rocket motors for their ballistic missiles."

Again, Fuller had presented a series of dilemmas. His report came when the president was close to signing a secret agreement to share peaceful nuclear technology, including supercomputers, with China. But the transfer of technology from China was in direct violation of the *Iran-Iraq Nonproliferation Act* that called for sanctions to be imposed on any nation exporting weapons to those countries. It was a perplexing situation for the president.

MacDuff quickly formulated a counteraction to Fuller's report for the press if the story was somehow leaked. Concerning China's exports of C802 ASCMs to Iran, he would claim that the sale was not considered destabilizing. Therefore, it did not violate the Iran-Iraq Nonproliferation Act.

Despite MacDuff's denial, the Iranians deployed C-802 missiles on the Qeshm Island in the center of the strategically vital Strait of Hormuz. The strait was very much like a control valve. Oil transported by sea from the Persian Gulf States must pass through the strait. It is the only route by sea to transport oil from Kuwait, Iraq, Iran, Saudi Arabia, Bahrain, Qatar, and most United Arab Emirates.

On the matter of Iranian military control of the area, the Iranian president pledged that military cooperation between Iran and Oman posed no threat to other countries. MacDuff said, "The military cooperation between Iran and other countries in the region, notably Oman, only serves to bring peace and security to the region, especially the Strait of Hormuz."

Regardless, ASCM sites on Qeshm, plus other Iranian ASCM sites on Sirri's and Abu Musa's islands, provided them the capability to close the Strait of Hormuz to commercial shipping. They had enough power to saturate the defenses of small naval forces.

While on the other side of the world, a Hong Kong–based company backed by the PLA had taken over part of the Panama Canal. By far, most of the traffic through the canal moves between the U.S. East Coast and the Far East, while movements between Europe and the West Coast and Canada comprise the second major trade route at the waterway. There were about 25,000 workers who died to build that canal, and, in return, it was ours in perpetuity. But now, Beijing controls a strategic waterway passage.

After a long pause, the president said, "What's the big deal, General? I'm sure the CIA, the DOC, the NSA, and others are on top of it. I didn't know anything about it."

"That's just it. Agencies don't share information, even with the chief executive. And we have no coordinated plan to counteract armament abuses."

After casting a protracted stare at Fuller, MacDuff said, "What do you propose?"

"First, I recommend that the secretary of commerce establish strict criteria for approvals of dual-use technology exports to China. This should include pre-license checks on the credentials of the end-user, the potential end uses of the commodities to be exported, and an analysis of the effects on national security," Fuller submitted.

"I'll look into it."

"Hold on, sir, I'm not finished. Second, I recommend that the secretary of commerce provide periodic reports to the interagency group on all dual-use licenses for China."

Fuller paused to observe MacDuff's reaction; at first glance, it was one of disapproval. Fuller went on, "The reports should include license and export control classification numbers, names of the end-user and/or ultimate consignee, end-use descriptions, and descriptions of the commodities to be licensed. We further recommend that the director of the *Arms Control and Disarmament Agency*, Joint Chiefs of Staff, secretaries of DOD, Commerce, and the secretary of state use licensing information contained in these reports. They can establish mutually acceptable criteria and guidelines for selection of other licenses for interagency review."

The president replied smugly, "Anything else?"

"That's it."

As anticipated, news of the missile sales to Iran leaked to the press. MacDuff scheduled a news conference in the James S. Brady Press Briefing Room. A flock of reporters with notebooks sat patiently while television crews set up and adjusted their equipment. Behind several rows of fold-up metal chairs, black electrical cords snaked across the floor, leading to power and signal boxes that connected the TV cameras. Bright spotlights targeted the lectern, which displayed the presidential seal. The flanks were the Stars and Stripes on the left and the presidential flag on the right, silhouetted by a royal blue backdrop.

The president strolled up and stood behind a cluster of microphones aimed at his mouth like cattle-probes. He cleared his throat and grimly said, "We are concerned about recent reports of Chinese exports going to Iran." He added, "But we believe at this stage that, in fact, the Chinese are operating within the assurances they have given us. We've not seen any reason to question their behavior.

"Actually, the Chinese foreign minister Qian Qichen gave us written confirmation that China will follow our missile control guidelines and parameters." He paused to scan the group of stoic reporters.

MacDuff glanced down at his notes. "In all likelihood, we will never spend enough on military hardware in the effort to bring the United States real security, in this new era of universal mass destructive capabilities. I realize my number-one constitutional duty is to provide for the common defense of our nation.

"But what we also need to realize is that most of today's threats are not just military. Environmental decay, weak markets, terrorism, infectious diseases, and human rights are far greater causes for concern than missiles."

The president had a point. Afghanistan, Burma, Cambodia, Indonesia, China, India, Malaysia, North Korea, Pakistan, Philippines, South Korea, and Sri Lanka were plagued with serious internal strife. "It is normal for some countries to have different views on human rights issues because of the different cultures and national conditions," MacDuff continued.

"The way to solve the difference is through dialogue, which will help promote the understanding of our standards and social values.

"Confrontation should not be resorted to because it will not help solve differences. But it would increase contradictions and disputes, and we should avoid this at all costs. We should be the keepers of worldwide peace.

"We should also share our technologies and our wealth. We should set the example, be proactive in solving international problems and be the model that every country will emulate.

"We need to emphasize working together in peace and harmony in everyday life. That's why we've convinced China and other nations to forego nuclear armament in favor of peace and tranquility."

Upon hearing the president's speech on TV, General Fuller commented to Colonel Gomez, "True enough. We don't want to go to war with China. But the president's approach is an open-door invitation to disaster."

17

U.S. DEPARTMENT OF COMMERCE

"The MEGA-Star computers are going to Taiwan to help them defend against China," MacDuff's aide explained to the DOC operative.

"I don't care how you do it, but don't leave any tracks. Got it?" The aide was a wretch of a man, a MacDuff goon. He was a shark disguised as a human being, packaged in a white shirt, a loud tie, and a frayed beige-colored polyester suit. His face was apathetic, dour.

"Okay, got it. But, do the people at MegaTronics know where these suckers are going?" said the DOC operative, a CIA washout. A small man, oily and mean, he was known to be money-hungry.

"No problem. The units will be first shipped to Certified Adjusters, Inc., a CIA front posing as an insurance agency in Fresno. From there, we'll ship them overseas. MegaTronics will think the systems are replacement units ordered under an insurance claim," he explained.

The wretch and the washout received their orders from the top. But they knew they violated the *Arms Export Control Act, Missile Technology Export Controls,* and the *Missile Technology Control Regime.*

Confident that the transaction was officially approved at a top level, albeit under a veil of secrecy, the DOC operative began setting up the logistics through his international trade network. And in the process, he negotiated a sizable kickback from his counterpart in Asia. The operative reasoned, *why not? People at the top do it all the time, and who's going to complain if the deal is busted? That bunch of pricks at the White House will have to protect me so I won't talk.*

The operation was code-named Albatross, and the MEGA-Star serial numbers were MC-1832434 and MC-1832435. The CIA agents at the phony insurance agency ordered the supercomputers and the operation was underway.

MEGA-Star computers were originally designed for the U.S.

Department of Defense and their coding was initially classified as top secret and banned from export. The president did not inform the DOD of Albatross, knowing that they would disapprove. MacDuff and the DOD had been at odds since he came into office, and using General Fuller as the main watchdog, the DOD opposed his ill-conceived, dangerous shenanigans.

Fuller was a dyed-in-the-wool leatherneck who clung to the old standards. He still boozed with his buddies at the Pentagon. He was not a conventional politician. He was a brilliant strategist with a blood 'n, guts attitude. His idea of politics was to do what was right, tell it like it is, draw the line and fight anyone who challenged him. "Pussyfootin' around with flowery talk and following strict administrative procedures is not my style," Fuller had said. He was self-disciplined and definitely not a pushover, even by the president. In Fuller's words, "MacDuff would be going against the wind to try and convince me to support him on what I believed to be wrong."

"Ted, we're going around those eagles at the Pentagon," MacDuff said. "I've arranged for MEGA-Star computers to be shipped to Taiwan through my contacts at the DOC. Those knuckleheads at the Pentagon don't know anything about it."

Whittington listened with a false expression of agreement, which he was good at. But inside, he felt very skittish about the scheme. He offered a suggestion, "Mac, even if we can pull it off with no hitches, have you set up someone to take the fall in case anything goes wrong?"

Rubbing his chin, MacDuff thought a second. "Damn, Ted, that's an excellent idea!" Why didn't I think of that? No, I haven't set up anyone yet, but I know just the guy for the slot." MacDuff had an evil grin on his face. He thought, Ted is mediocre, but occasionally, he comes through with some outstanding ploys. I think I'll keep Ted around for another term. He doesn't give me any guff, and he's good for PR, finding women, doing my dirty work, and taking the heat when necessary.

"We've got to protect our territory," the VP said. "The stakes are too high when it comes to the upcoming elections." Whittington was the only child of a wealthy businessman in Concord, Massachusetts. He was a plump, distinguished-looking man with a pinkish face, mousy-gray hair, average height. He had gone to Yale, where he first met MacDuff and entered politics at the city level.

"You're right. If we're not careful, we'll lose our focus," MacDuff responded.

"Sure, sure," Whittington said. "We need another four years to fulfill our agenda, but our foreign affairs problem is building into a hot issue." Whittington had been backed by his father's money and influential contacts but failed to excel independently. He was number 123 in a class of 150 and made the second string on the football team. He had a brief stay in the military, was mayor *pro tem*, and went to Congress representing the smallest district in his area. Finally, he ran for president but ended up as MacDuff's vice president.

"We'll just have to do the best we can to avoid any trouble in that area," the president responded. "I'm sure we can keep the lid on until after the elections."

In contrast to Whittington, MacDuff's academic credentials were extraordinary, and his quick rise to a high political position was striking. He graduated magna cum laude as an undergraduate, was in the upper 20 percent at Yale, and was a Rhodes scholar.

"Winning the elections is key," MacDuff said. "I refuse to accept defeat. I will not, absolutely *not*, accept it!"

The president and his cronies were of the baby boom age, many of whom developed a socially infectious attitude in the 1960s. Some formed a rebellious, greedy demeanor in the 1980s, followed by a penchant for power in the 1990s.

Many decisions made by MacDuff's cabinet were politically skewed. Congress was also confused about the majority of their constituents' attitudes since the silent majority *was* silent. Still, the so-called minority elements were loud and visible with complaints and discontent, occasionally laced with violent protests.

The mood in America was miserable. Strange events took place at personal levels: confrontations in retail stores, road rage, feuding in the streets, and the list goes on. People were venting their frustrations at an increasing rate. Frustration and malcontent were also stimulated by the mad race to outdo one another in a very competitive lifestyle. Material ownership, status, and other hang-ups became more important social traits than interpersonal relations and quality social values.

Senator Garrity spoke about social issues at a fundraiser banquet held at the Adolphus hotel in the Dallas financial district. A uniformed doorman greeted visitors at the carriage entrance of the hotel, which was built in 1912. *Objets d'art* enriched the lobby living room and the cozy alcoves, and the interior had a continental character that created an ambiance of the aristocracy. The banquet was held in the 5,200-square-foot Grand Ballroom, which featured a stunning *trompe l'oeil*, French Renaissance decor, and mirrored walls.

After being introduced by the mayor of Dallas, and a round of applause, Garrity declared with a wide grin, "It's good to be back home." The audience cheered. Then he put on a serious face and launched his speech: "My dear friends, in the past, we've enjoyed an atmosphere of prosperity and happiness, an atmosphere that is unlike the present. Today, we are afflicted with many social ills that are devastating to our quality of life. Unfortunately, this administration has failed to mitigate these ills, and in fact, has compounded the problem with a layer of inefficient bureaucracy and corruption.

"Our president gives a lot of lip service about social issues, but he and his cabinet have a halfhearted attitude when it comes to doing anything about it. They are focused more on political careers and less on serving the people.

"Most upsetting to me is—he continually uses our flag and the honor of those who fought our wars as a platform to further his political career. But he didn't serve.

"On one particular occasion, the vision was nauseating at the site of *Omaha Beach*—our commander-in-chief—but yet a proven draft dodger and a political adversary to U.S. military. He had prepared an eloquent speech about the veterans who fought for our country in Europe. What hypocrisy —he could win an Emmy as a clever practitioner of deceit and demagoguery. It's no surprise that military men and many businesses leaders spurn Ryan MacDuff."

Dante Martin, president of ComTech, Inc., was in the audience. And like Garrity, he had little respect for MacDuff. As a veteran, he loathed thinking of MacDuff standing in the sands of Omaha Beach and preaching patriotism.

The seashore was regarded as a sanctified site where many American soldiers gave their lives during World War II. They fought the Nazis for liberty, prosperity, and freedom enjoyed and exploited by war protestors. When American troops were sacrificing lives, these people were smoking pot, organizing protests, and urging people to dodge the draft.

Senator Garrity continued his talk at the Adolphus: "The president succeeds by the way he looks. Not in what he says, his actions, or his good intentions. He appears to really care. And people buy into this charisma without thinking of the consequences. He should be crowned the actor-in-chief!

"During the Vietnam War, I'm sorry to say, Ryan MacDuff put self-preservation over patriotism. His actions were politically motivated, and he wasn't willing to risk his life in a war. Besides, the cultural elite, the academia, and left-wing newscasters backed the protestors.

"Veterans were fighting on two fronts: the battlefields in Vietnam, and back home on the streets and campuses of America. In the first case, fighting foreign enemy forces and in the other, fighting cowardly opportunists at home."

Garrity paused to take a drink from a glass of water. At that moment, he had a disturbing flashback. He thought about a respected news commentator, William Krocker, a man who broke the neutrality code among major newscasters. He opposed the war on national TV. In a special report, Krocker said a trip to Vietnam left him "deeply disillusioned." He believed the war was futile and immoral. "We have too often been disappointed by optimistic leaders," he said to the public, "to have faith any longer in the silver linings of war." Shamefully, Krocker joined a group of Americans who denounced the war effort and undermined the loyalty of U.S. troops. Troops who risked their lives on the battlefield.

Garrity shook off the hurt from the past and concluded his speech: "Unfortunately, many protestors ended up in positions of authority and power. And I dread seeing the consequences of their actions, but I'm willing to fight on.

"I promise to preserve our nation's traditional standards and instill morality into the minds of our youth. We must persevere together as a unified nation. We can overcome the grotesque assault on the principles upon which we built this nation. And we shall defend ourselves from an enemy attack and the subversive schemes of global economic control," Garrity said. "As your president, I'll fight with you side by side. Together, we shall win!"

18

PRIVACY OF INFORMATION INSTITUTE, WASHINGTON, D.C

"Here's how it works. You open an account online, then print out forms to be signed and sent to the processing center. Once an account is established, you have the ability to view your records via the Internet, on the World Wide Web," Lindsey said into the phone.

"You can write electronic checks with secured digital signatures."

"Interesting," said Terence Dowling, managing director of the Privacy of Information Institute (PII).

Lindsey continued, "The only thing you have to do is send in proof of identity such as a copy of your passport or driver's license."

"Like the Automated Clearing House in the U.S. banking system," Dowling confirmed.

NetForum and Dowling's PII group feared that an international consortium was plotting to control global finances by using online banking and EFT via the Internet.

"Trouble is," Lindsey said, "you really have no idea who has access to your personal and financial information. Like our credit bureaus, it's a major drawback. We know the EFT consortium has a hidden agenda."

"You know, the privacy of information has just about vanished in a tide of online files," Dowling stated while shifting in his chair. "Information is merged, massaged, and passed around from one agency to another, in government and the private sector." He thought about the Internet's largest advertising company routinely tracking Web users' online movements by their actual names, addresses, and purchasing habits.

They linked query activities from site to site to a huge, real-world database whether a user made a purchase or not. The firm collected over 100 million files on individuals, usually anonymous, recording online behavior without their knowledge. The practice, known as profiling, uses cookies. Cookies are small pieces of information placed on a Web surfer's PC. They identify the remote machine and the user's activities for the site being visited.

"Thousands of Web sites are tracking you," Dowling said. "Your activities are exposed to sites dedicated to collecting information, then passing it to other collaborating sites. And this is not only happening in the U.S. We've found this to be true all over the world."

Dowling nodded his agreement. "Laws are designed to protect a privileged few, and ironically, lawmakers *are* the privileged."

"Yep," Lindsey replied. "Money and political status seem to be the dominant criterion. Nowadays, ordinary citizens have a sense of protest against rich leftists—the cultural elite—and a corrupt government that panders to them for support."

Before they broke their conversation, Lindsey mentioned that Dante Martin was elected executive director of NetForum. Martin had been proactive in expanding the group's activities.

Sitting in his small, cluttered office, not too far from the White House, Dowling realized PII and NetForum had a full plate. Over the past several years, he had warned his members of the subtle movement towards a single government that ruled the world. Emerging as a joint body, the UN, NATO, the World Bank, and the IMF set global fiscal policies—designed for a paperless currency system—which is near reality, vis-a-vis "cryptocurrency."

The consortium planned to integrate an international network of online bankers, making international online banking through the

Internet very easy. A network of on-the-ground correspondent affil-
iate banks would disburse funds or accept physical deposits on a
local basis. But the records would be kept in an electronic repository.

As global trading and currency controls increase, the power and
influence of the U.S. will diminish. The downward trend of U.S. trade
control since GATT was founded in 1947 would be perpetuated. Then,
the U.S. dominated half of the world's $25 billion in trade. Now, the
U.S. controls less than 17 percent.

After a series of e-mail messages, Dowling placed a call to Dante
Martin. His mission was to create an alliance between PII and
NetForum.

"Dante, how ya doing?" Dowling said.

"Well, I can finally put a voice to your e-mails," Martin
responded. "I hear you are on the verge of announcing a new, faster
CPU chip that will beat the MEGA-Star. Anything to that?"

Martin grinned sheepishly. "You know I can't comment on that,
but I will tell you I'm getting more and more excited about competing
with MegaTronics. Redding keeps my adrenaline flowing!" They
chuckled.

"Terence, we're mustering our forces here at ComTech, and if we
meet our goals, you'll see a lot of changes in the market."

"Good!" said Dowling. "Redding needs competition. He's got free
rein, and the market is too dependent on his products."

"Got that right!" Martin shot back.

"To be honest, I've even had visions of a computer monopoly
controlled by MegaTronics, much in the manner that the WEC, UN,
IMF, and the rest are trying to do in global financing."

"I know the feeling."

"I'm afraid our preoccupation with human rights issues has
diverted our attention away from the larger problems," Dowling said.

Martin thought of the president's ultra-liberal policies, the seamy
underside of his dealings, the breakdown of our democracy, and the
disarray of world affairs. "Our security and global economics are at
stake," he said.

"The White House goofed again," Dowling replied.

"I don't know what to think anymore. But I know this: we've got to get our act together. We need to start a grassroots effort with NetForum and get key people in each region of the world to pull together. We must fight the WEC and the EFT project. This could be the most dangerous, peace threatening development since Hitler and the Nazi movement."

"Pretty strong stuff."

"Well, the Asian market has not been stable in the past few years, and corruption still prevails in many of the Third-World countries. You have to consider, fifty-percent of Russia's colonies are of Islamic or Muslim religions. What happens if this kind of influence penetrates the WEC's control of EFT?"

"I admit, it's a chilling thought. I get apprehensive, especially when I think of the Middle East."

After a short period of silence, Dowling continued, "Why don't we set up a special initiative?"

"Special initiative?"

"If you're willing to outline the technical security issues on the Internet and the EFT problem, I'll draft up a paper on the subject."

Martin thought for a moment. "No problem. Can do!"

"Good. Then we can spread the word to gain the influence and participation of NetForum as a whole group."

"I can identify some key people who would probably participate. One, in particular, is a computer guru in Oslo, Norway. She's very skilled and knows the MEGA-Star system inside out."

"What's her status?" Dowling asked.

"Works for the Norwegian government. She's well connected."

"Great!" Dowling paused, momentarily eyeballing a stack of *Wired* magazines on his desk. He was reminded of an article about the Times Square New Year's Eve event. "Listen, why don't we tie this in with the New Year's gig? It fits like a glove."

"I suppose it would be good PR," Martin responded. "When can we get back together?"

"End of the week?"

"Great! Let's rock 'n, roll! The next time you're out this way, I'll show you the fun spots in D.C. I'll take you to a quaint place in Washington—even after dark."

"I'd like to, but I've been more or less sequestered on a special project," Martin said. "I see."

Martin paused and said, "Although the DOJ thing is coming up, I mean, I may have to go to D.C. anyway. The DOJ and the SEC wanna talk to me about MegaTronics."

"Really?"

"They're moving in on him pretty fast, but the White House manages to block the effort."

Martin lowered his voice. "Confidentially, I've already been approached to testify."

Dowling was quiet for a moment. Redding's swift rise to becoming one of the top five richest men in the world was astonishing. "Yeah, some guys don't know when to stop before greed sets in. I guess when you're that rich and powerful, your morals deteriorate, and right from wrong becomes a fuzzy concept."

"Anyway, gotta go. Talk to you soon," Martin said.

"Look forward to it."

Dowling and Martin were optimistic but knew they were up against tough odds.

Senator Garrity spoke at a corporate meeting held at the Hilton hotel, near Hartsfield International Airport in Atlanta. Service at the hotel was typical Southern-style, authenticated by the Southern drawl of the hotel staff.

Standing behind the podium on a small platform, Garrity began his speech: "Ladies and gentlemen, the subject of nuclear weapons and Russia go hand in hand. As you know, the Russian army was once very formidable. Now, economic decay has set in, and the Russian military has been reduced to shambles. But this is not all good," Garrity emphasized.

"The Soviets can hardly defend their European and Asian borders without nuclear weapons. This poses a serious complication for the rest of the world.

"If Russia or its military dependents engage in violent conflicts, there is a danger they will use nuclear weapons. Are we prepared? That's the question.

"The fact is, the GRU, the Soviet military intelligence, and the Chinese have been spying on nuclear technology and U.S. training activities for years. Particularly maneuvers designed for Middle East warfare. Consequently, the Soviets have equipped Iraq with modern weapons. And the Chinese have been supplying Iran with nuclear warheads. Now, we haven't heard anything about this from the president, have we?

"Since taking office, President MacDuff has claimed 'a state of nuclear disarmament,' a total of one hundred forty-seven times. On at least thirty-three occasions, he has unequivocally stated there were 'no nuclear missiles targeted against the United States.' They've implied the People's Republic of China has de-targeted its strategic forces from the U.S. The truth is, Beijing rejected the president's offer for a de-targeting agreement."

The senator paused. With a solemn face, he slowly panned the audience, seemingly looking into the eyes of each person. "Ladies and gentlemen, this administration is a farce. I urge you to write your representatives and demand a factual accounting of the nuclear threat situation. You owe it to yourselves to know the truth.

"And I will owe it to you, as your next president, to do my duty and cap this dangerous powder keg."

19

HEADQUARTERS, WORLD ECONOMIC COUNCIL, BRUSSELS, BELGIUM

Dresden Erikksen, chairman of the World Economic Council, greeted Sheikh El-Kansi of the Organization of the Islamic Conference. The OIC comprises fifty-six nations and four observer states. Acting as one voice, it represented the affairs of Muslims all over the world.

"Sheikh El-Kansi—a pleasure to see you."

El-Kansi gave a stilted nod. Somber-faced, he entered Erikksen's office.

His entourage of six followed. With his fleshy aquiline nose in the air, ElKansi scanned the room and its furnishings. Erikksen's office was more functional than flashy. It was equipped with a conference table, a built-in projection screen, and a small library.

El-Kansi rolled his eyes at the eclectic decorations. "*Salaam, chetouri,*" El-Kansi responded. He often spoke in his native tongue to muddle foreigners. El-Kansi flicked his hand towards the door. His band of assistants promptly streamed out.

Erikksen waited for El-Kansi to be seated at the conference table. Then he sat across from him and leaned forward. "Let me get straight to the point," Erikksen said sternly. "We would like the OIC's participation in the EFT project."

El-Kansi remained silent for a few seconds, staring at Erikksen stoically. Then he nodded mechanically. "Mr. Erikksen, we may be interested," he said in a posh, Oxford English accent. In his mid-thirties, El-Kansi was a wealthy Arabian aristocrat. He inherited a fortune in his family's oil business and garishly enjoyed the affluent lifestyle. On the spur of the moment, the consummate playboy often jetted off for a weekend of gambling and exotic entertainment.

Erikksen gave a lop-sided grin and replied in a flat, businesslike tone, "Splendid. Time is of the essence." Erikksen, a Swiss, was reserved and frugal. An astute businessman, he tolerated the arrogance of wealthy Middle Easterners. He himself had accumulated a small fortune as an art dealer and financier.

"I am happy the WEC is open to negotiations," El-Kansi muttered with a smirk. "Such an alliance would advance the formation of a much-needed world economic system." Bringing the WEC into the fold was key to ElKansi's grand scheme. The WEC would become *de facto* members of ElKansi's growing consortium of diverse organizations, whose individual agendas ranged from noble to outrageous.

In their madness, they shared a common desire to manipulate world currency markets and global commerce. There were also conflicts of interest; the IMF's goals contrasted with the scandal-plagued Bank of Credit and Commerce International.

BCCI's mission was to finance subversive Third World causes to support radical Islamic politics, including terrorism. BCCI was the main bank for the Islamic fundamentalists and terrorist groups led by Abu Nidal and the violent Maoist organization in Peru, the *Shining Path*.

Oblivious to the foundation of El-Kansi's group, Erikksen leaned forward and said, "Quite frankly, we can use your funding. And your influence."

"I see." Mildly averse to Erikksen's crude candor, El-Kansi wrinkled his dark eyebrows. "And what would the money be used for?"

"Expansion, advertising, and marketing. The operation must be streamlined and promoted in all regions of the world," Erikksen explained.

"And for us?"

"Equity."

"The cost?"

"One billion dollars."

El-Kansi hesitated, froze his demeanor, and showed no reaction. After a few seconds of silence, his black olive eyes looked Erikksen squarely in the eye and replied, "For the right percentage, I'll approach my associates."

Erikksen looked away and paused. "What's the 'right' percentage?"

"Majority ownership in the EFT clearinghouse."

On that, Erikksen developed a lump in his throat and swallowed hard. "Majority ownership?" Erikksen squeaked out the words, but he showed no emotion.

Poker-faced, El-Kansi gave a single nod. "Plus, five hundred million in gold bullion."

Erikksen's face went pale. He placed his hands on the table and slowly lifted himself to his feet. He turned and walked towards the window.

El-Kansi stifled a smirk. His group, which included OPEC, controlled the oil spigot that supplied over 50 percent of the oil consumed by developed nations. Oil had become the black gold of universal trade, and OPEC had an average trade surplus of 500 billion dollars. EFT was a vehicle to achieve their ultimate objective, hyper-intelligence—a networked system of imposing political and cultural values globally. Once established, one government, one—currency, one-language system of world order could be inaugurated.

His back to El-Kansi, Erikksen looked out the window. Thinking through the proposal, he was careful not to show distress. *If we don't go along, they may raise the price of oil again, wreaking havoc in the West. Can we succeed without them? Their inventory of gold is our ticket, but would we be giving up too much?*

Erikksen returned to his chair and sat down. "You have made a difficult proposal," he said. "But I will do my best to persuade my colleagues."

"Splendid."

"How soon can you release funds?"

"Sixty days."

They agreed to a secret rendezvous sixty days from the present date.

They shook hands, and El-Kansi left.

El-Kansi had an agenda. Electronic commerce and the electronic transfer of funds were central to the UAF conspiracy. And the expanse of the Internet made the EFT venture very feasible.

Access to personal information and EFT was already in place, and global commerce was increasingly robust in developed countries. The nucleus of the Net, a matrix of 200,000 independent computer networks, penetrated major economic regions. This could entice key nations into streamlining business transactions.

NetForum members had discreetly alerted their peers of the UAF's plot. Circumventing attempts by governments to filter and censor NetForum communications, NetForum continually gathered intelligence on the EFT movement. Armed with this information, Dowling and Martin formed a special NetForum task force to counter the scheme.

Dante Martin was addressing a group of graduating students of McDonough School of Business at Georgetown University. He talked about global politics, flaws of the UN, and the virtues of NetForum. The auditorium was packed with bright students, anxious to hear from a well-respected executive in the real world of business.

"Members of the UN are seasoned politicos," Martin said. "Each nation assigns its own agenda, pushed by its most provocative representatives. The UN system is also susceptible to geopolitical flux and favors those nations with the most economic resources.

"Take the OPEC oil consortium. NetForum is up against a powerful force. But the real strength of NetForum lies within its ability to bond together and work from the bottom up.

Martin continued, "NetForum is efficient. With e-mail, social media, and the Internet, our special task force can instantaneously aid other members, whereas the UN is strapped with bureaucracy and procedures. They have to spend a lot of time maneuvering politically. In comparison, NetForum is an organization with no such practices."

Martin had a sense of timelines—the world needed a grassroots system of communications—the cradle of humanity bypassing official channels. The students reacted. It was what they wanted to hear. It was time for unity, a new leadership, and putting the greater cause of human freedoms and compassion in the forefront.

"History attests to the intense volatility of the Middle East," Martin continued. "The conflict between the Jews and the Arabs, the oil consortiums, the religious wars, and of course, the outlaw terrorists of the region perpetuate the saga.

"Nevertheless, the region is rich in oil resources. The United Arab Emirates has grown to immense wealth and global influence." Martin's voice raised a few octaves as he approached a crescendo. "But to this day, peace in that part of the world is as elusive as a greased pig!"

Moved by his poignant words, the audience stood, clapped, whistled, and cheered.

Smiling warmly, Martin nodded and quietly murmured, "Thank you—thank you." He noticed the excitement in the seasoned students' faces—to discern every emotion that slipped through his consciousness. He had earned their attention and respect. They followed every word.

As the crowd began to sit down, Martin glanced at his notes, then at the audience. "Except for historical events, and before the 1950s, when we initiated oil production, the region was relatively obscure. But since the Six—Day—War between Israel and Arab nations in 1967, the world has kept abreast of the continuing strife and friction.

"We must accept the fact that OPEC has become the pseudo power broker, chiefly for the benefit of Arab nations and special causes. The might of the region concerns many scholars, and we must guard against the imbalance of power."

Martin's comments struck a nerve for those who studied the region and the pressures on Israel. For their part, with help from the

U.S., the Israelis remained ethnocentric and defensive about their region's position.

According to Israeli military intelligence, Syria positioned upgraded Scud missiles to hit Israeli targets. They targeted Israel's nuclear facility at Dimona, all of Israel's airfields, and most major cities. It would take just three minutes to reach targets in Israel.

Martin concluded his talk: "Unfortunately, much of the oil money finds its way into military uses. Israel is harassed, forcing them to take the offensive, as in Lebanon's invasion in 1980. Since then, a secretly backed terrorist movement has affected many parts of the Western world. This is why NetForum is continually alert in monitoring the teetering balance of world power."

He paused a long few seconds before his closing remarks. "Ladies and gentlemen, NetForum is a worthwhile, dynamic organization with a noble mission to establish peaceful coexistence. Please consider joining the movement. Thank you. We appreciate your support."

20

MEGATRONICS HEADQUARTERS

"The strategy is solid," Redding said to Mike Branston, his partner-to-be. "As long as we agree to the numbers, it makes perfect sense to do the deal." Redding's office was on the twelfth floor of the opulent MegaTronics I Building. His art deco office had dominating picture windows that faced the Pacific Ocean. The horizon unfolded into an expansive vista—a blazing sun, a thrashing sea, and puffy clouds hovering in an ice-blue sky.

"The board already approved it. Now we can do our thing," Branston said. He knew the advantages of joining up with Redding were immense.

Branston's company was something Redding wanted: a ten-acre manufacturing facility that had ISO 9001 certification, the highest quality rating for doing business anywhere in the world. Branston was cloning MEGA-Star-based computer systems at the new plant, and the capacity was enormous. Redding was hell-bent on conquering the global systems market on a fast track.

The plant was the vehicle to that end. He was entering the systems integration business, offering full-scale networks to emerging markets—LANs, WANs, and scalable computers—whatever the market needed. The merger would pose a formidable problem for companies like ComTech, which had fewer resources and a smaller market share. Redding's master plan was to lead computer consumers into complete dependency on his products. Every segment of business, government, and the consumer public were his targets.

Alliances with major computer manufacturers were key. The MEGA-Star chip locked customers into a technological trap because end-use software companies were forced to comply with MEGA-Star specifications. Spreading like wildfire, the proliferation of the MEGA—Star chip was worldwide.

"We have the dominant MEGA-Star technology, and it'll be some time before anyone can catch up," Redding boasted.

Branston put on a big smile, then exhaled a long sigh. "And the good news is, we can squeeze Dante Martin out of the market. No one else can touch us!" They allowed themselves a few moments of gloating over the prospect of being the biggest supplier of computer systems in the world.

Redding strolled over to the window and studied the soothing waves of the Pacific Ocean. With hands-on his hips, he stood silently for a second, then turned to Branston and said, "Don't worry about Dante Martin. I've been spreading rumors about them skating on thin ice. I think he'll sink deeper into trouble.

"My rumor mill is making the investment community afraid to back his operation. When he needs capital, he won't find any suitor. Besides, we have such a lead in the market, Martin has a very slim chance of making any headway," Redding said. His thin lips stretched into a sinister grin.

"Isn't that dangerous? I mean, spreading rumors like that? Can't he come back with a libel suit? Especially if the money guys blacklist him?"

Redding instantly became annoyed. He looked peevishly at Branston and grumbled, "Not really. I have inside information on ComTech, and a libel lawsuit is worthless if what is said or written is true. And I know it's true. I have actual accounting documents from inside ComTech."

Branston bobbed his head and smirked, "When we steal his customers, his cash flow and expansion capital should dry up pretty fast. Things will turn sour, and no one will touch ComTech. For sure, our combined market share will allow us to leapfrog way ahead of the rest of the pack."

Wearing a twisted grin, Redding said, "Yeah! You can say goodbye to ComTech!" They sniggered.

"What I wanna do is bury that son-on-a-gun Martin," Branston scowled. "He's been a thorn in my side since day one. He's been touted as some war hero, self-made man, and all that bull corn. In my opinion, he's just a lucky WOP from a crummy immigrant family."

Redding raised his brow and said, "Don't know about that. I checked him out thoroughly, and I couldn't dig up any dirt on him at all. No sexual affairs, no fraud, no kickbacks, nothing! No wonder people think he's a saint. I thought about starting a 'killing babies in Vietnam' rumor but decided it was too risky."

"Hey, that could've worked. Vietnam, killing civilians, looting, and raping. The Nam vets are slammed with that stuff all the time. And people believe it!"

"Maybe so, but it could've backfired." He paused. "The guy I wanna smother is his chief engineer, Bruce Lindsey. He's a freaking traitor. He gained his knowledge here, then jumped ship to ComTech. I don't like anyone pulling that stuff on me. I'm waiting for the day when that turncoat comes back around begging for his old job."

"Yeah, well, there are more important obstacles than Martin and Lindsey to worry about, like the DOJ."

"Don't worry about it," Redding said. "I'm working on it. The DOJ guys have been sniffing at my heels for a while, but they haven't built a case yet. I can assure you: the White House is with us on this. Our product is strategically key in the global scheme of things."

"Who are your contacts?"

"The top, Mike, the top. MacDuff is my man. Then it filters down from there," Redding bragged. "I don't screw around with under-lings." He spoke through a sappy grin on his face.

Branston was taken aback and didn't know what to think. "I knew you two were friends, but I didn't realize how close you were. This is great!" He paused a second. "Uh, who are you messing with down there?"

Redding laughed satanically but did not answer. "Mike, with the help of the president, we're attacking the biggest market in the world —China."

"Going after the bigger cheese? How deep are you?"

"Very deep. We enjoy special treatment. We have a contract working and a big lead over the competition. The MEGA-Star chip commands powerful leverage in the global arena because military systems rely heavily on our technology. Countries in emerging markets are keen to build-up their military strength."

"Sounds great!"

Redding grinned. "According to the president, we're considered America's commercial trump card. And we're gonna play that card every chance we get!" Redding uttered smugly.

"We'll dominate the world market!"

"I mean, big returns and plenty of cash," said Redding. "Like, real money in fat bank accounts?"

"Count on it." They high-fived, and Branston left.

Redding smirked as he thought about his larger ambition. He intended to discard Branston at the opportune time and rake in the massive profits the AMOEBA bug would generate.

Tiffany giggled nervously. "What's so funny?" asked Lee Redding. He set up a video camera between the dresser and television. They were in an upscale hotel in Reston, Virginia, near Redding's R&D facility.

"Are you sure about this? I mean, the tape." Tiffany flicked her hair away from her face, getting ready for a shoot.

"Relax. It will come off okay," Redding said. "Besides, this is just to test the equipment, only for the two of us."

Tiffany put on a coy smile. She was not concerned. If anything, such a tape could be more damaging to Redding as one of the richest men in the world. She was certain he wouldn't show it to anyone. It may even strengthen their bond.

What she didn't know was that Redding had made several tapes of other people in compromising situations—without their knowledge—the most recent being the president and Liz Ledgewick.

He had given the president a standing invitation to use his penthouse suite in Las Vegas. Known to only a select few, the suite was equipped with hidden cameras strategically placed in secret compartments around the luxurious bedroom. Redding had covertly taped people as a means to blackmail them if necessary.

"What's that wire for?" she asked, pointing at a standard coaxial cable between the camera and the TV.

"That allows us to see the picture in real time and make adjustments." He reached over and picked up a black device, also connected to the camera. It was a peripheral control unit with a joystick, similar to those used for video games. "This is a force-feedback joystick—something I've been experimenting with as a new product."

"What does it do?" Tiffany asked. She twisted her face into an uncomfortable expression.

Redding laughed. "Don't worry, it plays the video back on the television, introducing a sensory experience with dimensional sight and sound. Like in video games, it gives you instant feedback by simulating the physical and integrated components of a film."

"Physical and integrated components?"

"You can integrate music, special effects, and a host of other enhancements while doing a shoot. In other words, produce a film on the fly with all of these components preprogrammed."

Tiffany nodded but with a degree of skepticism.

"This special device only works with my force—feedback—enabling software. I can make camera and sound adjustments on the fly."

"Never mind, I get the picture."

"I should've known you had a business reason for making the tape. But what am I, some laboratory animal?"

Redding smiled and shrugged. "Funny. You know me, I mix business with pleasure. This device can be used in many ways, like missile guidance systems. Go ahead, give it a try." He handed the joystick to Tiffany and switched on the apparatus.

She took the device from Redding. The camera hummed. Tiffany moved the joystick to one side, and the camera responded slowly, panning the room. She watched the television screen as she moved into view. She stopped the camera on herself.

"Now, push the green button on the left."

She pushed the green button. Soft jazz music played through the television speakers.

21

DEPARTMENT OF JUSTICE

Tom Corrigan sat down on the slick, cobalt blue leather couch. It was fronted by a coffee table, on top of which sat a pitcher of water and two glasses. As the DOJ investigator on the MegaTronics-3D Systems merger, he met with his supervisor, Chad Phelps. Phelps greeted Corrigan, stood up from his desk, walked over, and sat in an adjacent chair.

"Let me put it into perspective," Corrigan said. "The merger will mean a tremendous gain in market share, and MegaTronics is already in the lead. It seems the motive is not to streamline the industry, as they assert, but to gain more control of the market."

The story had the same ring as others had had in the past. In his twenty-five years with the department, Phelps had seen the signs before: prosperity in a company spawning aggressive, monopolistic activities. "It looks like they're maneuvering into a one-stop-shop, monopoly position. That the way you see it?"

"Yes," Corrigan answered. "MegaTronic's chip, combined with 3D's operating software, is a powerful offering. It adds thrust to a clever marketing campaign to sweep the U.S. market. And eventually the world market. They only have one real competitor."

"ComTech?"

Corrigan nodded. "They don't have the financial clout to make much headway."

"Well then, that fact alone strengthens our case, doesn't it?" Phelps asked as he leaned forward to pour himself a glass of water. He hoped Corrigan would have solid evidence to prove collusion.

"This is an unprecedented case—a fast-moving target—hardly enough time to break new ground," said Corrigan. It doesn't stand still long enough to make any headway. New laws and regulations lag far behind."

"It's difficult," Phelps acknowledged. By the time we dig in our heels, circumstances change. Now that we're competing in the global economy, it's becoming a hot political issue," said Phelps.

Corrigan sighed. "Whatever happened to the simple days? When there weren't as many shades of gray?"

Phelps drank some water from his glass, shook his head, and said, "It's a nagging dilemma. But that's why we need to drive hard on the case. Get to the bottom of this thing."

"Got that going. I'm scheduled to interview Dante Martin this afternoon."

"I suppose we don't have enough of a case to stop the merger deal."

Corrigan wrinkled his nose and frowned. "Not yet, not enough information. No previous cases like this to reference."

Redding was investing a lot of money into his advertising and marketing campaign. "The blitz will convince consumers that they offer the best deal."

Phelps's eyes widened. "Slow him down," he said, with a sense of urgency. "His support is anchored in his customer base—a strong political contingency."

"I have a few ideas. The problem is, buyers are demanding MEGA-Star technology. And software vendors are forced into modifying their products for compatibility."

Phelps shook his head, held his hand up, and stopped Corrigan. "I already know the argument. 'It's a free enterprise system, and we're only appealing to the demands of the market.' Another one is,

'Let the consumers decide. They're the ones who stand to gain or lose.'

"If I've heard that once, I've heard it a thousand times! Yes, it *is* a free enterprise system. And we want to keep it that way. Free doesn't mean a company can practice collusion, price-fixing, and dictate market conditions. We call that corruption and antitrust activities"

Corrigan ushered Dante Martin into his office. A row of sage green file cabinets lined one wall, and a coffeepot sat on a small bar recessed in a corner near the window. "Thanks for coming. Make yourself comfortable," said Corrigan, waving him towards a chair in front of his desk.

Martin nodded blandly as he settled into a vinyl armchair.

"Now, this is not an official meeting," Corrigan said. "Don't worry about formalities. Any information we discuss stays between the two of us. Okay?"

"Fine."

"Help me understand. How was the MEGA-Star chip developed?"

"Don't quite know where to start," Martin said stoically. "It's a very sophisticated system. What exactly is your question?"

"Why is the chip so different from others?"

"It's not a silicon chip like the rest of them. It's new technology. It's made of synthetic molecules. The chip can store over *one trillion* bytes of information– nearly a thousand times more than regular storage media—on a chip smaller than your thumbnail."

"Amazing," Corrigan said. "I remember when a mere ten million bytes were stored on a disk the size of a hub cap."

Martin laughed and said, "Times have changed. How about this: shortly, with the new chip, we'll be able to replicate one hundred computer workstations in a device the size of a grain of salt."

"Wow! What is this stuff?"

"The technology was coined *molectronics*, a synonym for molecular electronics. The concept of molectronics-based computing has been under study for over twenty years. It's being perfected in a government-sponsored project at the Center for Molecular Electronics at UCLA. They—"

"Aha!" Corrigan bellowed. "That's the connection. I've been checking into Redding's background. UCLA—that's where they developed the chip."

"Right. He didn't really fund the R&D on the original MEGA-Star chip. The DOD and *Hewlett-Packard* funded the project."

"Yes, I know," Corrigan uttered scornfully.

"Anyway, the concept is rooted in the idea that the most powerful, complex computer—the human brain—relies on biological protein molecules to function. Not organic materials like silicon."

"Interesting, but aren't molecules soft? How does it work?"

"I know it sounds weird. First, let me give you an idea of what we're talking about. Processing speeds are up to one hundred *billion* times faster than the latest silicon processors. It can perform a quintillion operation on a single watt of power."

"A quintillion?"

"That's the number one, followed by eighteen zeros."

"Jesus. Now, how the hell does it work?"

"Basically, data is stored and retrieved by manipulating synthetic molecules in a chemical process. The process emulates a standard binary coding scheme—the same as we use now, making the data compatible with existing computers."

"Electronic pulses create the same kind of data in the molecules?"

Martin nodded vaguely. "Yes, it's still bits and bytes, written by a chemical process rather than using light beams. The researchers developed tiny molecular logic gates that are chemically moved with electrical characteristics into specific formations. They've connected these structures to titanium/aluminum wires and manipulated the molecules to perform the same functions as silicon chips."

"That's how they emulate other computers?"

"Yes. But the DOD, which has a broad range of applications, originally backed the design for military use only. The chip is small, nearly invisible—smaller than a pinhead—durable, and protected from radiation. It can work in computers weighing as little as two pounds to thin *Web pads*, now under development.

"For consumers, it can function wirelessly, running on low voltage. It handles multi-media, easily streaming video and DVD movies."

Somewhat bemused by the whole concept, Corrigan shook his head. "What sparked the idea in the first place?"

"It started with the study of biology combined with electronics, which evolved into molectronics. Actually, it really got launched when a joint effort by government agencies commissioned *the Human Brain Project* to support research that would lead to new digital tools for brain and behavioral research. The DOD became interested in military reasons.

"During the study to find out how small we could make chips, someone asked the question, 'Why don't we try replicating the greatest computer on earth—the human brain?' And in a way, they did. The structure and mechanics of the new chips were modeled after the brain. As a result, we've been able to make smaller, faster, durable, and more energy-efficient devices."

Corrigan looked skeptical. He had known about IBM's Blue Gene project to build a supercomputer that would simulate the biological process by which amino acids folded themselves into proteins. But it was entirely different. Compared to miniaturized protein-based computing, IBM's computer was to perform 1,000 trillion calculations per second, stood six feet tall, occupied 1,600 square feet of floor space, and included one million microprocessors. Martin peered at Corrigan and let out a short burst of laughter. "I'm not kidding! I know it's far out, but it's really true," Martin explained, scarcely relieving Corrigan of any doubt.

"Until now, the on-off switches in electronic circuitry used in digital computers have been etched into silicon wafers with beams of light, a process known as *photolithography*. And the ability to make conventional circuits smaller was limited by the wavelength of light in that process.

"But the molectronics researchers used chemical processes instead of light beams, making the on-off switches as small as a molecule. The molecules, called *rotazanes*, are synthetic compounds created by chemists and are partly made from common swamp bacteria."

His face contorted, Corrigan grunted, "Swamp bacteria?"

"That's what I said—bacteria taken from the swamps. This kind of technology represents a new class of machines, using sensors—microscopic sensors so tiny that they can even travel within a person's bloodstream, monitoring for health problems." Martin hesitated and studied Corrigan. "Still with me?"

Corrigan nodded, cleared his throat, and smiled. "Yes, I think so."

"Okay. Inside the skull, the brain sits in the middle of the membranes, suspended in pressurized cerebrospinal fluid. The fluid provides extra protection and acts as a shock absorber. In the same fashion, the MEGAStar chip is hermitized in a hard alloy shell that shields the storage media inside. The rotazanes—the brains of the computer—are injected inside the shell cavity, which is also surrounded by a special fluid."

"And that's how the molecules, or whatever you called them, are protected from radiation and shock?"

"Right on."

"And it's faster and more durable."

"Yep. That's why the MEGA-Star was deployed as a missile control unit. It can withstand unusually volatile physical conditions, especially the effects of radiation."

"Makes sense," Corrigan said, bobbing his head. "In case of a nuclear attack, the MEGA-Star will keep on ticking."

"Right. And for missile control environments, the casing that houses the entire system is also made of the special alloy."

"What about economics? Is the new chip any cheaper?"

"A lot cheaper," Martin answered. "That's a big advantage. Just think, using ordinary swamp gunk to make computers sounds ridiculous, but we're doing it."

"And it all started at UCLA. Redding is making big bucks at the taxpayer's expense. Shrewd move, but it stinks to high heaven."

The MegaTronics merger and the marketing campaign were a

tremendous success. Not surprisingly, Redding publicly accepted credit for developing the powerful MEGA-Star technology.

Profits of MegaTronics continued to soar as the MEGA-Star chip broke all sales volume and market penetration records. For Redding, this was the platform he needed to fulfill his dream of becoming the most powerful man in the computer industry. The prestige of owning MegaTronics propelled him into very influential circles, including the international arena. He was often invited to speak at fundraisers and political events, and foreign dignitaries sought out discussions with him.

Meanwhile, as Corrigan and the DOJ were discovering, the darker side of Redding was ubiquitous. They learned he once attempted industrial espionage. He obtained a new technology developed by a now-defunct competitor, Innovative Systems, Inc.

When Redding was discovered, he settled out of court and paid an undisclosed sum of money. Redding promptly hired the competitor's chief engineer, the new technology development leader.

Shortly afterward, Redding neutralized the competitor's leverage by introducing enhancements to the MEGA-Star chip. The changes rendered the competing product incompatible with the dominating MEGA-Star chip, which commanded the vast supply of end-user software. Eventually, he drove the competitor out of business.

COMTECH HEADQUARTERS, PALO ALTO, CALIFORNIA

"What happened at the DOJ?" Lindsey asked Martin.

Martin shrugged. "We just talked about the MEGA-Star chip. You would've been better at explaining it."

"Thanks, but no thanks. I'll leave the legal and politicking bull to you. I'll spend my time competing against Redding."

"Still think it's feasible to reengineer the MEGA-Star chip?"

"Yes, I think we can give Redding a run for his money."

Before joining Martin at ComTech, Bruce Lindsey was MegaTronics's top software engineer. He was the technical driving force behind the MEGA-Star success. But Lindsey never gained recognition for his work. And curiously, he never had access to all of the programs in the project.

Lindsey respected Dante Martin and joined ComTech for that reason. Lindsey's job was to conduct reverse engineering of the MEGA-Star chip and reengineer a new, faster chip. The new chip would put ComTech ahead in the race for the highest processing speed.

"How do you like it here?" Martin asked.

"No comparison. It's great."

"Heard Redding is a clever micro-manager."

"That he is. He took the lead and cleverly divided the MEGA-Star project into two teams: I had a team, and he had the other. Redding controlled the project, and the final integration of components was his responsibility."

"He did the day-to-day? Why?"

Lindsey shrugged. "I don't know, probably for security reasons. No one knew the whole puzzle except for Redding."

"Strange."

Lindsey grimaced. "Like rubbing salt in the wound, Redding had a way of extracting the best out of you, then pulling you down, a reminder that he was in charge."

"A scoundrel."

Martin quickly calculated the investment payback on producing a new chip. "We'll be running a tight budget on the engineering project," he said. "The expected payback is something our investors will look at very hard."

"Redding has bad-mouthed us all over town. Has that affected our fundraising?"

"Yes, it has. Some investors view MegaTronics as the Goliath of the industry and us as David. They overshadow us in everything."

"Not this time. We're going to be successful. We're gonna outsmart him!"

"Yeah, ya got that right! I've already lined up some backers."

"I think we need to monitor what's going on over there. It's risky, but it would help," Lyndsey said.

"He's ruthless, but I'm not afraid of the scoundrel."

"I have friends over there who are disgruntled with Redding. When I talk to them, a lot of times they open up."

"Good deal," Martin replied. "Maybe we should get some under-cover operatives in there—like my guys in Nam—get in, get the scoop and get the hell out."

22

COMTECH HEADQUARTERS, PALO ALTO, CALIFORNIA

Unlike Redding at MegaTronics, Martin gave Lindsey a free hand. The stakes were high, but Bruce Lindsey and his team began the secret reverse-engineering project with great expectations.

He organized a team of highly skilled programmers, system engineers, and cryptologists. Cryptologists are specialists in the breaking of codes. They named the project Omega-Alpha, a code word for ending MegaTronics' lead and beginning ComTech's advancement.

The Omega-Alpha team worked twelve hours a day, six days a week, and often went through the night when they were on a roll. The success of Omega-Alpha would reduce Redding's competitive edge and loosen his grip on world markets.

"To avoid legal problems, we'll divide the architecture of the chip into three components," Lindsey explained to Martin. "Then three different teams will work in different laboratories. The idea is to reverse engineer the three separate parts, then set up a team in Atlanta to do the final prototype."

"Steve tells me to keep system documentation in hard-copy form, then record it with the patent office at each milestone during the course of the project," Martin said. "Gotta have zero error tolerance."

"No question. It'll be a tough fight. Redding has deep pockets," said Lindsey. "And he's a rabid competitor." He recalled Redding winning lopsided court battles because of his sheer wealth and the clout of well-paid, aggressive lawyers. Redding out-lasted his adversaries by stalling until they ran out of money.

Martin was determined to win. "Stealth and perseverance—that's our game." Trained in the battlefields of Vietnam, he was prepared to bend the rules and use a fight-fire-with-fire approach. He had been gearing up for the battle with Redding for some time but needed a legal strategy.

Martin and Steve Rifken, his attorney, went over a checklist. They munched on coffee-dipped almond *biscotti* and sipped fresh *cappuccino*. "We're using strict engineering procedures to conform with patent laws— tight and well-documented," said Martin. "They should endure any audit team from the DOJ, patent office, or any other government agency."

"Excellent," Rifken replied. "One thing though, the fact that Lindsey signed a technical non-disclosure statement makes us vulnerable."

"But Chris said the MEGA-Star technology was 'public domain' material developed at UCLA."

Rifken got excited. "Tell me about it."

"Tom Corrigan at the DOJ mentioned this too. It involved a government grant. Corrigan is investigating Redding's connections to the university regarding the acquisition of design documents. Redding acquired exclusive access to MEGA-Star technology."

"Very key evidence," said Rifken. "Could be our ace in the hole." Martin smiled. "After he started his business, Redding managed to acquire exclusive rights to the MEGA-Star technology with no strings attached. I think President MacDuff set this up."

"Dante, we're on to something even bigger," Rifken said. He fidgeted in his chair and tugged on his ear lobe. A small man, his disheveled chestnut brown hair and black-olive eyes accented a scholarly demeanor. "If the president's involved, it's pretty heavy stuff," Rifken muttered. "As I understand, the DOD funded the MEGA-Star project with no private sources of financing."

"That's what I've heard."

"I think it was a classified military project, which could warrant a federal investigation," Rifken said. He sat up and leaned forward with excitement in his eyes. Thick horn-rimmed glasses rested unevenly on his Roman nose. "You know, Redding could be in too deep—a classic dilemma. If it was a classified project, that's a security violation. If the project were deemed public domain, it would've been *illegal* for Redding to have an exclusive on the technology."

"What's the bottom line?"

"Big trouble for Redding, and maybe for the president."

"What are our chances?"

"If my theory is correct, we could file a civil or federal case. We're looking at a breach of national security." Rifken grinned half-heartedly. "If that were the case, he would be facing an investigation and probably an indictment for a federal offense."

Martin thought a federal investigation would be a diversion for Redding. They would focus their attention and resources on defending themselves. He would be attacked from several angles. The DOJ suspected inside trading, illegal exports, and bribery.

"I like it!" Martin said. "No one has managed to snare that guy yet, not even the government. I'm willing to give it a shot."

"Worth a shot. I'm curious. Why would the government overlook the fact that it was a sensitive military project? It doesn't make sense. Collusion, maybe?" Rifken's combative juices began to flow. The thought of fighting an army of lawyers and winning against the odds was exhilarating.

The concept of winning was not out of the question. Rifken was a brilliant strategist. In one case, Rifken hired a handwriting analyst to refute claims of fraud against his client. In analyzing the handwriting, he proved his client innocent and simultaneously proved his opponent's guilt.

Martin and Rifken became acquainted in a neighborhood setting. When Martin started up ComTech, he asked Rifken to join his company to do corporate work. Rifken agreed, but his burning ambition was to become a trial lawyer—where the real action was. He sensed the time was near, his dream within reach.

"Okay, that's it. We've got a lot of work to do," Rifken said. "It's your show!" It inflamed Rifken's zeal for winning, and it whetted his appetite for a fight.

"Okay, you investigate Redding's ties with UCLA. Find out when and how he got the rights to the technology." He paused. "You know General Fuller, don't you?"

"Not personally, but Terence Dowling would give us an introduction. He and the general are pretty tight. Fuller is a straight-up guy, and I'm sure he'll understand where we're coming from. He doesn't go for all this corruption. I know he's had a few rounds with the president about it."

"Good. Get Dowling to help us gain Fuller's support. I'll bet Fuller didn't like Redding commercializing the MEGA-Star computer."

"Probably as much as the Chinese *loved* it!"

23

PRIVACY OF INFORMATION INSTITUTE, WASHINGTON, D.C

Martin entered with a broad smile. "Okay, where are those fun spots you mentioned?" He was dressed in a classic blue pinstripe suit—his banker outfits the one he wore to plead for more funding.

Dowling laughed. "Come on in, have a seat. We'll get to those fun spots later."

Martin looked around Dowling's unkempt office. Dusty newspapers and magazines were piled on his desk, topping file cabinets and on the floor. Books lay haphazardly in a built-in bookshelf. A mug half—filled with cold, murky coffee sat on Dowling's desk. A film of grime covered the window facing Fifteenth Street. "So, this is your war room."

Dowling shrugged his shoulders. "This is it. My haven for blasphemy. Have to straighten up one day. But then again, I wouldn't be able to find anything!" They chuckled.

"Actually, I spend a lot of my time down the street." Dowling jerked his thumb towards Capitol Hill.

"Are we set to meet with the senator?"

"All set. Ten o'clock. As I mentioned in my e-mail, Garrity

supports us on the AMOEBA issue. In fact, let's bring up the topic of global EFT with him too. Whaddya think?"

"Good idea."

"Great! I'm pounding on doors and singing the same tune practically every day down there," Dowling said. "A fresh face like yours will make a difference. Besides, he's a former Marine. You guys seem to stick together like a pack of wolves."

"You could say that. Whether in a foxhole, a bar, or Washington, we take care of our own."

Dowling respected the Marine Corps. He had helped them fight in some of their political battles. He lobbied against the air force erecting a memorial near the Iwo Jima monument. The Marines won. Another structure would dilute the legendary ambiance of the Marine memorial, making the area cluttered and gaudy. It was a matter of pride; a sacred ground being tainted.

Dowling said, "I've gotten support from Garrity in the past. He's a powerful ally to have in our corner. A bright guy, very informed on current events and the Internet."

"Okay. Let's go over the presentation." The two men rehearsed their pitch.

"Dante, we need to emphasize the fact that the Internet culture is becoming a driving force in world affairs. We should explain the trend of non-political groups joining NetForum. The message to Garrity is that NetForum now represents a strong worldwide lobby for peace."

"I haven't looked lately. What are the latest demographics of our group?"

"NetForum has several factions," Dowling said. "The majority is represented by a core group who believe the apocalypse will occur sometime in the new millennium."

"Interesting."

"The group formed on that basis. As it relates to Armageddon, they're concerned about the manipulation of private information and economics over the Net. The consensus is that some order should prevail," Dowling said. "It's a double-edged sword. E-commerce sales are expected to go beyond one trillion dollars in a few years. But the Net is also being used for devious, self-serving causes by criminals and political misfits."

"Over a trillion dollars? Need to get in that game."

Dowling raised his brow and peered at Martin. "It's easy to do. Ecommerce and on-line EFT are not regulated. This is where we have a slight dilemma, a double-edged sword."

"Think I know where you're headed, but help me out." Martin leaned forward.

"We need to launch a fight against the EFT consortium, but they're pretty tough guys. It's gonna be a balancing act. Don't wanna be faced with a bucket of worms."

Martin grinned and nodded.

Dowling continued, "The key point is, the success of the Internet is based on the free exchange of information and debate. We need controls, but too many restrictions would defeat the purpose."

"Catch twenty-two," uttered Martin.

"But Senator Garrity has found ways of getting around it," Dowling continued. "He's proposed a minor controls approach with his special committee on global commerce."

"It's time to pin something down in the Foreign Service department, at the secretary of state level," said Martin. "We've gotta do something to head off El-Kansi's group."

"General Fuller is tight with Peter Barrett at the State Department. And Fuller is on top of the Mid-east situation." Dowling paused, then smiled. "He can be our inside man. Make things happen!" They laughed.

"If anybody can get it done, it would be Bulldog Fuller. He's the most gung-ho Marine I know," Martin said. "And I think he knows how to deal with the Washington crowd, maybe sometimes through brute force. Let's see if we can get him on our team."

"It's really a tricky issue. Fuller will have to play it right. His political approach is usually dogmatic in nature. We'll have to set a clear agenda. We need to protect personal information carried over the

Net. And we want to promote free form communications and e-commerce according to global peace and prosperity."

Martin rubbed his chin and pondered the intricacies of their mission. "The key point is—we need some non-partisan governing body as we have with the Internet. It has to be a non-political organization, like NetForum, to set policies regarding usage and security."

Martin drew his conclusions from Internet history, founded by the National Science Foundation and the DOD. "The NSF still participates in some management, but several private bodies administer Internet addresses, technical control, and usage policies."

Martin continued, "Security remains a major concern. Over seventy percent of chief information officers in the U.S. do not use the Net as much as they could. In the meantime, the volume of Web pages and Internet users continues to grow. By the year 2003, there will be an estimated three hundred fifty million users on the Net, and electronic commerce revenues will reach one point two trillion dollars."

Dowling agreed. "What makes it more plausible is the fact that corrupt people are using the Net for espionage, sabotage, and fraud —the cyberwar thing."

"You mention 'war' to Fuller, and he gets fired up!" Martin quipped. "We know the Chinese are using the Net for espionage, political subversion, and arresting dissidents. Not to mention social engineering, such as the 'enhanced masculinity' of their male population. Ironically, we're going in the other direction!"

"We agree on that. Lately, there's been a movement called 'gender equality,' funded by computer oligarch Lee Redding. The movement has penetrated our military, but thankfully, it hasn't diluted our military power. This also goes hand in glove with Redding's connection with China's work in genomics, a biological study of genomes, the entire human DNA set. Through this unholy alliance, China has collected DNA data on an estimated 80 percent of American adults, which is a serious breach of national security."

Dowling nodded. "Yes, the privacy of information has all but vanished. American companies and our government should not meddle with the Net and sensitive data in those ways." Dowling was picked as the director of public relations because he was an effective lobbyist in Washington and headed up PII.

PII was a technical watchdog group dedicated to policing the rapid growth of information companies such as credit bureaus, mailing list companies, and other business information services that disseminated private, personal information for profit. This segment of the information industry was running rampant, and NetForum strengthened PII's political clout.

"We'll educate Garrity, Fuller, and others about the thrust of NetForum," said Martin. Since taking the job of executive director, Martin had organized and spearheaded several worthwhile initiatives within NetForum.

After a lengthy pause, Dowling said, "With the expansion of the Internet, more and more private information is recklessly being passed around without the knowledge or consent of the people affected. In some cases, the hackers are winning the race because of increased connectivity and access speeds.

"Even medical data is creeping into these channels. There seems to be a lack of concern from government agencies."

"What about the laws already on the books, dealing with private information?" Martin asked.

"The laws haven't sufficiently addressed the Internet, and some actually impair the privacy of information. The floodgates were opened to government records by the Freedom of Information Act. And the Fair Credit Reporting Act is like Swiss cheese—it has too many loopholes in favor of credit bureaus," Dowling said.

"More and more, information is used as soft currency," Martin said. "I saw this first-hand in my intelligence work." He paused. "I can tell you this. President MacDuff made secret alliances with foreign entities to fulfill his political ambitions. He colluded with them in information currency. This method is becoming the norm."

"The president actually instigated this situation during his first year in office," said Dowling. "The premise was that the Net was to be used as a tool for electronic commerce. MacDuff discreetly included a legal platform for the Freedom of Information Act as part of the same bill. It was a subtle, undetectable ploy to allow his use of privy information while in office."

Martin was familiar with the president's modus operandi. He said, "The main question is, how much freedom should the government have in collecting information on individuals? How much information do you think they have collected on us already?"

"You know, it may be worthwhile to use the Freedom of Information Act provisions to request the file the FBI maintains on us. Otherwise, how can we know that there is a file and what the contents are?"

The info age has brought about a new form of warfare that is subtle and difficult to manage," Dowling said. "Information warfare, known as 'cyberwar,' has become increasingly important to the military, the intelligence community, and the business world."

When he spoke to an audience at COMDEX, the annual computer show held in Las Vegas, Senator Garrity described the cyberwar phenomenon. The largest information technology marketplace, COMDEX, was held at Caesar's Palace in Las Vegas. Over twenty-two hundred exhibitors, over ten thousand new products, and close to a quarter-million attendees from over one hundred countries.

The show was held at the Las Vegas Convention Center, the Las Vegas Hilton, and the Sands Expo and Convention Center. Colorful displays, computer gadgetry, stage shows, and food and beverage kiosks filled the exhibit and pavilion areas. Visitors carrying tote bags stuffed with handout literature, promo items, and floor maps roamed around in the carnival-like atmosphere.

Garrity began his speech in a pavilion filled with four-hundred attendees: "Information warfare, or cyberwar, is both the offensive and defensive use of information and information technology. Cyberwar tactics exploit, corrupt, or destroy an adversary's information base and protect your systems. Actions are designed to achieve advantages over military, political, or business enemies.

"Despite the president's detraction from such serious issues, most of the U.S. military is planning ways of strategically incorporating this new genre of warfare. For example, the navy has made its plans for information warfare in a project known as *Copernicus*.

"The army has incorporated information warfare into its plans for the next century—they call their project *Force XXI*. Plus, the Marine Corps recently became proactive in the phenomenon. For starters, they've initiated a program of Internet-based war games for troops to exercise no matter where they're stationed. Furthermore, the air force may incorporate a strategy using information warfare."

Garrity sipped some water and continued, "The ballooning emergence of cyberwar—which carries an element of surprise—is something everyone should be concerned about," Garrity said. "The subject is discussed in a report entitled the *Principles of War in the Twenty-First Century*, a paper authored by the Strategic Studies Institute of the U.S. Army War College, at Carlisle Barracks, Pennsylvania."

The senator paused to review his notes. He had labored on his speech, only completing it in the early hours of that morning. His heavy schedule of commitments had kept him from a study-over, but his sharp mind and a sense of destiny were sustaining. "One interesting method of retrieving information, or tapping into a system, is to monitor the activity of a computer by detecting its low-level electronic emissions. This technology is known as *Van Eck monitoring*. Winn Schwartau suggests that the FBI used Van Eck monitoring to catch a spy within the CIA. Allegedly, such monitoring also played a role in the operation against the Branch Davidians at Waco, Texas. The military use of Van Eck monitoring is known as *TEMPEST*.

"In terms of economics, the National Counterintelligence Center is a federal agency charged with the responsibility of protecting businesses in the U.S. from information warfare and other forms of foreign espionage. The proliferation of the Internet and privacy issues adds to the complexity of the situation. We must guard against the offensive uses of information by an unethical few."

Martin studied transcripts of Garrity's speech on cyberwar. He was intimately familiar with the concept, having used the original Internet, and called ARPANET, during the Vietnam War. The embryonic ARPANET was an experimental network set up in 1969 by the Department of Defense. The system served as a test bed for networking technologies, mainly for DOD applications. The widespread use of the system created the expansive Internet, as we know it today.

Martin's computer experience in cryptography undoubtedly helped U.S. intelligence in the war effort and he feared its use by enemy forces. Martin said to Dowling, "Cyberwar activities fly in the face of NetForum principles. It counters the trend toward world peace through collaboration."

"Cyberwar is a snake hiding in the grassy web of the Net," Dowling said.

Martin nodded sharply. "We've already seen signs of counterintelligence activities. Stirring revolts could erupt in aggressive nations, particularly those with nuclear weapons and higher ambition."

SENATOR KENT GARRITY'S OFFICE, WASHINGTON, D.C.

Martin and Dowling shook hands with Senator Garrity and sat around a small conference table. After a few minutes of small talk, Martin took the lead. "Senator, we're here to solicit your support for NetForum, and the proper use of the Internet. The fact is, China and some countries in the Middle East have lobbied for the passage of special laws to ban NetForum from operating in their territory."

"Ganging up on you, are they?"

"Yes, sir. And they are pretty good at it too. But the nature of the Net does not easily allow censorship."

"Then, what are the options?" asked Garrity.

"Let's put it this way," Dowling responded. "Either you have a free flow infrastructure, or you have a controlled, censured 'intranet.' An intranet can be rigged with filtering software to restrict the free exchange of information within a network. The overwhelming consensus is that the Net should be free-flow."

"Senator, as a businessman, I concur," Martin said. "We conducted an independent survey, and the results were really skewed.

Despite security concerns, over ninety percent wanted open communications."

Garrity thought for a moment, cleared his throat, and said, "Well, I know a little something about it. According to my research, business organizations commonly use an intranet or a virtual private network. Strategically placed filtering devices can censure and restrict information from going in either direction. The filters would control data flowing in or out of Internet gateways. Such is the case in China." Garrity pressed on. "We've got to formulate an approach to resolve the problem here in the U.S. first. Then, most nations will follow. I'll work with you on it."

24

AMOEBA CLONES

The chattering by the gaggle of employees reverberated in Bruce Lyndsey's office. They were surprised by the discovery and the possibilities attached to it. Lindsey quieted everyone.

Dead silence.

He picked up the telephone and called Dante Martin. "Dante, I need to see you right away. We penetrated the bowels of the MEGA-Star chip, and we cracked the code!"

"Oh?" A trace of excitement was in Martin's voice. "We found an embedded bug in the software."

"Come on up."

Lindsey hurried up to Martin's office. He began explaining the discovery of a dormant bug.

"Why hasn't it popped up before? That OS has been running for a long time." Martin said.

"Apparently, because it's not time yet. We don't know when that time is."

Martin was slightly bewildered. "You mean, it's like a leftover Y2K bug?"

"Could be," Lindsey replied, nodding slightly with a pensive look.

"The AMOEBA caused a flaw in the algorithm that drives the real-time clock—the BIOS date functions. The date count started with the base year of 1970. Because the year 2000 was a leap year and one day off, the calendar is out of sync. The system can freak out anytime."

"No telling what a screwed-up calendar will cause."

Lindsey mumbled, "Yeah, a repeat of Y2K problems—only worse. This date bug moves around and replicates itself. It engulfs its prey, date-related programs it interacts with. Reproduction is accomplished by binary fission splitting–to produce two daughter amoebas. That's why we dubbed it AMOEBA."

Martin stared at Lindsey inquisitively.

"Remember your biology class? Amoebas clone themselves by a process that takes place in the nucleus of a dividing cell," Lyndsey offered. "It involves a series of steps which results in the formation of two new nuclei, each having the same characteristics as the parent nucleus."

"How did you find it?"

"We were going through some routine tests. We ran across a segment of code that didn't serve any purpose. We checked it out, and it linked back to a base date formula."

Martin's face was contorted. "What's wrong with that? Zero date calculations are often used for system calendars."

Lindsey shrugged and shook his head. "It dumped out in one of our mathematical modeling tests, and it had no bearing on the results of our model."

"What the hell is going on? There's an AMOEBA date bug embedded deeply within the MEGA-Star chip, and we don't know how it got there?"

They peered at each other in puzzlement. The ramifications of an AMOEBA date bug in the MEGA-Star chip were enormous. Finally, Martin mumbled, "Apocalypse. A computer apocalypse. It could cause catastrophes all over the world. Chris, timing is critical. Any way to find out where the systems are and what they're used for?"

"I don't think anyone knows, but I'll get on it."

"Setting aside business issues, let's work on the problem as a priority," Martin ordered. "Is it feasible?"

"I don't know," Lindsey responded. "It seems like a simple programming matter, but the amount of testing makes it a long, arduous task. But we can handle it."

"The larger question is, can we avoid disasters?" Martin said. "Do we need to collaborate with MegaTronics?"

"No way!" Lindsey stressed. "We'd expose our reverse-engineering effort."

"You're right," Martin said, nodding. He gave Lindsey a mischievous smile. "Got any plans for the evening?

Lindsey grinned. "I'll stay and spend some time on it."

"Good man."

They labored well into the night, brainstorming on the MEGA-Star chip's internal designs and the correct technical strategy. Next came business considerations. What resources would be needed, and how would it impact day-to-day operations?

The next day, Martin and Lindsey rallied a special team to participate in the project. Martin took the lead. Members would include Lindsey as the technical lead, Dowling as the NetForum liaison, and two systems analysts. Steve Rifken would serve in multiple roles as legal counsel, public relations, and the government liaison. Martin and Lindsey planned to launch a worldwide campaign through the NetForum membership.

One evening, Lyndsey called Martin. "Just got a call from one of my friends at MegaTronics. They're going to publicly announce the discovery of the AMOEBA bug tomorrow at noon. They're spilling the beans, but they're putting a marketing spin on it. They're selling the new MEGA-Star.1 chip as a solution to the problem."

"No kidding. Pushing the new chip? Very clever, but too obvious. I know the market is naïve, but surely, they'll catch on." Martin was surprised at the audacity of Redding's maneuver.

Lindsey shook his head and said, "People can be pretty stupid. As far as Redding is concerned, he may have known about the bug, but no one else in his company knew. Rumor is, Redding, planted it way back in the beginning."

"Wouldn't be surprised," Martin replied. "He'll probably lay the blame on the UCLA guys, the original developers."

Martin paused and said, "New ball game, Chris. Let's get together first thing in the morning."

MEGATRONICS CAMPUS, HALF MOON BAY, CALIFORNIA

Slivers of sunlight reflected off the building's gold-tinted glass, spotlighting the surrounding landscape. Redding stood at a podium on the front steps. A group of microphones extended out like metallic cattails. Over Redding's right shoulder, you could see the Mega-Tronics logo, a six-foot square *M*, the center of which was an embedded circle with raised riflescope crosshairs.

Lee Redding's nationally televised announcement in front of the twenty-story MegaTronics building was cleverly worded. He would portray the company as saviors, not profiteers. And the press would buy into it. Redding would claim the AMOEBA strain was a surprise —an unexplainable quirk left over from the original root program. He would claim they accidentally discovered the defect and would quickly offer the new chip as a fix.

Redding held his press conference. "In light of the situation, we want to make customers aware of the seriousness of the so-called AMOEBA bug. The flaw could trigger unpredictable consequences. We urge you to upgrade your systems with the new chip." As he stood there, the guru of supercomputers, a turbulent Pacific breeze ruffled his stringy hair and occasionally flipped up a lapel on his corduroy sport coat.

Redding continued, "In our quality assurance program, we found that the MEGA-Star chip has a defective date variable that will affect the transition to the New Year. But our dedicated engineers have repaired the defect."

Reporters accepted the bogus explanation and busily wrote notes.

"Rest assured," Redding continued, "you can easily replace the old chip with our new chip. As always, we stand ready to serve our customers in this time of need. Please call our toll-free number for more information. Thank you." Redding's brazen move duped a lot of people. At a discounted price of $150 each, Redding would make a killing.

Over fifty million computers were in the field. Redding had already prepared an inventory of new chips for the big rush. Not everyone would get the word about the bug. A vast number of MEGA-Star systems were destined to fail.

WUZHAI MISSILE AND SPACE CENTER, SITE #5, WUZHAI, CHINA

It was business as usual at this key nuclear site. The MEGA-Star system sat innocently, processing radar signals. Meanwhile, deep in the bowels of the system, the AMOEBA was doing its sinister work. The Chinese were unaware of the bug. Even if they were, they had no expertise to repair the defect.

Precariously, they were using the contraband supercomputer for a national-security application: monitoring the Chinese defense system.

The MEGA-Star computer was wired to a network of radar nodes strategically located along the coastal border. Any break in the barrier along the line would sense penetration of the military zone. A national threat alarm would be triggered at the central site. Jet fighters would be dispatched, and the system would launch nuclear missiles.

PRIVACY OF INFORMATION INSTITUTE, WASHINGTON, D.C.

"Iraq is a significant member of OPEC, which politically complicates our problems in the Arabian world," General Fuller said to Terence Dowling. It was an impromptu meeting. They discussed the Middle East situation and how NetForum might play a role in lobbying various governments, monitoring the balance of power. The Far East and the Middle East were extremely volatile.

"I understand, General. NetForum members in the area report other OPEC members go as far as secretly contracting with Iraq as surrogates to do their dirty work. Instead of dealing with their agendas openly and individually, other Arab nations to use Iraq as the enforcer."

Fuller grinned. "Well, I wouldn't put it that way to MacDuff. He would freak out! But it's close to being accurate. I think Iraq is delighted to have this status. Although, the CIA says Iraq's sponsor, the OIC, is really the mastermind behind the scenes."

"That concurs with my field reports," Dowling said. "The OIC is becoming the hub of the Arabian world."

Fuller leaned forward and lowered his voice. "I'm assuming this office is not bugged."

"Christ, I hope not. I'd be in big trouble!"

"What I'm about to tell you is highly confidential. I may need your help. I have to work around the Washington circus and get something done. Okay?"

"Yes, sir, General. I'm all ears."

"Mind if I smoke?" Fuller said. He pulled out a Cuban-made *Partagas* cigar from his inside shirt pocket. "I catch hell at my place from the nonsmokers."

"No problem," Dowling said with a small grin. "My dad used to smoke cigars. Ah, I miss that smell."

Fuller thumbed the lid open on his worn Zippo and sparked the wick. "These don't smell bad. I pay top dollar for my stogies." He lit the hand-made Corona size cigar and flipped the lid shut with its distinctive clink. He puffed a few times and waved the smoke away. "Terence, according to the OIC's strategic plan, they're doing a world-wide public relations campaign. They're promoting Sheikh El-Kansi as a world-class leader. Then, at the right time, he'll emerge, calling himself the *Prince of Peace*. Can you believe it?"

"Prince of peace? Ridiculous!" Dowling howled. "What an insult to Christians. He's a key player in the global EFT project. If we don't somehow stop it, his group will end up controlling the flow of global currencies."

"The CEFTS project? It's dangerous as hell. Could cause economic havoc."

Fuller puffed on his cigar vigorously and continued, "Let me tell you how it's supposed to happen: In his new role, El-Kansi will decree-law and order across the land. By default, he will assume absolute rule over Arabian nations and move for a single currency for Asia, Africa, and the Middle East—much like the EU and the Eurodollar.

He'll use his influence to implement a single world currency, possibly cutting a deal with the EU. That kind of alliance would make them the strongest economic entity in the world."

Fuller removed his cigar and poked it in the air to emphasize his point. "We don't know when, but sometime after they've covertly achieved economic control, they'll declare war on the West under the guise of *Jihad*.

"Know about the so-called *Jihad*?"

"Yes, of course, It's been a hot topic in the field."

Fuller raised his brow and chuckled. "I think you guys have better information sources than the CIA!"

"Possibly," Dowling said capriciously, with a thin smile.

Fuller took a couple of short puffs from his cigar and continued, "*jihad* implies a holy war. Islamic guerrillas such as the UAF conveniently use *jihad* to describe their abhorrent charter. According to their beliefs, the fighter who fights a *jihad*—or a *Mujahid*–will go straight to paradise as a martyr if he dies, and his enemies will go to hell."

Dowling said, "That's why they're so dedicated. Even to the extent of suicide missions."

"Exactly. The culture of jihad and the martyrs it produces is very pervasive in some Muslim countries. And it's an effective motivator for warriors. Remember the political conflict, the *Intifadah*, as they call it? The struggle against the Israeli occupation in Palestinian territories some time ago?"

"Yes."

"Well, anyone who was killed fighting or even accidentally killed in that conflict was considered a martyr by family members." Fuller flicked ashes off his cigar, drew in some smoke, and spewed it out the side of his mouth. By now, with the windows shut, the room was becoming more pungent with cigar smoke.

"General, how does it all fit together?"

Twiddling his cigar nervously, Fuller said, "The short version is, they've always been at war with us. We're just unwilling to accept that fact. The UAF cleverly uses jihad in the eyes of its fighters, the OIC, and the whole Arab nation. They're secretly promoting a *fatwa*, a religious decree ordering attacks on Westerners around the world. The fatwa is a micro war that's paving the way for the big surprise war. The engineer behind it is El-Kansi."

Dowling went quiet for a moment. "We've seen the signs. I mean, terrorist activities. Bombings, hijackings, and the buildup of biological and nuclear weapons. And we have that loose cannon, Bin Laden, running around."

"He's a freaking threat, too," the General replied. "I'd like to nail his ass. Most people think they're just splinter groups launching random attacks. I think these guys are part and parcel of the El-Kansi conspiracy. The cowards are especially dedicated to driving Americans out of the Persian Gulf region."

"Unfortunately, the OIC's economic control and political power intimidate our allies. A lot of Western nations respect El-Kansi."

Fuller grimaced. "And that's not the worst of it. The EU, the U.S., and other key nations are vulnerable to the dependencies of OPEC's oil."

"Arabs are capable of neutralizing the power of the UN and maybe even NATO," Dowling theorized, "making it difficult to swing votes in our favor."

"Hah!" Fuller scoffed. "The UN is nothing but a stumbling block. It's been an expensive political charade that gets us nowhere."

"They respond to El-Kansi's suave manner and clever politics.

He's got them conned! He not only controls a major portion of world oil resources but he's also revered and trusted."

Fuller puffed on his cigar and filled the air with dense smoke. "Like short-sighted factions who support the preservation of land and no new oil exploration. That's all right by me, but it's dangerous to put all our eggs in the OPEC basket."

Dowling sighed and shook his head. "Okay, the Arabs are getting the upper hand because of oil. What about China? What's their game?"

"Bloody good question," the General responded, twiddling his cigar. "Probably their military, their eagerness to conquer us- *foreign devils.*" China continues to position itself as a formidable force in the world, economically and militarily. It's hard to figure, but we know China has been too cozy with factions in the Middle East."

"Beijing's economic position has been strengthened through trade with Taiwan," said Dowling. "And since opening up to the West, their political image has been enhanced. But it's hard to predict whose side China's on. I think they're maneuvering to be a stand-alone force. Whatever alliances they form, they would breach to their advantage."

"Interesting," said Fuller.

"China is backing select countries, such as Pakistan, Iran, and others, supplying them with trade and military assistance. They're building an organization of allies—Asian countries in the Pacific Rim, comprised of APEC members. If you ask me, they're gearing up for a fight. But some of the pieces are missing." He puffed on his cigar repeatedly and fanned the smoke away.

Dowling said, "The balance of power is shifting. I can feel it in my bones. And the problem is compounded by the failure of Western nations to work together."

"You got it pegged," Fuller said. "*Failure of Western nations to work together* is the key problem. Historically, the U.S. has been able to pull everyone together, but weak foreign policies and disrespect for us have demoralized our allies." Fuller closed the conversation, shook hands with Dowling, and left. The cigar smoke dissipated, but the aura of his influence lingered.

A few days later, Fuller called Dowling. "Listen up."

"Yes, sir?"

"You heard El-Kansi finally made his move, didn't you?"

"Caught it on GNN last night." "Gonna trigger some bad stuff."

"I'll say. The thing is, El-Kansi now controls the gulf region—the source of energy for more than two-thirds of the world. If he shuts off the oil, he'll cripple the West."

"No question," Fuller said. "Listen carefully. El-Kansi and his band of nations are setting the stage for a takeover. It's not official yet, but the EU and its members are secretly assembling a joint military force, including the U.S. and Canada. El-Kansi tried to cut a deal with the EU, but they declined."

"Looks like we're in with the EU, and everyone is choosing up sides.

"When's this information going public?"

"As soon as MacDuff gets off his butt and makes the commitment. He's trying to negotiate with China, but it's not going well." The General paused. "He still doesn't get it. China's been straddling the fence, milking us of capital and economic development. Mark my words; they're likely to hook up with Russia and side with El-Kansi for leverage. Then they'll make their move—as you say—to stand-alone and conquer."

25

CALL TO ARMS

Martin placed a call to General Fuller's office. "Good morning, General."

Fuller replied, "Dante, good to hear from you. What's on your mind?"

"The AMOEBA virus, sir, the computer glitch."

"Oh, *that* problem. I thought you were calling about the UAF."

"No, but that's implicated. Lots of things can go haywire, General. According to reports, a large number of foreign countries are behind the eight ball. Unless we can head it off, computer failures are going to create chaos. What's happening in Washington?"

"We've made some headway, but not as much as I'd like." Fuller was having trouble educating his peers. "We're trying to keep up with progress here in the U.S., but the foreign landscape is another matter."

"Frankly, all hell's breaking loose," said Martin. "No other way to put it. Politically, we've got a world crisis brewing. The good news is, members of NetForum began a peace-keeping mission across the globe."

"A concerted effort worldwide?"

"That's affirmative, sir. All volunteer work, but hopefully effective."

"Well, I'm impressed. Good work, Dante. We need to preserve relations with our allies. Even when we get our act together, global economics and national security issues are still serious concerns."

"More serious than most know," Martin said dismally. "The AMOEBA virus could reach epidemic levels. The monster will soon rear its ugly head—a kind of *HAL* coming back to haunt us," Martin said in seriousness. "HAL?"

"Yes, only the real thing this time. The bug is pervasive. We need to come up with a fix and control it before it overtakes us. Like the movie version of HAL, it can cause a meltdown of processes the world depends on. It can trigger catastrophic events in defense systems, crater financial institutions, and the list goes on."

"I understand the part about defense systems all too well," Fuller replied gravely. "Exactly what is your group doing? What is your idea of heading this thing off?"

"First, we're desperately trying to come up with a fix. Second, we're acting as consultants to help people deal with the anomaly across the world."

"Fine, mighty fine," said the General. "We need all the help we can muster. I don't see the absolute end of the world, but the coming New Year could mean doomsday in a lot of cases."

"I agree."

"How soon will the virus take effect?" asked Fuller.

"Like the Y2K bug, most systems will experience problems immediately after December thirty-first, some sooner than that. Computer programs will produce incorrect results or crash altogether. Some will falter before that date, with the same consequences."

"Problem is," Fuller said, "except for Senator Garrity and a few others, people up here have a false sense of security."

"Exactly. When are they going to wake up? This is the real thing. Many operations are already experiencing early failures."

"What you're confirming is, our military readiness is in serious jeopardy."

"Affirmative, sir. Worse than that, accidents can happen with our enemies and us."

OMNI HOTEL, RICHARDSON TEXAS

Senator Garrity was at a fundraiser at the Omni Hotel in Richardson, Texas—the heart of Dallas's "telecom corridor." The main topic was the AMOEBA virus and its impact on the telecom industry. The event was held in the luxurious Renaissance Ballroom, accommodating three hundred fifty executives from Alcatel, Ericsson, Lucent, SBC, Nortel, Verizon, WorldCom, and others.

Garrity began: "As chairman of the special committee on the AMOEBA virus, I'm making a call to arms. We must resolve the matter for the sake of preserving economic and social stability and our national security.

"I know that many of you network service providers are faced with grisly choices, as you try to decide how to spend limited resources in the face of the upcoming events. And for many, the only option is to delay the new product's rollout in order to fix the bug. But I believe telecom providers have more to lose than other industries.

"Perhaps delaying other projects to repair the glitch is a reasonable course of action. We're talking about a network infrastructure that covers the world, in which most of you are involved in some way.

"We know you're making a strong effort already. In fact, one large carrier plans to spend five hundred million on the project. Another is spending about three hundred fifty million. Seven other telecom carriers are spending a combined total of two billion dollars. But the good news is, I understand about eighty percent of the networks accessed by the general public will not be impacted.

"But this doesn't guarantee that a single point of failure won't wreak havoc, I am told. Individually, major carriers expect to complete their efforts by December fifteenth, which is cutting it close. Many are scrambling to beat the clock at the last minute. Ladies and gentlemen, I hope none of you fall into this category!"

The audience appeared to be mesmerized.

Garrity paused to drink from a tall glass of water. He briefly glanced down at his notes, then looked up. "We're also concerned about the fourteen hundred smaller carriers that handle about two percent of the nation's traffic. According to a State Department survey of overseas carriers, one-quarter of these firms is not fully aware of the AMOEBA bug! Only interlaced testing will provide accurate results in a global setting."

Garrity continued, "The other day, the FCC commissioner said to me, 'We just don't know all the ways that a failure of one piece of the network could trigger failures elsewhere in the system.'

"Ladies and gentlemen, I'm here to tell you we are doing something about it in Washington. Our committee convinced the president to extend the 'good Samaritan'- legislation intended to protect companies that share information about fixing the defect. The administration has also extended the cap on litigation.

"With little time remaining, and the looming threat ahead, it is imperative that we act *now*. We cannot afford to be casual about it.

"We are counting on you to join us in a partnership to eliminate the AMOEBA bug. I encourage you to work with your government representative on any issues we can help you with. Good luck and Godspeed!"

General Fuller was determined to learn more about the technical aspects of the AMOEBA problem. He arranged a meeting with Dante Martin in California.

"Welcome to my world, General."

"Good to be here. I can feel the vibes of the bustling high-tech-industry. It's quite different from the Washington scene," Fuller said, smiling. He settled into an armchair, propped up his elbows, folded his hands, and cradled his chin with his thumbs. "I need to get more educated about the AMOEBA problem. I'm sure everyone gets sick of hearing the downside, and I'd like to inject some factual knowledge into my discussions. What's involved?"

"A lot, sir, a lot," Martin said. "To start with, it takes experienced people, proven methods, and an intricate process to arrive at a fix. But there is a shortage of qualified people."

Fuller nodded. "Yes, I know. And—we have a critical due date."

"Precisely. There are two options to consider: either modify or replace the defective chip. Most professionals would rather put in logic patches, that is, modify programs on the existing chip."

"Why?"

"Replacing the chip can be risky. Programs are running okay on the old chip, but may not be compatible with the new chip. Also, when you modify programs on the old chip you're dealing with a known quantity, taking the path with the least resistance," Martin explained.

"I see. How do you modify the programs?"

"You first have to find the date bug inside each computer, then insert logic to go around the bad spot. One technique is windowing. Once we know the date, we can avoid the trigger by specifying parameters that circumvent the anticipated time slot. Or we could compress one bite into two bytes or use a base date calculation.

"Base date is where you start with a zero date and count the number of days from that point. That establishes a calendar by the number of days from the base date. If it's not done right, this method can also create erroneous calendars."

Fuller grinned sheepishly. "You know what? I don't understand a thing you said. But I get your drift!" The two men laughed.

"Bottom line. What's it gonna take?" Fuller asked.

"Good people and a lot of tedious work. Depending on the number of programs, the repair of programs can be immense. So far, I've referred to open-architecture systems—embedded computer chips are another matter."

"How's that?"

"Embedded chips are extremely tough to repair. They reside inside non-standard equipment that performs specific, dedicated functions. You have to rely on the vendor or the maker of the equipment to repair those chips.

"Unfortunately, the AMOEBA time bomb can affect life or death situations. And there are thousands of machines out there.

"If you're talking embedded chips, there's a lot more than thousands—more like twenty-five billion in the U.S. alone," Martin explained. "And there are nearly as many vendors as there are types of machines. These units are preprogrammed with set functions and are not easily repaired by programmers off the street."

"Seems like an impossible task," Fuller said, shaking his head. "What about missile control units?"

"Actually, the MEGA-Star chip was first designed and used in military systems as an embedded chip. The system clock was shrouded with encrypted security codes, making it difficult to change."

"Jesus, we'll have to get through this fast," Fuller said.

"We have no choice," Martin replied. "But given enough time, resources, and cooperation, we can do it."

"How can we find and fix all the links in the network chain?"

"Excellent point. The Internet uses a web of landlines and satellite links, tying together millions of computers worldwide. We'll have to get schematics from Internet companies, map out the total network. Each node has to be identified with branch nodes. Then we trace the lines to target computers."

"Christ, the impact of AMOEBA is mind-boggling!" the General said. "A complicated maze. This is as important an issue as I can remember over the past several decades. God help us."

26

GRAND HOTEL, OSLO

Dean Cordell swept his eyes across the ballroom at the majestic Grand Hotel, searching for a familiar face. The hotel was in the heart of Oslo, near the city's air terminal and the fairgrounds.

Dean was a relative newcomer but was included on the guest list —one of few from the secretive THAAD facility. Technically, he *was* on a diplomatic mission.

Guests drank exquisite wine and nibbled on an assortment of European cheeses. The American ambassador was intent on socially mixing local dignitaries with U.S. compatriots. The atmosphere was formal but relaxed. A quintet of tuxedo-clad musicians played classical music in the background.

Suddenly a breathtaking face caught Dean's eyes—a stunning blonde, draped in a passion-red dress. Not someone he knew, but someone he instantly wanted to know. When their eyes met, she stared at him momentarily. Dean's heart jumped. He could see no one else in the room.

She turned away.

Wasting no time, Dean maneuvered his way through the horde of people. He edged beside her and suavely made his presence known. He extended his hand for a handshake. "Hi, I'm Dean Cordell."

She hesitated, smiled, and said, "Karina. Karina VanDegarde." Her voice was throaty, pitched low, and with a distinct Norwegian accent. She offered her hand. "Pleasure."

Dean's grip dwarfed her slender, delicate hand. Her silky, flaming —sun golden hair was stylishly short. It crowned her milky face nicely. Dean liked short hair on women. It gave them that professional look, blended with a cute and saucy bearing. That turned him on. It was also easier to kiss the neck of a woman with short hair.

Dean looked into her sky-blue eyes. He sensed a warm, utterly enchanting person. He burned inside with a wonderful delight. He had not been with a woman for more than twelve months. He broke his trance and glanced around the room. "Lots of people here tonight."

"Yes, quite." Karina liked the resonance of Dean's deep masculine voice and the softness of his dark brown eyes. His strong, well-structured body towered above her eye level.

"Don't know many here," Dean said. He studied her clear, oval-shaped face. Her body was lean and poised. It was outlined by a plunging neckline and a classic hip-hugging evening gown. The gown perfectly revealed the tempting boldness of her figure. Dean smelled her perfume. His heart raced.

Embarrassed by the sudden burst of passion, Dean struggled out of the rapture and grappled with composing himself. "Uh, what line of work are you in?"

Amused by his awkwardness, Karina spoke through a small grin. "I work for the Norwegian government." She admired his mahogany brown hair, not too short, in an executive cut. It framed his handsome, rugged face nicely. His thick eyebrows and bristling mustache finished off his professional appearance.

"Really. Which department?"

"Census Bureau—computer programming."

"Programming? Whaddya know, I'm into computers too!"

"Oh? And where do you work?" She tilted her head in a classic pose as if to pronounce her fine-planed cheekbones.

"I'm on a special assignment with a joint U.S.-Norwegian project. Hey, it's really no big secret; it's the missile base on the coast."

After an evening of small talk over wine and cheese, they wandered out to a wide terrace overlooking Oslo. Built-in 1874, the seven-story, 287- room hotel was historic. It had been renovated in 1996, fitted with updated decor while maintaining its traditional quaintness. Outdoor tables and chairs were uniformly scattered about. But few people were present.

Karina sensed an exciting experience was forthcoming. Under twinkling stars and a bright moon, an unusually romantic feeling had enveloped her. "Where are you from?" she asked, leaning against the wrought-iron railing.

"A small town in Texas," he responded. "Joined the army right out of college. Special Forces, Intelligence Unit."

"Special Forces? The Green Berets?" Karina's eyes flashed excitement. "Yeah," he said, nodding with a coy smile. "Served in Vietnam."

"Intelligence Unit?" She giggled ineptly but asked in a serious tone, "Were you a spy?"

"No, not really. I mostly did political work in small villages, working with the local Vietnamese compatriots. I did political indoctrination, gathered information, and monitored radio signals. I was a cryptanalyst. I deciphered coded messages."

"That's what you do now?"

Dean shook his head. "Sorry, can't really say much."

"What do you think? I mean, about the war in Vietnam."

"For me, I wanted to stop the growth of Communism. But overall, I thought it was a disaster."

Karina nodded acknowledgment and lowered her eyes. Then she looked up and said, "Were you on the front lines?"

"No. I worked with a group of people in the mountains. A place called *Ban-Me-Thuot.*"

Karina's eyes sparkled with interest. "Tell me more."

"It was in the Central Highlands, a region on the border of Laos.

Ban Me-Thuot had a cool climate at higher altitudes. I worked with the local *Montagnards*."

"Monta..."

Dean chuckled. "We call them 'Yards' for short. The name is a French idiom for mountain people." He paused, shook his head, and grunted a laugh. "I feel like I'm talking to a reporter." Karina laughed.

"Anyway, the Yards used crude weapons, but they were excellent jungle fighters. We worked with the SOG guys." Karina's curiosity about Vietnam strengthened Dean's ploy to lure her with mystique. He would just as soon forget about the war, but there were some things he could talk about without feeling trauma. So, why not?

"SOG?"

"Yeah, the Studies and Operations Group." He paused. "SOG activities were considered -black operations- Meaning the missions were top secret. At the time, the U.S. government denied its existence."

Karina's eyes glistened with anticipation. "Oh, how interesting! Tell me, what kind of operations?"

Dean shrugged. "I don't mind telling you. We did a little of every-thing. Unofficially, we operated in Vietnam, Cambodia, and Laos. We'd go on reconnaissance missions. We monitored roads, trails, rivers, and, at times, pulled off some slick prisoner snatches."

"Behind enemy lines?"

Dean shook his head slowly. "No enemy lines in that war."

"What else did you do?"

"We did wiretaps, planted sensors, placed bad ammo in cache sites, and distributed counterfeit money."

"Interesting. I've always been intrigued by wartime stories, espe-cially spy stories. I mean, how did you feel?"

Dean had a melancholy look. "At times, I felt strange. There we were, in the middle of the jungle fighting a war—a war protested by our people back home. Some guys really got messed up on drugs..."

"I understand," said Karina.

"Actually, while in Nam, I first discovered the serious buildup of missiles in China. Even back then, they were aimed at the U.S."

"Really?" Her intellectual eyes gleamed with a judicial inquiry. "So, this has been going on for some time?"

"Yeah. Despite what people think, they're still aimed at us."

Karina was mildly surprised. "Why, I thought Russia and Mideast countries were the main threats."

"Sure, and they'll always be a threat. But I bet the Chinese will join the foray if something goes awry with the Sino-U.S. trade. Nuclear weapons are a hazard to world peace—something to be feared—something we need to be prepared for. That's what led me here, to work at the missile site." A short period of silence prevailed.

"Anyway, what about you? Tell me about yourself," Dean said.

Karina fidgeted in her chair. "Oh, compared to yours, my life would seem boring."

"Try me."

She spoke timidly. "Okay, here goes. I attended the *Universitetet I Oslo* and received a computer science degree."

"Hobbies?"

"I like reading, doing artwork, and playing tennis." Karina paused briefly to analyze Dean's qualities. She saw the epitome of a clean-cut, handsome American—the *John Wayne* type—a rare, dying breed, she thought. She felt at ease.

The embassy social wound down to an end. The crowd thinned out. "Can I call you next week?" Dean said, now feeling confident in his pursuit.

"Maybe we can do lunch or dinner."

Karina grinned, showing snow-white teeth. "Okay, sure."

Dean raised Karina's hand to his mouth and gently kissed it. His tongue whisked her skin lightly and fleetingly. Karina felt a tingle down her spine.

Karina said goodbye and walked away. As she approached the door, she turned to get one last glance at Dean—a sure sign she wanted to see him again.

The Oslo missile station was a key post for nuclear defense. During the post-war era, both the Marshall aid and the common commitment to NATO contributed to the strong bond between Norway and the U.S.

Thanks to the healthy state of this bilateral relationship, Oslo's mission was focused on expanding the success of the Norwegian Atlantic Committee, *Den norske Atlanterhavskomité*, established in 1955. Its objective was to work towards peace and understanding within NATO through political, economic, and cultural cooperation. Programs included work in NATO alliance policies, security issues, and negotiating arms control. In fact, the U.S. and Norway jointly worked with Russia to preserve the Arctic and the Barents Sea. They also helped the Baltic nations find their place in the new Europe.

Norwegians are a proud, determined group of people. For centuries, Norsemen had aggressively exercised their will. They regarded information technology as the top priority. But dealing with Lee Redding became difficult. Redding was unable to intimidate them, as he had done in other markets. Unlike others, the Norwegians challenged his audacious refusal to include their language within the MEGA-Star operating system. Redding's response was, "It is not economically feasible to include the Norwegian language file. It's a business decision."

But the Norwegians were forced to use the MEGA-Star system as a mandatory component in the joint military THAAD project. After World War II, the U.S. military formed a pact with the Norwegian military but dictated specifications on what systems to use.

Ironically, Karina VanDegarde was well versed in the MEGA-Star chip. As a director of NetForum, she was in close touch with Bruce Lindsey at ComTech and Terence Dowling at PII. She was working with Lindsey while studying the AMOEBA problem. Karina discovered it's possible to change user date programs, and the system continued to fail. She had reported this to Lindsey two years ago.

The U.S. military was also working on the AMOEBA strain. But they were mired in red tape and impeded by the *laissez-faire* attitudes at MegaTronics.

One brisk autumn day, Karina and Dean had joined up at a popular sidewalk café in Oslo. They drank espresso and nibbled on warm, buttered croissants. The bright afternoon was tinged with a sunny palette of pastels and a sharp afternoon breeze. Oslo's climate was invigorating, a boost to one's energy.

"So, how's work?" Dean asked before biting into a flaky croissant.

"Working on AMOEBA. Surprised?"

Dean paused to sip some espresso. He was sworn to secrecy in his sensitive post but saw no harm in discussing the AMOEBA fix project. "I hear ya. Same here."

"Making any progress?"

Dean shook his head. "Not really. I'm stuck–just plain stuck."

"How's that?"

"I've got a dilemma. I can't get any support out of MegaTronics. They simply don't respond. The replacement of the MEGA-Star chip will not work for us," Dean explained. "Our programs are highly customized with low-level integration."

Karina took a sip from her demitasse and nestled the cup back onto the saucer. "Can't get *anybody* at MegaTronics to help?"

Dean chewed on the last of his croissant, swallowed, and said, "Negative. I think they're too busy making piles of money. We've come a long way, but we're not there yet. Our programs accept any year we put in, but end-to-end processing always fails."

"You too?" Karina said. "I've got the same problem." They looked at each other in puzzlement.

"We don't have a clue," Dean said. "Programs work individually, but when it comes to full system testing, they crater!"

Karina perked up. She had struggled with the problem for some time. Now she could compare strategies with Dean. "Sounds weird, but this stuff turns me on. It's a challenge."

"Then maybe you can give me some ideas."

"Perhaps." She paused. "Ever hear of NetForum?"

"Net what?" Dean was so enamored by Karina, and her gleaming eyes were magnetic. He grinned mischievously and gently touched her left hand, which clutched the saucer. Their chemistry sparked a mutual passion.

Karina lowered her eyes and blushed. She sipped her espresso, lifted her eyes to Dean, and said, "NetForum. Do you know about NetForum?" Her voice was soft, inviting, like music to Dean's ears.

"Heard of it but don't know much about it."

Captured by Dean's penetrating eyes, Karina's face again went flush. She paused and swallowed hard. "Well, it's a consortium of people who support world peace," her words trailed, and her voice became monotone. "I work with other professionals in information technology."

"When did it get formed?"

"Oh, I would say about two years ago. The group evolved from a chat room we started on the Net. There were so many people; we formalized the group by electing directors and setting guidelines for communications."

"Who runs it?"

"Now, the two main driving forces are Dante Martin and Terence Dowling. Dante is the president of ComTech, and Terence heads up PII— the Privacy of Information Institute."

Dean abruptly snapped out of his lascivious fantasy. "Dante Martin? I know him."

"Really?"

"What a small world. I know him from the war in Nam. We worked on a couple of missions together. You know the guys at ComTech?"

"Not very well. Just through e-mail. I've formed a good relationship with Bruce Lindsey, his technical guru, and others working on the

AMOEBA bug."

"That's great!"

After a short pause, Dean uttered, "Why don't we work on the MEGA-Star bug together?"

"Excellent idea! But would there be security problems?"

"That's something I'll have to check on, but don't think there will be any conflicts if we set it up right."

"Can I tell the people at NetForum?"

"Sure, but no details, please."

"Okay."

"Now, how about that dinner date?" Dean said. "Still on for next week?"

Karina smiled and answered in a sensual voice, "Wednesday—my place, eight o'clock."

27

COMTECH HEADQUARTERS

Bruce Lindsey studied Karina's e-mail with interest. "Infected systems are popping up everywhere!" Her message vaguely explained how the defective MEGA-Star computer was being used in a sensitive operation in Oslo.

The AMOEBA puzzle had become a top priority. ComTech had increased spending and appointed special programmers to analyze the code. They combined resources of the AMOEBA effort with the Omega-Alpha project. The team would have to repeatedly duplicate testing on the same code using a different set of parameters. Lindsey felt Karina was a key person in the effort.

Karina's introduction of Dean Cordell came as a surprise to Dante Martin. When he recalled who he was, it spawned emotional, ambivalent feelings about the Vietnam War, including a brief rekindling of the heady taste and thrill of war. *Ah yes, Hill 33-Charlie, near the villages where Cordell worked. I remember it well. He did wonders, convincing locals to join the cause.*

At that time, Martin was disenchanted with his particular assignment. He was in the CIA-backed *Phoenix* operation, which was not his game. Authorities had set unreasonable quotas for neutralizing Vietnamese civilians. The initiative soon got out of hand. It became an instrument of counter-terrorism—psychological warfare—that often did little to win the Vietnamese people's hearts and minds. Martin eventually transferred to regular combat duty.

Martin thought *I could use a guy like Cordell.*

Lindsey, his team, and NetForum members collaborated to avert a global meltdown, which could lead to a nuclear war. But the question of how to implement a global computer fix was a nagging issue. They worked feverishly to devise a plan for repairing a myriad of infected computers worldwide. One thing was definite. The mammoth undertaking required razor-sharp project management skills. Business-wise, the campaign was risky, but Martin was a risk-taker.

He reasoned that if ComTech provided the service to customers on a delayed payment plan, they would do business with ComTech in the future. Besides, General Fuller and Senator Garrity were providing fiduciary support.

Without warning, a dreadful predicament emerged. A team of avaricious lawyers at MegaTronics filed a lawsuit against ComTech. Redding issued orders to pursue ComTech with a vengeance at any cost. Against these odds, Lindsey's crew became demoralized. They had not resolved the bug, and time was running out.

Late one evening, Lindsey was printing out a test report. Abruptly, someone on the network had locked one of the program files. Lindsey checked to see who was accessing the file, but he saw a strange, unrecognizable name.

Lindsey wandered through the vastly empty departments to seek out the intruder. As he rounded the corner in the main hallway, he noticed the outside back door swinging shut. Lindsey sprinted down the long hallway and rammed the door open. He stepped outside, looked from end to end, and saw nothing but darkness. Seconds later, he heard the roar of a car leaving the parking lot. Too far away to read the license plate, Lindsey helplessly watched the car around the corner and speed away.

The guard on duty told Lindsey he saw someone entering the elevator a few hours earlier.

"Who was it?" Lindsey asked the guard.

"Don't know, sir. Only saw his back. Didn't see his face."

"Well, what did you see?" Lindsey noted the guard's description of the man and left.

Later, ComTech's network administrator reported his audit findings.

The bogus user was established shortly after they had hired three new programmers for the MEGA-Star project. Lindsey studied personnel records for new hires and came up with Derek Junger's name, a developer assigned to the Omega-Alpha project. Junger had not reported for work since the incident.

A few weeks later, a private investigator uncovered ties between Junger and MegaTronics. Junger had, in fact, passed sensitive information to Redding.

"The guy created a gaping hole in the project," Lindsey revealed.

"Set us back several months. Could even destroy the mission." Martin's face dropped in despair.

Lindsey spoke softly. "Apparently, he buried a piece of code that causes a major diversion from defining a solution for the MEGA-Star bug. We're wasting a lot of time chasing the bogus target.

"In reverse engineering, that kind of diversion causes a complete fallback to the last reference point. At least two months of effort went down the drain."

"What's the next step?" Martin asked.

Lindsey hesitated.

"Start at square one."

"This is a bust!" Martin said, shaking his head, pacing the floor. "Where is this guy? Can't we have him arrested?"

Lindsey shrugged and threw up his hands. "Resigned months ago. He's long gone, out of the country. We think he's holed up somewhere in the Caribbean."

Martin sat down, dropped his shoulders, and slumped over his desk like a rag doll. "I can't believe it! A low-life spy crushes our project. We can't back out now. We'll lose money, time, and prestige. Maybe not enough time to beat the clock. Or Redding."

After the episode, doom and gloom penetrated the atmosphere.

Morale was at an all-time low. An attitude of defeat spread throughout the company.

Two weeks later, MegaTronics launched a massive lawsuit against Dante Martin and his company.

At the White House, MacDuff was jubilant. He found a blemish on Fuller's Vietnam record.

It had to do with a VC-infested village named *Son-My*. The long-past *Son-My* search-and-destroy operation was under Fuller's command. The mission was linked with the infamous *My-Lai* massacre, wherein an army officer was convicted of war crimes by court-martial. The president's propaganda squad put a spin on the *Son-My* onslaught and leaked the story to the press.

They said Fuller had been investigated in the raid for alluding to "...the elimination of the Vietnamese 48 Local Force Battalion, once and for all." In the two-day operation, seventy-five VC and three U.S. soldiers were killed. The general was never charged with misconduct, but the incident tainted his record. The excruciating guilt, the psychological turmoil, and the discord caused by religious beliefs were haunting.

The general was especially distraught over his family being dragged through a slur campaign during elections. For weeks, negative thoughts of the past flooded his mind. He plunged into a deep depression. To find solace, Fuller turned to his favorite drink—vodka martinis with a sliver of lime. Eventually, one drink for relaxation in the evening evolved into four or five doubles.

One morning, after a bout of heavy drinking, Fuller and Caitlin were having coffee. Fuller sat at the kitchen table in his robe, unshaven, his head low. The bloodshot lines in his eyes resembled a topographical map of the Rocky Mountains.

"Wish you wouldn't be so down on yourself," Caitlin said affectionately. Her neatly trimmed eyebrows curved into a compassionate frown.

"Hard to explain," the General said, curling his hands around the warm coffee cup.

Caitlin went over and hugged his thick neck. "Chet, I'm worried. This is not like you."

"Yes, I know. The decision to tangle with the White House could do me in. Guess I'm not too good at this game."

"Aren't you blowing things out of proportion?"

Fuller jerked his head up and snapped, "That's easy for you to say!" She quickly pulled away.

Fuller slammed his meaty fist on the table. His cup bounced up, overturned, and splashed coffee in all directions. "Now, look what I've done!"

Eyes wide, Caitlin was stiff with astonishment. She had never seen him this way before.

"Don't you understand? We could be finished!" Fuller snarled. "Leave Washington and start all over." He sighed and bowed his head in thought. *What's happening to me? I've been outnumbered before—during school, in Korea, in Nam, the Gulf War, now I'm letting wimpy, stuffed-shirt politicians get to me. I can't let that happen. I just can't.* His face turned beet red with frustration and confusion. He moved his eyes towards Caitlin.

"Sure, I can understand how you feel," said Caitlin, studying the hulk before her, his powerful body, his large, heavy-boned hands, his blunt facial features that she always thought so manly. *Yes, I know you, Chet. You're tough yet compassionate and sensitive. Your approach to conflict is direct. Your heart drives actions, and you're often spontaneous. But you're a good man. I love you.*

Their brief but memorable courting period had been cut short by his burning desire to fight in the Korean War. He joined the Marines before completing his freshman year. He said, "I wanna go where the fighting is!"

Unlike Fuller's modest background, Caitlin was the daughter of a prominent Texas rancher and state politician. She had a world of privileges in front of her. Her femininity, love of pretty clothes, her participation in extracurricular activities made her very popular on campus. She had an outgoing manner, and the pride in her heritage projected astute political awareness.

And yet, she fell in love with a down-to-earth patriot—an ambitious young cadet whose thoughts and aspirations were conservative but exciting and distinct.

Chet, you've been a driving force for everyone around you. I remember the gleam in your eye, and when you're confident, how your chin juts forward with determination. With a strong inner vision, you've penetrated the walls of hardship and discouragement time and again. "We just have to deal with it like we always have," Caitlin said evenly, head held high.

Fuller paused, slowly regaining composure. He raised his eyes to Caitlin. *God, I love this woman. I still remember when I first saw her. She was like a magnet. She was vivacious, attractive, intelligent, sassy, and sensual all in one. It didn't take long, and the wedding was simple. Our family and a few friends gathered at the little church in New Braunfels.*

She's right. It's that same feeling—that night in my damp bunker near Khe Sanh. The booze, being battered for six straight hours by enemy fire. My mind was one messed-up psychosis. Will we survive? Yes, I lost hope for survival. Damn near gave up altogether. But we did survive! The Hueys came in—the unforgettable sound of rescue—just when the NVA launched their final attack for a certain victory. Self-indulgence—I've scorned men for it. Now here I am. I hate it! Hate it! It's time to take hold, straighten up.

"Okay, Chet, what's it gonna be?"

The General lifted his head again. He looked at her with remorseful eyes. "Sorry, honey. I think it's the booze. Need to get away for a couple of days, clear out my head, get my game plan together."

Caitlin sighed in relief. She could see the familiar glimmer of confidence reappear in his eyes. She smiled broadly, showing cute dimples in her cheeks.

Fuller rose to his feet. They embraced.

28

KARINA VANDEGARDE'S APARTMENT, OSLO

Karina and Dean worked all day testing the MEGA-Star code, to no avail. Testing led nowhere. The program subroutines under test turned out to be dummy lines of code designed as a diversion. The code would wander from the main program, perform meaningless functions, then abruptly end with IF KEY-DATE = Y, THEN GOTO REG_RESET. It made no logical sense.

The GOTO command linked with either another meaningless branch or back to the main program, basically where they started. It was a programming maze. After discussing the regular occurrence of fake branches with Lindsey, Karina learned he was experiencing the same thing. So far, the combined count was over 200 identifiable dummy branches in the system.

It was déjà vu for Karina. At one point in her career, she had been a tester of new software. During that period, she developed a penchant for squeaky-clean code. As part of her procedure, she would also test inactive lines of code. If the inactive code did not serve a purpose, it was deleted from the program. This also saved memory. Luckily, this procedure was a lasting habit for Karina.

Karina and Dean were going over a segment of the code when Karina spotted an odd-looking -REM- statement. In a programming language, REM was used to make notations within a program or deactivate code lines from execution. In this case, the REM statement involved a section of code that made sense. If activated, it actually performed a complete function.

That evening, Karina removed the REM word from the program and executed it to see what would happen. After going through the normal testing series, the crucial moment came when she ran the AMOEBA date cases.

The first case was executed fine. No big deal, it's normal. The reactivated code did not adversely affect the system. The second case was executed again; everything ran okay. Karina's interest was growing. But the code was a bit too complex to analyze on the spot.

Karina proceeded to the next test case, and it too ran okay with no negative impact. Hold it, she thought; the system should have failed. *But it didn't!*

Now, only one more test case to go. The next test would prove the viability of using the code and indicate how it affected correct operations under New Year conditions.

Her adrenaline flowing like river rapids, Karina carefully entered the data for the last test case. She was at the crest of success or abrupt failure. She keyed-in the data and paused before hitting ENTER. Karina finally pressed the key. She gazed intently at the screen, waiting for output. Her heart was thumping. The passing seconds seemed like minutes and the minutes like hours.

Seemingly in slow motion, the system painted columns of positive data on the screen. Karina studied the rows of data for a few seconds. After gaping at the screen results, she was in a mixed state of shock, puzzlement, and glee. Everything ran okay! Karina dared to reason. *Could this be the fix?*

Karina was elated, but as a well-trained professional, she didn't allow her emotions to override her analytical thinking. She slowly stood up from her worn secretarial chair. She walked over to the bar and poured two shots of vodka in a whiskey glass.

She sipped her vodka and thought about Lee Redding: What crass, professional indignity! If you're guilty of planting and disguising this code as an AMOEBA fix, it was a stupid blunder! I've always thought you were technically inept, and now I know. It was too easy. The code could've been disguised a hundred different ways, but you chose a sloppy, amateurish approach.

Karina threw her head back and gulped the last of the vodka. Like a goddess, she stood and gazed across the room. The vodka gave her a warm, calming glow. She immediately called Dean and described the finding, play-by-play.

Both were pumped with excitement but wisely decided to finish the night. Dean planned to return to Karina's apartment in the morning. Karina put the receiver down and squinted at the monitor in disbelief. She was totally fascinated with the thought of discovering Redding's secret. She developed a set of test cases using the new code.

She worked into the early morning hours.

Testing was a long, arduous task. Karina and Dean had spent the entire day going through a variety of test scenarios. They decided to call it a day.

"How about dinner?" Karina asked.

"Sure!"

Karina prepared Chateaubriand steak stuffed with shallots, chives, cayenne, garlic, and salt; sautéed asparagus and new potatoes were on the side. Karina and Dean had finished dinner and were sipping a glass of red Bordeaux.

Stretching over the small dining table with her head slightly angled to the left, Karina's soft lips grazed Dean's lips lightly. They moved towards the couch and sat in tandem. They kissed passionately.

The telephone rang.

Startled and frazzled, Karina wondered who would be calling. The telephone rang in bursts of two rings at a time. "Must be something important," she said.

"Lousy timing," Dean complained. He drew in a deep breath, exhaled, and reluctantly stood up.

Karina got up from the couch and answered the phone. *"Hallo, denne er Karina,"* Karina answered.

"Karina, this is Bruce Lindsey. Sorry to be calling so late."

"No problem."

"I think we've found a piece to the puzzle!"

"Really?" Karina cupped the mouthpiece with her hand, turned to Dean, and mimed, "Bruce Lindsey."

"Can you talk?" Lindsey asked.

"Sure. I've found something too."

"Great! We're definitely on-to something. We discovered a routine called *REG_RESET*. It functions as a clock switch in the BIOS.

"The code was cleverly camouflaged in a divergent nest of meaningless routines. At first, we were stumped. Then I remembered *REG_RESET* is a system-level command we used for low-level testing and resetting memory registers. But today, most of that stuff is built into the BIOS. Anyway, we investigated further."

"What did you find?"

"The command actually resets the internal clock."

"That would account for programs bombing out."

"Right. Now we have to search through each program to find out where this thing is executed, trace the logic flow, and determine what the intent is."

It was no substitute for Dean's foreplay, but Karina became enthralled at the thought of resolving the AMOEBA dilemma. "Amazing," Karina said. "I think I have the other piece to the puzzle."

Dean began putting on his shirt. He knew by the conversation that the solution to the AMOEBA problem was imminent.

Karina explained her discovery to Lindsey in great detail, with the caveat that there was more testing to be done. Meanwhile, Lindsey's team would continue to test the REG_RESET routine on their end.

Karina hung up the telephone. She recounted her conversation with Lindsey to Dean.

"I'd better go," Dean said. "Otherwise, this could turn into a really long night."

"I know. I want you to stay, but..."

There was a long pause as they gazed at each other. Dean shrugged his shoulders. "Another time."

Karina smiled. "We'll take up where we left off."

Dean's heart leaped and pumped up his blood pressure. He gave a low grunt. He pulled her body against his, wrapping his arms around her. They kissed, breaking off just short of getting steamy again.

"Talk to you tomorrow." Dean turned and walked towards the door.

Karina followed. Drained of energy, she leaned on the doorjamb and said, "*Adjo, elske du.*"

"Love ya too." Dean entered the elevator and waved as the doors came together.

Karina shut the door and set the lock in place. A menagerie of thoughts swirled in her mind. What a night! No telling what could've happened with Dean.

Then she considered the bug fix project. If I join the ComTech pieces of the program with what I found, would this fix the date-related code? Thorough testing would bear out my theory.

Karina made some strong espresso and continued testing. The results of her efforts would be very revealing.

29

HILTON HOTEL, MIAMI, FLORIDA

MacDuff pushed the blanket back and answered the phone at his bedside. "Yes?" he said hazily. "What? Ted in an accident?" He was muddled by the call from an aide at two o'clock in the morning.

"God, is he okay?"

The aide hesitated. "Mr. President, there were no survivors." At first, the words did not register. "Oh no. Christ, not Ted!"

"What's the matter, Mac? What is it?" Liz Ledgewick stirred, struggling to open her eyes.

MacDuff put the phone in its cradle and rubbed his tired eyes. "Ted was in an accident." He paused. "Total wipeout." Anguish was in his voice. The blood had drained from his face, giving it a ghostly appearance. Then it turned a putrid yellow.

"What, what happened, Mac?" Gleaming dark hair rested gently on her shoulders.

Stunned, MacDuff plopped his head back onto the pillow in a state of shock. Gazing at the ceiling, he said, "Plane accident—no survivors."

"Oh no!"

"Need to tell his wife and family," MacDuff said in a throaty voice.

"Gotta control the news media." Face vexed, his eyes welled with tears. Liz rolled towards him and said, "Mac, how terrible." She sat upright. "Think I'm gonna be sick." She slid out of bed and rushed to the bathroom.

Five minutes later, Liz appeared at the threshold of the bathroom. Her face was pale, her eyes sunken. She was trembling. "Sweetheart, you look terrible," said MacDuff, visibly concerned.

"Why are you shaking?"

"I, I don't know. All of a sudden, I got nauseated and had to vomit. I've got the chills." Her face turned white; she shuddered all over.

Patting her pillow, MacDuff urged, "Here, honey, come back to bed. I'll get you something."

MacDuff summoned the Secret Service agent stationed in the hall. He instructed him to fetch some *Alka-Seltzer* and aspirin. He also briefed him on the news about Whittington.

Sallow and weak, Liz slowly climbed back into bed. Lying on her side, she pulled the blankets up to her neck, drew her knees up into a fetal position.

MacDuff dialed his campaign manager, Jack Blake. Blake was a loyal protégé, capable and ambitious. He was very proficient at crisis management. But too often, he used a crude, rabid approach that ruffled people.

"Hello," Blake answered. "Jack, heard about Ted?"

"Just got the word. Anyone knows what caused it?"

"No, not yet. A witness said the plane exploded over Texarkana. Investigators are on the way."

"What was he doing in a chartered plane? Where was Air Force Three?" "He stayed over in Dallas for a business meeting," MacDuff replied.

"The crew was doing the pre-flight check on his plane, and they discovered a problem—something about hydraulics. So, Ted chartered a private jet to meet us here in Miami." MacDuff pondered a moment. "If only he hadn't switched freakin' planes."

"You're not going on with the fundraiser, are you?"

"No," MacDuff answered. "I'm going back to Washington, but we can get the governor to fill in. We also need to postpone the Salem trip. We'll be tied up with this thing for at least a couple of weeks."

"Okay. I'll take care of it. I'll join up with you in D.C."

The next day, photos of strewn rubble—remnants of a Cessna Citation biz jet—were plastered on the front page of every major newspaper in the world. Witnesses explained how the plane exploded over a wooded area outside Texarkana, Arkansas; the time was about 11:45 p.m. No clues as to the cause of the crash were apparent. At the crash scene, a full investigation was underway. The FBI, the FAA, the National Transportation Safety Board, and the National Security Agency were busily searching through the ruins for clues.

Investigators combed through the wreckage, taking notes and bagging small pieces of evidence.

At the White House, MacDuff and his press secretary were hassling with news conferences. They had assured the public that it was not an act of terrorism. The UAF had publicly issued threats against the U.S. recently, and the press had already fabricated such a story.

ARLINGTON NATIONAL CEMETERY

"He was one of a kind, a dedicated father and a dear friend. Ted Whittington was a loyal public servant." MacDuff delivered an eloquent eulogy at Whittington's graveside. It was a chilly, overcast day. A purple quilt of threatening clouds muffled distant thunder.

Throngs of people gathered at the ceremony. Dark clothing cast a black hue against the vivid green grass at Arlington National Cemetery, *Field of the Dead*, where orderly rows of white crosses blanketed the rolling landscape.

The casket was horse-drawn in a military procession, traveling past Fort Myers to Arlington Ridge Road. Across the country, flags were flown at half-mast. The elaborate funeral was televised, and the nation was in mourning.

Whittington's wife, Emily, and son, Jeremy, sat beside the bronze casket and wept. Friends paid their respects and offered condolences.

Secret Service agents wearing concealed radios were strategically dispersed. His roaming eyes camouflaged with sunglasses, one agent stood near the cordoned area, guarding family and friends.

"His memory will live forever in the hearts of his family, friends, and the American people," the president said somberly.

NATIONAL PRESS CLUB, WASHINGTON, D.C.

"And what did the doctor say?" MacDuff asked Liz over coffee and Danish rolls. Omnipresent Secret Service agents stood in the marble-floored hallway and at the entrance of a private meeting room.

The National Press Club was in a drab, concrete building of 1940s architecture. It was situated on Fourteenth Street, in the heart of Washington. It was a powerful organization and members of the club included top national and international media people. MacDuff often used the club as a forum to announce new policies, maintain his bond with the press, and for special private meetings.

Liz bent forward and whispered, "I'm pregnant."

MacDuff stopped chewing and froze. He gaped at Liz with a ghostly face. He spoke in a hushed tone. "I hope you're kidding."

Liz shook her head. "I'm not kidding. I've had morning sickness ever since Miami." She was strangely nonchalant about the matter.

Suddenly, the contents of MacDuff's belly turned into a sickening puree ready to erupt. "Oh no!" His eyes swept across the room. "Sorry, Liz. I should've been more careful."

Liz shrugged her shoulders. "No need to blame yourself. Anyway, I was on the pill. It was just a slip-up. An accident!" Her eyes glimmered with tears. She had mixed feelings. She appeared momentarily stunned with an uncomprehending impression on her face. She thought *I'm not really prepared for this—having a baby or having an abortion. On the other hand, if I have the baby, it may force a permanent bond with him.*

"Let's stay calm," MacDuff said smoothly. Though the small room was void of others, he quickly craned his head, scanning the area. "We'll figure something out." He paused. "The doctor doesn't know about us, does he?" MacDuff had a deep frown. A sex scandal could kill his re-election.

"No problem. He's an old friend of mine practicing in New York. I flew up there to avoid local exposure."

"Good." MacDuff's eyes reflected apprehension, and at the same time, compassion. "Does he do abortions?"

Liz lowered her eyes and said nothing for a long while. "No, I don't think so." She turned away abruptly, looked up at the ceiling, then the floor. Her eyes had filled with tears.

"What do you want to do?" He looked at her with strained anticipation. Liz sipped her coffee, cognizant of his eagerness to hear her response. "Mac, if this leaks out, what about your family, your career? What are the consequences? I'm confused. How can we handle this?"

"Don't worry. We'll come up with something." MacDuff's face now appeared relaxed. He lowered his head and momentarily stared into his cup of coffee. He looked up and said, "How far along are you? I mean, how much time do we have?"

"Two months."

"Then, we have a little time yet." *Enough time to consult with Jake Blake on this.* "Look, hang in there. We'll work it out. I've gotta go. I'm late for a meeting. Let's get together in a few days. Okay?"

Liz nodded. "Okay."

MacDuff got up, bent over, and kissed Liz on the cheek. Escorted by the Secret Service, he ambled through the demure building.

Liz stayed behind to finished her coffee. She thought about her father, a career officer in Britain's diplomatic corps. A scandal would surely affect his sensitive post in Washington. She removed a tissue from her purse and gently blotted the tears.

At every opportunity, General Fuller refuted the claims that no missiles were aimed at the U.S. Over twenty nations had ballistic missile capabilities, and the U.S. did not have an adequate missile defense system. ICBMs in Russia, China, North Korea, Syria, Libya, and Iraq posed the most serious threats.

Fuller was also concerned about the White House's lack of response in addressing the AMOEBA virus. The general feared the bug could severely impair national defense systems. They had passed legislation to mitigate computer-related disasters in 1999, but President MacDuff had not followed through with a sense of urgency. An interruption of normal systems could heighten social animosities and create economic chaos.

During a speech at Georgetown University, McDonough Hall, Fuller said, "On the financial front, spending is out of control. Look at the fact that our national debt is at six trillion dollars—a burden our children and grandchildren will have to bear. This could mean another tax increase and over half our income going to the government for decades to come.

"Our education system is failing pitifully. Normally a leader in education, we've fallen behind other nations. We need to recover the values and high standards we once enjoyed." Fuller reached under the podium and took a drink from a glass of water.

"The drug culture is corrupting the minds and bodies of our citizens. We must declare and fight the war on drugs. We must preserve the integrity of our culture. We must strive to eliminate selfishness and bias in the news media and the entertainment industry.

"Accept the challenge. Write your representatives and express your concerns about the publication of decadent, trash, especially to our children. "Most importantly, we must protect our beloved nation from enemies within and outside our borders. Today, we are faced with more complicated, hybrid enemies. But the strength of our armed forces has been drastically diluted, and we lack readiness. We are as vulnerable to attack as we have been in the history of our country. "We are faced with enemies in terrorism, commerce, and politics, including hidden electronic enemies–infected computer systems that can impair our defenses, our social and economic welfare.

"Specifically, we are threatened by the AMOEBA virus. Remember the Y2K scare? We should consider that as a drill for what may really happen." He glared into the audience. He leaned closer to the microphone. "I have to tell you, if the AMOEBA time bomb goes off, we *can* expect tragedies," Fuller said in quieter, softer words. A wave of mumbled conversations moved throughout the audience.

Fuller paused to drink some more water. He had brief flashes about the recent news of extremist criminal activity in the U.S. About groups that professed an apocalyptic view of the new millennium. According to the FBI's Project- Megiddo, militias- and adherents of racist belief systems such as Christian Identity and Odinism could be problematic. General Fuller cleared his throat. "The approaching New Year may unfold with some critical effects." The crowd was silent, hanging on his every word as if waiting for a call to arms. "But this is not a time to panic or to interpret any calamities as the beginning of the end. We can't solve the whole problem at once, so we should first address mission-critical systems."

He took in a deep breath and delivered his closing remarks. "My dear friends, I implore you, be proactive," he said in a louder voice. "Communicate with your representatives, write letters to the president. Talk to your neighbors, get a consensus of where your state and local areas stand.

Get prepared on these issues." He paused. "God bless America."

THE OVAL OFFICE, WASHINGTON, D.C.

"Paris? Have the abortion in Paris?" MacDuff whispered discreetly to Liz over the phone. "What about time off work—what's your story?"

"I've been thinking about working over there for some time now," Liz answered. "I've worked in Paris before. Actually, I feel like another tour may help my career."

"Yes, but it would separate us."

"If I stay over there for a while, we can avoid the rumor mill altogether."

"I need to think this over." MacDuff paused momentarily. "Liz, honey, I... I love you."

"Really?" Liz was pleasantly surprised. This was the first time MacDuff said the words she longed for. She wanted to think he was sincere, but only time would tell—she had been let down before. She had given a great deal of thought to their relationship, wondering what would come of it. But instinctive common sense warned her against a deeper involvement with the president—what it could do to her status, her veritable career.

Ten days later, MacDuff received a phone call from Hayden Boyd, director of the CIA.

"Mr. President, I need to see you right away," Boyd said with urgency. "It's crucial."

"If it's about the Gureyev Yalinsky defection, I heard about it yesterday. Congratulations. Good job!"

"No sir, not about his defection."

"Listen, I'm in the middle of drafting a speech. Can we meet sometime tomorrow?"

"Sir, it really can't wait. Something you should know right away." "What's it about?"

"It's a matter of national security," said Boyd, a veteran of twenty years in the spy business. For him to call an impromptu meeting, it had to be important.

"Okay," the president replied. "Three o'clock."

At precisely three o'clock, Boyd appeared in the Oval Office and shook hands with the president. He looked as if he'd been on an all-night binge. His eyes were bloodshot; he had an overnight beard and his suit looked like he had slept in it.

"Hayden, you look haggard. Need a drink?"

"Don't mind if I do. Scotch and water, please." He paused.

"Actually, I'd advise you to have one too." Boyd slid into one of the wing-backed stuffed chairs in front of the president's mirror-like mahogany desk.

"Sounds serious," uttered MacDuff. He fixed two glasses of ice, poured a jigger each from a spouted bottle of Johnny Walker Black Label. He added water and stirred. MacDuff delivered a drink to Boyd and headed for his chair. "What's up?"

Boyd sipped his scotch and waited for MacDuff to settle behind his desk. "I've got some bad news. We've been grilling Yalinsky all night, and he's telling us stuff we didn't know."

"Stuff? What stuff?"

"About Ted Whittington."

"Ted?" MacDuff asked in puzzlement.

"Yalinsky told us the KGB blew up his plane."

Taken aback, MacDuff squinted at Boyd. "Are you joking?"

Boyd shrugged, then shook his head in a steady motion. "No, sir, I wouldn't joke about a thing like that. I'm dead serious. I've been up all night. We checked the guy out. I assure you: it's not made up." Boyd leaned back and studied MacDuff's reaction.

Fuller said, "But why? Why would they wanna kill Ted? He was no troublemaker."

"Don't know," Boyd replied.

MacDuff peered suspiciously at the CIA chief. "Don't know? Tell me, what *do* you know?"

Boyd drank a bit of scotch. "He was... well, he was working with the KGB."

"With the KGB!" MacDuff shouted in a booming voice. "Hayden, is this some kind of sick joke? We just buried Ted. Show a little respect!"

"Not so fast, Mr. President; I wouldn't canonize the guy yet." Boyd sat still and said nothing for the moment. The news was bad enough. He knew the president was in a state of denial.

"No way—this is nonsense! I can't believe it!" MacDuff shouted.

Boyd leaned forward in his chair. "Believe it, chief. It's been confirmed," Boyd said, his tone ending on a high note.

"Why? How? Tell me what the heck is going on, Hayden!" MacDuff lamented; his face reddened with frustration.

"Yalinsky explained to us how Ted was positioning himself to be the next president. Apparently, Ted was working with the Russians to set you up in a KGB-sponsored sting operation. You were to end up in an ugly scandal." The president sat quietly for a moment, staring into the distance.

"Bizarre. That's a bizarre story, Hayden. Ted was smart, but he wasn't that cunning. I don't think he had the guts to pull off anything like that. If he *was* involved, it was probably for money," MacDuff said, searching for logic or reasoning.

"Money wasn't an issue. He didn't need money. He's wealthy. He inherited a fortune when his father died last summer." Boyd paused.

"Yalinsky said Whittington just wanted you out of the picture."

"Ridiculous," MacDuff scoffed.

"That's what he said—out of the picture. They were planning to link you up with a contrived KGB spy ring here in the States. You were to be portrayed as a well-paid traitor, siding with the Russians. You walked right into their trap by making those speeches about 'no Russian missiles aimed at us.'"

MacDuff turned and shot Boyd a riveting glare. "What's *that* supposed to mean?"

"Most everyone knows the Russians have missiles pointed at us. You made it sound like they were nice guys, really cooperating with us in the nuclear non-proliferation treaty."

There was a long period of ocean-deep silence. MacDuff was noticeably agitated by Boyd's words. Perplexed, he frowned intensely. Then his face turned pale. He bowed his head and gradually accepted the story. Appalled at the thought of Whittington doing such a thing, he said, "For the presidency? That's why he did it?" MacDuff pursed his lips, and his nostrils flared.

"Yes, Mr. President. In my estimation, the vice president felt he would finally be the boss instead of a second-string lackey. Then, of course, the Russians would have *their* man in the most powerful position in the world."

"Incredible!" He hesitated, stroking his chin. "But why did they have to kill him?"

"According to Yalinsky, he backed out of the deal at the last minute. They were going to pull the trap on you during the Salem fundraiser. Whittington was to leak the story to the media. And the Russians would supply members of the spy ring to corroborate the story.

"He met up with his KGB contact in Dallas to discuss the final steps.

That's when he supposedly told them the deal was off, and he was backing out." Boyd slurped the last of his watered-down scotch. "The

KGB was pissed so much that the man in charge of the operation made an unprecedented decision to terminate him. They loosened fittings on Air Force Three, enough for it to be grounded. Then they hid a bomb inside the cargo bay of the chartered jet at Addison Airport."

Stupefied, MacDuff managed to exert slander upon his VP once again. Now *that* sounds like Ted. I knew that piece of work didn't have the guts," he muttered.

"I think the Russians figured they had too much to lose at that point. Whittington became a threat, and things could have backfired on them. It could've been a scandal for the KGB. So, they whacked him." Boyd paused. He cocked his head, smiled, and looked at MacDuff. "Ironically, they didn't know Yalinsky was going to defect, so the whole damned thing backfired anyway!"

Boyd went on, "Mr. President, I need to tell you, when the KGB screws up like this, it feels better than an orgasm. They really blew this one, and it will take some time for them to recover."

"You mean about Ted or Yalinsky?"

"Both."

MacDuff stared across the room in bewilderment. "I need another drink! Want one?"

"Hell, yes. I'll fix it this time." Boyd got up and went to the bar. "I think you'd better stop pacing and sit down. You haven't heard the worst of it yet."

"Worst of it?" Emotionally drained, MacDuff plopped himself into his chair, swung around, and faced the window.

Boyd mixed two drinks, this time doubling up on the scotch. MacDuff quietly gazed out the window at the lush green White House lawn, wondering what was next.

Eyes bloated and teary, MacDuff spun his chair around and lamented in a voice choking with emotion, "How did Ted get mixed up in this in the first place? How, who, when?" MacDuff's face was flush, a bright pink color. A spy scandal would put his campaign in imminent danger. And Ted Whittington, of all people, was the villain. For the first time in his political life, it could dramatically expose his failings. This scandal could resurface his numerous sexual excursions —one of which involved his sexual romp with two young porn stars in a Los Angeles hotel room a few years ago. And over the last ten years, there were payoffs from labor unions and foreign agents posing as commercial officers—agents from Russia, Iran, and China, to name a few. Notably, a large amount of Chinese money made it into MacDuff's re-election campaign, with the tacit understanding that it would improve U.S. China trade relations. China had secured over $5 billion in trade deals and directly influenced U.S. foreign policy.

Then there were the illegal donations received from cocaine-supplying countries such as Columbia—resulting from a web of transactions ending up as deposits in MacDuff's account at the Banco Nacional de Panamá.

MacDuff anxiously waited for Boyd's response.

Boyd handed MacDuff his drink, sat down heavily into the soft armchair, tipped his glass, and waited for the scotch to trickle down to his tailbone. He leveled a piercing stare into MacDuff's eyes. "It was Liz Ledgewick. She's back home, in Russia."

30

SENATOR KENT GARRITY'S OFFICE

"How about the latest—the Whittington-Ledgewick scandal?" Garrity said to General Fuller. "A real shocker, wasn't it?"

Fuller nodded slowly. "I understand she really fell in love with him. Who knows, if Whittington hadn't backed out and if she had his baby, that would've cinched the deal!"

"Never mind the press," Garrity mused. "The Russians are spymasters. She knew what she was doing. Love or not, she meant to get pregnant."

"No telling what kind of mess MacDuff got us into."

"Yes?"

"Been getting a lot of feedback through the Omega-Alpha project," the General said. "Combined with what's coming out of Beijing, a *real* scandal is shaping up."

The senator paused and looked at Fuller admiringly. "Chet, been meaning to tell you, I'm impressed with the work you've been doing."

"The Alpha-Omega project? They're a bunch of dedicated people," Fuller replied. "Pretty damned effective at what they do, and they cover a lot of territories." Fuller had been making the rounds talking with top Foreign Service officials and key politicians on the AMOEBA crisis.

Garrity's office staff of six followed the White House scandals very closely—doing research, telephone surveys, and staying up on current events. Plus, they had documented the transfer of missile technology to China, the AMOEBA problem, and economic issues.

"Actually, I was referring to your work pushing for missile defense and keeping tabs on corruption in the White House," said Garrity. "They really got caught with their britches down. MacDuff was gouging Redding for big bucks, and Redding was draining big favors from MacDuff!"

Fuller shrugged his shoulders. "Flat greed. Had to catch up with them sooner or later."

Garrity leaned forward and lowered his voice. "Chet, you should know, we're organizing a hearings committee on corruption and negligence within the government. We're digging up a lot of stuff on MacDuff's administration." "How bad is it?"

After a long pause, Garrity said, "I think we're only seeing the tip of the iceberg."

Fuller shook his head. "Well, I do know the Chinese ripped off Redding and MacDuff on demo units. That will cause definite problems! And Redding is ripping off his customers with the upgrade necessary to fix the AMOEBA bug."

"Do you know how many systems are still out there with the virus?" asked Garrity.

"Hard to say. It's like guessing how many cars there are in the world with a defective ignition switch that fails after so many turns. Some are still out there waiting to hit that elusive failure point. We know this much: AMOEBA-infected computers *will* fail."

"Will they fail at a specific time?"

"Not necessarily. They can limp along with work-arounds."

Garrity bowed his head and said solemnly, "Need to take care of the military units first."

"Yep. And fast!" Fuller responded. "The AMOEBA snafu is the worst manmade threat in centuries."

Garrity squirmed in his seat and scowled. "My committee is pretty pissed at the president for dragging his feet on this."

"You know, even the big reputable corporations are still behind the eight balls. They're not keeping up with bug fixes," said Fuller. He leaned forward with a deadpan face. "It's damned scary."

After a long period of silence, Garrity said, "About the Mid-east situation. I've got a feeling that's going to erupt soon."

"Gotta head off the guy behind the UAF and the EFT scam." He paused to study the senator's face. "Know who I mean?"

Garrity furrowed his brow and looked Fuller in the eye. "Yes. Sheik El-Kansi and his sneaky bunch of bandits."

"My sources say they're putting an offensive together."

"I'd like to muster a battalion of Marines, fly over there, and finish what we started in the Gulf," Garrity said.

The two men grinned broadly at each other, savoring a moment of vengeful fantasy.

"*Semper Fi!*" pronounced Fuller. "*Semper Fi!*" Garrity replied.

The two men chortled.

"El-Kansi is the kingpin," Garrity said. "Everyone respects him as a world-class leader, but he's really a snake in the grass. The OIC is supposedly on the up and up, but something's really fishy."

The General nodded. "Reminds me of Nam."

"How's that?"

"El-Kansi has people convinced that we're the bad guys. It's psychological. I mean, we need to roll up our sleeves, get in there and work at it—as we did in the villages of Vietnam—convincing the ordinary people. Once you do that, they'll support you. The simple concept sometimes eludes us."

The General paused, looked away momentarily, and continued, "We've got to shore up our political clout in Europe and Asia. Look what Zemin and Putin have done with the SCO organization. After they form an ally like that, next comes a military coalition. Then we have a horse of a different, dangerous color."

There was cause for concern. In central Asia, a disturbing paradigm was taking shape. The Chinese and Russians had formed a united front against the U.S. plans to build a missile defense system. SCO, the Shanghai Cooperation Organization, planned to build an economic and security bloc in central Asia. SCO was a means of countering growing U.S. and European investments in the region. And it was a strong lobby against the proposed U.S. missile defense shield.

"Now, the consortium of missile defense critics includes rogue nations, factions of the EU, Russia, and major powers in Asia," said Fuller.

SCO favored the Anti-Ballistic Missile Treaty, a relic of the Cold War. Beijing and Moscow also warned the U.S. proposal might trigger a fresh arms race. SCO members included China, Russia, Kazakstan, Kyrgyzstan, Tajikistan, and Uzbekistan. The SCO group of six nations replaced the Shanghai Five, a loosely knit forum created in 1966 to resolve border disputes and to fight rising Islamic militancy. But priorities changed over the years.

The Russian president said, "Cooperation in economics, trade, and culture is far more important than military cooperation." Whatever the rhetoric, military expansion in the region was still an agenda —nuclear arms sales by Russia and China were brisk.

Nonetheless, China was eager to gain access to new energy sources for its expanding economy and lessen dependency on U.S. trade. Trade between China and Russia exceeded $8 billion a year, less than a tenth of China's trade with the U.S. Russia also depended on the West for desperately needed investments in its faltering economy.

Garrity absorbed Fuller's words, cocked his head, and looked at him with a serious eye. "Chet, have you thought about politics? That is, running for public office?"

"Not seriously."

"Frankly, I think you would do well. You're gutsy, motivated, and you have a grasp of world affairs."

"I'm flattered, but not sure I can put up with the political bull. I'm a grunt Marine, not a politician."

Garrity guffawed at the comment. "Yes, to be in politics, you do need the skin of a buffalo. But there can be a lot of personal satisfaction too. Chet, I want you to seriously think about something. I'd like you to be my running mate as vice president."

Fuller's eyes lit up. He peered at Garrity in wonderment. "Jesus, now I'm really flattered!"

"I know I hit you cold with the idea, but you're the kind of guy I need."

Fuller gazed across the room, his mind swirling in a long period of thought.

Garrity piped up. "Listen, you don't need to decide now. Think about it. Talk it over with your wife and family. Get back to me in a couple of weeks. Okay?"

31

SAN FRANCISCO EXAMINER

"BEIJING EXECUTIVE ABDUCTED IN HOLDUP"

SAN FRANCISCO– The SFPD and the FBI are investigating the abduction of a top executive on tour from Beijing, China. The executive, Mr. Wang Zhang, is the managing director of the China National Aero-Technology Import & Export Company, a member of a trade delegation visiting high-tech companies in Silicon Valley. Details of the abduction were not disclosed, but theories about a robbery and kidnapping for ransom were discussed. The delegation is on a mission to explore business relationships with Megatronics Corporation, among others, for the production of computer hardware and software products. China's high-tech industry is growing at a rapid pace and ventures with U.S. firms are part of the President's aggressive approach to global expansion.

A White House spokesman said, "The President and the American people deeply regret this tragedy involving our Chinese friends. It is not indicative of crime in the majority of our fine cities. We hope this incident does not deter further visitations by foreign trade delegations. Every effort is being made to investigate and search out the whereabouts of Mr. Zhang. The FBI, the San Francisco Police Department and others are making this case a top priority."

Despite the President's message, the abduction will indeed make

Chinese and U.S. officials think about tighter security for foreign delegations. China is one of America's prime target markets, particularly in high-tech industries. China's computer industry has grown an average of 31% annually in the last two years. With its market potential, their supply of engineers, computer scientists, and a pool of low-cost, semi-skilled labor, China plans to emerge as a global producer of low-end hardware and software products. China is competing with its neighbor South Korea, but China has nearly 4 times as many computer engineers as South Korea. The estimated size of China's computer market is more than $1 billion, with an expected growth rate of 42% annually. In China, there are over 50 high technology projects in various stages of development.

"We're still putting the pieces together," Chief Tony Kowalski of the San Francisco Police Department said to the FBI China specialist. The case officer, Scott Brummell, had been dispatched from Washington as the lead investigator on the Wang Zhang disappearance. The two criminologists were in the downtown Northern California federal office building in a colorless, dark room with a metal desk, a row of filing cabinets, and four chairs.

In his mid-thirties, Brummell was dressed in a blue blazer, tan slacks, a white shirt, and a red tie. He groomed his short, pecan brown hair in a clean executive style. "Whaddya have so far?" He asked. His young-looking face was serious.

"Witnesses saw Zhang with two male Caucasians. The two guys waited for Zhang in the hallway, grabbed him, and whisked him away," Chief Kowalski explained. "At a glance, the garage attendant remembered seeing Zhang in the back seat of a dark green Jeep Cherokee as they left. They turned north. He was able to give us a description of the two assailants." A gruff, rock-hard man, Kowalski started as a cop on the beat, long before "police brutality" was coined. He stood at six foot three, had a crew cut, a ruddy complexion, and deep-set aqua-gray eyes.

"Was Zhang alone in the hall?" Brummell asked.

"Yeah. Zhang's group was having lunch in the hotel restaurant when he complained about stomach pains. Zhang got up, went to the gift shop, bought a bottle of *Pepto-Bismol,* and went up to his room. A maid got a glimpse of the two men just before Zhang arrived."

"Motive. What's the motive?" Brummell said. "Kidnap-for-ransom?"

"Maybe. But we haven't heard from them yet."

"This is turning into a political nightmare," Brummell uttered. "They're saying Zhang has 'fallen prey to the crime-ridden streets of a decadent American city and the criminals will get away with it."

Kowalski flinched. "Ridiculous."

"That really pisses me off too. All the more reason why we need to get our butts in gear!" Brummell growled. "Have to show some results."

"Got my best detectives on it," the chief added.

Brummell stood up, propped his hands on his hips, and walked a few paces towards the window. Below, you could hear the buzz of traffic on Sutter Street. "Okay, the name of the game is, keep digging locally. I'll coordinate with General Fuller at the Pentagon and the CIA guys in Beijing."

"You mean, the CIA's involved?"

"That's affirmative. They're into everything. Specifically, checking into the possibility that Zhang is involved in intelligence gathering in the U.S. They're still investigating China's spying coup at Los Alamos and other nuclear facilities. Missing disk units with nuclear secrets have yet to turn up."

"Still?"

"Affirmative. Key principals have scattered like rats in a fire. They're having a hard time proving anything. It's bad," complained Brummell. "The Chinese have succeeded in the kind of capers we should be doing. We're always one step behind."

Kowalski shook his head in disgust. "I really find it hard to accept that nonsense. When I was in Army Intelligence, we were always at least one step ahead! What the hell's going on with national security?"

"Any news from Beijing?" chief Kowalski asked Brummell. "We've flat run out of clues here." In Brummell's unmarked car, the two men were going to the crime scene. They would first have lunch. They drove down Ennis Boulevard through a seamy industrial area of South San Francisco.

After a mile or so, they approached the gate at Hunter's Point, an abandoned navy shipyard still owned by the government. The solo guard politely directed them to a parking area off the main road. The quaint bistro was just inside the chain-link fence, nestled on a sloping bank that bordered the shoreline at the rear of the building.

The structure was nostalgic. White stucco veneered the establishment's exterior shell. The cuisine was ethnic—easily clued by the name, *Dago Mary's*. The landmark eatery had opened in 1931.

Kowalski and Brummell parked the car in a lot across the street.

When the two men stepped inside the building, it felt like a different time zone. Black and gold velvet wallpaper, Italian marble columns, and hand-carved mirrors gave the room a look and feel of a gold-rush bordello. Sculptured window panels and high ceilings harmonized with burgundy-colored carpeting and white tablecloths.

"Man, oh man, what a place." Kowalski rotated his head up to the ceiling, down and around. A colorful, old-fashioned Wurlitzer jukebox was couched in a small corner near the front door. A cluttered yet inviting California lotto kiosk filled the opposite corner.

"Hey, check out the bar!" said Brummell, bracing his foot on the brass rail, leaning against the shiny countertop.

The huge antique structure was the triple-arched type, measuring about fifty feet wide. Bottles of every size, shape, and color reflected against inlaid mirrors, surrounded by scalloped dark oak. The carved faces that adorned the back bar were arcane, horned devils accompanied by other less demonic creatures. The front rail was onyx, and the bar itself was made of rich, quarter-sawn oak.

The two men were escorted to a table in the rear of the building, next to a large window framed the curvaceous bay. Across the glimmering water, a line of dockyards was silhouetted against a deep blue sky.

After the men ordered two iced teas, Brummell waited for the maître d' to leave. He leaned forward and said quietly, "We found out Zhang is really with the PLA—the Chinese army."

"What? Thought he was civilian."

"Supposedly. But unlike our system, the Chinese military is deeply embedded in the business sector. They're into different industries. Even the arms trade. Can you believe it? When they come over here, these characters pose as civilians," Brummell said. "Can't tell who's who."

"It all ties to the system in China. The PLA wants our technology, and one way is to obtain information through legitimate businesses. Besides, the system is so corrupt that they use graft in China and the U.S. They find ways to grease the rails, so to speak."

They took time to study the menus. A matronly waitress appeared and asked for their order. Kowalski ordered lasagna, Sicilian style, and Brummel chose roasted chicken with Marsala gravy. After the waitress noted lunch details and retrieved the menus, Kowalski asked, "How old is this place?"

"Been here since World War Two," she answered curtly. "A lady named Mary Chiorzio started the place. Back then, it was really a hot spot. Something going on every night. Live entertainment, seven-course meals, and lots of good fun. During the war, it converted into an officer's club."

So *that's* what it is, Kowalski thought. The ambiance radiated a wealth of unwritten history. For a moment, he envisioned ghostly figures of uniformed soldiers bent over the bar laughing, drinking, and telling war stories. Kowalski could even hear Glenn Miller's *Little Brown Jug* echo in the background.

Brummell craned his head around the room, then broke the silence. He said, "Frankly, our spooks are scratching their heads over this Zhang case. We even checked with the Chinese Public Security Bureau, and PLA intelligence. Nothing doing there." He whistled quietly. "Boy, they're one freakin' tough bunch!"

"Something has to give," muttered Kowalski. "The local Chinese community is having a fit. They're stirring up a lot of political disruption."

Brummell sighed. "My friend, we're in the same boat. It's raised a big stink in Washington too. The Chinese spooks are snooping around D.C. I understand they're here too, in the Bay Area."

Kowalski nodded. "Probably staked out in Chinatown. Give me their MO, and I'll put a tail on 'em."

"We're already tailing them. But check your sources in the streets. See what's going down."

"The Chinese are pretty damned tight-lipped. But we'll make a run at it."

"Okay, ace. I'm counting on you."

32

LE RIVAGE RESTAURANT, WASHINGTON, D.C

Senator Garrity strolled past the bustling high-tech bar toward General Fuller's table on the deck. Garrity pulled out a chair and sat down across from the general. "Hullo, Chet. What's the occasion?" The deck overlooked the Potomac, a boat dock, and the Maine Avenue seafood market outside a panoramic window.

Poker-faced, Fuller loosely disguised a thin grin. He wore civilian clothes—an open-collar white shirt, tan sport coat, and dark blue slacks. He looked distinguished, rather dashing, in civvies. His cropped hair was the only obvious giveaway to being military.

When the waiter appeared, Garrity ordered iced tea, and Fuller's choice was coffee.

Fuller watched the waiter leave, then said, "Thanks for coming on such short notice. Things have been a little tight on planning." He looked from side to side, then placed his forearms on the table and leaned forward. Fuller spoke in a low voice, "Listen carefully. Suppose I told you I could arrange a meeting with my Beijing contact, Lame Duck. Interested?"

Garrity cocked an eyebrow. "Hell, yes."

"Good. Here's the setup. Can you be at the Manassas National Battlefield Park, tomorrow, say, at eleven in the morning?"

Garrity thought for a second, then nodded. "Sure. Let's go for it."

"Right, eleven o'clock sharp. We'll be parked at the Stonewall Jackson monument."

Garrity nodded again, then paused to sip some tea. "By the way, what's the latest from Beijing?"

"We've been tracking down missile units and making AMOEBA repairs."

"Good."

"We've also got some unexpected help."

"And who might that be?"

Fuller lowered his voice. "Get this. A small band of Montagnard mercenaries in deep cover, posing as peasants. They're feeding us vital information about China's missile sites. Just like they did in Nam."

"I know the Yards. I was stationed at the American embassy in Saigon. I read the reports."

"What a coincidence!" Fuller said excitedly. "I was at the embassy too!"

"We recruited the Montagnards in 1961. We armed, trained and paid them to help us. But, in the end, we essentially abandoned them."

General Fuller bowed his head. "Yeah, I was there when we pulled out of Saigon. In fact, I was in charge of the evacuation. Let me tell you, that was one helluva operation."

He momentarily gazed across the room. "The Vietnamese swarmed around the compound like a flock of hornets. They hung from helicopters, shouting pleas to take them with us. We ended up evacuating over fourteen-hundreds of them. We were lucky to get out that many. It was a freaking mess, but we did it."

During the Tet Offensive, Saigon was under siege. Tan Son Nhat airport was unfit for normal transport aircraft, and the only way out was by helicopter. Undercover fighter aircraft from offshore carriers, helicopters landed at the airport on rooftops, and in parking lots to rescue people. Marines from the Ninth Amphibious Brigade were flown in especially for the operation. All but a handful of the 900

Americans were evacuated. The last helicopter lifted off the roof of the United States embassy carrying the Marine Security Guards.

Deeply emotional, Garrity and Fuller reminisced about the traumatic experience.

"Well, as it turns out, the CIA guy in Beijing was on the original team that recruited the Yards in Nam. Somehow, he made contact with them again and set up another alliance. It was good timing because the Chinese were elusive about the whole AMOEBA project. They've been asking for source programs on the MEGA-Star, but not saying much about their missile units."

"What are they up to?" said Garrity. "Why are they holding back? Could they be planning a military operation?"

"They probably are, but the timing's off," Fuller replied. He paused to take a sip of coffee. "Beijing's attitude has changed. They've beefed up internal security and are zapping political dissidents hard."

"What's your take, Chet?"

"China has always spurned Western-style democracy," the General answered. "They have a strong propensity for crushing any threats to the Communist regime, and their goal is to dominate the world. But they're also faced with a dilemma. With global economics in play, opening up their markets and converting to a market-driven economy has encouraged a democratic mind-set. Beijing doesn't like that."

"I think they're in a panic mode," the General continued. "The Public Security Bureau has kicked into high gear. They closely monitor the Internet for the signs, and if the political mood seems to shift away from party lines, they crack down and round up dissidents." Only recently, a Chinese rebel who tried to develop an opposition party was rounded up and sent to a labor camp. Another, campaigning for democracy, was arrested and locked up indefinitely.

"I remember the one guy getting caught on the Internet," said Garrity. In a well-publicized case, Beijing caught a dissident named Xu Rongmin while he was using e-mail on the Internet. He was a factory worker who served an eight-year prison sentence for organizing an independent labor union during the 1989 protests.

Zeng Wu, who edited a dissident journal during the Democracy Wall movement over twenty years ago, spent twelve years in prison. His trial was coming up soon, but in China's kangaroo court system, he was likely to get life no matter what his defense would be.

Garrity drank some more iced tea. "In terms of trade relations, Beijing is in a pretty good position. They've amassed a trade surplus with the U.S. of over fifty billion dollars, second only to Japan. So, when China's economic growth slows, they limit foreign competition." He was right. The finance ministry controlled the foreign exchange movement out of China and restricted any foreign business expansion within China. They were making life in China very awkward for Westerners, jeopardizing millions of dollars of U.S. investments.

"And I would guess that includes MegaTronics deals too," responded Fuller. "That debacle is going to cost us a bundle." MacDuff, Redding, and their partners got too greedy, he thought. "They had no right to roll the dice on American taxpayer dollars. China will get what they want, then slam the door shut."

MANASSAS NATIONAL BATTLEFIELD PARK, MANASSAS, VIRGINIA

It was cold and gray, typical of December weather in Northern Virginia. Patches of early morning mist floated in the air, surrounding the statue of Stonewall Jackson perched on his horse.

It was here, during the Battle of Manassas, that the Confederate general acquired the nickname Stonewall. The Park was a quiet place with few visitors, especially today, a weekday.

General Fuller's black, bulletproof limousine sat ominously among the trees. Dark-tinted windows camouflaged the figure of a man in the back seat. Eyes wandering, Lame Duck constantly looked over his shoulder, expecting gun-wielding PLA agents, the *Ke Ge Bo*— or a hit man from the fearsome *14K triad* gang—to emerge from the forest at any moment. He peered at the low blue clouds that threatened snow flurries. Beijing was not above hiring the triad to do its dirty work. Lame Duck reasoned that snow would provide good cover for the cunning crime family, an omnipresent mob that put fear in everyone.

The triad was formed after World War II, when the Maoist Communists won the Chinese mainland. A few of the nationalist troops and supporters fled to Hong Kong and formed a 14-K Triad Society group. The group established branches in Hong Kong, Taiwan, and other countries around the globe. But the 14-K was the most prominent faction—the bedrock of Chinese organized crime that controlled much of the heroin flow from Southeast Asia to Europe and North America. In fact, U.S. law enforcement agents believed the 14-K Triad, not the Mafia, provided 70 to 80 percent of all heroin smuggled into New York City.

Fuller stood to the side of his limo, puffing a Partagas cigar. Two FBI agents were on guard. One agent was stationed at the rear of the car. He wore a flak jacket overlaid by a dark blue business suit. His automatic Koch MP5 tactical carbine had a switch that enabled the rifle to fire two rounds with a single squeeze of the trigger. The switch was on.

The other agent, clad in a flak jacket and a lumpy chauffeur's uniform, sat behind the steering wheel. He had a holstered 9mm semi-automatic pistol, and a semi-automatic Colt AR-15 rifle stretched across the front seat.

Suddenly, the sharp crack of a rifle echoed from the forest. The FBI agent at the rear of the car dropped to the asphalt surface. Fuller instinctively dove to the ground. He sensed the shot came from a group of trees at the foot of a small hill, about two hundred yards away. Adrenaline rushed through every vein in his body. *The rifle. I need to get the rifle.* The agent's carbine was lying twenty feet away.

The driver started the limo, opened the door, and shouted to Fuller, "How bad is he?"

"Can't tell. Not much blood, though. He got hit somewhere in the head or neck. I'm going over to get his rifle and check 'em out." Like a giant lizard, Fuller belly-crawled to the agent—he was still breathing.

The bullet had grazed the right side of his skull and knocked him unconscious.

Fuller grabbed the MP5 carbine and snaked towards a small ditch on the left side of the limousine. His eyes swept across the tree line, from side to side—no sign of movement.

Then another shot cracked like a thunderclap. This time Fuller saw a flash, the flicker of a gun barrel near the forest on a grassy knoll. He settled into a low spot, propped his rifle on the small embankment. "He's still breathing! He should be okay!" he shouted to the driver. "Shots are coming from the right side of that clump of trees. At your four o'clock."

"Roger, four o'clock," the driver replied. "General, your man is on the floorboard, safe from gunfire." A protective cocoon, the executive car was encased with half-inch-thick metal plating, making it impenetrable by rifle fire. "Can we knock him out?" the agent said in a strained, tight voice. "Or should we put my partner in the car and get the hell outta here?"

"Let's nail 'em," replied the feisty General.

"Okay, sir. Coming out. Cover me." Hunched over, the driver picked up his rifle, slid out, and squatted close to the pavement. He duck-walked to the left front fender. The agent lifted his rifle on top of the car's wide hood and looked for the shooter. From his vantage point, the trees were to the right of Stonewall Jackson's statue. "See him?"

"Negative," said Fuller. "I'm gonna fire off some rounds to root him out." He squeezed the trigger, and the rapid-fire rifle spurted out a string of rounds.

Eyes riveted on the clump of trees; Fuller caught a glimpse of a man dropping down from a tree. The gunman ran over and hid behind a large oak. "I see him!" The General said. He aimed his rifle towards the oak. "Behind that big tree on the right."

Suddenly, the piercing sound of another rifle shot reverberated in the woods. The driver grunted sharply, slid down the fender, and fell to the pavement.

Fuller snapped his head around. *That came from our rear.*

Another sniper! *We're boxed in!* He called out to the driver, "Talk to me. Where ya hit?" Silence. Fuller turned his attention back to the first sniper. At that moment, he saw the sniper run and crouch behind another tree. Fuller leveled his rifle and waited in anticipation. Seconds later, the sniper jumped out and sprinted across the pasture toward another tree. This time the General was ready, his finger firmly on the trigger.

Peering through his telescope, he allowed the exact lead between the man and the crosshairs. He continued to squeeze the trigger. The rifle recoiled, discharging another batch of rounds. Through his telescope, Fuller saw blood splash from the back of the man's head. The sniper spun around clockwise. His rifle flew off to the side, and he dropped to the ground.

Fuller's Expert Rifleman badge on his chest was symbolic, attesting to years of high scores on the rifle range. And in combat, there's no denying his kills were real. Like an uncanny haunting from the past, the park's fusillade mimicked the historic Battle of Bull Run. More vividly, it reeked of bloody wars that Fuller had fought, alongside buddies whose lives were snuffed out with no warning.

But Fuller had no time to savor this scant victory. Another rifle shot blasted out of the forest. A cartridge buzzed by his left ear and ricocheted off a boulder.

Fuller spotted a shallow culvert fifteen yards away, near the front of the limo. He sprung to his feet and sprinted toward the convenient trench. Diving headfirst, he curled his chin into his chest, somersaulted in mid-air, and slammed his left arm to the ground to break the fall. He ended up flat out on his back—a maneuver resulting from the general's reflexive judo skills.

He rolled into a prone position and lifted his head to look around. His rifle propped up, he hunkered down, again sighting the carbine crosshairs. He glanced toward the driver on the pavement. The agent was silent, motionless.

The agile Marine nestled in the crevice and faced the sniper in the woods. Luckily, the trench was over a foot deep with pasture grass a foot high, providing cover for his long, bulky body. He peered over his rifle and again surveyed the line of trees, about 100 yards away.

He searched the dense forest for the hidden enemy—very quiet, very dark, very vulnerable—just like Nam. The only thing missing was the distinct sound of the UH-1 Huey rotor blades flapping in the distance. Combative juices flowing, the general's innate instincts for survival had reached a peak.

He aimed at the tree line, squeezed the trigger and the rifle violently pumped another burst of rounds. The loud noise from his carbine echoed against the scenic Virginia forest. Still no movement, no return fire. Fuller checked his watch. The dial read 11:15, and no sign of Garrity. They're late!

An image suddenly appeared from the wooded area. The shooter emerged from behind the line of trees but quickly vanished in a cluster of tall grass. Fuller pulled the trigger and fired into the grass. The sniper fired back. A bullet whizzed by and punctured the soft Virginia soil just inches away. Out of the corner of his eye, Fuller glanced at the bullet hole and winced. He angled his head on the rifle stock, peered down the sight, and slowly squeezed the trigger. *Click!* Out of ammo. It was a death notice. The general was covered in sweat, and his body shivered.

Within seconds, the sound of Garrity's car resonated in the woods. A quick calculation told Fuller they were several minutes away. *What to do? I can't run—I'd be an easy target. The best bet is to play dead and hope to hell Garrity's bunch shows up in time.* It was an excruciating waiting game.

To position for a better line of sight, Fuller rolled over on his back, feet at the forest side. Lying quietly, he heard footsteps in the thick underbrush, creeping at first, but the sniper soon broke into a zigzag jog. The footfalls and the crackle of underbrush became closer.

The cagey gunman slowed to a walk, more like a crawl. To Fuller, the footsteps were like drumbeats. He felt his bowels tighten, and he was screaming inside.

Judging from the roar of Garrity's car, Fuller estimated they were still a minute or two away. Outta time.

The gunman stopped, cautiously stepped closer, then stopped again. Fuller was dead motionless. Through slits in his eyelids, Fuller could see the blurred silhouette of the man standing to the left of his outstretched legs. More vividly, he saw a long rifle pointed directly at his nose. *Here we go!*

Fuller reached up with his right hand with catlike speed, grabbed the rifle barrel, and pulled it down across his body. The rifle fired inches away from his head with a deafening blast.

The bullet drilled into the ground just under his armpit. He grunted, pivoted his right leg up, and swiftly kicked the bent-over assailant in the head. The sniper groaned and let go of his rifle. In nanoseconds, Fuller sprang to his feet and assumed a karate stance.

The hit man babbled incoherently. He shook his head to regain his faculties. He was Chinese—a *big* Chinese.

33

WASHINGTON, D.C.

Locked in a chilling stare, Fuller and the hit man stood face to face. Hands crimped karate style, they maneuvered in a circle, arms in motion.

The Chinese shouted, lurched forward, and threw a hard karate chop to the neck. Fuller took one step back, raised his leg parallel to the ground, and rammed his foot into the gangster's throat.

The blow stopped the man in his tracks. He clutched his throat with both hands, and gurgled, gasping for air. His larynx had collapsed.

Seizing an opportunity to finish him off, General Fuller cocked his right arm back, bent his palm upward, and curled his fingertips to deliver a punch. He intended to drive the man's nose bone into his brain with the heel of his palm. But the general hesitated, then changed his mind. He clenched his meaty fist, stepped forward, and threw a powerful right cross, hitting the sniper squarely on his left temple.

Instantly paralyzed, the man's legs buckled, and he dropped heavily to the ground. His body stiffened, and his left leg twitched profusely. Finally, Senator Garrity's car drove up. Fuller heard the tires screech on the asphalt road. With pistol held high, a bodyguard came running.

"Jesus! What's going on, General?"

"Two assassins, after Lame Duck." Fuller nodded towards the man on the ground. Then he turned and pointed to the sniper in the field. "Another one out there. Think he's dead."

Fuller leaned over the sniper on the ground. He unbuttoned his camouflage jacket and ripped open his olive-green undershirt. "Triad. He's a freakin Triad. Look at the tattoos." Star-like tattoos covered each shoulder, signifying a high-ranking officer. His mean, ruddy face was scarred.

Fuller pointed at the agent behind the car. "Take care of him. He's still alive."

After checking the downed agent, the bodyguard radioed his partner. "Attacked by assassins. One of ours dead, one wounded. Get the hell outta here!"

After a short pause, the voice from the radio said, "The senator says negative. He wants to go through with the meeting. Secure the area and report when clear." Garrity figured as long as the area was clear, it would be better to make the meeting now rather than chance another rendezvous or forego the meeting altogether.

"No, no. Go, go!" the bodyguard insisted.

Moments later, the radio voice came again. "Still wants to go through with it."

Reluctantly, the bodyguard responded, "Roger, we'll secure the area." First, they called the local police, and an ambulance was dispatched. Then the lead bodyguard went to check on the sniper in the field. After inspecting the results of Fuller's marksmanship, he trotted back and said, "The guy's a goner. A bloody socket where his right eye was and a gaping hole in the back of his head." The agent rounded his thumb and index finger together, illustrating a large hole. "Good shot, General." He turned towards the man on the ground. "And a good street fighter!"

Fuller grinned modestly. "Don't know 'bout that. After that little fracas, I'm deaf in one ear, and I think I broke my freakin' hand!" He chuckled softly, brushed his uniform off, and picked up his smoldering cigar. "Can't let a good Partagas go to waste." He pulled out his Zippo, flipped the lid back with a clink, and sparked the wick. He re-lit the expensive cigar, puffed a few times, and went to check on Lame Duck.

The bodyguard radioed Garrity's car. "Area secured, proceed with caution."

Garrity's Lincoln Continental limousine eased up and stopped near the scene. The lead bodyguard approached Fuller. "Sorry, sir, need to check him out first."

Fuller opened the back door of the limo where Lame Duck was now sitting upright.

The bodyguard got inside and frisked the man from Beijing. He nodded, then stepped out of the limo and gave a signal.

Senator Garrity made his way to the car and slipped into the back seat with Lame Duck. Fuller stubbed out his cigar and followed. "Kent, let me introduce Mr. Wang Zhang—otherwise known as Lame Duck."

Garrity shook hands with Zhang and exchanged greetings with the friendly agent.

"My pleasure to meet you," Zhang said. He was wearing sunglasses. Zhang appeared tentative, preoccupied, and distant. He had small bandages near the corners of his eyes and on his chin. Zhang removed his sunglasses, as politeness required, exposing shades of purple under his eyes. He nodded vigorously, showing a great degree of respect for the two American leaders. He smiled broadly and bobbed his head again. "Sorry for the trouble, Chet."

"No sweat," said Fuller. "Frankly, I haven't had this much fun since Nam." The remark prompted small grins from the men, an understanding of camaraderie among warriors.

Zhang was short and stocky in his late fifties. He had tiny sprinkles of gray in his thick, smoky black hair. The skin on his square face was smooth and unblemished; probably from Jilin Province, near the Korean border. He wore an oversized charcoal trench coat and the familiar golf cap.

Garrity furrowed his brow, cocked his head, and said, "Wang Zhang,

Wang Zhang? Isn't that the name of—"

"That's right, the missing Wang Zhang, the executive with the import-export company. The man who got kidnapped in San Francisco," Fuller acknowledged.

"I'll be," Garrity mumbled in amazement. "Nice job, Chet! You faked out a lot of people."

"Sorry to blind-side you on this, but the operation, code name Quick Change was touch-and-go. We had to impose tight security."

"I thought Lame Duck was military, PLA intelligence."

"He's military, all right. The PLA owns the import-export outfit Zhang headed up. They operate a ton of companies in China."

"I understand," Garrity said. "Christ, it's hard to tell who owns what! The state and the military still own a big chunk of the industry, and they're involved in a whole maze of joint venture deals."

Garrity glanced at Zhang. "What about protection?"

"He's in the witness protection program under a new identity.

Actually, he's wearing a bulletproof vest, and we gave him a piece to carry: a Smith & Wesson nine-millimeter, but we disarmed him before this meeting. We've also issued the usual gadgetry like Mace pepper foam with UV dye, an eighty-thousand-volt stun gun, and a set of Kevlar bulletproof seat covers for his car. He also chose to carry an Italian-made eight-inch stainless steel switchblade. He's fully armed all right!"

"Going to establish the usual?"

"The plan is to keep him secluded for at least six months before relocation. Then we'll set him up in a small business."

Zhang sat quietly and listened intently. Except for Fuller, he was somewhat uncomfortable and intimidated by his new *Meiguoren* comrades. "What's with the bandages?" Garrity said, studying Zhang's face.

"Plastic surgery. His eyes and chin were altered," Fuller replied.

"He's a new man!"

Garrity turned to the man from Beijing. "Well then, Mr. Zhang, how do you feel?"

Zhang dipped his head slightly. "Fine, sir. I need time to know America again. I like very much." He paused. "I am tired and weary now."

"We appreciate what you've done for us," Garrity said. "Especially concerning China's nuclear program."

"I have much more to say," Zhang replied. "Now I can report to you. One thing I learned: Beijing had the triad assassinate your President Chalmers."

"Are you sure about that?" Fuller said.

"Sure, sure," Zhang replied. "They want Mr. MacDuff to be in charge. China has many plans for the economy and nuclear weapons. Mr. Chalmers would be a problem. So, they kill him. They got a lot of spies all over the world. They help the enemies of America with nuclear weapons too much.

Big trouble, Chet. Big trouble!"

Fuller and Garrity gaped at each other. It was quiet for a few seconds.

Garrity asked, "Chet, what's his rank?"

"Full bird colonel."

"Colonel Zhang, thank you for the invaluable service you provided us," said Garrity. "I speak for the American people. You have endangered your life for our sake."

Zhang bowed his head sharply and grinned. "Thank you, Senator. When I come to college here, Texas A&M, I always love the American people, the freedom. In China, we are not free, really." Zhang lowered his eyes. He felt a twinge of remorse, but only for a second. He thought about the cultural differences between his homeland and America. "*Ch'i kan*-I am not worthy," he mumbled. "But I must return to America. In China, there's *Luan*, how you say, political chaos, corruption. There, I am a dead man."

"A&M, that's where Zhang and I first met," Fuller blustered in an attempt to lighten the atmosphere. "His American name was Wayne Zhang, and we used to hang out, go to ball games together. I was a short-timer, but we were both in the Corps of Cadets." He paused. "Go, Aggies!" Fuller roared. The group of men chuckled.

Garrity grinned and did a thumbs-up. He turned to Fuller. "He'll be debriefed soon?"

"Yes. We'll compile a full report." Fuller put on a serious face. "The situation is getting worse. I think Beijing's talking to El-Kansi. That partnership spells bad news."

Garrity turned to Zhang. "Glad you're with us, Colonel." Zhang nodded thankfully.

34

THAAD DV-8 SITE, OSLO, NORWAY

In the midst of the loud, garrulous fanfare, Dean shouted into the phone, "Karina, you should be here. You're the lady of the day!" Karina's solution to the AMOEBA computer problem gave cause for the THAAD crew to celebrate. Her discovery of the hidden code was a tremendous victory. Tests confirmed the characteristics of the bug.

Thrilled, Karina smiled broadly. "I'm flattered, but we still have a way to go."

"I realize that, but I wanted you to enjoy a moment of glory. You should be here, with us."

"I would like to be there, mainly with you—for more reasons than one," Karina said in a breathy voice.

Dean organized and mobilized an implementation team. Concurrently, Karina e-mailed the fix to Lindsey, who was developing an installation program to invoke the fix.

The conversion routine would streamline the process, minimize mistakes and salvage valuable time. Karina's fix program would monitor the system's clock and BIOS date functions. If an error should occur, the fix routine would immediately correct it.

Considering the catastrophic effects computer failures would have on world financial markets, NetForum's special EFT task force assigned top priority to the AMOEBA project. A flurry of e-mails addressed impending issues. The momentum eventually attracted the help of more technicians.

Meanwhile, Dante Martin monitored the group's progress. The overwhelming interest was extremely encouraging. It sparked a renewed source of confidence in the project. Martin felt he was on the cusp of successfully pulling it together again.

The NetForum EFT task force had galvanized a massive number of resources to work on the MEGA-Star plague. They joined up with ComTech's Omega-Alpha team. The force was now large enough to implement an AMOEBA fix worldwide, at little cost to ComTech.

All told, there were more than 1,300 highly qualified computer professionals working on the project. To Lindsey and Martin, it was like manna from heaven. Finally, resolving the problem and neutralizing Lee Redding was within reach. A strong sense of enthusiasm rapidly built within the ComTech camp. The group quickly set the project and allocated parts of the code to team leaders.

A virtual project was established, utilizing volunteers in every corner of the world. They formed an intranet—a private communications network—to maintain tight security, control, and integrity.

Bruce Lindsey then organized a NetForum task force to deploy the fix. He broadcasted a questionnaire in search of system locations, the highest priority being military sites. He communicated with NetForum members in China, Russia, North Korea, India, Iran, Iraq, and other countries known to have missile systems. He instructed all NetForum members to plan and execute a massive worldwide notification program about the fix, using whatever local media available. The fix would be deployed using secured file transfers over the special intranet. A code message *Priority Red* was broadcast to all NetForum members. In another broadcast aimed specifically at heads of nations, the names of respective NetForum contacts were listed. They assigned a contact to appropriate government departments, and supervise the effort. Members formed local citizen action groups. Using their influential contacts, they convinced officials in missile-laden countries to participate in the effort.

Fear of a nuclear war was widespread.

Dean's team was hard at work installing the AMOEBA fix at the THAAD-DV8 site. Short of time, they opted to do the install without testing.

Dean advised the team, "The estimated install time is ten minutes from the 219 time the system is shut down. This means we will not be operational for at least seven minutes into the New Year."

The control room was quiet. Team members cringed with worry. One man gazed at his notepad and nervously doodled. The possible consequences of crossing over into new, untested waters were daunting.

11:50:19 pm, GREENWICH MEAN TIME

The crew completed shutdown procedures on the system. "All logs cleared, files rehashed, execute shutdown sequence," announced the supervisor, Jack Stracker. Technicians sat at their workstations in a maze of flickering screens around the room.

The control room was concentric, stretched out in a giant wagon wheel configuration. The main computer server represented the hub of the wheel in the center of the room. Surrounding the hub were ten monitors sitting on countertops. Thick operating manuals lined the overhead shelves like literary soldiers standing at attention.

Some monitors glowed with multi-colored block charts. On others, columns of ciphered numbers reflected off the sweaty faces of technicians staring at their screens. Wearing lightweight earphones linked to the launch pads, the engineers spoke into tubular boom mikes and tapped computer keys in rapid succession.

"Shutdown complete. Prepare for installation," Stracker commanded.

Like a pressure-cooker, the room was filled with fever-pitch tension.

11:55:30 pm, GREENWICH MEAN TIME

Engineers gazed at monitors. Perspiration covered their faces. It was risky. A myriad of things could go wrong. For one, several relays were leading to the radar sites, and a failure at any point would break the connection. This could set off a string of war alerts.

On the main monitor, the dialogue messages appeared sequentially: the FIRST STAGE DONE! CLICK NEXT TO PROCEED.

Stracker moved his mouse, pointed it, and clicked NEXT. He glanced at the clock on the wall—it unceremoniously ticked past midnight. Several technicians glanced at the time, rolled their eyes, and sighed. Others anxiously flipped through installation manuals in anticipation of what might happen next. After several long seconds, the control monitors displayed the message: SYSTEM ACQUIESCANT—CONNECTING REMOTE UNITS.

WUZHAI MISSILE AND SPACE CENTER, SITE #5, WUZHAI, CHINA

Like diamonds in an ocean of darkness, the sky was studded with stars. Whereas deep below the horizon, giant nuclear harpoons pointed at the heavens. The spine-chilling missiles were encoded for disaster. The clock inside the MEGA-Star computer had advanced past midnight. Without warning, the AMOEBA virus clobbered the system. Erroneous signals triggered the automatic firing sequence. Two nuclear missiles were ready to be launched—Missile #1 was programmed for Wall Street, and Missile #2 was aimed at the Pentagon. Sirens wailed. Metal doors slammed shut, alarm bells rang, and red lights pulsated. Camouflaged dome panels, topping the cryptic silos, peeled back and disappeared into the landscape. A minute later, a deafening rocket blast shook the earth as the first missile ignited. Seconds later, Missile #2 fired.

Streams of bright orange flames violently spewed from the rockets. Billows of gray smoke engulfed the launch pad. The ICBMs slowly lifted from their moorings, lumbered away inch by inch, toward the tranquil sky. At a nearby airbase, Chinese pilots scrambled to their Russian-made Sukhoi30 jet fighter-bombers.

Hysterical Chinese soldiers scurried in crisscrossed paths pulling levers, shouting orders, and seeking cover from an invisible "enemy attack." A rotund Chinese officer yelled at a sergeant, berating him for being away from his post. The sergeant, standing face-to-face with his superior, was a slight man with a narrow, pockmarked face. He was shaking in his boots. His gut fermented just short of upchucking. "*Hao! Shur, shur,*" he stammered. "*Okay! Yes, yes.*" His head pounded with fear and frustration. He did an about-face and rushed to investigate the emergency.

At an altitude of 2,000 feet, the missiles rapidly built-up velocity from the 27,000 pounds of thrust generated by the GE X-405 rockets. At 4,000 feet and building to a speed faster than light, the weapons angled towards North America. With pinpoint precision, the satellite-driven Global Positioning System would guide the warheads directly to the strike zone. GPS figured time within a millionth of a second, velocity within a fraction of a mile per hour, and target location within a few meters. *These missiles were objects of a final battle.*

At the THAAD DV-8 site, the main monitor displayed two buttons: FINISH and BACK. Stracker clicked FINISH. "Install complete!" he happily announced over the PA.

Cheers and laughter at CR base headquarters and site number ten was deafening. Stracker immediately notified the Norwegian MOD and other officials, the White House and General Fuller. Lindsey and Omega Alpha team members were keeping abreast of their counterparts across the globe. They had a videoconference link with the DV-8 site. But the joy was short-lived.

Moments after the broadcast, several large red beacons mounted on the ceiling lit up and rotated. Ear-piercing sirens blared. Faces dropped. The festive mood had reverted to intense fear. Someone hit a button to stop the sirens.

The radar screens eerily displayed two moving objects: the ICBMs from China were tracking on course. The projectiles were at an altitude of 500 miles, six seconds apart. The missiles' geographical position was fifteen degrees latitude north and thirty-seven degrees longitude west, just off Spain's southwestern coast.

The monitor flashed: ESTIMATED FLIGHT TIME TO TARGETS: 7 MINUTES 12 SECONDS.

The DV-8 crew scurried to their battle stations. The alert message to Norway's MOD was transmitted: *Quick alert! Quick alert! Two bogeys off the coast of Spain; trajectory heading, continental U.S. Request counterfire!*

Simultaneously, a crew member transmitted the quick alert to the NORAD Command Center in the U.S.

NORAD, located in the subterranean maze in Cheyenne Mountain, Colorado, acknowledged the message. "Roger, THAAD. Understand two bogeys heading continental U.S. Request counterfire. Standby." The high-tech facility was designed and equipped to deal with Armageddon-type wars—the so-called Star Wars.

NORAD immediately sent an alert to the Advanced Missile Warning Center, which circulated the THAAD site's message. They communicated the entire process of confirmation and issuance of counterattack preparedness within four minutes. NORAD also notified U.S. officials at the White House and the Pentagon.

President MacDuff briefly deliberated with his advisors. Despite their advice, he chose to make a safe, political decision. He issued a proxy order through NORAD to Norway, giving them the authority to order a counterattack "at their discretion."

The Norwegian MOD could fire at will, potentially starting World War Three.

Meanwhile, General Fuller had closely monitored the work being done in the Omega-Alpha project. When notified of the threat, Fuller promptly contacted Martin at ComTech. He requested his immediate assistance in repairing the main system at Zulu-Zulu 99 in Norfolk, Virginia.

As part of the THAAD defense network, the Norfolk site controlled the eastern seaboard defense radar perimeter. The MEGA-Star computer was responsible for launching counterattack missiles.

Having followed the building drama of the impending disaster,

Norway's MOD hastily reached a decision: "Fire at will!" Then he gave the cipher lock release code to Stracker, "Code 465-0730."

Stracker punched in the code and shouted, "Fire one!" Precisely two seconds later, he ordered, "Fire two!" Another two seconds, and he roared, "Fire three!"

They had launched state-of-the-art MIM-99 *Eagle* anti-nuclear missiles. The two ICBMs and the Eagle missiles resembled tiny white bugs crawling toward each other on the radar screens. And the five ghostly dots bleeped across the display at a steady pace.

The Number One Eagle closed in on the Chinese ICBM. Flying on course, the Number One Eagle appeared to be heading straight for the target. Dead silence.

"Detonate," the launch engineer proclaimed.

Surprisingly, when the Eagle was to strike, the two targets were still on the screen. Instead of exploding, it zoomed right past the ICBM!

It was a miss.

35

WUZHAI MISSILE AND SPACE CENTER, WUZHAI, CHINA

Set off by the failure of the radar control units, shrill alarm bells rang violently.

Sergeant Hui, the senior engineer at the center, was bewildered by the mysterious missile launchings. Having shaken off the reprimand by his superior, he regained control of his frenzied troops. He ordered an examination of the erratic computer systems.

Nestled on Beijing's northern outskirts, the site monitored the air defense radar along China's eastern border. The colossal facility was lit up with color monitors, flickering control panels, and bright overhead spotlights.

In an uncanny sense, the radiant complex resembled a giant Christmas tree's entrails, decorated by the sheen of modern instrumentation. The Russians, OIC nations, and profit-minded Western countries had endowed the Chinese with much of their technology.

The octagonal-shaped, thirty-foot-high room housed China's latest radar and missile systems. A collage of control units was linked to the remote missile launch pads. High above, near the ceiling, a large screen projected a video of the missiles. The backdrop wall was plastered with large, colorful Chinese war slogans.

Behind a half-moon-shaped row of monitors, racks of computers and modems were inside a secured room. A group of high-strung technicians alternatively sighted monitors and the video screen, fingering keyboards.

They attempted to make ready the apocalyptic weapons for a counterattack.

Puzzled by the rapid turn of events, technicians laboriously worked on the idle computers. Hui finally discovered part of the problem. When they launched ICBMs, a drain on the electrical system—a brownout—had shut down a network segment. Hui recycled the power, deactivated the remaining ICBMs, and resumed his investigation of the "invasion." But they could not find the cause for the accidental launch without innate knowledge of the MEGA-Star CPU chip.

When the clock ticked past midnight on the key date of December 31st, the control unit defaulted to a false state. When in a false state, the system had interpreted signals from radar sensors incorrectly, indicating multiple unidentified missiles were penetrating the defense zone.

The condition triggered the AMOEBA time bomb.

The key-date algorithm circumvented a launch wait period, causing the missiles to fire instantaneously. Even if the Chinese had discovered the fault, they did not possess the knowledge or skills to correct it.

During the mayhem, communications with top Chinese officials were botched. In fact, a *War Alert Briefcase*, carried by the Chinese minister of defense, contained deactivation codes that could've averted the catastrophe. But the host MEGA-Star machine also controlled the briefcase.

GENERAL FULLER'S PENTAGON OFFICE

"There's a helluva lot of confusion over the missile firing," the CIA analyst reported to Fuller. "Get this—Beijing thinks Taiwan was behind it. They reasoned that Taiwan was using reunification talks as a smokescreen and actually played a part in the attack."

"What? Taiwan attack them?" Fuller shrugged. "What are they thinking? Beijing is overreacting. Things have flared up before, and we've been able to moderate the situation."

"They think it was a conspiracy—essentially a U.S.-backed offensive," the CIA specialist said.

"This vendetta has been going on for over 50 years now—fifty since their civil war. Why the hell would anyone force the issue now?"

"Remember when Taiwan's President, Lee Teng-hui, pushed for state-to-state relations with the mainland?" the analyst asked. "Not all Taiwanese agreed. Over the years, Beijing agents organized a Taiwanese group who protested this policy—they wanted to keep the one-China status. In truth, Beijing has had a subversive political initiative going in Taiwan for at least a couple of decades, using operatives in high positions of influence."

"And they're pretty damned strong."

"Beijing has Taiwanese agents spying for them across the globe." The CIA specialist paused. "And the OCBs. They've amalgamated overseas Taiwanese together with Mainlanders in the U.S."

Fuller paused briefly. "And they succeeded. They reshaped Taiwan's politics, psychologically swaying them to Beijing."

The CIA analyst nodded. "And so, down deep, they've leaned towards reunification in some form."

Fuller nodded. "Yeah. Always had that nagging feeling..."

"Here's the picture," the analyst said. "They did it in two stages. First, they maintained the status quo—you know, bickering back and forth. Then insurgents gradually penetrated politics and converted the Taiwanese over to the Beijing side. We've had our finger on that pulse for a long time but weren't sure how things would end up. Actually, they surprised us! All they needed was a trigger, and that snafu missile-firing served the purpose."

"What a freaking mess," Fuller said. "It's still weird, the Chinese figuring we attacked them. Why would we want to start a war with them—a quarter of the world's population?"

"It doesn't make sense. But the Chinese have been paranoid about a lot of things lately," the agent responded. "They don't have a good feel for where we stand. And maybe, just maybe, it's the fact that we haven't paid them off—in other words, placated them—keeping them docile in their nuclear threat. Otherwise, they're set on a military buildup, especially their navy, which is far bigger than ours."

"Good point," said Fuller.

The agent continued, "There's been some doubt about us really favoring a one–China arrangement. I can see how they might be suspicious. We say the words, but we've lacked follow-through. Our foreign policies have confused them."

"Reminds me of a similar incident—NATO's accidental bombing of China's embassy in Belgrade. I still get pissed when I think about how Beijing claimed it was intentional. A freaking ruse. On top of that, we paid them four and a half million dollars."

The analyst gave a small chuckle. "In this case, Beijing thought we were in a conspiracy with Taiwan. Go figure."

"Not too surprising after all," the general replied. "Think about it. For years, while in China's intimidating shadow, Taiwan managed to walk a thin tight rope. This was okay as long as we defended them. "Then, Taiwan got overly confident and abandoned the one-China policy, proclaiming de facto status as a nation-state. Beijing warned they were playing with fire."

The analyst nodded his agreement.

"Beijing construed this as a bold, strictly pro-West attitude," Fuller went on, "and hypothetically, they could reason a joint U.S.-Taiwanese attack wouldn't be out of the question."

"And when Taiwan made a move, Beijing was convinced they secured our military support, including nuclear weapons. I don't know why their agents didn't dispel the theory."

Fuller shifted nervously in his chair. "I think our administration spawned this whole notion. We screwed up royally. After Taiwan made its proclamation of independence, we mishandled the whole freaking deal.

"The president gave a lot of lip service and no firm action. He touted Taiwan as a symbol of democracy in the region, but it backfired. We let it happen. We forced them into a corner. Consequently, we ended up on the bad side of both China and Taiwan."

The analyst said, "This sounds quirky, but when Taiwan became aware of China's attack, maybe they thought we schemed the encouragement of China to conquer them. This, of course, would've simplified our relations with China: no need to be a big brother to Taiwan."

"Hard to figure," the general said, shaking his head. "Taiwan has been in the middle of a fragile situation for a long time. Maybe they just got paranoid." He recalled when the U.S. tried to include Taiwan under the Theatre Missile Defense system, and Beijing strongly protested. They demanded we exclude the island from the defense umbrella and stop selling arms to Taiwan."

"Our Taiwan relations have soured," the specialist said. "Beijing has been adamant on the issue of Taiwan. However, in the economic revolution, Beijing's Communist Party's grip on power became fragile. It's an anomaly—we ought not to overestimate its strength, nor underestimate it. It doesn't all add up."

"Frankly, nothing has to add up when stuff like this happens," Fuller responded. "The president has resisted providing arms to Taiwan, implied contempt, and got in bed with Beijing. What else is Taiwan to think? The sweetheart deals, the payoffs, and the high-tech transfers to the mainland were proof enough."

"And now, it backfired on us," the specialist said. "After the accidental missile launch and a brief skirmish, Taiwan and China declared a cease-fire. Then Beijing's operatives on both sides of the strait headed it off and put the deal together."

"All over a mishap!" exclaimed Fuller.

"Yes, sir, how true. Then there's the matter of Taiwan's investment in the mainland. They provide China over sixty billion dollars in hard currency every year."

"A serious factor," said Fuller. "Beijing had to have known Taiwan was not a principal in the attack." The general shrugged his shoulders. "Beijing's operatives succeeded. They convinced Taiwan to join the mainland and fight against the West. The missile accident was just a trigger."

Fuller paused. He looked troubled. "What about our troops in Taiwan? What's the status?"

"Sorry, General," the analyst said solemnly. "One of the first actions taken by Taiwan was to round them up and hold them hostage. But, as far as we know, they're still alive. They're okay."

Fuller snarled, "I knew this would happen. Damn the politics! We'll have to go in and get them. And I don't care what anybody says."

The CIA specialist bowed his head, turned away, and thought for a moment. He returned his attention to Fuller. "It may not be that simple, General. The situation has totally changed."

"Whaddya mean?"

"Consider this. China is now the big kid on the planet. And reports are they're getting North Korea and Russia to join them."

"Okay. So, it's happening. The power forces are uniting."

"Yes. All these years, Russia has never forgotten our Korean War involvement and its goal to 'bury the U.S.' The first step was joining China in the Shanghai Cooperation Alliance."

The U.S. administration had ignored the systemic repression in China—Beijing's reluctance to proclaim a free Tibet, their nuclear arms buildup, and China's unfair competition in business. These were all signs of a self-centered, arrogant Beijing regime. U.S. businessmen complained China's markets were largely still closed, and the military buildup in the region was threatening their investments.

China had not been trustworthy.

For the past twenty years, China had exported dangerous weapons to enemies of the U.S. At a minimum, China supplied nuclear reactors and bomb designs, ring magnets to enrich uranium, and technical knowledge to produce nuclear weapons. China has sold nuclear reactors and uranium enrichment equipment to rogue nations, along with Silkworm ground-based anti-ship missiles and chemical weapons.

Fuller had a nagging sensation. *Is war imminent?* All that night, he meditated in his office.

Encouraged by the turn of events, the United Arab Front rallied its forces. They busily recruited: all the League of Arab Nations, China, Russia, and others—not knowing China, and Russia had their own motives.

Central to the UAF's strategy was the use of terrorists such as Iran's Hizballah Ummah, which had already established its network of cells across the U.S. Not surprisingly, El-Kansi emerged as one of its top officers and the chief strategist in the takeover movement.

The OIC officially joined the UAF, providing funds and augmenting UAF military forces. Predictably, they immediately threatened to shut off oil supplies and the EFT operation.

No one could have fathomed such an extraordinary predicament. China, North Korea, Russia, and the UAF forces were now unified. They were poised to launch a joint offensive against the West. Peace talks were not an option.

A nuclear war hung in the balance.

36

CRITICAL MISHAPS

Holy moly!" The technician's voice was strident, tight with stress. Everyone stopped as if frozen in time. The control room was shrouded in a blanket of tension. The wired-up crew watched in amazement as the Number One Eagle missed the target.

They peered at the two radar blips on the flickering screens, anxiously anticipating the electronic drama. The Number Two Eagle missile slowly merged with the *Number Two* ICBM. A final bright glow flared on the display, then faded away.

It was a hit!

But sudden relief turned into an instant panic.

To everyone's surprise, the Number Three Eagle veered off course and missed the other ICBM. The crew speculated the explosion disturbed the onboard radar device, causing the missile to veer off course.

But wait, the Number One ICBM had also changed directions. It turned north, towards the North Pole. It was flying away from the U.S. coast!

Another wave of relief swept across the room.

"A reprieve, guys," Stracker said evenly. "We've got some time to recover."

Emotionally drained, the men helplessly gaped at the solo white bug inching to the north. The stress was too much for some. One man felt dizzy and lay down on the floor. For others, the thought of a missile hitting the U.S. brought tears to their eyes.

At other THAAD sites, the bug fix effort was going painfully slower than expected. They needed extra time. The missile path to the north offered no guarantees. The hope was the missile would fall on an unpopulated, desolate area. There was also a very slight chance the missile would run out of fuel. Everyone was in quiet anticipation.

THAAD SITE ZULU-ZULU 99, NORFOLK, VIRGINIA

THAAD technicians at site Zulu-Zulu 99 previously tried to use the new MEGA-Star.1 chip to no avail. However, General Fuller, heavily involved in coordinating the effort, gave them the new AMOEBA fix program. He arranged for Lindsey and Martin to provide technical assistance.

As a backup plan, Fuller alerted commanders at Andrews AFB in Maryland, Cherry Point MCAS in North Carolina, Beaufort MCAS, and Charleston AFB to deploy missile interception. These facilities were equipped with the *Sidewinder*, the *Sparrow*, and the *Phoenix* air-to-air missiles.

The intense scene at the Oslo site was mirrored at the Zulu-Zulu 99 sites. The tedious process of installing the MEGA-Star fix was still underway. The Zulu-Zulu 99 CR resembled the one in Oslo. In fact, it served as the base model, with some exceptions.

Norfolk was lined with a three-inch steel wall and situated in a forty-foot-deep underground bunker. A square, red-brick administrative office building, surrounded by a fifteen-foot chain-link fence topped with barbed wire, sat inconspicuously at ground level. A fingerprint/voice recognition system secured access to the facility. Only personnel with special privileges could enter. Management officials escorted visitors.

In Norfolk, the CR buzzed with chatter, computer fan sounds, and Bud Mintzer's announcements, the supervisor. They were in the final stages of the install.

The monitor glowed, FIRST STAGE DONE. CLICK NEXT TO PROCEED. As the supervisor clicked NEXT, all personnel were standing at their battle stations, ready to act when queued. In the meantime, radar systems were inactive, and incoming ICBM was not being tracked. After excruciating minutes of waiting, the main monitor displayed CLICK FINISH TO COMPLETE. The supervisor clicked FINISH. The system sluggishly performed a file check and displayed: ENTER TIME. Mintzer keyed in the correct time: 23:38:44 EST.

The control panel monitors printed the message, ALL SYSTEMS ACQUIESCANT. There was a cautious sigh of relief. Gradually, the radar scene brightened with a single white image. It was vectored at 25,000 feet heading north. The fatigued crew watched the white blip inch towards the North Pole.

Suddenly, faces were contorted in horror. The ICBM strayed off course again! The crew stared at the missile as it made a wide turn to the west. "It turned again," the duty engineer shouted. "The bogey made a turn to the west!"

The runaway warhead continued the turn and straightened with a southwesterly heading, towards the U.S. Frustratingly, it was out of range. No U.S.-controlled missile defense stations were able to strike. Mintzer executed the normal procedure: he verified the president and General Fuller were informed and requested another clearance for a counterattack. He connected with the White House within seconds. But the president and vice president could not be reached.

He switched to General Fuller's home. With the red phone pressed to his ear, he radioed the secretary of defense, Charles Atkins, who gave him approval.

Meanwhile, the MEGA-Star system faltered. It was giving erroneous radar readings, then shutting down altogether. The incoming radar site data was automatically rerouted to a backup system. But it failed too. Data was again rerouted to yet another backup system. It indicated not one stray missile but a massive raid of ten missiles!

Was it a defective fix program? Or could it be one of the remote radar units in the field?

No time to prognosticate. Mintzer chose to reinstall the fix program. He promptly began the process. But not before the false raid was transmitted to U.S. military bases around the country, initializing a Quick Alert status.

In the confusion, a SAC duty officer directed all standby B52 crews to man their aircraft and start their engines—a total of 100 airplanes. But none of the aircraft took off. NORAD and THAAD had communicated a false alarm, but at the same time, verified the Chinese ICBM code named "NX2" was still flying toward the U.S.

At last, Mintzer completed the installation. The monitor read: CLICK FINISH TO COMPLETE. Mintzer clicked FINISH. This time, the remote radar units connected without a problem. The main monitor positioned the renegade missile 800 miles from the U.S. border.

And then, without warning, the radar screen faded like a worn-out picture tube. "System failure!" the supervisor cried out, cursing under his breath. He knew a whole process of diagnostics would have to be done.

Mintzer ordered network engineers to run programs against the AMOEBA fix program, a long, arduous task. Luckily, within the hour, his crew found the problem and came up with a logic patch. After the system came up, the radar screens illuminated the Chinese ICBM, now at less than 300 miles off the U.S. coast!

A Secret Service agent was cuffed to a nuclear briefcase with the day's cipher lock codes in Washington. His orders were to be no more than three seconds away from the president at all times. When contacted about the impending threat, the agent responded, "The president is being contacted— standby one." Five seconds, ten seconds, fifteen seconds, twenty seconds.

Exasperated, Mintzer howled, "Listen up—we need to fire these missiles. We'll be blown to smithereens!"

Finally, the president approved the order to fire. Fuller had had his nuclear briefcase opened and ready, so he intervened and gave the order. He shouted in a booming voice, "Zulu-Zulu 99 abort Able One, go to Bravo Two!" Without missing a beat, Fuller issued the command: "Niner-niner zero, two five eight. Fire!"

Mintzer entered the cipher lock code 990-258 and ordered the launch. He lifted the security caps covering the firing button. The seasoned veteran sang out in cadence, "Fire one! Fire two! Fire three!" Huge puffs of gray smoke smothered the launch pads at coastal missile site Zulu-Zulu 99.

In pursuit of salvation, three phallic-like MIM-99 Eagle missiles trudged through the black sky.

37

THAAD SITE ZULU-ZULU 99, NORFOLK, VIRGINIA

Like three white bugs attacking a larger white bug, the Eagle missiles converged on the Number One Chinese ICBM. The gap slowly closed. They clashed.

The screen flashed a brilliant splash the size of a quarter. Then it disappeared. The Eagle missiles had knocked out the Number One ICBM! The earth-shattering explosion was widely seen and heard along the north-eastern coast.

Both control rooms rumbled with applause. The scene at each site was bedlam. People jumped for joy, hugged one another, slapped each other on the back, and high-fived. The nightmare was over. Bottles of champagne mysteriously appeared in Norway, and the U.S. crews at the sites toasted to victory.

Ron Blevins, a senior radar technician, plopped down at his workstation to drink a glass of champagne. Relaxed, he began to wonder what his wife and two young daughters were doing. Dealing with the missile crisis had urged him to call and tell them to take cover, though the danger zone was far away.

In times like these, crew members had to rely on local emergency systems to protect their loved ones from a strike. How widespread could it have been? Did the missile contain lethal chemicals? The danger of chemical and biological weapons is infinitely worse. But the public knows little to nothing about protecting themselves. He thought *we must overhaul our civil defense project with more education, prevention, and preparedness.*

Blevins noticed movement on the radar screen out the corner of his eye as he sipped from his glass. He turned toward the screen and was stunned. A small blip had appeared. It was inching toward the U.S. coast. He studied the dot closely. His heart pounded. Loose bomb. "It's a loose bomb!" he shouted. "The ICBM had multiple warheads!"

Blevins sounded the alarm. Sirens blared, and red lights rotated.

Startled, Mintzer yelled into the mike, "Battle stations! Battle stations! Quick alert!"

People looked at each other in shock. They scrambled back to their workstations.

"Course heading two hundred fifty miles east of Maine. Closing fast," Blevins said in a wavering voice. His hands were trembling.

"Ready firing sequence," Mintzer ordered. "Target locked," the fire leader replied.

"Niner-niner zero, two five eight. Fire!" Mintzer chanted.

The code was keyed into the computer, and he punched the red button. Nothing happened! The fire leader pushed it again. No contact. The control monitors reflected: INCORRECT CIPHER LOCK CODE.

"Wrong code!" Mintzer cried out. "Quick, get me the general." Seconds later, Fuller was on the phone.

"Sir, the missile had miniaturized, propelled warheads," Mintzer explained. "One broke loose, and we tried to shoot it down. But we had the wrong release code!"

"Stand by," the general said calmly. He put Mintzer on hold and called the Pentagon Command Center.

The unrelenting crew stuck to their monitors. They gawked at the small dot moving along the East Coast.

"Trajectory heading Maine, two hundred miles and closing," Blevins said.

Mintzer waited apprehensively, the phone pressed hard to his ear. His face was wrenched in fear. Sweat streamed down his face, his bloodshot eyes still alert.

The room was dead quiet. Elbows propped up on his desk, one man held his head in his hands with his eyes shut. Another made the sign of the cross. The crew watched helplessly as the bomb proceeded on its fatal path.

Fuller came back on the line. "Mintzer. New code, three four five-seven. I repeat, thirty-four fifty-seven."

"Got it." Mintzer turned and yelled, "Thirty-four fifty-seven. Fire!"

The fire leader keyed in the code. He pushed the red button. The screen displayed MISSILE NUMBER 4 LAUNCHED.

Mintzer did not fire a second missile. The approaching warhead —was already too close to land. Another missile would surely hit land.

Missile Number Four was the only chance of destroying the warhead– a slim chance.

The harmless-looking white dot crawled across the screen like a deadly spider. In contrast, the bigger missile Number Four was moving faster. But the gap was wide. Around the room, glasses of flat, fizzled-out champagne sat undisturbed. Crewmembers quietly consoled each other.

The number four missile closed in on the warhead, now forty-five miles from the U.S. coast. Would our missile catch up? No one was certain.

Blevins stared at the small white bug as it scaled across the screen. What size is this thing? Could it be a megaton, the power of one million tons of TNT? Or was it smaller? Is it nuclear, biological, chemical, or radiological? Will, it hit land or drop into the sea?

If it were nuclear, the initial radiation and residual radioactivity would be devastating in a populated area. The electromagnetic pulse associated with a nuclear explosion- could destroy or disrupt communications, and impair rescue operations. A large number of fatalities and long-term radiation effects would occur.

Sweat was pouring down his face, and Blevins's tired eyes

squinted at the screen. There was still a gap between the missile and the bomb. He faced reality. Time had run out. It sapped the energy from his body. His shoulders dropped. A chill crept down his spine. He watched the dot turn into a bright glow, then disappear. Resounding groans came from the crew.

Tears came to his eyes.

38

ELKINS, MAINE

The citizens of Elkins were unaware of their plight. They were in the direct path of the oncoming missile.

Radio and television stations sounded an emergency broadcast alert for the northeast coastal region. As much as they tried to mask it, the normally calm newscasters' voices were streaked with terror.

Residents from Maine to Virginia were instructed to seal their premises and take cover. Or evacuate to the nearest shelter.

By all standards, the residents of Elkins were affluent. The majority of its 6,575 citizens were in the upper-income bracket. Luxury homes with plush landscapes dotted the quaint town, the easternmost point of the U.S. Islands, peninsulas, coves, and bays profiled an irregular coastline. Picturesque harbors were colored with a marina and a series of piers and docks. The beautiful seascape offered a grand view of the ocean, a perfect gateway to Acadia National Park. But fate was fast approaching. Sadly, the tranquil setting would be abruptly demolished.

When the nuclear warhead exploded over the Atlantic, huge yellowish-orange flames sprayed the sky. A mass of black smoke ballooned as glowing cinders fanned out and fell into the ocean. The blast formed an aquatic crater 2,000 feet wide and 400 feet deep.

The ten-million-degree fireball raised a dome of water 250 feet high. The aftermath shock wave drove out air bubbles, turning the wavy surface into a layer of snow-white foam. A vortex of water shot straight up from the pit like a giant, spewing fire hose. The water spouted 700 feet in the air and was capped by a large, umbrella-like plume.

A frightening after-shock tremor shook the earth, clobbering a wide area of the eastern seaboard. Shock waves stretched as far as Washington, D.C. The tip of the Washington Monument cracked and shifted several inches off-center. In New York, high-rise buildings precariously swayed from side to side, shattering windowpanes throughout the city.

A gust of thermonuclear heat, traveling at over 250 miles per hour, flattened the islands near Elkins. Large trees were snapped and scorched like smoldering toothpicks.

The blast instantly killed two fishermen on the beach. The force blew them 100 yards from the beachhead. Shortly afterward, their lifeless bodies were buried in sand, washed up by the raging tidal wave that followed. The blinding flash and the rush of intense heat had melted their eyeballs. Shreds of singed clothing covered what flesh was left on their baked carcasses.

The wave of compressed, heated air swept through the town of Elkins like a hurricane. It shattered windows, scooped up cars, and bulldozed power line towers like toys. Downtown, tall buildings toppled over like dominoes. The force hurled tree limbs, rocks, broken glass, and other objects like shrapnel.

The only recognizable landmarks were a few concrete abutments and crumbled building foundations. Rubble covered the streets and, in some places, was piled over six feet high. Parked cars were crushed by falling buildings and buried by bricks and debris.

The electromagnetic pulse generated by the nuclear explosion caused an immediate blackout. Radio, television, electricity, and telephone lines were knocked out. Darkness enveloped the township.

Hours on end, disoriented people carrying flashlights and lanterns wandered around aimlessly. They searched for loved ones, belongings, or shelter. People shouted out names of the missing, only to hear no response.

Soon after, radiation-laced rain showered the area. The persistent rainfall leaked through the roofs of makeshift tents and seeped through the flooring. According to dosage, the fallout could cause anyone exposed to die a slow, painful death. Radiation collects in the body in several ways. It can be absorbed through the skin, inhaled, or eaten. When the accumulated amount reaches a certain level, radiation sickness is a disease that attacks the bone marrow and other parts of the body.

The people of Elkins were ravaged. Those who ingested the radiation would be tainted, deformed, or they would die. Radiation sickness causes nausea, vomiting, and diarrhea, followed by anemia, hair loss, skin sores, and infections. Victims would die from poison in the blood, lungs, and brain tissue. Over time, leukemia and other cancers would decimate the infected.

At the break of dawn, over half the population of Elkins was homeless. Makeshift emergency centers were set up in churches, schools, or any suitable building still standing. Supplies were trucked in. Nearby airports and other transportation systems were inoperable. Pandemonium prevailed at bus terminals, train stations, grocery stores, and gasoline stations.

The calamity had reduced many wealthy people to refugee status. They were battered and in a state of shock. They stood in lines waiting for food, water, and medical treatment. Children accustomed to getting anything they wanted squirmed and complained, having no idea of how to cope. They loathed standing in line, being without the modern comforts of life. Some eventually became vigilantes. Civil unrest and looting were spreading, and random fights broke out. Some took up arms, either for protection or for aggression.

An orderly evacuation had turned into panic. Desperate acts of survival led to the formation of plundering mobs. Neighbors became enemies. Rather than helping each other, people hoarded food and water and became self-centered. Within hours, hysteria set in.

With no water supply, sanitation conditions quickly turned bad. Infectious diseases would soon spread. Many of the town doctors, nurses, and public officials were killed or maimed by the blast. Burn victims moaned in agony, with disfigured faces and hideous red blisters on their bodies.

At one emergency center, a young girl sat on a bench sobbing. "Mommy, I can't see. I can't see!" She lifted her little arms towards her mother for help. Her vision was blurred, and her nose was bleeding profusely. The girl's mother was no better off. She was suffering from the same symptoms—the radiation effect.

Elkins was an eerie scene. The landscape was flattened and scorched. Over 200 000 people were killed. The remains of Elkins resembled Hiroshima and Nagasaki after the atomic bombings.

Henry DeVille and his family stood drenched inside a Red Cross tent. They were oblivious to the harm of fallout rain. DeVille, his wife, and his daughter wore the only clothes they had. They survived on food rations and bottled water handed out by the Red Cross. DeVille paused to think about the lifestyle that they enjoyed just a few days ago. It was a vague dream.

A successful businessman in his mid-thirties, he looked around and wondered. Would Elkins ever be rebuilt as the community it once was? He said to a relief volunteer, "In our neighborhood, most homes were destroyed. Restaurants, schools, churches, and stores were wiped out." Foremost on his mind were the essentials—food, clothing, shelter, and medical treatment.

He was preoccupied with terrifying illusions. If we survive physically, how will this affect us mentally? What impact will this have on the rest of our lives? Is this the beginning of World War Three? How many other cities are in the same boat?

DeVille's wife trembled from a mixture of cold, hunger, and fear. Her face was haggard with a taut frown beneath her wet, curly, blonde hair. "It's despicable. Gangs are roaming around looting.

Something ought to be done!" The town's only sheriff and a handful of law enforcers were missing.

The DeVilles' three-year-old daughter sucked on her thumb and held her mother's hand tight. She was bewildered, her face was soiled, and her eyes were glassy from trauma and lack of sleep.

"I'm a well-paid psychologist," Deville's wife said to the volunteer. "Now look at me!" She gestured at her mud-stained skirt, dirty shoes, and socks. She sobbed, tears running down her gritty face.

Across the room, a teenager dressed in designer jeans, a football jersey, and a pea jacket said to his friend, "Hey, dude, I've seen bad stuff like this on TV. But this is our town." He attempted to conceal his fear but failed. "It's different, man," he said in a quavering voice, "when it's you, your family, and friends. Know what I mean?"

His friend, empty-eyed with scruffy hair hanging down his forehead, cast a glance over his shoulder and slowly nodded. He slipped earphones over his head, switched on his Mp3 player, and lyrics from "*Suicidal Dream*" pounded his eardrums. He bobbed his head in cadence with the music, seemingly buffered from the tragic surroundings.

Suddenly, a brash emergency broadcast signal interrupted the music. A disc jockey anxiously announced, "This is an emergency alert broadcast. We've interrupted this program to bring you a special message from the president of the United States." People hastily huddled around anyone with a phone on speaker.

An uncanny hush spread across the land. The voice on the broadcast said, "Ladies and gentlemen, please stand by. The president of the United States will be making an important announcement."

39

NUCLEAR CRISIS

I n the Elkins aftermath, the governor of Maine declared martial law. Citizens were instructed to refrain from entering or leaving designated radioactive areas. The police and the National Guard manned the perimeter borders and were ordered to shoot curfew violators and looters. "Widespread looting may be expected," reported one TV station. "But law and order will prevail. Please stay home. Stay away from the martial law zone. Casualties are high. So, if you live outside the danger zone, we urge you to donate blood at the nearest Red Cross station or hospital in your neighborhood..."

Televised shots of National Guardsmen scrambling out of three-quarter-ton trucks projected a terrifying scene to the world. Clad in olive green battle fatigues and Kevlar helmets, the Guardsmen wielded M16 rifles and fiberglass riot shields. The scene was like a war zone.

THE WESTIN CENTRAL PARK SOUTH,
NEW YORK CITY

Given the crisis and the impending missile threat, MacDuff had his wife, Claire, flown to Dulles Airport after the Times Square speech. Secret Service would then escort her to a safe house some-where in the Virginia countryside. Meanwhile, the president returned to his hotel.

MacDuff slumped on a couch in his hotel room, partly dressed in pants and an undershirt. His eyes half shut, he reeked of the heady odor of booze and cheap perfume. On a glass coffee table, next to a half-filled whiskey glass, four rows of cocaine were neatly lined out. Earlier, there had been six.

A flashy bimbo nicknamed Chastity sat on a chair, legs crossed, smoking a joint. She stared at the man on the couch and wondered how he became president.

The phone rang. MacDuff struggled to lift himself in to a sitting position. "Yes?"

"Mr. President, I need to see you in private," said Special Agent Meier, the president's trusted bodyguard. "It's urgent!" He was calling from the anteroom, just outside the presidential suites.

"What? What's that you say?" MacDuff slurred. "Oh, Kurt, it's you. What's happening?" Through small slits, his bloodshot eyes glanced at Chastity. He waved her off. She promptly put on her coat, picked up her purse, and started toward the door. "Come on in," he said to Meier.

Meier opened the door and waited for Chastity to leave. As she brushed past Meier, she gave him a scornful look. "Goodbye," Meier sneered. He firmly shut the door behind her and rushed over to the president. "Mr. President, a nuclear missile hit Maine!"

"What?" MacDuff shook his head radically. His mind was dull, irrational; his speech was slurred, often incoherent. "Missile, hit Maine? Oh yeah, damn Chinese missiles. No, no!" he mumbled, sitting at the edge of the couch. "Thought we got that sombitch!" MacDuff's face was ashen. He dropped his head and gazed at the carpet, taking long, deep breaths. By all indications, senility and hopelessness appeared to set in.

Meier suggested, "I'll get you something." He radioed his partner in the anteroom. "Bring the usual. You know, ammonia capsules, oxygen, Tylenol, and the rest." Meier turned and briefly examined the president's condition. The cocaine and heavy drinking had greatly impaired him. "Sir, NORAD is standing by, waiting for orders. Should we give General Fuller the authority to... -to assume command?" he said cautiously. Fuller had also tried to reach the president from the war room at the Pentagon.

Still, in a daze, MacDuff looked up at Meier with glassy eyes. "Yes. I mean, no! Hell no!" MacDuff had visions of all-out nuclear war, and it was going to be his show. He was the commander-in-chief, the man in charge, not Fuller's subordinate. MacDuff immediately declared China's missile strike as a war alert. He was hell-bent on retaliating.

The medical items arrived. Meier broke the ammonia vial and passed it under MacDuff's nose. The president jerked his head up and opened his red eyes wide. He shouted, "War! Get me to Cape Canahhvrill." According to procedures, he would be immediately evacuated to Cape Canaveral at the sign of a nuclear threat. Meier had already radioed ahead to prepare Air Force One for takeoff.

The Secret Service agents rushed to get the president dressed and on his way to Kennedy International Airport. Flashing lights and blaring sirens filled the sparsely occupied New York streets as the police escorted the presidential convoy.

At the airport, Air Force One was on the tarmac with engines running, ready to taxi. MacDuff and his entourage hurried on board. They were cleared for an immediate takeoff.

During the flight to Cape Canaveral, MacDuff frequently held an oxygen mask over his face and inhaled deeply. By the time they reached the cape, he had gained some coherency but was not totally detoxified. His brain was still in shock, not firing on all cylinders.

They landed and hurried to the launch site. In the briefing room, MacDuff and his aides, who had arrived earlier, were outfitted in space suits in the briefing room. After a quick orientation, they were escorted onboard the national emergency command translunar integrator, Necktie, the Star Wars command-center satellite. The crew gave the top-level passengers last-minute instructions and strapped them down, horizontally, in their seats. The flight crew went through a checklist. The control tower cleared them for takeoff.

The control center read off the final countdown in one-second intervals: "Five, four, three, two, one. Launch!" The rockets ignited, and the spacecraft began to shudder violently. The rocket engines spat out a burst of orange flames. Puffy clouds of smoke enveloped the launch pad as the satellite slowly lifted off.

At 500 feet, it rapidly gained velocity. Leaving a trail of white condensation, the spacecraft finally shrunk to a mere dot in the peaceful sky.

Rising above the earth at neck-breaking speed, MacDuff was enthralled with the experience. The cluttered instrument panel flickered. The spectacular view through the portholes was marvelous. More than anything, he was ecstatic over the idea of exercising supreme authority in a military conflict.

This was an opportunity to save face, wipe out scandals, to embellish his tarnished legacy. It was his chance to go out of office in blazing glory. A sudden flashback of the Cuban missile crisis came upon him. What would Kennedy have done?

Once Necktie was in orbit, they initiated communications with the air force, navy, and army command modules. All were pinpointed for time and distance from Necktie, with exact coordinates.

The radar system located objects in space by GPS triangulation, using signals from a minimum of three other orbiting satellites. Necktie calculated a specific location by measuring the triangle between itself, the target, and the other satellites.

MacDuff placed a call to Jiang Zemin, the president of China. But the interpreter in Beijing returned the message, "President Jiang is indisposed."

"NORAD on channel one, sir," MacDuff's aide said. "I've already given them the cipher release codes."

The NORAD silos were beneath the surface at desert sites in the U.S. But its command center was at Cheyenne Mountain, a granite mountain near Colorado Springs, Colorado.

MacDuff keyed the microphone. "This is the president. Who is this?"

"Piender, sir. Colonel Russ Piender. Deputy base commander,

the officer on duty," he said. Colonel Russell "Peepsight" Piender was formally the commanding officer of a tank battalion, and he was hungry for action. As a tanker, Piender was accustomed to pulling the trigger and inflicting more damage with one shot from a big gun than what a platoon of ground troops could do at the same time.

"Colonel, I'd like to send a volley of five missiles."

"Understand five missiles. Identify targets, sir."

MacDuff's aide momentarily studied a topographical map of China's missile sites. He pointed out the predetermined target codes. The president read off a series of codes.

"Roger, sir. Stand by one." Seconds later, Piender said, "Targets are L14, L-15, L-22, L-34, and L-38." He used corresponding codes for security reasons. The codes translated into long-range missile sites in China: Wuzhai, Chuxiong, Jianshiu, Lianxiwang, Xi'an, and Tongdao.

MacDuff matched Piender's codes with his list. "Right. Target codes confirmed. What's the ramp-up?"

"Fifteen minutes."

"Okay, launch in thirty minutes. Got that?"

"Affirmative, sir." Looking at the twelve-inch zone clocks on the wall, Piender said, "I'll commence sequencing at twelve-fifteen Zulu time. That is, Greenwich mean time, sir. Blast off will be twelve forty-five Zulu—six forty-five in the morning, eastern standard time." Unlike his days in Afghanistan as a tanker, sweeping the main gun from side to side looking for targets, Piender had a computer fix on the targets, and someone else would give the order to fire. But it was still an awesome responsibility, a chilling duty.

In Nam, his M 48 tank would fire at tree lines, aiming at muzzle flashes, hoping to hit the concealed enemy. The hot brass shell casings from the 90mm rounds covered the already cramped turret floor. It was like a blazing-hot oven. You could literally feel the heat, especially his loader. Now, he was in an arm's length war, an air-conditioned room—a war of politics, computers, switches, and buttons. It was all the same, though, death and destruction, suffering and remorse.

"Confirmed," MacDuff uttered into the microphone. "Launch scheduled for six forty-five eastern standard time."

The aide said, "Mr. President, General Fuller's on the line. And he's pissed!"

MacDuff pushed the transmit button. "Yes?"

Fuller replied, "It's too soon for a missile strike, sir. It would be better to—"

"Sorry, General. You've had your glory. Now it's my turn," MacDuff snarled. He released the transmit button, gesturing to his aide to cut the connection.

"Warnings issued?" MacDuff blurted.

"Yes, sir. The EU, UN, and friendly countries have been notified," replied the aide.

"Military commanders in orbit?"

"They're in orbit, contact made. Proton weapons being tested." They armed Necktie and military command modules with highly accurate proton beam weapons. The high-tech devices would help defend the U.S. and the orbiting space ships from a missile attack.

"Inform the chiefs: launch set for oh-six-forty-five." MacDuff resorted to military jargon.

The president switched to the NORAD channel. "Base Ops, this is the president."

"Base Ops. Go ahead, sir."

"Let us know when you're ready for the countdown. We'll link you up to the squawk box."

"Roger, sir," said Piender. "I'll patch that line in at minus sixty seconds from launch." He had already keyed in the release cipher codes and escalated the status from Orange Alert to Red Alert. Crew members busily entered commands into their computers as muffled voices from launch areas rattled off individual checklists.

At 06:43, Piender said into the mike, "Approaching countdown. Two minutes from the countdown."

MacDuff went into a self-induced trance. He had a smirk on his face and a melancholy gleam in his eye. *The time has finally arrived. I can make my mark in history!*

"Mr. President, Senator Garrity on channel two," the aide said. "And he's really distraught. He says you must abort the mission!"

MacDuff shot a defiant look at the aide and lazily shook his head. "Tell the senator he's too late."

At 06:44:00, the fire controller started the countdown. "Sixty seconds and counting."

Launch procedures would culminate in the simultaneous turning of two fire control keys, one by Piender and the other by the controller. Piender thought, *God, this is it. I've fired off a lot of ammo, but this takes the cake. Right now, I don't know what I feel. I've dreamed about this scenario umpteen times, but now that it's here—*

"Ten seconds to launch," the fire controller chanted. "Begin countdown," Piender ordered.

"Nine," the controller called off.

The crew was petrified. Fingers glued to their keyboards, they watched masses of numbers and messages scroll down the screens.

"Eight, seven, six, five," the voice echoed simultaneously at NORAD and in the Necktie command module.

The president's aide said, "Sir, Senator Garrity is still demanding that you stop the launch."

MacDuff shook his head and said nothing.

Back at the NORAD command center, Piender thought, *any second now, they'll abort.*

The countdown continued. "Four, three, two."

Lights in the command center flickered from a brownout. Piender's entire body went numb. *No orders to abort yet. God, it's really happening. We're gonna fire the big ones!*

"One," the controller said. In a protracted second, the word was followed by an eerie silence. Everything seemed to be frozen in time. Piender ordered, "Activate all systems." On that, Piender and the fire controller simultaneously turned their keys, arming the firing mechanism.

Peering at his monitor, the controller said, "All systems activated. Missiles armed."

The controller lifted five protective caps covering the fire buttons.

Piender gave the order to fire each missile at two-second intervals. "Fire one. Fire two. Fire three. Fire four. Fire five."

The controller pushed the red buttons after each command in sequence.

"Launch complete," Piender announced.

Piender's report reverberated in the NORAD center and the Necktie command module. Many crew members cheered. Some dropped their heads in regret.

When he heard "Launch complete," MacDuff flinched, snapping out of his trance. *This is my moment. My moment in history. I've got to present a clear, concise view of this event for the sake of my legacy. The image must be exact. It is my destiny.*

MacDuff pondered for a long while, formulating his words and imaging his demeanor. *This historical event will certainly brand the minds of every citizen of the U.S. and the world.*

He took in a long deep breath and exhaled. He switched to channel three on the communications panel. It was linked with the emergency broadcast system—a network tied into every U.S. radio and TV station on the air. "Citizens of America, this is your president speaking," he said in a calm voice. "I come to you with a grave message. Do not panic. As most of you know by now, we've been hit with a bomb on the East Coast. We know where it came from."

He paused. "And we've retaliated."

40

CHINA

Each nuclear blast created a twenty-million-degree fireball, scorching hundreds of miles of earth. The missiles hit the Chinese targets with amazing accuracy. The explosions completely demolished the targets, killing over 150 million people and maiming untold numbers.

Victims nearest the targets were a ghastly sight. The blast of heat stripped the flesh from their bones and left scant remains of their carcasses. Smoldering piles of human bones were lying about. The massive inferno altogether disintegrated many.

Survivors were showered with nuclear fallout in the form of radioactive particles mixed with rain. Refugees walked miles in hopes of finding food, shelter, and medical help. Along the way, many were forced to leave behind those who were too weak to continue. These unfortunate souls would likely die from radiation poisoning.

In the first few hours, a moderate level of 50 rems (Roentgen Equivalent Man) per hour of fallout blanketed the target areas. An accumulated dosage of 450 rems per hour would kill half of the people not protected by the adequate shelter. In the first four to five days, the fallout level would reach 2,000 rems per hour, killing anyone exposed and increasing the cancer risk for those who were fortunate enough to be sheltered.

The bombings wiped out transportation systems and utilities, severely disabling emergency services. There was an acute shortage of food, shelter, and medical supplies. Water and gas distribution was shut down because of a loss of pressure, caused by powerless water and gas pumps. What little water that flowed was contaminated with Iodine 131. Floating sparks from the nuclear blast ignited fractured gas lines. Multiple gas explosions occurred; the singed earth spat out orange flames in scattered locations.

Homeless victims swarmed to stopgap medical facilities and emergency centers. Many suffered from the early symptoms of radiation. It didn't take long for the medical staff to quickly abandon the normal procedures for decontamination. Instead, patients were stripped of their clothing, given hospital gowns, and assigned an area for treatment. Doctors separated the very sick from the moderately sick, but few received sufficient medical treatment. Critical patients were given painkillers, allowing them to die in some form of comfort.

People turned away from the crowded facilities clustered in the streets, having no place to go. Separated from their families, many died alone, broken-hearted, and in despair. Their decomposed bodies polluted the environment with bacteria. A putrid stench saturated the air.

Liu Cheng, director of the CCPIT, had luckily escaped the nuclear onslaught. At the time of the bombings, he was with relatives in northern Shaanxi province, a good distance away. As he listened to reports, he painfully realized his work in building China's economy through foreign investment was literally going up in flames. He solemnly commented to his wife, "We have overcome a great many problems, and made strides to reform our economy—only to see it come to this. Humanity has a method of self-destruction that defies explanation."

Visions of the last seven decades flashed before Cheng's eyes. He remembered Mao Tse-tung's Great Proletarian Cultural Revolution, his brazen Red Guards sweeping the countryside with new policies;

Chiang Kai- shek's Nationalists fled and established Taiwan's independent nation; Deng Xiaoping's bold economic reform policies.

One of the old guards of the Chinese Communist Party, Deng, became secretary-general in 1954 but was purged by Mao in 1966 for his strong objections to the excesses of Mao's ill-conceived program, the *Great Leap Forward*. Many suffered under the plan to industrialize China by building backyard factories, resulting in famine, extreme pollution, and other catastrophes.

By 1974, Deng Xiaoping had been rehabilitated and returned to power. After Mao's death, Deng became the *de facto* leader of China. During his reign, he established the foundation for China's reformation. In 1989, Deng chose Jiang Zemin as his successor. Deng lived on for eight years as Jiang's protector but eventually grew too feeble to rule.

Jiang was anxious to take over the reins. Ironically, the Tiananmen episode was the turning point for his career. They quelled the protests, and three weeks later, Deng named Jiang as the new general secretary of the Communist Party. Though his record was unspectacular, Jiang had gained recognition as a tough decision-maker.

Before the Tiananmen protests, Jiang had fired the editor of an independent, liberal newspaper in Shanghai called the *World Economic Herald*. This act convinced Beijing hard-liners of Jiang's worthiness. After Deng Xiaoping died in 1997, Jiang Zemin finally stepped out of his shadow and preserved Deng's vision. One of his first acts was to boldly declare the privatization of most of China's state industries.

But most vividly, Liu Cheng remembered October 1, 1949, when Mao Tse-tung stood at the Gate of Heavenly Peace, proclaiming a Communist People's Republic of China. Evolution is a revolution in China. Over the past fifty years, Cheng thought, there was little doubt the economy had improved under Communist rule.

Most of China's 1.3 billion people now have more freedom, are better educated, live longer, and have a higher standard of education. But it's equally obvious that they had indeed paid a heavy price.

Millions of unjustly persecuted Chinese died under Communist rule. He thought about the bloody crackdown on pro-democracy demonstrators and the infamous Tiananmen Square massacre in 1989. In reality, since the revolution, the Chinese people had yet to truly gain political freedom and civil liberties.

Liu Cheng was livid over the turn of events. Beijing prepared for a nuclear counterattack against the U.S. They ordered a general troop mobilization, initializing strikes against the closest U.S. bases in the region.

At a short-range missile site, a young Chinese officer carefully drew circles on a regional map, identifying U.S. targets in all of Asia. While outside in the streets, a swarm of protestors strongly chanted, *"Enough is enough!"*

GENERAL FULLER'S OFFICE, THE PENTAGON

Hayden Boyd called President-elect Garrity and reported the Chinese launches were accidental. Garrity immediately called General Fuller and organized an emergency meeting in Fuller's office.

As Fuller waited for Garrity and the others to arrive, he rose from behind his desk, walked over, and stared out the window. The sun had faded away, and gray stratus clouds filled the sky. Then it dawned on him that within minutes, he was to discuss the fate of his country and the world. He sensed Garrity would rely heavily on his judgment. Suddenly, he felt overwhelming loneliness.

Garrity; his aide, Derek Stevens, and Colonel Gomez hastily paraded into Fuller's office.

"By every account, the experts say, if we continue a nuclear confrontation, we are likely to destroy our opponents and possibly ourselves in a matter of days," Garrity said.

Fuller nodded his concurrence. "Anything can happen. Besides China, we've got the UAF, the Russians, and others ready to come at us. It's gonna be a free-for-all."

"Gotta pull in our allies, ASAP," Colonel Gomez jumped in. "Any feedback from the Brits, the European Union?"

"The UK is ready, but the EU committee is holding up a majority decree. They govern like you've never seen before. It's a freaking zoo!" Fuller grumbled.

"By the time they reach a decision, Beijing could seize a big part of Asia," said Gomez.

"Gentlemen, we're certain we can win a war against China," Garrity said. "But that's not the issue. For God's sake, we're talking about World War Three!"

"And, a nuclear war at that," added his aide, Derek Stevens. "Some of us would survive, but we're looking at the possibility of complete annihilation!"

"I say beat 'em to the punch," Gomez cut in, eyes flaring with aggression. "Knock out China, and the rest of 'em will take notice and back off. We must go on the offensive." He punched his left palm with his fist, making a slapping noise.

Garrity thought for a moment. "Well, I understand where the colonel is coming from. It's true that in the last several years, we've been viewed as tentative and feeble in our position. Everyone knows we have a strong military, but we have pandered to many on so much that our credibility to stand firm has all but disappeared."

"Which theater are you referring to?" questioned Fuller, his face furrowed in a frown.

"For example, the Palestinian issue. We're caught up in the chaotic power struggle between Israel and the Palestinians. The minority groups are getting nailed, but we keep sending money over there like none of that is happening."

"How's that?" queried Gomez.

"For one thing, we send money for housing developments, but the housing in Palestine is kept to a minimum. The minority elements in the West Bank and Gaza are basically squeezed out. We should use our money in equal fairness, not placed selectively."

"Never heard that before," commented Gomez.

"Here's how it is? Since 1996, because of terrorist attacks, a ruling made by the Israeli military has imposed restrictions on the movement of people into Jerusalem. Border closures have harmed the

Palestinian economy—the policy violates basic civil freedoms." Garrity paused. "But we're always preaching human rights to the world, appearing hypocritical in our foreign policies. Some perceive us as imprudent and vacillating. Not a good image for a superpower with the greatest military machine on earth."

"Exactly," Gomez replied. "We need to act like a superpower. I say give China an ultimatum. If they don't agree to a cease-fire, we wipe out all their missile sites and move in for a takeover."

"Bold talk, Colonel, but not very good diplomacy," Stevens retaliated, enduring Gomez's cold, piercing stare.

Gomez shot back. "Nothing diplomatic about a freaking street fight!

And that's what it is. You don't pander to your opponent and expect to win."

As the debate went on, Fuller privately struggled with his thoughts. *My rationale is with Stevens, but my passion is with Gomez. And how casually we talk of it all but always hoping that something, somehow, will prevent the ultimate ending—a nuclear holocaust—what could be the final battle of humanity. This is a moment of history, and we'll shape it as we see fit. God help us.*

"Gentlemen," Garrity spoke up, raising his hand to calm the bickering between Stevens and Gomez. "I know it's difficult, but we must keep emotions out of this. We must be logical, collaborative. I think the best course is to devise a plan of action contingent upon the outcome of each event. After all, this is not just a skirmish with China. Again, we're looking at the start of *World War Three*."

The notion of a world war was a harsh realization. There was a sudden stillness in the room. Through a partially opened window, you could hear the faint sound of Washington's traffic. The atmosphere was very somber. Gomez and Stevens no longer brooded over their differences.

"Okay, here's the game plan," Garrity said. "I'll neutralize MacDuff— keep him out of it. Chet, I want you to negotiate a cease-fire with Beijing. As a backup, come up with plan B, plan C, and so forth. It will take a little time to devise our master plan, drawing from our so-called expert advisors' opinions. But we have no time to waste. We must move fast."

"Right," said Fuller. He turned to Colonel Gomez. "Get an interpreter. Then get Jiang Zemin on the phone."

Gomez immediately beckoned a staff officer, a Mandarin interpreter. They placed a call to Beijing. China time would be mid-morning. The interpreter was told President Jiang would call back in one hour.

Later, when the Chinese statesman came on the hotline, Fuller said, "President Jiang, there's been a mistake."

"We did not attack," Jiang replied rashly.

"Yes, we now know your launch was accidental."

Jiang paused, then said, "Too late."

"We've issued a cease-fire," Fuller said.

"There's much destruction. Many people are dead, suffering. American aggression is an act of war!"

Fuller listened to Jiang's harsh words in silence. Jiang continued, "We shall fight!"

"But you realize we were hit first with one of your missiles," Fuller countered. His patience was running out.

"We did not fire missiles. It was an accident."

"It was the missile control computer," Fuller said emphatically. "There is a flaw in your system. That's what caused it. We know you are using our supercomputers. The defect caused the missile launches, and by the way, we know they were pointing at us all along." He anxiously waited for Jiang's response.

After a few tense moments, Jiang iterated, "I know nothing of these computers."

"Okay, we'll play it your way," Fuller snapped. "But I would suggest you investigate the missile firing. You're in direct violation of the ABM agreement. You have broken our trust that China would not use our computers in the military."

Fuller knew, diplomatically, he shouldn't have forced Jiang into a corner. But a third world war, a nuclear war, was on the brink. He felt it was too late to use smooth negotiations and diplomatic protocol.

"We'll give you twenty-four hours to announce a cease-fire." The arrogance of his ultimatum was a calculated one. He hoped the Chinese statesman was sensible enough to know it was the rattle before the strike, a shot across his bow.

President Jiang was silent for what seemed like several minutes. He had taken great pride in what China had accomplished in the last twenty years. But he also feared the political strength the PLA had built up in the process. If he were to unleash military force in an outright war against the U.S., the military could usurp power and severely limit Beijing's control. Should he call Fuller's bluff, there was also the cultural fear of *luan*–chaos, and disorder among the citizens. At last, Jiang spoke in a quiet, conceding tone. "I will talk with my comrades."

"Twenty-four hours," said Fuller. He hung up the phone.

41

GRAND HOTEL, OSLO

The wedding was spectacular. A thirty-member choir sang, and the scent of ten dozen cream-colored roses filled the air. Dean and Karina were married in an elaborate ceremony held at the Grand Hotel, where they first met. Karina was stunning in her ivory organza gown. Soft, frontal curls and swept-back golden hair framed her smooth, silky face. A diamond-studded crown accented her flowing Belgian lace train. Four bridesmaids wore lavender-pink gowns, closely matching the backdrop of roses.

The extravaganza attracted over 300 guests, among whom included high-powered American and Norwegian diplomats. Yet, a sense of warmth and intimacy infused the fanfare. One guest commented, "It's like a royal wedding with the aura of a close-knit family." Karina's father gave her away, but the U.S. ambassador honored Dean as his best man. After a brief honeymoon in Monaco, Dean and Karina moved to the U.S., joining Dante Martin at ComTech.

Amid one of the most scandalous presidencies in U.S. history, Garrity and Fuller won the election by a landslide. Their platform was simple: eliminate internal corruption, patch up foreign relations, and control the nuclear threat.

China had begrudgingly ceded. NetForum membership flourished. The task force was running at full steam, deploying the AMOEBA fix worldwide. When news of the accidental missile firings broke, responsible nations hastened to cooperate. They deactivated sensitive high-impact computers.

The public was outraged over Redding's swindle. Lawsuits were filed, forcing Redding into bankruptcy and driving MacDuff out of office. It forced Congress to authorize funds to correct problems caused by the AMOEBA bug. The National Security Agency contracted with the ComTech/NetForum team to fix MEGA-Star computers, giving special priority to foreign military systems. Mega-Tronics would make retributions through residual assets.

The world had been severely traumatized by the nuclear crisis. Addressing a committee on strategic defense systems, General Fuller, now vice president, gave a briefing on the missile firings, "For the most part, credit should go to Karina VanDegarde and the team in Oslo for finding and repairing the defect. And for the Norfolk crew in the U.S., they're commended for retarding the missile attack.

"Thank God, the Omega-Alpha initiative essentially avoided an all-out nuclear war with the UAF. In fact, as I speak, the team continues to alert users of MEGA-Star computers throughout the world. The mission is especially focused on the global military community—East and West, friend and foe. My fellow Americans, there is no room for partisanship. As you now know, chances of starting a nuclear war by computer malfunction are real. It is, in the best of cases, still a very fragile situation.

"How many other time bombs like China are waiting to go off? We don't really know. How many other units exist in clandestine operations? We don't know. But I can tell you: we must not be lured into a false sense of security. We must gain positive control. We must stamp out the AMOEBA epidemic!"

The horrifying missile catastrophe would leave a lasting impression on all who would see nuclear destruction effects. Epic television accounts illustrated the nauseating scenes of blood, devastation, and the unseemly defacement of earth. Traumatized victims expressed their demise on television for the world to see. Whole families had been wiped out.

The malaise fostered the mobilization of extreme religious groups. Predictably, they had prematurely professed a time of repentance. They interpreted the calamity as a sign of the final battle—the Apocalypse—the Second Coming of Christ. They believed internal revolutions, continuous wars, pollution, abnormal weather, earthquakes, and devastating diseases would soon follow.

In the aftermath, Garrity and Fuller were able to quell several war initiatives spawned by the Chinese mishap. For the time being, the fuses of World War Three had fizzled. Humanity had been spared the dregs of another war, perhaps the final war.

42

CAMP DAVID, THURMONT, MARYLAND

"The Triad bugged my study at home, but they didn't get anything there," Fuller said to Garrity. "Turns out, a local OCB—a restaurant owner in Chinatown—tipped off Beijing. He found out about the safe house where Zhang was."

"How?" Garrity asked.

"The underground buzz in Chinatown. There were Chinese agents staked out all over the place." He chuckled and shook his head. "Of course, when we approached Beijing, they adamantly denied any knowledge of the spy network or the plot to kill Zhang. They strongly rebuked us for the implication. They said they were 'insulted.'"

Monumental meetings had been held at the presidential retreat in Catoctin Mountain Park. Fuller and Garrity sat at a table inside the lodge named Aspen.

Garrity was drinking a glass of California Chardonnay. Fuller had a tankard of English dark ale. The fireplace crackled with freshly lit firewood, topped with dancing orange flames.

"That's okay, as long as Zhang is safe," Garrity remarked. "After his plastic surgery, they wouldn't know what he looks like. And he's pretty much secluded where he's living." He glanced out the window, inspecting the three-hole golf course and the skeet range just east of the main lodge. A thin blanket of snow covered the golf course. Glistening snowflakes gave it a type of sanitized glow.

"Walters should find out what Beijing's strategy will be soon," Fuller said. "I'm betting they will blow off Zhang's defection and preserve trade relations."

"And I expect them to use Zhang's political asylum as a negotiating point."

"Good point," said the general. "Another try at it would be political suicide." The Chinese were not stupid. The U.S. investment in their economy and the huge trade deficit were serious factors. It wouldn't make sense for them to knock off Wang Zhang after the exposé. One failed attempt was enough.

"On the other hand, we have the confession from our Triad prisoner. When the scumbags tapped the phone lines at my house, that linked them directly with Beijing." Fuller paused. "And we have the Russians. Since we've neutralized China, Putin is willing to talk about a missile defense shield."

Garrity nodded. Following a few seconds of silence, he asked, "Did you read the report about the Council on Foreign Relations, the CFR?"

"Yeah, pretty freaking amazing, isn't it?"

For a moment, the two men thought about the implications. According to the CIA, the CFR had actually invested millions in the UAF movement. Playing the odds, and in their quest to conquer the world economy and politics, they backed the sinister ploy of the UAF. The elite's inner circle was comprised of central bankers, international banking families, global banking cabals, and wealthy families in several countries. The news media, some industries, labor unions, universities, the financial world, and even the Supreme Court were represented in the so-called shadow government. "Scary," Garrity replied solemnly.

Historically, the CFR was actually part of a movement launched back in the 1760s under the name *Illuminati*. Adam Weishaupt was its founder. Born a Jew, Weishaupt had later converted to Catholicism and became a priest. But the newly organized House of Rothschild soon convinced Weishaupt to abandon his religion and establish the Illuminati.

Mayer Amschel Rothschild, who died in 1812, once said, "Give me control over a nation's currency, and I care not who makes its laws." The Rothschilds financed the initial Illuminati operation and, beginning with the French Revolution, every major war since. The Illuminati has establishments worldwide, such as the British Institute of International Affairs in England. There are secret organizations in France, Germany, and other nations operating under different names. They continuously set up numerous front organizations that infiltrate every phase of a nation's affairs.

Allegedly, the conspiracy masterminds control the mass communications media, especially television, radio, the press, and Hollywood. Some think Illuminati/CFR conspirators were also behind the creation of the United Nations, which has promulgated many of the CFR objectives. Many backers of the UN also favor a one-government rule. They're comprised largely of the social elite.

Here in the U.S., a stepping stone to the CFR and the elite was the Skull and Bones society at Yale University. It's a senior year society where new members are chosen in their junior year. Each year, only fifteen students are selected, and they only spend their senior year with Skull and Bones. The most likely candidates were from a "Bones" family. But all members were sworn never to admit being members of the secret society.

Selected students were usually political, amoral team players. The power of the Order guaranteed honors and financial rewards. But the price of these honors and rewards was to sacrifice for the goal of the Order.

"I mean," Garrity continued, "who'd ever think the elite, a bunch of rich and powerful Americans, would go to such extremes?"

"Kent, we're surrounded by the enemy," said the general. "We can't afford to let our guard down. Anytime, anywhere. Especially within our own borders."

43

THE EXPOSE'

After considering the consequences of a CFR connection, Fuller and Garrity vowed to assign the NSA, FBI, and CIA to follow the group closely.

After a long period of silence, Garrity said, "Speaking of being on guard, why is it taking so long to fix the AMOEBA bug?"

Fuller spread his hands in a gesture of frustration. "There are more infected computers out there than we thought! Export controls under MacDuff were in shambles. And Redding never publicized the number of units he sold overseas. Frankly, I don't think he even knew. As long as the money was rolling in and he gobbled up rich markets, he was happy."

"At least we've repaired the missile-control units in China," Garrity muttered. "Lame Duck and the Yards really helped out there." Lame Duck had gathered a paper trail of the systems, and the Montagnards confirmed the sites. And because of their input, the DOJ was able to trace units found in Russia and China, leading back to MegaTronics. The solid evidence would cinch conviction once it got through the courts.

Fuller chuckled. "Hey, forget about counting computers. What about the Redding-Tiffany case? That was a real deal. Tiffany really bashed those jokers, didn't she? She and MacDuff's aides did some damage."

Tiffany had testified she was "afraid of the goon squad." And that she was forcefully implicated in White House conspiracies. She also confessed to her affair with Redding and the extraction of classified documents from the White House.

"MacDuff didn't have a chance," said Garrity. To gain clemency, Redding also poured his guts out about MacDuff. He even provided videotapes of the president and Liz Ledgewick—tapes that were a hole card against MacDuff. Garrity spoke of the inside trading, pay-to-play schemes, kickbacks from our enemies, drugs, and reckless sexual escapades.

"I knew a lot of that," said the general. "I had a pipeline out of the Bureau. Now I can tell you who he is. Scott Brummell, code name *Blue Jay*. That guy stuck his neck out big time, a true patriot. If it weren't for him and his buddy Kurt Meier, MacDuff would've steam-rolled over everybody."

"Kurt Meier?"

"You know, MacDuff's bodyguard."

"Ah!" Garrity nodded.

Fuller took a swig from his beer mug and grunted. "It's ironic. The Whittington-Ledgewick scandal neutralized the Russians and the Redding-MacDuff scandal softened the Chinese threat."

Garrity paused, then cleared his throat. "One thing I'm puzzled about. Why didn't the infected systems in Russia fire off missiles?"

"Luck!" the general replied. "Would you believe their power system went out? And get this: the AMOEBA strain caused it. Their equipment is so archaic there was a power outage when a MEGA-Star computer was due to fail. The missiles never got the signal to fire!"

The situation was indeed amazing. The Russians were spending just 15,000,000 U.S. dollars to repair their aging computers. And out of that amount, the U.S., through the World Bank, contributed 80 percent—12,000,000 U.S. dollars.

"Another bit of irony," Fuller continued, "the Russkies may elect to fire off nuclear missiles at us any day. And we're the ones fixing their screwed-up computers. Go figure." He drank more ale, unintentionally slamming his tankard down on the oak table, making a sharp noise.

The general wiped the residue from his mouth with a napkin and said, "Need to beef up our intelligence. We should appropriate more funding for the CIA and put them back out in the field where they belong. Today, the freaking terrorists are too bold, too arrogant. We also don't know enough about the technological capabilities of our enemies.

"Also, about Russia," Fuller continued. "We know they've relied heavily on PCs and midrange computers rather than mainframes. Many of their programs are written in non-standard languages.

"For the last decade, they've been converting their code to more universal languages. In actuality, a group of scientists at the University of St. Petersburg and companies like IBM has teamed up to help, but have fallen short."

"Which reminds me of the AMOEBA fixes," said Garrity. "What's the latest?"

"Apparently, Redding was careful to ship clean computers as demo units," said the general. "As a result, two of the long-range missile sites were not affected. But they deployed other systems in non-military labs and industrial operations."

Garrity sipped from his wineglass. He again shifted his eyes towards Fuller. "And what about those units?"

"Basically, the Chinese are in a dilemma. Ninety percent of their software was pirated. Consequently, they cannot consult with foreign owners on how to fix bugs. The Ministry of Information trained and dispatched five thousand technicians across the country. But they're still in deep trouble. The Yards say they don't know what the hell they're doing."

"Speaking of which, what should we do for the Yards?" Garrity said.

"Why don't we bring them in under special protection, as we did with Wang Zhang?"

"Right, sounds good. Let's do it."

At that moment, the red telephone rang. The two glanced at each other curiously. Garrity answered. "Yes?"

Fuller studied Garrity's face intently. At first, it was impassive.

Then, Garrity's eyes grew wide as dinner plates.

"Who was your source?" Garrity asked anxiously. Then came a pause. "Okay, thanks."

He cradled the telephone and turned to Fuller. "That was Hayden Boyd. It's been confirmed. Another high-level Chinese defector gave us new information. Several informers corroborated it. The Triad killed Bradford Chalmers."

Fuller sat quietly for a moment. "Yep, and another reason to knock off Zhang. They thought he knew about it."

"Probably."

The general grunted. "But *proving* Beijing was behind it is altogether another matter."

"There's more," said Garrity. "We've realized our worst nightmare."

General Fuller slid to the edge of his seat and leaned forward. "Yes?"

"The *Princess*. The Chinese sunk the *Princess*."

The two men dropped their heads and reflected on the disaster. A long period of silence passed. They quietly pondered the historical events in past months.

Fuller slid back in his chair and roared, "Jesus, what a phenomenon! Beijing kills Chalmers to get in bed with MacDuff. They get pissed at the EU deal and blow up the *Princess*, and the AMOEBA virus nearly starts a freaking nuclear war!"

Garrity shook his head and silently contemplated the ramifications of it all. He enumerated the latest statistics, adding up the increasing number of missiles in unfriendly hands. *Wait a minute.* "Chet, how many long-range sites did we bomb in China? Wasn't it six?"

"Yes, six."

"Can you name them?"

"You bet. Wuzhai, Chuxiong, Jianshiu, Lianxiwang, Xi'an, and Tongdao."

"We need to be sure. According to Lame Duck's report, there were a total of *six* long-range missile garrisons. He mentioned a top-secret site called Tai-Hang."

"Tai-Hang?" Fuller stroked his chin. "Don't remember that one."

"He said it was a long-range site equipped with a MEGA-Star computer."

After a long pause, the general said, "Kent, I haven't read Zhang's full report yet, but I know we didn't hit Tai-Hang, and we didn't repair any units there." Silence.

Then Fuller's eyes widened. "Think I know which one it is—the missing 'Albatross' unit. The one MacDuff sent to Taiwan."

44

MOSCOW

Inside a KGB apartment, just a quarter mile from the American embassy, two spools of tape turned slowly on an old Sony tape deck. An operator with large headphones sat listlessly in front of the equipment. The sound of a ringing telephone came through his headset.

Across Moscow in Baumanskaya, Liz Ledgewick picked up the receiver and put it to her ear. "Allo?"

"Comrade Elizabeth," a voice said with a crude British accent. "This is Oleg. Sorry to disturb you, but I bring you important news." Liz stood motionless. Oleg Sarkalov was a top KGB officer, a director at headquarters. Since her return to Moscow, she had had minimal contact with him, rendering the call unusual and surprising. "Just spoke with the Czech embassy," Sarkalov's raspy, vodka-soaked vocal cords rattled in faultless English. "President MacDuff is here to visit you. He is traveling incognito. We have made all the arrangements for him to see you."

Liz was stunned. Her jaw dropped, and her hands began to tremble. Tears welled up in her eyes. After a while, she regained her composure. "When? When is he coming?" Her voice was strained with emotion.

"Tomorrow night. My men will escort him to your apartment. You must understand this is in the strictest of security. He is here under his own free will. He is not under the protection of the U.S. embassy."

"Yes, I understand," she answered, with a hint of confusion in her voice. "Comrade, what does that mean?" *Is he in exile?*

Sarkalov hesitated. Oleg Sarkalov was extremely prudent in his thoughts, actions, and his words. He was a veteran field agent, a spymaster. He was a career sleuth who came in from the cold. After twenty years, Sarkalov had earned a reputation as a hawk in his dealings with the West. A Middle East expert, he was friendly with all its leaders and had a good working relationship with the U.S. secretary of state, Peter Barrett.

When he came back to Moscow, he had, in a sense, been demoted. Russia was a new scene. An old spymaster did not fit quite as well. Most of the younger generation did not appreciate the Communist ideology. The attitudes of replacement were more Westernized.

Sarkalov was installed as head of counterintelligence. But party officials needed a cunning, bold man for this special assignment. He was charged with the responsibility of cracking down on internal dissent. Russia was in a crisis, on the brink of complete collapse.

The tally of achievements in Russian-style democracy was shriveling fast. Despite the growing control of corporate interests, the new Russia was not a civil society. The Russian Mafia had been wreaking havoc in the new democracy. Corruption was now openly rampant.

After the break-up of the Soviet Union, there were still no political parties to mediate between the state and its people. Of course, the exception was the Communist Party, a large part of which remained committed to destroying all vestiges of parliamentary democracy.

Oleg Sarkalov had a full plate. Indeed, he himself walked a tightrope daily. His powers swayed with the unpredictable winds of Russian politics. "I have no instructions for you," he finally said in a monotone. "We consider this a personal matter. But comrade Elizabeth, you are a good servant, smart and intelligent. We trust you. You will know how to deal with this."

"Thank you, sir, but, *ya ego lyublyu!*" she blurted uncontrollably. *I love him.*

It was a bold move for Liz. She had taken a chance by expressing her true feelings. The KGB thought lightly of agents succumbing to the weaknesses of romance and materialistic Western standards. But in her case, she *was* Western, a convert to Communism.

The top spymaster shrugged and dismissed the remark with a scornful grunt. He cradled the phone.

45

THE RENDEZVOUS

Liz had gone to the hairdresser for a cut and set, a manicure, a complete makeover—the works. Although very much excited, she felt ambivalent and apprehensive about the rendezvous. What was the meaning of the visit? Was she making false assumptions? She couldn't be sure of any hypothesis, but she wanted to be prepared. And she wouldn't allow herself to jump to conclusions, a trait she had refined in her training.

After thoroughly cleaning her flat, Liz bathed and dressed herself in a rather provocative royal blue dress that tightly hugged her body. It was cold, so she wrapped herself with a bulky white shawl. She felt like a fresh lily, rejuvenated and smelling of expensive perfume.

She looked at herself in the mirror. Her beautiful creamy face, framed by shiny dark hair, was vibrant with expectation. Her dark eyes sparkled like snowflakes gleaming in the sun. She fixed herself a double vodka martini in a tumbler—she had none of her refined tableware with her. Liz settled into a small, lumpy armchair. She didn't know exactly when MacDuff would arrive. The KGB, called the *Federal Security Service* since the collapse of the Soviet Union, never gave set times.

As he anxiously waited, Liz tried to keep her mind busy. She thought about all the possible scenarios. Surely, he would come to Moscow for no other reason but to see her. Maybe to defect? No, that's ridiculous. The scandal and lawsuits that ensued in the U.S. had stripped him of power and dignity, but not enough to drive him out of his own country. He was a survivor, wealthy enough to over-come any scathing. Besides, his political acumen empowered him to deal with the most difficult of situations.

She got up, went to the window, and peered down at the street below. A few tourists were roaming about, undoubtedly under the strict eye of internal security or the KGB.

An eerie white mist floated in the city air, radiating a bright aurora around street-lamps. *Ice fog*, they called it. When the moist air freezes at fifty-five below, it makes fog. Liz shivered, turned from the frosty window, and settled into her cushioned chair.

It had been just under a year since she left the U.S. It seemed like a decade. What would it be like to see him again? She took another sip of vodka to calm her nerves and warm her body. A few minutes later, she heard the Kremlin tower's huge resonant bells clang six times. It was a familiar sound to Muscovites.

Metro Baumanskaya was located near the Golden Ring, a group of ancient Russian towns to Moscow's northeast. On the map, the path that links the group of eleven towns forms a shoe-like curved line, the toe of which rests in Moscow.

These historic sites were often called "museums under the open sky," where Russian architecture's unique monuments are preserved. Liz savored the intriguing atmosphere and had chosen it to be her place of retirement.

Nervously anticipating the moment, Liz was startled by the knock on the door. Adrenaline rushed through her body. Her heart pounded vigorously. She stood up, quickly primped her hair, straight-ened her clothing, and went for the door.

MacDuff stood on the threshold when she opened it. He was wearing a heavy brown coat, a Russian mouton lamb cap, and a broad smile. Two hard-faced KBG agents with black felt hats were at his flanks. With a smug grin, MacDuff said, "Thought you wouldn't see me again?" His cold-dried lips stretched the grin wider.

Liz noticed his face was surprisingly gaunt compared to the last time she saw him. She smiled, nodded, and stepped aside to let him in. "Please stay in the hall," she staunchly ordered the agents in Russian. MacDuff moved inside. One of the men started to follow. The agent had the face of a worn-out boxer, unshaven, scarred, and wrinkled. A pair of mean, tar-black eyes accompanied his large, crooked nose.

Liz raised her voice. "I said—"

"*OK. Ya znayu to, chto ty skazal!*" the agent snapped. *I know what you told me.* He shrugged, backed off, and mumbled an obscenity to his partner.

Liz glared at the oaf, then shut the door in his face. She could not accept the crude methods of the KGB in Russia.

After all, she had not personally taken part in assassinations, directly ruined careers, or destroyed lives. She conveniently vindicated herself: she was merely a small thread in the huge web of the KGB.

She was always at arm's length, in a buffered zone as it were. A zone encased by a professional career, diplomacy, and luxury. Fortunately, other agents were charged with the despicable acts of her trade.

She latched the door and pirouetted to face MacDuff. Their eyes were momentarily locked, probing for a sign. Was it really love? Their solemn faces soon broke into wide smiles. They embraced. The contours of their bodies pressed hard together as if they were one.

"Oh, Liz, I've missed you."

She began to weep quietly. "And I've missed you." They kissed passionately.

When they broke their embrace, Liz asked, "How, why are you here in secrecy?"

"Friends. That is—never mind, it's too complicated." He scanned the room, certain of eavesdropping by the KGB. He pressed his index finger to his lips and whispered, "Later."

Suddenly, the faint cry of an infant drifted from a back room.

MacDuff stepped back in astonishment. "What—"

Her eyes glassy, Liz nodded. She said in a wavering voice, "It's our little Ivan."